A thumbnail of this Chicago-born author reads like that of one of his characters – a fellow who, in his mid-fifties, has seen a bit more reality than is often healthy but has come away with P. J. O'Rourke's sense of humour instead of angst. **Charlie Newton** has built successful restaurants and hotels, raced thoroughbreds that weren't quite so successful and sold television and film in the Middle East to gentlemen who often weren't. Generally speaking, he's lived a life in the borderlands (literal and figurative) where stories like *Calumet City* happen. And survived to enjoy it.

To find out more about the author visit his website at
www.charlienewton.com

CALUMET CITY

Charlie Newton

BANTAM BOOKS

LONDON • TORONTO • SYDNEY • AUCKLAND • JOHANNESBURG

TRANSWORLD PUBLISHERS
61–63 Uxbridge Road, London W5 5SA
A Random House Group Company
www.rbooks.co.uk

CALUMET CITY
A BANTAM BOOK: 9780553818727

First published in Great Britain
in 2008 by Bantam Press
a division of Transworld Publishers
Bantam edition published 2009

Addresses for Random House Group Ltd companies outside the UK
can be found at: www.randomhouse.co.uk
The Random House Group Ltd Reg. No. 954009

The Random House Group Limited supports The Forest Stewardship Council (FSC),
the leading international forest certification organisation. All our titles that are printed
on Greenpeace approved FSC certified paper carry the FSC logo. Our paper
procurement policy can be found at www.rbooks.co.uk/environment

Typeset in 11/14.5pt Granjon by
Falcon Oast Graphic Art Ltd.
Printed in the UK by CPI Cox & Wyman, Reading, RG1 8EX.

2 4 6 8 10 9 7 5 3 1

CALUMET CITY

OFFICER PATTI BLACK

There's this place in Chinatown.

Off Wentworth Avenue in the 25th Ward, where the four-story walkups lean out over the street. Buildings not yet leveled by urban renewal, mattress fires, or debts to the wrong politicians. The kind of neighborhood that scares people who look too close.

A block east the 'L' screeches overhead, sharp like it's mad, metal-on-metal that bitters the back of your throat. Amtrak runs up there too, on iron bridging painted gray to match the concrete it shades. Above and below and beyond the trains, twenty lanes of loud expressways rumble and honk in four directions. Everything at ground level vibrates, the sense of movement so strong you can lose your balance.

During the day Great Lakes sailors and bus–tour adventurers shop for trinkets and a glimpse of something that isn't here; at night it's a Mexican border town selling vice in Mandarin. Behind the pagoda storefronts and across the alley, the Outfit runs dice and card rooms, and the Chinese Merchants Association with their teenage hitmen run everything else.

Me, I'm sitting in a side-street restaurant with faded Chinese characters for an address and six tables for locals who should know better. It's dim in here, and that's unusual. The floor's dirty, and that isn't. Rice kettles and radiators steam the stale air humid. Back by the kitchen an old woman sits smoking unfiltered cigarettes down to her fingertips and has for as long as I can remember. We don't speak, her and I; we stare out the front window. Her eyes hide behind the smoke and that's probably a good thing – she hears what I hear: the echoes of a long, violent struggle between me and the devil.

The devil has a man's first and last name – you need to believe that – he's got saliva, busy hands, and a Bible he quotes, and shoes that are always new. But he's the devil just the same.

And he's out there beyond the glass. I've seen his footprints. And so has she.

For the last seventeen years I've come to this restaurant, always alone. Every Friday night since I came on the job. Back then Patti Black was a tough–talking twenty-one, but it was bluster. At heart I was a little-white-girl orphan with bad history and worse dreams, hoping to hide inside a uniform from history that won't let you hide.

Seventeen years I've sat at this same table, looking out this same window, me and a nightmare secret that's kept me a well–armed coward. Tonight I face it: We finish here. I'm bruised and cut, there's a pistol in my pocket that doesn't belong to me, and the taste of its barrel in my mouth. You might say the clock's running. 'Cause it is.

Chapter 1

SEVEN DAYS AGO

It's Monday in Chicago, which is actually worse than it sounds.

Our bookies, palm readers, and civil servants are all doing double-shift overtime. We're in an end-of-season baseball thing – the Cubs and Sox are still alive. A planetary alignment so rare that today's *Herald* suggested biblical implications.

It's also election eve.

And then there's the other *thing* – nineteen hours ago a 'lone gunman' tried to kill our mayor. Three bullets. High caliber. All into the airspace surrounding his and his wife's expensive haircuts.

As you might imagine, our police department is experiencing a bit of discomfort over this. At least above the rank of sergeant there's a bit of discomfort. Below the rank of sergeant we're more focused on policing the city, saving mankind, and stealing the odd apple here and there. Don't get me wrong, I like the mayor – his wife Mary Kate's a bitch, but that's another story – and I don't think Hizzoner should die in office. And as long as my sergeant's not frustrated or hungry, neither does he: big, badass Irish Sonny Barrett.

At this moment Sonny's face is mostly two-handed sandwich. But neither the breaded steak nor the Dan Ryan's southbound trucks lumbering overhead slow his comments on my appearance. 'I'm tellin' you, Patti, and no shit now, you gotta drop a few.'

I'm only 5'6" and change, but I have a pistol, and although Sonny can't see it under my faded windbreaker, he knows it's there. He's seen me use it. 'Really? You think?'

Sonny nods across the battered fender that separates us, eyes my figure or his opinion thereof, and keeps eating. The other five officers in our Tactical Unit (TAC) are doing the same, enjoying Sonny's lounge act with their Ricobene's – medium-sized, breaded-steak footballs with tomato sauce.

'Don't mind workin' with fat chicks, but shit . . .'

I weigh half what he does and often think Sonny and I would be better off if he were severely wounded in the line of duty. Had he not saved my life on Seventy-ninth, over by St. Rita's, I would've shot him long ago. And I still might. See, we have sort of an unwritten rule in our crew – my personal appearance and your opinion, compliment, or critique, don't need to mingle. But Sonny's safe today and knows it. After this tailgate lunch we're serving a stolen-property warrant on a Gangster Disciples building. A warrant that requires all seven of us be alive. There are thirty thousand members of the GDs nationwide, probably a third or more headquartered in Chicago. Many, if not all, can be on the violent side of unpleasant.

I, on the other hand, am a model of self-control when responding to my sergeant. 'And your freight-train ass is modeling underwear?'

My partner Cisco Pike reaches to mediate and sloshes coffee

across the hood of our Ford, stammering something nobody understands. Cisco has a speech impediment when he's flustered; I think it makes him semi-adorable, but not enough for what you're thinking. Like Cisco, my fellow TAC officers are chuckling, trying to imagine Sergeant Sonny Barrett BVD-clad and runway-ready. Only I bother to wipe at the coffee.

This TAC vehicle, like all the others, is a beater – five years on the job, one hubcap, and two-thirds of the paint it had when new. In Chicago TAC officers only drive what the detectives won't. The dicks wear department-store blazers and knowing expressions. We wear body armor and quick-draw holsters, clothes you could garden in, and tomato sauce on our sleeves – although that's primarily Sonny. Many of the brass and media rate TAC officers only slightly above the outlaws we police. We invite both groups to ride the ghetto with us. Better still, without us. Bring the wife and kids; make a day of it.

District 6, where we work, like districts 2 and 7, is not a good place to be. For anyone. There's plenty of harsh on both sides, plenty of animosity, enough to poison families for generations. Trust me, I know: I came from a place like this. Bosses and reporters ask me why I don't work Traffic instead. Traffic doesn't help and that's as far as I can explain it. I want to help, and most of the folks down here get so little, it wouldn't add up to pity.

Sonny hard-eyes me across the fender and taps the hood. '*How 'bout you break-this-shit-down, Patti Ann, one last time for da brothers.*'

Good sergeants let you run your own warrants; mine wants a replay of the raid diagram while he looks for a street-corner high-five to go with his modified pimp roll. He looks stupid, sort of a cross between a grizzly bear and an Irishman two beers into the parade, but I know why he's doing it. A focused and loose crew makes fewer mistakes.

Cisco smiles at Sonny's act, then at me. Without me, Cisco would be three times dead, and there isn't a moment when that statistic is lost on him. If luck is real – and it damn sure is – then I'm his and he's mine. Other than his tendency toward fad cologne, Cisco's perfect. *Almost* perfect – there is the occasional smatter of night-school psychobabble. Since spring, his college homework has often been focused at me and the illusion that I have shortcomings. 'Issues,' Cisco likes to call them now that he's educated: 'An unapproachable self' – figure that out while you're rolling through the ghetto. 'Avoidance of thread' – another simple one he says has to do with 'connecting the dots of one's life.' And yesterday's comment, that I still play rugby every weekend and won't wear nail polish. That one I get. I have trouble being a *girl* girl, but that's none of his fucking business, is it? Then there's this other rumor, that I only take criticism well as long as I don't hear it.

Sonny burps and says, 'Okay, cowboys, saddle up.' He's done eating, so the rest of us need to be. 'We gon get us some stereo equipment.'

The attempt on the mayor ceases to matter, as do our cultural differences on the Cubs and Sox. We toss the coffee, pack the papers, and bag the cups. I keep everyone's edible scraps; they help sustain most of the stray animals in 6 and save me from buying them emergency hot dogs.

Everyone checks their pistols. Mine's the only revolver, and they mention that all the time too. Three of us check shotguns. I draw the plan a second time on my hood. Everyone nods, the levity fading, the adrenaline coming. Two of the boys will handle the Chicago bar and the sixteen-pound hammer. I'll do the door since I know the perps. They'll hear, 'Better to live till tomorrow,' then it's up to them. And occasionally GDs make very poor decisions.

Sonny drops his chin, eyeing all of us; he's lost two partners where we're going, one dead, one to a wheelchair. 'These are bad people, kids. None of us die today.'

We all nod. Eloquent he's not, but Sonny Barrett's always on the money.

This far south, Halsted Street looks like what it is. And the seven of us look like what we are – three TAC cars rolling fast in convoy, passing street-corner lookouts with junior high educations and only one question: *Where?* They're part; we're part, everyone mixed into the swizzle and swazzle. Sonny's Ford makes a left on Vincennes; he has the lead, burning oil we can taste.

Three blocks and we'll be at the dead end of Gilbert Court. Two uniform officers died there in '03, shot fifteen times in their car. My heart's starting to ramp, keeping time with the song in my head. Springsteen's 'Born in the U.S.A.' Cisco's smiling, at what I'm not sure. He does that with some frequency.

Sonny's Ford is pushing 50 and so's ours; the brick storefronts start to blur, hand–painted signs mush into one sentence, 'Big Julie's Suit Up, Temple Mercy, Time Out Lounge, Esta's Chicken Wings.' The shotgun bumps heavy against my vest; I've never had to kill anyone. You make me, and I will, nobody on these streets doubts that, but I lose sleep over a split–second decision that's *right here, right now* all the time.

Two blocks. This neighborhood is ten square miles, parts of which most Americans wouldn't believe were in our country. I've been here since I was twenty-one, watched it change from white to black, working-class to poor, then poor to ghetto. Plywood covers more windows than glass, and not because it's cheaper.

One block. We're doing 60 now. I know all the people who operate these stores, people who try like those who tried before them. Their lives can't be fixed with sermons or promises. Both are popular but useless down here; it's a war zone in every sense of the term – poverty, dope, and gangs, gangs like small countries have armies.

Cisco hits the brakes.

Lookouts yell, '5-0! 5-0!' and scatter.

Our three cars make the turn. In an instant Gilbert Court is flooded by seven white cops with dead-serious expressions, two with shotguns running to the building's rear, me with a twelve-gauge charging the front. Cisco has the Chicago bar, Eric Jackson the hammer. We're on the steps and I'm knocking with my foot. Sonny and the boys are right behind us ready to pour in when the door goes.

'POLICE. We got a warrant, Carlos. Open it NOW!'

Three, two, one. I stand back, Cisco wedges the bar, Eric slams the hammer. The door and frame splinter, a good sign. Fortification usually means armament.

Big flash. Then the roar. The door and frame explode in our faces. *Machine gun.* Cisco's down and Eric Jackson's firing. I'm bent sideways and blind. Pistols bang from behind. I can't see and drop to a knee. Eric sails over the railing. Concussions run together; the air's cordite and flashes. Can't hear – hands grab me, something clubs me in the face. An arm chokes my neck . . .

I fight, kick, claw – *anything not to be taken*, can't see to shoot. I'm headlocked, being dragged by a gorilla with four arms. Big shotgun blasts from the back. Guys yelling. Three gangsters rush past; the gorilla pushes me toward the center.

'Hostage, motherfucka! Hostage 5-0!'

Sonny's firing. I'm choking out and slam a crotch with my shotgun. *Big blast* from mine and behind, then another, and I'm down on a knee. The four-armed gorilla becomes two GDs who drop me and sprint retreat through the apartment. They slam open the back door and I'm chasing before I realize I'm standing. In the tiny yard our backup shotguns are engaged by GDs with pistols banging from the building's corners. My two make it into the alley and across, running for the nearest six-flat. One turns to fire. I duck; he falls, we scramble up, both running again. I can't afford to shoot into the six-flat and miss. He doesn't give a shit and fires twice.

Shotguns roar behind me. At the neighbor's stoop I stumble, don't think, and bolt into the hallway. Five steps in I see both GDs sprinting out the back and something surreal charging up out of the basement stairwell. Two white ComEd workers hit me like linebackers. I'm down, suddenly swimming in gasoline and there's no air. The white guys run out a door into daylight. I cough blind and try to stand. More gunshots make me duck. Framed in the doorway a white van squeals away. I fan through the fumes for GDs – none on the floor; none on the stairs. Cough; blink. Gasoline's everywhere.

Gasoline.

'FIRE! FIRE!'

The basement has to be full of gas, and the building's three floors full of people. I pound on first–floor doors nobody in their right mind would open. 'FIRE! FIRE! Get out!' If anyone's smoking anything, I'll be a torch. I take the stairs higher two at a time. 'Out! Out!' More doors, more pounding. A woman opens and I grab her. 'GET OUT. Building's on fire!' She balks and I jerk her into the hall. 'OUT! OUT!' Doors crack; white eyes; children crouch, heads peek down through the stair railing. Nobody's safe here, ever; nobody's sure. I smell like a bomb. 'C'mon people, out in the alley. Now. Now. NOW.'

Dogs bark and run everywhere. The six-flat's empty – thirty angry, scared citizens have been pushed through the fences to Gilbert Court. No one has belongings, no picture frames or dishes. Gilbert Court is chaos; the neighborhood's already marshaling, jeering from the windows and shaking their fists. Squads scream in. Two white cops are down but alive. Two black gangsters are dead in the blood, glass, weapons, and wood shards. Brass casings and Cisco cover the stoop. Cisco's staring at me from his back, eyes cloudy, his speech impediment half there, half not. 'Smell like a S-shell station. Whata happen?'

Before I can help him a hand grabs my shoulder. I spin and punch and it's a fireman staggering back. We're both confused. Another one points at me, 'Your clothes, asshole. C'mere,' and he shoves me with a small hose. An EMT rushes Cisco, I get a shower.

A cold one. The fireman tells me to 360; the water pressure's triple my shower at home and I have to brace against it, eyes closed. Cisco's laughing, ringside for a body-armor wet T-shirt contest. The water quits as Cisco's EMT pats him and flashes thumbs–up to her partner. I stumble, fogged on adrenaline and still smell like gas, just less so. Two more EMTs have Eric

Jackson standing, but not under his own power. He looks loopy but his feet are moving, scuffing past the youngest of the dead GDs. I squeegee water and slick back my hair, trying to find steady, then recognize the sprawled body; I know the dead boy's mother.

I turn back to help Cisco and his EMT. The fireman in my face says, 'Strip,' then points to another fellow like they do this all the time, 'Give her a jacket.'

I give him the finger. *In your fucking dreams, homes*. He shrugs at stupid and joins firemen running across the alley. Cisco's on a gurney. My eyes jump to the gasolined six-flat expecting flames. No flames; no occupants died. Deep breath – *c'mon, baby, slow it down*. Dying in a fire is a bad way to go, old people especially. They seem to just curl up in a corner and wait for it to take them. More sirens; our uniforms have the perimeter of the whole block. Our own small army, like every cop in 6 and 7 is here. It's a weird picture for the citizens and always is – the ghetto's rhythm just floating along, then BANG, 5-0 every-damn-where. Makes you wonder what the vibe's like after we're gone.

Sonny's at my shoulder, his pistol pointed at the pavement. 'You all right, P?'

'Huh? Eric's okay, right?'

'Vest stopped it at the shoulder, knocked the fuck out of him, though. Dislocated it.'

I spin to find Cisco. Sonny watches Cisco waving weak as he's put in the ambulance and says Cisco's gonna be off work a while, but he's too educated to die. My knees weaken as the adrenaline dies off and Sonny grabs my collar. I fracture a smile and don't knock his hand away. 'Lotta bullets for some stereo equipment.'

Sonny appears to be having similar thoughts but doesn't share.

'Gonna be more medals for this, P; soaked in fuckin' gasoline and evac-ing a building.' He shakes his head, tilting toward Ireland like he does after five beers. 'I'm hatin' to admit it, but you a gutsy bit a skirt,' and he headlocks me to his vest, a tear in his eye. I know Sonny Barrett; it's definitely the gasoline.

Within minutes Gilbert Court is surrounded by angry citizens. Three media trucks arrive followed by the Homicide dicks who'll run the crime scene while OPS – Office of Professional Standards – watches, waiting to write up the officer–involved shootings. An OPS officer's already eyeing me and my shotgun. This means it will be a long day of interviews after the dicks clear the scene.

The crime-scene techs arrive while the uniforms push back taunting citizens, then string miles of yellow tape. I notice our Watch LT from 6. He's the lieutenant who runs our shift, an 'empty-holster motherfucker' it has been said by those less respectful than I. He and an assistant state's attorney are shoulder-to-shoulder, arms folded, second-guessing our actions. The black bodies aren't covered and look strangely potent on the pavement. Now they're focal, not random and nameless. They're connected to consequences and careers. A black woman I know calls me to the tape.

'Why you kill those boys, Patti Black?'

Although it seems really simple, it isn't. 'You know, Drea. When they shoot at us, we're gonna shoot back.' I point at the two converted TEC-9s in the street. 'Those aren't TV machine guns.'

The boy next to her isn't four feet tall. He's watching from under the tape and says, 'Like on TV?' Drea shoos him away but he just loops her hips and tugs at my jeans. 'You all wet.'

I squat and my knees hold. His little hand squeezes water from my sweatshirt and he laughs. I point at the fireman. 'That man gave me a shower. Thought I smelled bad.'

The boy squints. Drea says, 'That's Ruth Ann's boy, Robert. Ain't it?'

I nod, imagining Ruth Ann's face on her porch twenty minutes from now when they come to tell her Robert's dead. He'll be her third. I wince and tell the pavement: 'Really hate it shit like this has to happen.'

And I do.

Our Watch LT has moved to my left so Channel 7's sunbrites can pick up his name and the glint from his silver bars. He tells a Homicide dick, 'She does love our African Americans.'

I turn into the Homicide dick's answer – 'Almost as much as she does the reporters.' He stares right at me. 'Clears two or three murders, bitch thinks she's a dick.'

Our Watch LT frowns agreement and checks the camera. 'Does *not* hurt to have the superintendent's ear either.'

The dick smiles, adding volume: 'Ain't just his ear.'

He and I are sharing eight feet of pavement and Channel 7's camera lens. I make him forty pounds over and figure his wife has a boyfriend, hopefully two, and different colors.

The fireman who hosed me steps between us and says, 'You might want to look at this.'

I can't tell whether he's refereeing or he really has something. If he does, he needs to talk to the dicks running the scene, not me. I walk with him mainly because it's away from my temper and my two fans with rank. As we pass the second body, a *Tribune* reporter I know yells my name. I say, 'Sorry,' and point at the guys in the blazers and keep walking.

The street deputy arrives with his entourage. He's a deputy superintendent, the highest CPD rank who responds to crime scenes and wields the superintendent's authority. All the man-power that doesn't migrate to him stays focused on the shoot-out crime scene. So far, only the firemen are interested in the gasolined six-flat – it's theirs until they release it. As we cross the alley to the six–flat the fireman comments that it's odd the building has a Gilbert Court address, then says, 'Fuck those two. That move took balls, lady. You come to work for us whenever you want.'

He registers as honest, a nice change from most men. His eyes linger a bit longer than they should; probably a compliment but it just makes me fidget. 'What're we looking at?'

'Basement.'

Downstairs, the six-flat's basement is flooded twenty-four inches and already stinks. I stay on the stairs. He looks at me like more water can't hurt, but he doesn't have to buy my gym shoes. The other firemen are ringing back from a wall section they hacked up by the furnace. I squat and squint. One shines a light that reflects on the tricolor water. There's something white in the rainbow. A bone. No, a hand, palm up with long rigid fingers and no skin. The floating hand's connected to a sleeved arm and part of a body buried in the wall.

Don't see that every day.

The fireman waves me over. I slosh across – a mistake, since this basement is now a homicide scene. Up close, the bones wear a woman's velour jacket popular in the '90s; she's crunched, facing away and tied with leather ligatures that run from neck to wrist. One ligature has snapped with age. I try to see her face but can't. The fireman points his light inside the crypt over dead

20

worms and roaches at what looks like fingernail ruts in the wood.

He exhales in a whoosh, then says, 'Went in alive.'

The hand's floating near my shin; her fingertips are jagged. Above them her wrist bones have a metal wrist restraint, *perv-manacles* we call them, sex-crime equipment that vice and child services see more often than us.

My wrists have manacle scars too, hard welts I avoid when I wash. She's barefoot. I wasn't allowed shoes when I was pregnant at fifteen. It was in the Bible and kept me from running away; they wanted the baby. The ankle bones glint in the light, but I don't look. There might be manacles on them too. The basement shrinks; fouled air thickens, gasoline water wants to rise over my head. I stumble, flashing through years of piecing together a me, making a person out of the wreckage. I don't want to fall, not in this water, not near the hand with the manacles. And I won't, if I quit thinking.

About all the things I've spent twenty–three years not thinking about.

Chapter 2

MONDAY, DAY 1: AFTERNOON

My afternoon is eight hours of interviews at 111th and Cottage Grove, the Area 2 Detective Division, sometimes referred to as ADD by tired and shaken patrol officers who take issue with repeatedly answering the same question.

Each interview is done separately, but the questions don't change, nor do the dour expressions and sidebar conversations. First, it's the Homicide dicks who already interviewed you at the scene; then one at a time, it's the rest of them – OPS, the ASA (Chicago's version of DA/district attorney), our Watch LT, and the street deputy backed by his entourage. They all want to know why you didn't do it differently.

I don't complain because I understand why we're doing this; people died, people with families and maybe even futures. Today, the intermissions are worse than the interrogations. I keep seeing the body in the wall and the hand in the tricolor water. And the manacle.

After our Watch LT finishes the gunfight segment of his questions and his third sidebar with an assistant state's attorney who wasn't introduced, our Watch LT asks me again,

'Why chase the perpetrators across the alley into the six-flat?'

He's been marching toward the conclusion that I abandoned my fellow officers to make the 'hero move' – like he'd have an idea what that was. His name is Carson Scott, *Lieutenant* Carson Scott if you wish less shit to fall on you during your workday. Thankfully, I don't see him often unless something awful like this happens. He's an asshole – a racist and a weekend golfer who keeps his nose embedded in the rear seam of any plaid-pants that might get him lifted to captain or feather his ambitions for public office.

'I was protecting my fellow officers by giving chase, by remaining connected to the shooters.'

He jots down my answer a third time. Privately, we call him 'Kit' Carson and speculate that a ringmaster position in a wild west show would be the proper promotion.

'And that's why you abandoned wounded Officers Pike and Jackson?'

'*Abandoned*?'

'Please answer the question.' He's looking at the blank line where his pen will record the answer.

I repeat the same explanation. He writes it down again, then checks it against the previous lines. His pen taps and he curls his lower lip under expensive teeth. Kit Carson has family money he didn't earn and a law degree from DePaul on the Northside. If you don't know the city, Chicago has a 'north/south thing' – the city's separated into two distinct tribal nations by a river engineered to flow backwards from Lake Michigan: the Southside says it works for a living, while the Northside pays five dollars for coffee and has maids to open their windows.

Kit Carson says, 'Hmmm . . . IAD may need to look at this.'

IAD is the Internal Affairs Division. There's no way IAD needs to look at this, and won't unless Kit Carson files a CR number (complaint register investigation) on me, a complaint that would have the same basis in fact as pudding would in the foundation of the Sears Tower. My mouth moves before I can cover it.

'Gimme a break, Kit. Jesus.'

'What?' He two-hands the pen and leans toward me.

'There's no violation of policy. No 'abandonment.' All I did was what we're supposed to. You'd know that if you ever left your desk.'

Lieutenant Carson writes that down, taking time to recheck the grammar. 'That will be all, Officer Black.'

But it isn't. I can assure you that these interviews are why the police would rather not shoot anyone. And when the interviews are over you cap the twelve–hour, two–death day by dodging accusations from neighborhood politicians waiting outside with the cameras, then doing paperwork until your hands hurt.

My day finally finishes because people like Kit Carson have other things to do and even the bad days end – an elemental truth sane cops learn early, along with no one's solving shit out here. Little victories are all you get. Live inside those and you can still hope to make a difference . . . for somebody. Cisco for one. So, I stop by Christ Hospital, where he looks comfy, all dopey and bracketed by two red-eyed parents still tie-dyed from the '60s (hence his name) and student nurses who like their heroes with bullet holes and sidearms. Good guess is he'll be milking this for days, pun intended. Eric Jackson has already been released to his wife and kids and a barber shop business he'd rather tell you about than hit the lottery.

24

The Dan Ryan is its usual twenty-four-hour river of chugging metal and frustration, inching me toward my duplex, and I don't care – my Celica feels like an armchair and if I still drank, it'd be Miller Time. I no longer partake, other than the miniature bottle of Old Crow I carry as a keychain talisman. See, my Miller Time became somewhat extended – every day all day, age sixteen to twenty. All the Old Crow a little white workin' girl could hustle and swallow.

Traffic stays miserable to the Y at I-57, then eases for the last two miles to 111th. In between Ramsey Lewis and U2 my radio says both the Cubs and Sox won today. More overtime for everyone; Mardi Gras has come to both sides of the river.

I'll be home in just blocks and should be smiling. But I'm not, I'm thinking, scattershot, like I do when I don't get it and probably should: I see the two GDs sprawled on Gilbert Court and frown deeper. Dead teenagers – even GDs with machine guns – tend to mar a day's 'little victories.' I also see two white guys with gasoline in a part of town where white guys, even ComEd workers, need armed guards. They filled the basement with gasoline ... *Shiver*; I'm not a big fan of basements ... and God knows we don't need a multi-block ghetto fire like in Philadelphia.

I make a turn without looking. No way I knew the body in the wall, but her terror's familiar enough. My hands change position so I can't see the scars on my wrist. I make three more turns on residential streets; the last one avoids Tripod the neighborhood poodle.

There's a parking place at my curb. God has shined on me at last. I kill the engine, take a deep breath that doesn't taste like city, and I'm finally a civilian. *Get me Dorothy's red shoes and a parasol*. Out front, my flowers look great, especially the marigolds. My marigolds have everything but major medical and a Social Security number.

I turn and consider my street; it's crowned more than normal and when it storms the rain rushes to the curbs. 'Quaint' you might call it, little bungalows and little lawns, about half old people and half Chicago cops or firemen. Mount Greenwood. It even sounds quaint. The younger guys with power mowers mow the widow ladies' lawns. The trees drop leaves the size of catcher's mitts. If they still delivered milk twice a week, my street would be the milkman's favorite.

I reach to key the lock and—

Son of a. Beneath the CPD star and the voodoo doll hanging from the knocker my door's a B&E. The clothes bag drops out of my hand; I draw, step through. Instantly *my* living room's gunsight narrow and threatening, nothing in it mine.

Who's here? How many?

My heart adds beats. Both hands on the pistol. I step slow, cocked forward to fire – kitchen, clean. Bedroom. Clean. Bathroom. Clean. Closet, pantry, under the bed. Clean. My second pistol's in the drawer where it's supposed to be. Porch, backyard. Clean. *Motherfuckers*, this is my house.

Neighbor?

I run out front and pound on Stella's door. Stella's a home beautician and too old to hear her own radio. I pound again, get nothing, step back to kick in the door and it opens; Stella looks more confused than usual. Probably the gun and my foot in the air.

'You all right, Stell?' Beyond her shoulder there's—

She squints and says, '. . . Ah, fine?'

'You are?'

She feebles up her usual grin and reaches for the blond pony-tail exiting my Cubs cap. 'Tricia, such pretty blue eyes, but your hair. Always such a fright. You'll never get a man.'

Relief. We're back to the basics. I holster the pistol that Stella doesn't acknowledge. Next will be a comment on the Cubs fixation – a distinctly Northsider trait that's not too popular on our side of the river. Or else she'll say my work clothes do *nothing* for me. She goes with the clothes. 'Tricia, no man wants a waste-basket for a wife.'

'Stell, honey, did you happen to see someone by my door?'

She steps out past her screen and looks at mine. 'You should fix that, Patti. What if company came?'

I nod because it's easier. 'But did you see anybody? Today?'

'Busy, busy.' She reaches for my hair again. 'We'll fix you tomorrow.'

One of our neighbors is in Stella's chair with the hairdryer space-helmet on. She smiles; I smile. Stella closes the door in my face. I step around my broken door. Front door. Not my back door. A choice that demonstrates a level of brazenness one associates with drug-induced stupidity or knowledge of the neighbors.

Inside I check stuff that matters.

Jezebel and Bathsheba are swimming like champs. No doubt they saw the intruders but goldfish make shit witnesses so I don't ask. My TV's still there, the stereo too. Strange, both are hophead magnets. I had a John Coltrane CD on last night and its case is where I left it. The Johnny Cougar album is still fronting my LP stack – the last one before he went back to John Mellencamp.

My living room seems unmolested. This is not true of my

bedroom. My bed's mussed. The perps sat on it, facing my dresser. Then probably stood – *assholes* – and looked close at the pictures wedged into the mirror's curved frame. Pictures that take up so much mirror there's no reflection, pictures of me caked in mud, arm-in-arm with rugby teammates Tracy Moens – a hardass, max-competitive, prima-bitch reporter with the *Chicago Herald*, and Julie McCoy, my best pal and owner of the L7 Bar.

Pictures of me with my TAC crew at CPD picnics, Cisco and Sonny and Eric Jackson trying to look all gunfighter. I can't help the grin that crosses my face. They are *da* boys – 'the Magnificent Seven' if you count me, alpha-male hell, but I love them. Even Sonny Barrett if I don't think about it too hard. They and Julie are the brothers and sisters I never had.

I have lots of pictures and can't tell if any are missing. Three for sure aren't. One's the superintendent of police in full uniform when he was the chief of detectives. Then there's me and '60s all-star Ernie Banks at Wrigley Field on fan day – *how cool was that?* Me and Ernie talking home runs and . . . And there's a beautiful baby, a day old and pink. His picture has yellowed with years, taped to the mirror at eye level. PANIC. I check behind the mirror. The envelope's still there, still yellowed too, still taped. The deep breath helps—

A quarter inch from my Kleenex box there's a dust line. I stare, reliving the morning: Did I bump the dresser, sit on the bed? I check the second pistol again. Nope, we're okay; it really is in the drawer. That stops me. Wanna explain why we do a B&E and don't take a gun? That's like leaving a bag of gold. Pistols are illegal inside the Chicago city limits, hence they bring big dollars from the fences and street gangsters. The only way we left this is if we didn't see it.

And the only way we didn't see it is if we didn't look.

Then why the hell break in here in broad daylight?

Which is now gone. I'm supposed to be practicing at Grant Park right now, downtown by the lake – we have the big game this Saturday against the Bay Area SheHawks. My rugby cleats and kit bag are in my locker at 6 where I left them. Exhale; shoulder sag. I'm way too tired to deal with repairing the broken door locks or this ... this witless B&E. No-showing practice when my friends depend on me won't work either; ditto spending the night alone with two dead teenagers and a manacled woman in the wall.

I strip, figuring to don the rugby shorts and jersey a respectable fly half would wear (sans the prissy-ass eyeliner Tracy Moens will be wearing), then quit for two reasons – my rugby gear's not here – duh? And no real desire to participate in the world of the living. I grab unironed jeans, my pistol and star, refind the car keys, and feed the fish. *Love you girls: Promise we'll do water world on Sunday.* I know, I know, filling the bathtub for their weekly excursion may seem stupid, but it's no different than taking your dog to the park. I even have underwater props. And the happiest goldfish in Chicago.

And I'm gone, heading east to anywhere. Lights veer in behind me, filling the mirror. In the glare I see that basement, the fingernail ruts clawed into the wood, the expressions on the firemen's faces ... Bony fingers reach for me – *Stop it* – like a B horror movie, but I don't go to horror movies. Denial's my copilot; I'm an expert at burying the day's depravity ... except there's my wrist and the scar; and there's the bony hand—

Horn. LOUD. Shit! Brakes – miss the guy's fender. Jesus Christ. Sorry. Sorry. Get a freakin' grip, Patti. Two hands on the wheel.

Deep breath. Steer ... Doing fine, doing fine. You're a cop, remember? A gunfighter. Patti Black. *The* Patti Black, okay? You know how to drive. So I do and a ghost whispers, 'Chinatown' to the back of my neck.

Rugby practice is five minutes from over when my Celica decides to stop at Grant Park. Why it drove here I don't know, but now that I have, it's best to make an appearance. The younger girls on the sidelines nod, less than pleased with my absence but not inclined to push it. Last week I played with them in the She-Devil 15s tournament and not particularly well, something a brave few mentioned when we lost. My excuses weren't good so naturally I made several, including being thirty-eight.

They toe the grass with their cleats and continue talking with their significant others, mostly about the assassination attempt on the mayor. Their theories range from *Ryan's Hope* to *The Godfather* in complexity. Me, I'm voting for the same 'lone gunman' who shot our Mayor Cermak back in the '30s and JFK in the '60s. Lone gunmen, like serial killers, have earned wide acceptance in the media and general public. If you don't have a suspect in twenty–four hours, either of those fits like twenty dollars does 'Hey, baby' on Soul Street.

One of the rugby girls isn't trading theories – it's my stellar teammate, Miss All-Everything redhead, Tracy L. Moens, known to her fellow reporters as the Pink Panther. It's not a compliment. Tracy has the body language of an anchor relay sprinter already set in the blocks and the compassion of concrete on a cold day. I want her and Sonny Barrett to date, drink heavily, and maim one another.

She tosses the ball away but stays at the sideline and smiles like

I'm the only person she ever cared about. 'Tough morning, huh?' It's likely she's the only one here who knows about the GD shooting on Gilbert Court.

I nod, then wince at the hamstring I'm attempting to stretch instead of talk to her.

'Care to talk about it?'

I stare. We also have an unwritten rule, Ms. Moens and I. No work stuff at practice or matches. Anywhere else is fair game. But not here and not now. She only forgets that when it's important to her.

'BASH is gonna be a bitch, Trace. Let's focus on them.'

'Thought I'd ask.' She flashes the reporter smile that conveniently hides her sharpest teeth. The others are perfect.

My pal, Julie McCoy, hasn't spoken to me yet because she's busy doing what I'm supposed to be doing. Rugby's her whole life since the motorcycle wreck in Nice ended her cello career. My teammates finish running lines and plays and Julie finally appears. She starts by appraising my street clothes.

'Damn, Patti, forget how to play?'

'Technically, yeah.'

'Tracy looked sharp tonight. She's younger though.'

I add, 'And prettier.'

'That too. Lots more money, boyfriends. Really something, isn't she?'

'Technically, yeah.' I try not to smile. Julie's very good at this for a big blond saloon keeper.

'So? Practice for BASH or just show up Saturday and cripple your teammates?'

Cripple? Maim? I can't help but glance at Tracy sparkling in the lights. Julie laughs. I start to answer and she drapes her arm over my shoulder, 'Come with me, stay upstairs, have a pizza. Be a Northsider for the night. You can borrow a good shirt for work if you don't get any blood on it.'

A one-night vacation across the river in yuppie land. Won't have to worry about the locksmith or phantom B&Es that make no sense.

'Can we ride in your BMW and wave at the poor people?'

The L7 is a 'women's bar.' Take a look at the L and the 7 and you'll figure it out. Julie's version is brick-wall retro, a Beat generation coffeehouse combined with a full bar, behind which is a long mirror centered by a twenty-foot grainy photo of Julie and her Ducati café racer splattered into a sidewalk bistro in Nice. Four years ago on the anniversary of the crash she got drunk and autographed ten feet of photo in aerosol orange.

The music is usually loud and bluesy – Bessie Simone, k. d. lang, Billie Holiday. The ceiling's high and serpentine with flex A/C ducts painted like snakes that only get that big in your nightmares. Julie's walls are covered with autographed rugby jerseys and pictures of her heroes: Jack Kerouac, Allen Ginsberg, Ken Kesey. At the back there's a small stage, in front there's a loyal clientele strange enough to be in a John Waters movie. Actually, there's a picture of him too, autographed by Johnny Depp and kissed bright red by Traci Lords.

We do not have this type of spot on the Southside, nor do we have the asshole comedian up there doing deaf-guy humor. He's reading something, mimicking Lou Ferrigno's impediment, and nobody's laughing – at least you gotta give these Northsiders that. Guys like Cisco and Mr. Ferrigno deserve better; it's got to be hard wearing your weakness for everybody to see and still having the balls to press on anyway.

The TV above the bar is on but soundless, and I focus on it instead of the comedian. The running lines are the reporter reporting on the assassination attempt backed by video of the mayor and his wife. Julie leans across the bar, glances at the stage, then refills my water.

'So?'

I shrug.

'Talk, sweetie. You don't miss practice. Ever. Other than your fish, we're the only life you have.'

'Thanks. I miss one day and Ms. Moens is playing my position?'

'She and I *are* the sponsors.'

Tracy and Julie are partners in the L7. They were lovers once, but no longer, at least that me and the public know about. I shrug, not wanting to get into my day, the stuff I did and saw.

Julie says, 'Don't make me come over there.'

She's much bigger than me, but I have a gun and mention that.

'Seen it, sweetie.' She grabs my hands. 'Is this about the mayor? Talk to me. No kidding.'

So I do. But not about the body in the wall. I talk about the Gangster Disciple shooting, about knowing the kid, knowing his mom. All the shit you don't want to know, don't want to share, and don't want to relive after seeing it firsthand and then reporting it for eight goddamn hours to the wrinkle–free blazers.

The comedian finishes about when I do, and now the small crowd applauds – so much for my new faith in the Northside. Better still, he pulls up a stool next to me, smiles so warm I almost blush, and stays with the deaf guy impression, talking directly to me from too close. I notice a cell phone on his belt and consider shoving it up his ass, then turn back to Julie because I missed what she said. The guy puts his hand on me and I'm off the stool before he can finish, my hand close to my pistol, eyes hard in his.

'*Do not* put your fucking hands on me.' I seem a bit on edge.

Julie tells my cheek, 'He can't hear you.'

'He can hear a .38.' I'm still glaring at him.

'He's deaf, Patti.'

I glance at Julie. 'He's a deaf comedian?'

'He's a poet. The comedian's going on now.'

I glance at the stage; there's a girl with a bad haircut mounting it. The deaf poet is walking away, his back to me. I start to yell an apology but realize that won't do much good. Julie's eyes are burning my cheek. I look. Her frown's bigger than before.

'*Shit*. I'm sorry.'

Julie spoon feeds guilt across the bar. '*Men*, thinking they can compliment a single woman sittin' alone at a bar.'

My phone vibrates my hip. It's the superintendent of police. He wants to see me, at the Berghoff Restaurant, State and Adams. NOW.

34

Chapter 3

MONDAY, DAY 1: 11:00 P.M.

Eleven p.m. at the Berghoff Restaurant is a strange place to meet the superintendent of police. Then again, somebody doesn't take a shot at the mayor every day. And in Chicago, the mayor appoints the superintendent of police, who appoints all our big bosses, from the captains to the chiefs. So, if the mayor goes, by bullet or ballot, so does most of the brass.

I'm a patrolman, a ghetto cop. Why talk to me?

The homeless man facing me at Adams and Wabash doesn't answer. I'm in the Loop and completely out of my element. The Loop is the financial district where all the rapid–transit trains come together overhead in a – you guessed it – loop. If you saw the car chase in *The French Connection*, that's how it looks. Except better, since we're in Chicago, not New York.

At my back two lions guard the Art Institute; tonight they're animated, peering through the banks and insurance companies at my ass and licking their lips. Like most civil servants I'm a little leery uptown: I owe mortgage payments to one of these skyscrapers and car payments to another. It takes two more blocks of imposing buildings before I figure the superintendent's summons: This is about Kit Carson. Lt. Milquetoast phoned his golfing buddies at IAD and I'm about to get—

I stutter-step to avoid a second homeless man dressed similar to me. I apologize and he demands money or 'some pussy.' I decline both and continue west. Maybe the superintendent uses the Berghoff to avoid the reporters camped at HQ 24/7. The Berghoff's basement dining room would be a good spot to meet with outsiders. Could be he just wants to chat when his dinner's over. *Right*.

Much more likely this is about – *much more likely?* Who're you kidding? There isn't one thing about this summons that's 'likely.' Or it could be the superintendent just wants me to mow his lawn.

Our superintendent is . . . how do I say this . . . a bit unusual, a nice fellow who could easily have been a professional wrestler or governor of Minnesota. His name is Jesse too and his close friends still call him Chief. Chief Jesse Smith is of distant Native American extraction. He's a Hohokam, so the 'Chief' part works both ways and you gotta be careful. The other 85 percent of him is the standard mix of white European and not all that happy.

He's also childless and thirty years divorced from an upwardly mobile woman who's now married to the wealthiest radiologist in Illinois. Other than the chief's marital choices, I like him and he likes me – I'm sort of the daughter he never had; he was my boss in 6 before becoming the fearless leader of our 13,500 blue uniforms. Unlike Lieutenant Carson and the *little dicks* in the department – *dick* is short for detective; *little dick* is a bit less flattering – Chief Jesse does not think I'm a grandstander. Chief Jesse has, however, made the occasional comment on my attitude. I think 'therapy' was mentioned in one heated exchange; it was off the record, but not real far. Other than this lapse in judgment, he is an astute judge of character. Definitely a man I listen to when he has something to say, especially when it's prefaced with my name.

Nine feet before the Berghoff's basement door Chief Jesse's uniformed aide steps into my path and points me toward an idling '05 Town Car. A driver is standing against the rear fender waving traffic past, pretending he can't see me or anything else.

Inside, most of the leather backseat is the superintendent. The windows are up tight. Someone smoked in here then tried to deodorize it, that or it's a hooker's perfume. We'll call that nervous humor – a very strange day is getting stranger. The superintendent of police is staring at me. So I ask.

'Hi.' Not much of a question, but I'm a bit off balance. There's a personnel file in his lap, and my name's on it. He nods at me, a habit when he's displeased; his thick fingers drum on my file. 'An interesting day, Officer Black.'

Our meeting doesn't seem to be about our Democrat mayor or the Assassination Task Force formed *very publicly* yesterday by our Republican governor and the Cook County State's Attorney's Office. So this meeting *has* to be about Kit Carson and his chicken-shit CR numbers. Instead of anger I feel a shiver that I shouldn't, a feeling that doesn't fit, same as when you know there's something behind the shower curtain but still need to get in naked.

The highest-ranking police officer in Chicago says, 'Our *Republican* governor and his State's Attorney's office believe the attempt on Mayor McQuinn is connected to next month's mayoral election, not an attempt to interrupt the casino license vote . . . as if the two aren't interrelated.' Chief Jesse shakes his large head and it's not hard to imagine a headdress. 'Either they

37

don't teach "follow the money" in law school or the professors have never been in a casino.'

I sigh relief that I don't show. Evidently this *is* about the mayor and the casino license, a license that will significantly alter the city's balance of power.

'Should there be another attempt before the election, and the assassination is successful, Alderman Leslie Gibbons will become our new mayor as well as our Democratic incumbent in the election.' Chief Jesse glances away, investigating Adams Street beyond his window. I follow his eyes and can't tell any difference from last year, other than Adams is dark and none of my drunk teammates are with me.

'Alderman Gibbons is black.' *Black* hangs against his window; and it should since the alderman's racial make–up is not new information. 'Gibbons would then run against this year's extremely well-financed Republican challenger. And although there is no assurance that a black candidate cannot be elected again, our Republican opponents believe Gibbons would be significantly easier to defeat than Mayor McQuinn.'

I do the political math. *'The governor hired Rush Limbaugh to hit the mayor?'*

Chief Jesse returns from the window with a frown that flares his nostrils. Obviously I have missed a crucial bit of information. That, or once again, my mouth has outpaced my command of city politics.

'Republican malfeasance is one possibility.' The superintendent's tone isn't good, although the picture of Limbaugh on the radio trading his prescription dope for hitmen is pretty funny. I notice no such fantasy on the superintendent's face and don't describe the vision.

'Another possibility is Alderman Gibbons. Alderman Gibbons is from District 6, your district. As is Louis Farrakhan and his bow–tie army of Muslims. While the State's Attorney's Office stumbles about with their high–profile task force, would you mind terribly if you were asked to do the same?'

'Sir?' I'm not following him. I'm still riding the rush, enjoying that this isn't about Lt. Kit Carson's hard–on for my *hero move* or the manacles in the wall.

'My office would like to know, *quietly*, what, if anything, the citizens of your district think is going on. There's been strong opposition to the mayor's casino plan throughout the black community. Are members of the black community making a move against Mayor McQuinn? An effort to place their spokesman in the chair at a crucial point in the city's future?' Pause. 'Can you accomplish a quiet, informal investigation, Officer Black?'

'Absolutely, yes, sir.'

'Should there be participation or collusion on the part of those in your district in the attempt on the mayor, you and the unwounded members of your team would be capable of discerning same?'

I'm recovering a bit. 'It would be our pleasure, sir. To serve and protect. *Quietly*, of course.'

'You understand that this means no formal channels, no written reports, no accusations later that the mayor's campaign strategy or his support of the casino license was racially motivated.'

Knowing the climate and the players, *my* participation in this clandestine fact-finding mission makes less than perfect sense to me, given that Alderman Gibbons is at the moment rallying the ghetto against the GD shootings my warrant and raid caused. The first pickets were already in front of 6 when I finished writing my reports four hours ago.

I say I understand even though I don't. Chief Jesse nods, looking away again, then adds, 'They ID'd your skeleton.'

'W-what?'

'The body in the wall. Annabelle Ganz, Calumet City.'

My hands go prickly and pin-lights flash in my eyes. I block most of the name, trying to focus on 'city,' the only word that doesn't hurt. It's been twenty–three years, not nearly enough. I reach for the armrest, try to steady.

That's not a name you can say out loud in the dark.

Annabelle Ganz was my foster mother.

TUESDAY

Chapter 4

TUESDAY, DAY 2: 3:00 A.M.

My cell phone vibrates and I pat blind until I find it.

I'm under a blanket. Cisco's talking – I think – still high on painkillers and young blond attention. His voice turns into Sonny Barrett's – either I'm dreaming or Sonny's at Cisco's bedside. I rub my eyes. My room's curtains are sheer; moonlight silvers the end of my single bed. Where am I? I glance at the door; it's double locked. My hand bumps my pistol . . . under the pillow?

Sonny's voice says, 'Whas up wid da what up?'

Julie's upstairs room. I'm above the bar at the L7. Why's my .38 sleeping with me? Sonny slurs more ghetto-speak – good chance Sonny's had a few, probably not enough to ask a girl who doesn't charge for a date, but enough to think he could.

'I'm sleeping.'

'How you doin', gunfighter? Hear we got injuns.'

A reference to my meeting with the superintendent. How my sergeant knows this is interesting. 'Could be. How's your patient?'

'Cisco? *Shit*, Cisco don't talk right, but he bad, honey; Forty-seventh Street bad.'

This is the first time Sonny Barrett has ever called me 'honey' and I have known him all my adult life. In deference to his condition and the loose nature of cell phone transmissions, I'm happy to discuss his attempt at camaraderie or sexual banter, two conditions I'm sure he wouldn't attempt when sober. 'Fuck you, *honey*.'

I hear two men laughing. Sonny burps, says he's sorry to someone else, then tells me. 'Kit Carson thinks you're an asshole. I couldn't argue and sound convincing, so—'

'Gee, that's news.'

'So I says he should soak his ass in gasoline, see how fucking brave he felt.'

'We could use him as a flare.'

Sonny pauses and I hear Cisco say 'ask her' in his modified speech. Sonny clears his throat into the phone and says, 'You coming to work tomorrow, right?'

Julie's clock glows on the nightstand. 'In five hours.'

'But you're coming.'

I'm too asleep to register how weird that sounds until after I answer. But the question hangs there, like some of the things Chief Jesse in the backseat—

Calumet City. *Annabelle Ganz*.

The covers fly off and I jump out of bed; my eyes snap to the door, then the window. It's not possible, Annabelle Ganz, back again, and in my district, not five miles away.

Sonny's voice is tiny and talking to my hip. 'Patti? Hey, Patti?'

The room is . . . empty, safe; it looks empty. The phone keeps calling my name and I fumble it to my mouth. 'I'm here. Go to bed. I'll see you tomorrow.' My thumb kills the phone and I stare at the moonlit room. What the fuck is going on? The room doesn't answer. Neither does the window. Leaves blow across the sidewalk below. Annabelle Ganz. A demon in a gingham nightdress. Cold, slippery hands. The devil's wife and mother and . . . *Stop, Patti.* Me and Richey and Little Gwen. *Enough.* Three of us children lost in hell, too ruined to help ourselves or each other.

A cab passes slow. The storefront neons are dark; the Northside and its nursery-rhyme life is asleep – butcher, baker, candlestick maker. My hand clenches the curtain and the fabric brushes my cheek. The attic had curtains, but they didn't move, neither did the moldy ones in the basement. My eyes squeeze shut, but I don't like what's there either. Me, Richey, and Little Gwen . . . three empty shells sitting together, then not; always finding somewhere else to look.

I want to hide.

Am I coming to work tomorrow? I blink back to the present. Why *wouldn't* I?

TUESDAY, DAY 2: 6:30 A.M.

And five hours later I do.

From inside Art's on Ashland I can feel the sun rising behind the building and see the day coming. The sun never quite hits Art's, except in the early summer; the rest of the year it shines elsewhere. I've eaten breakfast here six days a week for seventeen years, preferring the booths to the stools at the cigarette-burned counter. The booths have an equal amount of electrician's tape and vinyl. Square windows frame the ghetto changing from night-shift gangsters to poor working people trudging to jobs that don't pay enough. There's hope in that somewhere and on the better days I find it.

The door opens. Two older GDs stop just inside, both with jackets. 'Older' in gangster parlance is twenty–five and they are, by far, the most dangerous. But Art's is a ghetto DMZ. Cops and bangers eat here and generally leave one another alone. It's also the only white–owned restaurant that's survived the economic spiral.

Me and the GDs stare. We all know each other by job description; they nod small and so do I. That's today's agreement – no shit in here unless they start it. One is from the same set as the two we killed on Monday, the same set that fired first and put my partners in the hospital. He sits facing me with three empty booths between us. His partner lounges with his back to the window. Either one could be here for me or for the toast and coffee.

Anne brings bacon and eggs and news of her daughter's separation. She adds coffee left-handed and an opinion that the husband wasn't Jewish so it's no big loss. The GD whose hands I can see is dipping silverware in his spotted water glass, a move all regulars make, including me. His partner sneaks a side glance in my direction, then away. He's medium black with high African cheekbones that catch the harsh light; his cap is spotless and off center; his shoulders are hunched to accommodate the lack of space between his table and him.

If you saw this setup most places you'd think: breakfast.

Today, that's not what my instincts think.

Until today, I've never drawn my pistol in Art's. Now it's gripped tight in my lap, but unless I commit to putting it on the table, it won't be useful. Either GD could have a sawed-off or a

46

TEC–9, and then it won't matter anyway. I slip a finger inside the trigger guard and hesitate ... There's a certain amount of street pride in showing no fear. Watch a prison movie: Street pride is necessary for survival, even for cops. It's not that I don't draw three or four times *every day*; but being empty-handed confident down here is big face, big armor.

My toast is getting cold. The Gangster Disciple facing me isn't looking away – not right at me either – but close enough that he can see me move. The hair rises on my neck. If I carried a cannon like my Magnificent Seven partners, I could shoot through all three booths. Hell, I could shoot through an engine block. The GD lounging starts to turn, his shoulders coming with his cap.

Heartbeats. If this is it, this is it ...

The front door fills with Sonny Barrett and, 'Yo, Anne, baby, how you doin'?' Sonny has both eyes on the GDs and one hand visible. The lounger eyes him back; the one facing me shifts just his eyes to Sonny's voice, then back to me, and right at me this time.

Sonny passes their booth too slow to be polite, nods less so, and says, 'Gentlemen.'

The lounger raises his chin. Sonny steps to a stool, leans his back on the counter, and shows his gun hand full and a thick finger on the trigger. The grin doesn't match his bloodshot eyes, but Sonny's voice is happy. 'Anne, how 'bout some coffee?'

Anne steps between Sonny and one of the GDs to pour their coffee. Not the move I would've made. Anne is smart but has less fear than she should, and once chased a ticket walker three blocks. Got her ass kicked too.

Sonny hard–eyes the GDs, but bitches about me, 'You *gotta* sit by the window?'

It's where I always sit.

The GDs don't touch their coffee. We all sit and wonder what's next. Sonny announces to no one in particular, 'Funerals ain't today, no reason to be all jacked till then. Me? Shit, I'd grab a forty and forget about it. Maybe some bitches too. Party, you know, till it's time.'

The GDs don't look at him. Both get up. Both glance at me. And leave. The last of their oversize jackets passes through the door and Sonny says to me, '*Get the fuck out of the window*. Jesus Christ, what's wrong with you?'

I dip the cold toast instead of answering. Sonny cuts to the Seventy-fourth Street windows, waiting for the gunship. I figure to hit the floor beneath the sill if it happens. If not, still being in the window when they pass reinforces what I've been telling this neighborhood since they were schoolboys. 'I live here too, homes. Me *and* you.'

Anne has remembered where she works and found a reason to be in the kitchen. A blue–black Impala slow–passes on Seventy-fourth and the driver stares – he isn't one of the two who were inside – not a good sign. The Impala waits on traffic that isn't there while the driver makes sure that I am, then makes a slow right onto Ashland. The cook behind Sonny acknowl-edges the tension; it's tight across his face and chest, the stained apron deflating when he lets the breath go. I know why I'm working down here, but honestly have no idea why he is.

Sonny asks for coffee again, slips into the booth, and says, 'The mayor, huh? They think *these shitheads* tried to clip him? Put fucking Ayatollah Gibbons in office?'

My toast stops mid-arc. I add two blinks and wait for Sonny to continue. He doesn't. The bread is raisin and more aged than toasted. Sonny's a lot of things, most of them A-male Irish and blunt to the point of painful, but he isn't telepathic. I know better than to bite on anything but the toast, so that's what I do.

Sonny accepts coffee from Anne in a cracked cup, comments on her having lost weight since yesterday, and turns to me. 'The mayor, right?'

'The mayor . . . what?'

'Somebody did try to kill him, remember?' Sonny's eyes are ponds. '*Jaze*, I feel like shit. Drank half the night with Cisco. Boy's got every nurse in that building working his room.'

'You called me, remember?'

'Cisco called you?'

'You.'

'Cisco called me?'

I check my toast. 'How'd you pass the sergeant's exam? Your cousin take it?'

Sonny winces at the coffee, then frowns an inch over his shoulder toward the kitchen, as far as his neck allows. 'So, what'd he say?'

'Who?'

'Cochise. Who the fuck do you think?'

I try a change of subject, one I'd prefer not to broach but can't help needing to know more, if there is more. 'The body in the wall, they ID her yet?'

Sonny says, 'Ask the dicks.'

'They're not, ah, my biggest fans.'

'So ask . . . Who gives a shit anyway?' Sonny wrestles with the hangover. 'Could be interesting, though. White broad in 6, buried alive in a ghetto wall.' He smiles. 'Has to be a hooker or some Ted Bundy shit.' The smile broadens to his ears. 'Hope it's a Ted; we'll be Dennis Farina.'

Dennis was a Chicago cop who made it in Hollywood. 'It is interesting, Sonny. Ask, okay? They'll talk to you, a big swingin' dick who speaks the language.'

Sonny checks his crotch, 'Got that right,' then back at me. 'So what'd Chief Jesse say?'

'How's it, ah, you know he and I did dinner last night?'

Sonny blinks again, almost like he's mad. His hand flexes and he slides it under the table. 'You and him . . . *are* an item?'

'Baby shower's this week. After IAD charges me for dereliction.'

Sonny leans back, eyes tighter.

'The superintendent and I are registered at Field's.'

Sonny reads my eyes, then hardens up. 'Fuck you.'

Now I think I've hurt his feelings, not that anyone would believe Sonny Barrett has any. 'Listen, this is quiet, okay? That's why he said it to me.'

Sonny nods, looks at me straighter but doesn't lean in to hear.

'He wants to know if folks from here,' my fingernail taps the table between us, 'are part of it. Farrakhan and Alderman Gibbons in particular.'

Now Sonny leans in, 'Shit, I thought I was jokin'.' The beginning of another smile competes with his hangover and whatever reason he's pissed off. 'You absolutely gotta be shittin' me.'

'Nope.'

His neck flexes back into his collar. 'So much for the civil rights movement.' Sonny gets the implications better and faster than I did. 'We got cameras and pickets three deep at 6. This could be big, Patti. Big.'

50

And it could be. Messy too. No one would mount an attempt on the mayor – an operation this complicated – without serious players on the inside. Looking at Sonny's face it begins to dawn on me how serious this is if Alderman Gibbons or Louis Farrakhan's Nation of Islam is involved, even peripherally, if one can be 'peripherally' involved in a coup d'état.

Sonny goes back to the coffee he couldn't drink a second ago. 'Who else knows?'

'How'd you know about my meeting last night?'

Sonny shrugs. 'His driver, Fatso Leary.'

I wag my index finger.

Sonny frowns, not unlike how he frowns when he has explained something to the crew that none of us captures. 'Fatso's married to Kelly, my older sister, the one in Humboldt Park. She called all excited that one of my crew was having dinner with the superintendent. Wanted to know why, since Fatso wouldn't tell her.'

'That right? The guy driving him last night might've weighed one–fifty tops. Tall too.'

Sonny screws up the rest of his face. 'So fucking what?' He leans almost to my nose and waits until he has my undivided attention. 'All of a sudden you and me ain't working together for seventeen years? I ain't somebody you talk to?'

I smooch the air between us. He startles back; I grin. It's the best thing that's happened to me in twenty–four hours.

Sonny growls, 'You got any fuckin' idea what it'll be like, sticking our hand up the asses of Gibbons and Farrakhan? Without being on the record?'

'Won't be good.'

'*Won't be good?*' Sonny shakes his head, 'It'll be shit city if your boyfriend decides to front us. We'll be out there alone, fucked sideways, is what it'll be.'

'Why'd you ask if I was coming to work today; why wouldn't I?'

Sonny keeps staring; he's no–shit angry and gets like this when he isn't provided answers or feels threatened by the system. The explanation I want will have to wait.

'I got this assignment directly from the superintendent, so I get to pick. You and the boys take Farrakhan. I'll do Gibbons.'

Sonny stands, 'This is fucking bullshit,' and glares at everything he can, including down at me. 'We been together a long time, Patti; do not lay down on me or the guys.'

'*Me?*' My face flames. '*Lay down?*' Where the hell did that come from?

I'm not thrilled about this assignment either, mixed up in a backroom mayoral-mob fistfight that may or may not be real. Cops are paranoid by nature and mystery shit like this isn't good for our digestive systems. Sonny exhales but doesn't move.

I push out of the booth and into his face 'I'll do Gibbons. You try to remember who you're pissing on *after seventeen years.*' I bump his shoulder as I walk past, out into a ghetto changing from standard early–morning to Byzantine maze.

Some say the Chicago Police Department murdered Fred Hampton.

Alderman Leslie Gibbons is one of them. He was there in '69 and says he should know. His version of December 4 had no warning, just the apartment door splintering at 4:30 a.m., then one hundred rounds fired *inside* the Black Panther Party headquarters on West Madison – all but one fired by CPD – seventy-five of them into Fred Hampton's bedroom.

Alderman Leslie Gibbons says Fred Hampton was badly wounded in the shoulder but survived the attack only to face two Chicago police officers who stepped to his bed and executed him with a shot to the head. In front of his pregnant wife.

That's what she says too.

For eight years prior to being incarcerated for his role in the Black Panther Party, Alderman Leslie Gibbons marched with Martin Luther King, stood with him in Selma and Birmingham and Marquette Park until King was murdered in Memphis. A major résumé.

Leslie Gibbons is a hall-of-famer in the ghetto, and pissing on him in District 6 would be the closest thing to suicide any street cop could conjure. Not pissing on him in the dwindling white neighborhoods of the Southside where they refer to him as 'the Ayatollah' would cause the same reaction.

So, that's what I was doing instead of working. Pissing. My TAC unit is max-shorthanded today with Cisco down and two of our other guys in court. I'm on the street alone. This happens more often than you'd think and more often than any of us prefer to discuss with outsiders, especially those we police.

I'm asking good guys and bad guys wha–sup. Anybody hear shit? Stuff about the mayor, you know? Why somebody gone shoot him, and like that? That's how it sounded in my head, but not how I said it; I meant the same thing, just without the Sonny Barrett homey lingo. Asshole.

Connie Long, CTA bus driver, didn't know; Auntie I. L. at the Fried Right didn't know; Shirl-the-girl transvestite hooker knew, knew for damn sure – the white devil wanted the Southside for hisownself. Motherfuckin' Irish.

I went where I could, talked to people who knew me, people I'd helped, people I'd arrested and would again. It wasn't street winter, but it wasn't hearts and flowers either. See, it's not like TV where you good- and bad-cop the bad actors. They don't *have* to talk to you. And they don't have to be nice or respectful or anything else. They can just not understand, give you slumped shoulders and blank, watery eyes. Or in the afternoon, after the 40s are down, give you the peeled lips, rap-rhythm, 'Uh-huh,' while they chew gum and check out all the shit around them that they've been looking at all day.

You get that a lot; Sonny thinks there's a school for it hidden under one of the radio stations the El Rukns or the Vice Lords own: The Post-up, Bad-motherfucker Pimp School of Chicago. Cisco says it's a shame no one does tours from the colleges and corporations, 'live–fire exercises' to go with the textbooks and tuition. Cisco has not yet worn a button–down shirt to work, but he will. If he brings a pipe we've decided to shoot him.

Anyway, that was the morning, most of it interspersed with angry stares – some leery, some not, fifteen or twenty raised chins mumbling insults, and four in-my-face accusations that we/I murdered Robert, Ruth Ann's boy.

Lunchtime is better. I share it near Maxwell's Dumpster with Rasta-Dog, a rangy spaniel the shorties and taggers spray paint when they have extra. He and I discuss mayoral politics while he eats his hot links and the occasional bit of gravel. Rasta-Dog has no insight on Chief Jesse's assignment but his tail wags when I talk.

We call it even and I do another hour of detective work that yields additional votes to canonize Alderman Leslie Gibbons and a crack whore warning that the GDs are more unhappy with me than usual. At 2:30 I do backup for a uniform car under the viaduct at Eighty-first and Wallace, just down the tracks from Gilbert Court. The stop is loud and angry, but no one gets shot, and the uniforms drive off with two felons when it's over. I don't; I sit in my Ford and listen to the engine knock echo off the viaduct's walls, thinking about yesterday's dead GDs around the corner . . . And the gasolined six–flat across the alley.

I drop the Ford into drive and spit gravel with the tires before I can decide to turn into Gilbert Court. Going in there alone is . . . there isn't a term for how stupid that is.

By mid-afternoon no one has accused the Republicans or Alderman Leslie Gibbons of plotting to kill the mayor, although a Blackstone facing five to ten said he may have heard something and would say so if I can 'help him out.' I do two stolen vehicle stops, assist another uniform car with a woman threatening to kill a man for talking to her child, and now I'm passing Gilbert Court's dead–end entrance again. And this time I begin to turn.

'5-0! 5-0!'

I jerk the wheel mid-turn and miss a GD lookout sprinting toward Kerfoot Liquors. My tires buckle on the passenger side and the Ford skids sideways at a utility pole – *son of a* – then back onto Vincennes. Horns blare. Two trucks scissor to the shoulders. I split them and shoot through the viaducts bordering Simeon Vocational. Instantly I'm sharing my side of the street with bangers from four gangster sets and blue-and-whites working the daily fight and occasional massacre when class lets out.

I try driving like I know how and only in my lane. A uniform waves; I gulp quick, then wave back and flip a U just beyond the school. Trains rumble over the viaducts I just left, two of them in the same direction and covered in graffiti. I'm about to cruise by Gilbert Court a third time. *Annabelle Ganz is dead, okay? The dicks ID'd her.*

The daylight quits when I enter the viaducts. The mold smells stronger than my basement memories, but the confinement is suddenly the same and I hit the gas. *Like the dicks haven't been wrong before?* And why in my district? It's a city of three million, goddamnit – why was she in my district? My right hand pounds the seat. 'Not fucking fair! Not fucking fair!'

A truck driver wide–eyes me going by. I reach Gilbert Court and its goddamn basements and this time look away toward the tracks. And decide to do something only slightly less dangerous.

I stop by Ruth Ann's Emerald Avenue apartment instead. Her street has cars parked on both sides. Directly opposite her porch six GDs lean against an old Ford Galaxy. Ruth Ann's outside, shoulders folded into her chest, hands folded on her lap. Next to her, one of Alderman Gibbons's flunkies fills a chair he borrowed elsewhere or bought for the occasion. Five other women sit various boxes and cartons. There are no GDs on the porch; Ruth Ann is not a gangster fan, a vocal opinion that is tolerated but considered treason.

A storefront preacher I know from the Lazarus Temple sits the steps, a Bible in hand, sneakers on his feet, and a pained expression in his eyes. He's what they call 'African,' a shouter, a denomination of one who intends to lead his flock back to Africa. Of all the bullshit artists selling religion down here, I believe this fellow means it. He's about thirty, give or take five, college-educated and confrontational – with both sides – the gangs and us. And alive by accident. For the believer's sake, I hope he's not another FBI plant.

And then there's me. I can tell you that walking a sidewalk on this block, alone and white, is not smart. Not Gilbert Court stupid, but close. None of my mistakes will be lost on those here who don't like the police in general and me in particular.

Ruth Ann's fifteen feet of sparse yard separates us. I smile sad. The preacher stands, as does the alderman's flunky at Ruth Ann's shoulder. This is a good show by the flunky, although Ruth Ann and I know they never seem to be around when the gangsters are ripping the neighborhood apart. Anyone who tells you that the gangs are an essential part of the 'fabric' are in sociology class on the Northside. Gangs are a plague, pure and simple. And the politicians, like the one about to brace me with his righteous indignation and thousand–dollar suit, haven't done shit about it other than swallow money and blame someone else.

From three steps above me the alderman's flunky says, 'You're not welcome here.'

'Ruth Ann. I wanted to stop by . . . to pay my respects.'

She looks past the flunky to me and the preacher who's now at my shoulder. I can smell the preacher's spicy lunch and the sweat in his clothes. It's new sweat, like he's been working hard at something today. You can't hate a guy for that.

The preacher adds his opinion. 'You're not learning, are you? Watch the news, the Gaza Strip, the West Bank – the police can't kill us all.'

'Ruth Ann, I'm sorry about Robert. The whole thing. I'm sorry . . . about it.'

She doesn't invite me up, although I've been on her porch several times and in her apartment when she needed help with

Robert and his friends. The flunky steps between her and me, then down one step closer. 'As the attorney representing Mrs. Parks, I'm directing you to leave her property unless you have a warrant. In which case produce it.'

'Ruth Ann, I—'

'*Officer Black.*' The alderman's flunky–lawyer drops another step. 'Civil rights. Civil procedure. Get-off-the-property.'

'Ruth Ann, I—'

Her face is so tired I feel it from here. Then the flunky is on the sidewalk, making the show, too close to me and he knows it. 'You are not the occupying army. You will not murder my client's son and—'

'Stand back, asshole.'

He doesn't and inflates. 'You're threatening me? On Mrs. Parks's property, in front of all these witnesses?'

'I'm the police.' My tone is a mistake, a big one. '*Stand the fuck back* when I tell you.'

He does, one step, then another that wasn't necessary, then raises both hands to block my mythical line-of-fire at Ruth Ann, grieving mother. Instamatic flashbulbs pop. A camcorder appears. It's like they've been waiting for me.

TUESDAY, DAY 2: 5:00 P.M.

Sonny Barrett shakes his head when I finish the story, as does Eric Jackson back from his barber chair and half-day, dislocated-shoulder leave. My afternoon post-up at Ruth Ann's acts as an icebreaker with Sonny. He's being distant but not so far away that I feel threatened. Distant doesn't feel good, but it's better than where we were at Art's.

58

Sonny's day was all Nation of Islam and he looks more spent than usual. Looking into the Nation of Islam and their temple on Seventy-ninth Street is not as easy as it sounds, if in fact it sounds easy. Sonny's day had no cameras and/or pickets, so by a degree, his went better than mine.

'You won't make the six o'clock,' says Sonny, 'but count on the ten.'

Eric Jackson concurs. 'Scalps, yours for damn sure, as soon as Chief Jesse hears.'

Sonny nods and takes another sip. It leaves the Guinness mustache he thinks adds Richard Harris to his lip. We're doing the Irish end-of-watch *slainte* at Dell's, a cop bar on Seventy-ninth Street in the DMZ. I don't come in here much – first, it's the drinking thing that I'm not doing as hard as I can, and second, it's the painted glass window that represents all the armor between us and a drive-by that the GDs threaten ten times a day. 'Happy hour,' I've heard them call it.

I ask about Farrakhan again. Sonny shrugs and glances past me to the black patrol officers on my left, then back. I ask a third time. Sonny shakes his head, meaning we'll talk about Louis Farrakhan somewhere else with fewer black faces. Eric Jackson, who's black, puts down his Old Style and leans away deeper into the booth. He eyes me so I notice, then shifts his eyes and mine to the barstools at the bar. I look but don't recognize the backs of anyone seated or their dim faces in the mirror. Our table is suddenly very quiet.

I say, 'Why'd you ask me if I was coming to work today?'

Sonny squints, 'Huh?'

'We been through this once. Last night, you called from the hospital and asked me.'

Shrug and a Guinness sip. 'Must've been Cisco or one of his babes.' He smiles at Eric. 'Man, he had some babes in there. I am not shittin' you.'

Since I'm not sure why or how long Sonny intends to run this game, I decide to retire, head home, and see if the locksmith came. Maybe let Stella assault my hair while I consider a life without Sonny Barrett and his private-agenda, alpha-male, Irish bullshit.

Outside, I'm about to get in my car and a blue-and-white stops, then a second one behind it two feet from the bumper. The passenger door of the second car opens and Kit Carson, Watch LT and all-around asshole, steps out. Although this is his district from 8:00 to 4:00, he's rarely out in it and generally never as night falls. The two uniforms with him are his answer to dusk.

'Officer Black?'

He knows who I am, he's trying to get me to stop. If I shoot him now, right now—

'Officer Black. I need a moment.'

Technically I don't work for Kit Carson because I'm TAC and we have our own LT, and technically I do because he's the Watch LT. It's confusing, and if my LT wasn't on vacation I'd be much more likely to shoot this asshole and hope for a review board that could see past the lieutenant bars. But that's not the situation, even in Fantasyland, so I stop on the sidewalk just steps from safety and an evening at home with music and my fish.

'Yes, sir. And what will it be, sir?'

One of the two patrolmen with him chuckles behind his hand; his partner winks.

Kit says, 'Could you *possibly* be more stupid?'

'Sir?'

60

'The community is picketing 6 and you go to the mother's *house*? Gibbons said you were there to threaten her.'

'If you mean Ruth Ann, I went to say I was sorry.'

'Sorry?' Kit Carson swells to full departmental height. 'Alderman Gibbons has filed a formal criminal complaint against the department naming you, charging harassment and assault. These new charges dovetail with yesterday's accusations of brutality, violation of civil rights, and "the police-sanctioned murder of innocent Afro-American citizens." Unquote. Report to IAD downtown, now.'

'Bullshit.'

'Now. That's an order.'

A big shape that's Sonny Barrett steps out of the bar semiblinded even at dusk and yells, 'Patti. Patti, wait a sec.' He gets what's left of the sun behind him, sees the LT and his bodyguards, and stops. He slows, his head swivels with his shoulders as he sizes up everyone on the wide sidewalk, including the civilians trying to size it up too.

'*Jazus*, Kit. It'll be dark soon.'

I choke into my hand. The bodyguards bend away, trying not to laugh. Kit Carson reswells to full height and rank, glaring at Sonny. '*What?*'

'No shit, man. *Dark*, like no fucking light at all, you know? And felons, motherfuckers come outta the woodwork. Evil sons-a-bitches like that one.' Sonny points at a crack merchant we've put in County on gun charges twice this year. 'This is not a safe neighborhood . . . sir.'

Kit Carson is crimson, as red as I have ever seen him, except last Valentine's Day when he beat a handcuffed prisoner unconscious for kicking his secretary in the crotch. Kit's wrapped a little tight in a lot of ways that aren't immediately obvious and he closes the distance.

'What did you say, Sergeant?'

Sonny stops smiling and I realize he's not a drop drunk and might be doing this for me. Might be. Sonny leans 250 pounds closer to our Watch LT. 'I said, sir, *empty-holster-motherfucker*, is what I said.'

If I haven't mentioned it before, Sonny Barrett, drunk or sober, armed or not, is not someone you screw with, and everyone south of the river who needs to know that, knows it.

'I said it to Officer Hazleton, sir; that mick shithead next to you. And I'll say it again if you'd like. Sir.'

There's a reasonable chance that Kit Carson does not want to die on Seventy-ninth Street. And he's having trouble gauging Sonny's condition. More than one cop has died when the day's internal stress was marinated in whiskey and badly chosen words. I don't know if Sonny's playing – his whole act since my gasoline shower has been a bubble or two off – but I'm glad he's standing there. And that feels funny for both reasons.

Kit Carson looks at me. 'IAD, now,' and waits until I'm driving away to turn and face Sonny. The last I see of Kit is he and Sonny are squared up, Kit Carson backed by his patrol officers. It looks like a fair fight, even backwards in my mirror.

My cell vibrates before I can get fifteen blocks to the Dan Ryan. It's the superintendent's secretary. The message is: 'This evening's IAD appointment has been postponed. Contact the superintendent at 0–900 hours tomorrow.'

Strange . . . but good. At least I think it's good; now I have time to wallow in the list of charges Kit Carson just said were brewing, any one of which would end my career if Gibbons can make it stick. Hard to figure why smart people aren't lining up to do this job. My phone announces it has more messages. Eleven, in fact. Five from Tracy Moens and one from Julie. Julie's is the best: 'Box seats tonight! Cubs versus Cardinals.'

Yeah, baby! I only get to attend two games a year, always in the bleachers, and never before in a pennant race. I punch–dial instead of steer. 'Julie. It's me. I—'

'C'mon. Right now. Park in my space and we'll walk down.'

'Maybe thirty minutes,' I check the Dan Ryan looming ahead, 'maybe an hour. Tell me again how to get there.'

Sadly, I can't find anything on that side of the river unless I'm following someone or the directions begin at Wrigley Field. That's the truth except for a building up in Evanston I visit once a year – next month will be the seventeenth time – I stop out front but never go in, so it doesn't really count.

Julie does the directions twice, then adds, 'Someone wants to meet *the* Patti Black.'

Every bit of me slumps. 'Not tonight, okay?'

'Cowboy up, girl. We're trading you for tickets Mayor McQuinn couldn't get. Give 'em ten minutes of small talk at the bar and we're four rows back of the dugout.'

'Who is it?'

Julie pretends static interrupted us and makes me repeat my question while she thinks up an answer. 'Could be a suitor,' heroic pause, 'maybe a Northside gentleman. Clean underwear *and* fingernails, the whole package.'

I veer ten degrees to avoid a drunk chasing his bottle into Seventy–ninth Street. 'Why me? Tracy's dance card full?'

Julie laughs. 'So full, sweetie, you can't imagine.'

* * *

It took seventy-three minutes. Why? Because the Northside is designed to confuse anyone who didn't attend graduate school. I had to call for directions three times, each time Julie became less respectful. When I finally arrived, the L7 was a pre–game festival of sporty women who looked it and small groups of Cardinals fans who had no clue *why so many women hung out here*.

My suitor was Tracy Moens and no part of her was looking to get laid, much to the chagrin of the male St. Louis fans. We had thirty-five minutes till leadoff and walked out right after I arrived, Tracy, me, Julie, and the deaf poet from last night. I got my apology in, then Tracy dragged me next to her and started bitching.

'I called five times. We have a deal, Patti. I expect you to honor it.'

Two of my fingers remove hers from my arm. 'Thanks for the tickets.'

'You met with the mayor last night.'

She's mistaken but I don't give a shit. 'It wasn't a "meeting." We had dinner, a few laughs, kissed around; nothing serious.'

Tracy's frown doesn't fit her usually glowing face. That makes me happy, possibly number two on the day.

'You met with him out of the office, alone, and in his car. Fifteen hours later, Alderman Gibbons – *next in line* should the mayor die in office – filed two criminal complaints against you. And now a number of residents of District 6 have come forward – all with the blessing of Alderman Gibbons – saying you spent the day asking questions about said alderman.'

I sense Kit Carson at work and keep walking; the sidewalks

are crowded with fans who are suddenly lots happier than me. 'Top secret, okay? The mayor and the alderman are lovers — poodles, KY, sweaters, the whole thing.'

Tracy grabs my arm again. 'You can talk to me before we print the story or apologize later, up to you.' Miss All–Everything redhead smiles all the way to the sharp teeth. 'Power of the press. A lot like your handcuffs.'

I try to think positive while we walk; try to blot out Her Fabulousness as a living being, her threats, but not her tickets. This is a pilgrimage and I must get my mind right. My team needs me.

Wrigley Field is home to the 'Addison Street Miracle' or any number of names used to define the never-even-a-bridesmaid Chicago Cubs. The names usually become less flattering as the season progresses. This in spite of once being owned by the *Chicago Tribune* and attendance records that locusts couldn't match. To be a fan of these fellows one must have sins; it helps if they're serious and unforgivable in any other way. But that's ninth-inning talk and tonight's game hasn't started; we're not behind yet.

Inside, Wrigley looks glorious under the lights – if you could package this it would outsell hope. I'm smiling ear-to-ear, even with the Pink Panther seated at my shoulder. She's been on her cell since we arrived and bent away so I can't hear, like I give a shit what she's into. The deaf poet seems to be having fun, signing on Julie's leg and pointing like a fifth grader, no different than me. We catch each other's eyes several times and he shies as often as he doesn't. Julie buys peanuts and three Old Styles. Tracy spills hers on my sneakers and I remember I'm wearing yesterday's socks. She pats at the mess with napkins. Her fingernails are perfect. I'm surprised the two handsome men in front of us don't fistfight to do her clean-up.

Julie nudges me. I look at her looking at the dugout. Alfonso Soriano, 136 million, the next Sammy Sosa. So close I could touch him, swear to God. Alfonso's smiling at the crowd and, man, does he look like a baseball player. No, Alfonso isn't smiling at the crowd, he's smiling at Tracy. Oh my god, he's waving. She waves back in that perfect benediction it takes movie stars all day to perfect. Suddenly I'm surprised she didn't sing the national anthem.

'Want to meet him?'

'Huh?' Up until Alfonso Soriano became Tracy's friend I would've cleaned his house daily; now I want to deport him for selling slaves in the Dominican Republic.

Tracy smiles wider at me, then back at Alfonso before he runs his cute little ass out on the field. 'We can meet him if you want. No problem.'

'And that would cost me what?' I adjust my butt in the seat, hoping she can feel my pistol in her ribs.

She pushes red hair out of her eyes and all the men this side of third base stop breathing. 'Cost? You're a civil servant. I just want to ask questions about your job. Off the record if we have to, but then Alfonso might be,' she adds a so-sad grimace, 'too busy.'

I look at left field. Me and Alfonso, talking baseball, maybe in the dugout, spitting every few seconds. Cisco and Sonny would shit a mountain. *And pictures*, 8 × 10s – bullshit – posters. I'll borrow a uniform. I'll throw out the first pitch, like the mayor does —

'Okay, we hang with Alfonso first, then we'll talk. Off the record.'

Tracy moves the hair side to side, doing the VO5 Shampoo commercial. 'Sorry. We have to talk now, tonight.'

'Why?'

'*Why?*' Tracy fouls her perfect features. 'They're about to put you in the blocks.'

'Who's they?'

Kerry Wood throws a strike and Wrigley goes World Series. It's the first pitch of the first inning. You have to be a Cub fan or a horseplayer to understand – 'enjoy it early' is the theory.

Tracy hasn't looked at the field since Alfonso left for work. 'Patti, you don't want to be the lightning rod for this election. Way too much at stake; *lots* of casualties before it's over.'

Casualties is a stopper, even after Wood throws his second strike in a row. 'Casualties? Like dead people?'

She leans back. 'Could be.'

Tracy is All-Everything, but she's out of her league if we're talking about a string of murders to be, especially if they start with the mayor. I lean sideways and stare. We occasionally eye one another like this on the rugby field when the other's play may have caused personal discomfort. The term is *hospital pass* and it's used when the ball is passed poorly resulting in the receiver taking an unnecessary beating. There are rumors that she and I are vindictive enough to have done this on purpose.

'Bit of advice, Trace. If you know something, call the cops. Now, before the Cubs bat.'

'Oh, god, Patti. "Casualties" means political death, a metaphor. I'm a journalist.'

'You're a pageant winner.'

Tracy smiles because she is. 'I meant "political" casualties and we both know it. Talk to me about you and the mayor, and I'll leave you and your friend the superintendent out.'

Wood throws strike three from somewhere out in Waveland Avenue and Wrigley goes apeshit. That helps me not hit her, that and she'd be a handful to fight fair. When the cheering dies to human levels she stares at me too long and adds, 'After the game we'll need to talk about the body in the wall too.'

WEDNESDAY

Chapter 5

WEDNESDAY, DAY 3: 12:02 A.M.

The Cubs won. I should've been too happy to breathe.

As it was I don't remember much after Tracy and I left our seats, after she said the magic words: 'Annabelle Ganz' and 'Calumet City.' I shouldered out hard, past the boxes and Andy Frain ushers. She caught me outside the gates, under the huge Wrigley Field sign they always show on TV. The crowd celebrated past me but Tracy stayed in my face.

'Last night Area 2 Homicide identified the body you found as Annabelle Ganz. Two hours ago – in a dazzling feat of police work – the late Mrs. Ganz was ID'd as the same Annabelle Ganz involved in a 1987 Calumet City murder – an adult male in a foster home she co-parented. A very strange one – the murder and the home.'

I try to sidestep her and the words but Tracy and the crowd won't let me.

'*The Black Monday Murder*. Fairly famous at the time: October 19, 1987, biggest stock market crash in history. The victim was a business associate of the late Mrs. Ganz and her husband, Roland. Roland disappeared, everybody knows that, and—'

Roland Ganz repeats in my head; a picture flashes with it. Then filmstrips of pictures, 8mm grainy awful – *Roland Ganz* – a name I never think and never say out loud. Roland Ganz booms up and down Addison Street and sucks the life out of my chest. Tracy's still telling me things I already know intimately when I bolt. Full out, sprinting through headlights and horns and men cursing; sprinting through couples and dogs and piles of leaves; over curbs and across gardens, across streets and more streets, and alleys . . . until I can't breathe, until an old red-brick wall overhung with oak and elm branches blocks me. The gate has metalwork, foot-and handholds that I scramble up panting, tearing Julie's shirt. My sides hurt; I'm lost, and over the top before considering what the gate and wall protected.

I land hard on my shoulder. My heart pounds while my eyes adjust. It's a park. With rolling hills, and full of stone in deep shadow; the inside edge is barely lit by the overspill of Clark Street's glow. Demons can make you a sprinter. My demons are Olympians. And it isn't a park, it's a cemetery.

And it's dark. Serious dark the deeper I go. My heart slowly finds a tolerable rhythm and the tingle in my fingertips stops, the traffic noise outside the wall dies to nothing. I brush a plaque that I can barely see. My fingers trace 'Graceland Cemetery.' The quiet intensifies, if quiet can do that. I creep farther toward the center, groping with my left hand extended. Ornate buildings built in miniature catch what little moonlight there is, but only at a marble corner or a padlocked door.

Mausoleums. And scented night air. Dead flowers, marigolds I think. The path is gravel or maybe a weathered road twisting through headstones I can't see. Old ones probably, like on the

Southside, old trees too— Fast *whoosh* to my left; I jump, stumble . . . and into hands all over me. Not hands, leaves, an untrimmed branch sweeping the ground. I suck air, step out, and the tree's weakest leaves blow dead over my gym shoes. I let myself fall. The ground is soft. And the leaves keep blowing. I don't move. My heart slows and warm tears tell me I'm crying.

The night air swirls in and out for an hour, blowing leaves and tears and dead flowers I can't see. A storm's gathering in the east. There's much to say, very bad things, but how, and to whom? Maybe I'll sleep here, find a dry place among the forest of spires hidden by the dark, bed down with these ghosts who mean me no harm.

My people. They know I've always been more ghost than person. A teenaged boy at the Salvation Mission once told me I was an unfinished song – we were the same age then – a lyric with more breaks than words and nowhere to put the notes. He had pimples, shoes that didn't match, and a guitar and ran away that same week. I ran a week later.

A shiver shakes through my back and shoulders. I'll think about something else, call Stella, ask her to feed Jezebel and Bathsheba. My hand flattens on the unreadable marble by my hip and I wonder about the life under it, what it accomplished, wonder what my headstone will say and how soon it will say it . . . a thought sneaks through the blackout memories and self–pity: This is a famous place on the Northside, a bunch of famous Irish gangsters from the '20s are buried here.

Why think that?

Annabelle and Roland don't want to think about Irish gangsters and push them out of way. Annabelle and Roland want the family together again.

I'm up and moving because moving is suddenly better. A dim line of light shimmers through shadow trees. The light must be Clark Street. The gravel path snakes toward it, then away, and finally a section of wall materializes. Squirrels or rats run from my approach. The 'L' passes somewhere behind me in the dark back to the east. Graceland begins to feel bad, like a dark cemetery would to most people, all your fears peopled in these corpses and religious superstition. That's someone else's terror. I know mine. It's got a name, shoes, saliva . . .

This section of wall has a gate too and is easier to overcome. A yellow cab passes. I don't want to go home, not where they can find me.

Who's they?

You, me, them . . . Get a cab to the L7. Hide out till morning.

The cab will be six or eight bucks; not like I've got it to burn, but I have no idea where I am. Another cab slows and he doesn't stop either, then a gypsy does – I'm white and a girl – the cabby knows the address or pretends. We catch stoplights as it starts to rain, mist first then heavy drops; the boulevard becomes smeary headlights and shadows. And the traffic signals are brighter than usual, hot, like red spotlights.

My driver checks me in his mirror for the tenth time, eyes all scrunched up. I show him my star too fast and up tight to his ear. 'Drive, asshole. Worry about the road.'

He cows, wishing he had a thick plastic partition.

Nice, Patti. Real nice. 'Sorry. Sorry, just drive, okay?'

I slip back heavy into the seat, then startle. Annabelle Ganz is here too. She thinks I should wonder how long she was in District 6. I slap her part of the backseat to prove it's empty. The driver checks me again. Parts of District 6 were white back in the '80s and early '90s. But what was Annabelle doing there, other than the twelve years Tracy said she was buried in the wall? My fists ball. No telling who was with her either. They – *God, Roland too* – he could've been there. Probably was—

Big shiver. I might puke.

The cab stops outside the L7; the driver eases his eyes back into his mirror. Either a lesbian fantasy or he expects a cop to stiff him. He gets ten instead and watches my ass. I really want to shoot somebody, start to turn but don't. Maybe I'm not finished crying and just can't admit it. Julie's out front under her awning watching the rain.

'Where the hell have you been?'

'Took the train. Next time my date is your ex, spare me, okay?'

She slides sideways and blocks the door. 'Trace said you ran. *Away?*'

I hard-eye her, then say, 'Too happy to stand still,' and try to pass. She grabs at the shirt she lent me and I knock her hand away. 'Not tonight.'

Julie floats her eyebrows and looks down her nose. But she steps out of the way. As I walk through the bar to Julie's backstairs, Tracy waves me over. I take the stairs from Julie's office instead. My phone vibrates and I answer without looking.

It's bar noise and Tracy saying, 'We have to talk. I'm coming up.'

'Maybe tomorrow.'

'No. This is importan . . . for you—'

'I said no.' Every part of me clenches. '*Do not* fucking do it.'

In the room I do the door locks, sit on the single bed, and want to cry for so many reasons I don't know where to start. Tracy doesn't come, nor does Julie. I lie down and kill the lights, then cover my eyes. My son's face is with me in the pillow, the face I made up for him. The face isn't his and I've never seen it, but it's what I have. Tonight he's not enough.

WEDNESDAY, DAY 3: SUNRISE

The night's all sleepless dreams, hazy and frightened and guilty and then sunrise finally hints at my window, ending a night not unlike drowning. My cell and my pistol share the bed. I check the clock – the superintendent wants me to call at 9:00; this time it won't be a surprise mission, it'll be about IAD and the criminal complaints Alderman Gibbons has stacked atop Kit Carson's CR numbers. I turn on the cell and punch Stella's number before checking messages.

Stella clears her throat, then says she's been up for an hour watching HSN and drinking the hot chocolate I bought her. I ask her to feed Jezebel and Bathsheba. She already has and says no locksmith has been by, then wants to know why I don't think it's important to fix things. It should be a matter of pride, at the very least. We make a deal – I promise to try harder and she promises to make sure that I do.

Now to the messages. The one that matters is the superintendent's. He wants to talk at breakfast and *in person*, before I report to 6. That won't be easy since I'm not at home where he thinks I am; north–to–south rush hour separates us. I only have time to take the aerosol shower and a handful of Altoids, hoping the combination makes me presentable. A TAC officer does not keep the superintendent waiting. I leave

Julie a note saying I'll explain after work, positive I won't.

The early traffic into downtown is on the way to awful but not quite there yet. I run the summons possibilities – this is my second restaurant meeting with Chief Jesse in three days, this time in Bridgeport, the stronghold of the Daley machine, and in public, not the backseat of a Town Car. The superintendent breakfasting with me could be a show of force or a personal blessing. If I were Chief Jesse, this is the last thing I'd do.

Unless he knows stuff that I don't.

Duh?

But what? Why parade me when I'm radioactive?

Think *Southside Irish*. Who do they hate more than the English? The smile makes my eyes squint. I'll stop for a paper as soon as I recognize the geography.

Outside the Bridgeport Family Restaurant I buy a *Herald*. Page two has my answer. The stacked, one–column header reads: 'Hero Cop Threatened by Alderman.' I believe they call that spin. Big exhale, like half the firing squad temporarily ran out of bullets. I look up. Inside past the glass, Chief Jesse is waving me to his back booth.

On the way there I accept a handshake from a stubble–faced flannel shirt. One of his pals pats my shoulder. Both think, 'The fuckin' Ayatollah shoulda died on West Madison back in '69.'

The captain who vacates the superintendent's booth, says, 'Proud of you,' and gives me a pat too. For a few moments, it's me who won the beauty pageant. Then I'm alone with the superintendent, surrounded by steamy clatter and Irish accents, and he says, 'Nice work.'

I can't tell by his expression whether he means it or not. The waitress brings coffee I didn't request, smiles like I'm her sister with the mortgage money and steps to the next booth. For sure I'm coming here tomorrow. I'll bring Cisco and Sonny.

The superintendent asks, 'And the word in the ghetto is . . . ?'

I report on yesterday's Gibbons–Farrakhan missions. The superintendent listens without comment. Not that I provide much to comment on regarding a possible coup d'état.

'You're transferred to 18, effective an hour ago.'

'*What?*'

'Phone transfer. Enjoy.'

'Bullshit.'

Chief Jesse now has a pained expression on his face as he balls his left fist, either *really* angry at me or a heart attack working its way down his arm. He hesitates until whichever it was passes. 'We are less than a month away from the election, and only two weeks from the casino license vote. The governor called the mayor's office last night. Threatened us both with the FBI. The governor feels the FBI should be involved in the assassination attempt. Alderman Gibbons wants them in too – a federal probe of "systematic civil rights violations by the Chicago Police Department," the most recent being your Gilbert Court shootings and yesterday's "criminal altercation" between you and his grief-stricken lapdog.'

My eyes roll. 'It wasn't an altercation.'

'As you know, I am appointed by the mayor; if he goes, I go.' The superintendent doesn't seem to care what I think. 'The governor and Alderman Gibbons would like that and never miss a chance to suggest that we do not "serve and protect" to their elevated standards. Nor are they shy about charging rampant police corruption.'

Rampant police corruption charges are not new and tend to precede every mayoral election. This year is no different.

'Among the many other recriminations offered me by His Honor last evening, it was suggested in the strongest possible terms that you, Officer Black – soon to be *Detective* Black if you don't fuck it up here – are not to speak one word to your media pals, on or off the record, about Alderman Gibbons or Monday's unrelated firefight at Gilbert Court.'

'Unrelated to . . .'

Chief Jesse leans across his plate, staring all the way. 'The two dead Gangster Disciples on Gilbert Court are *unrelated* to the assassination attempt on the mayor.'

'That's easy.'

'And the assassination attempt is *unrelated* to the body found in his wife's building across the alley.'

Whoa. The mayor's wife?

'According to His Honor, and this is a quote, "his re-election does not need a smear-campaign rabbit trail from Gilbert Court to Calumet City and its sixty years of malfeasance." Am I clear?'

I'm having trouble breathing normally as the Bridgeport Family Restaurant fills with smoke only I can see. 'Ah, did you say the mayor's wife is tied to Calumet City—'

'It's in the paper, for chrissake.' The superintendent clenches and unclenches his fist again. 'Annabelle Ganz, her husband, and two of their foster kids have *all* been MIA from Calumet City until you and the fire department found Annabelle in the wall.'

He frowns at the *Herald* and then the window onto Thirty-fifth. I follow his eyes, hoping there's something out there that

79

changes what he just said, especially the part about it being in the paper.

He looks back and says, 'Not that I give a damn about Calumet City, except that the mayor's wife once owned the building Annabelle's buried in – a gift from her grandfather as I remember.' His voice lowers. 'And I lived there in the 1970s when I first came on, as did a number of other rookies working 6, 7, and the Deuce.'

The lovely and talented Mary Kate O'Banion owned Gilbert Court? And Chief Jesse lived there? I wonder if I wake up, where I'll be. No wonder this is all in the *Herald*. And Mary Kate has her own 'colorful' history. Besides being the mayor's wife, Mary Kate is the granddaughter of Dean 'Dion' O'Banion, a famous Capone–era gangster now remembered fondly as 'local color' in spite of the twenty-five murders he committed.

'Certainly her once owning this building and my residence therein is a coincidence. But a coincidence that your media pals, including Tracy Moens, will fan into three days of additional sales, followed by well-timed political attacks on His Honor and myself.' The superintendent looks at me as if I understand the political ramifications. 'So, Officer Black, you are news yet again, this time at the center of an election-related civil rights smear. And when that news dies, the new epicenter of said smear campaign will be the former owners and occupants of Gilbert Court.'

'No need to transfer me. Tell me to shut up and I will.'

'District 18. Am I clear, Officer Black?'

'Ah, yeah, but—'

'There are no "buts" in the Chicago Police Department this month. *Stay out of all three cases* and *away* from Alderman

Gibbons.' The superintendent offers a small unreadable smile. 'Go forth and make the Northside safe for BMWs and baby carriages until I tell you different.'

'What about IAD and the criminal charges—'

'District 18. Now.'

The superintendent stands as a photographer approaches, then he grabs my hand and smiles like the professional politician he isn't. The flash is soundless but loud. He tells the photographer, 'P-a-t-t-i,' pats my shoulder as he passes, and shakes hands out the door. I look at the *Herald* so I don't have to meet any eyes and blink like I did when the flashbulb hit me at Ruth Ann's. The caption under the picture in the *Herald* reads:

'Annabelle Ganz. Murdered in 1993, missing since 1987.'

WEDNESDAY, DAY 3: LATE MORNING

Three hours later most of my brain is still swimming with what I heard the superintendent of police say in Bridgeport. And why it was said, and why it was said in front of an audience and a camera. I'm a TAC cop, a ghetto action figure; this is Perry Mason from the '50s.

My new partner is showing me my new neighborhood, using one hand to turn us left on Division Street. He's young and excited, a two-year TAC officer in 18. Their stationhouse is across from the ghetto high-rises on Division, the projects – Cabrini Green – the only area north of the river I've seen that resembles what I'm used to. It's also where Mayor Jane Byrne and her army of bodyguards lived to prove 'public housing is safe,' a point that no one could prove. And since she gave us our union, I'm a fan no matter how stupid a stunt it was.

Yawn. Last night's catching up with me; my eyes are heavy and my right shoulder aches like somebody kicked it until they tired. On the bright side, Cisco's doing fine in the hospital; his voice in my phone an hour ago sounded as smooth as Mel Tillis singing, like painkillers and student nurses were definitely the way to go. He didn't know I'd been transferred and I didn't tell him. My new partner finishes the turn and says, 'Patti Black in the flesh. Either I'll be dead or make detective by the weekend.' He smiles like that's a compliment. 'No offense, but you're kinda young to be on the job seventeen years.'

Exhale. 'Guess so.'

He's about thirty and surprisingly, not an asshole. I say surprisingly, because he's wearing light–colored pants and has peppered me with cop slang – attributes one needs to be the TV police, a rank of limited value in a gunfight. He's also wearing a wedding-ring tan line and has a second gun I can see, but he does have on the right shoes. Shoes tell you a lot about whether a cop plans on working or not. We're passing buildings that mean nothing to me. Same for the early street gangsters out from Cabrini Green – crack's a 24/7 business now – that much is the same.

'Young 'cause of the history, you know, back in the day. LT said you rode with Denny Banahan.'

Denny's name makes me smile. Denny Banahan didn't drive a desk like most bosses or field offers from Hollywood. He didn't mince words either. Denny Banahan showed me and Sonny and every other gunfighter in 6 how to be the police. The gangsters tagged him with 'Zorro' and with good reason. If you were a banger, Denny and the law met only occasionally; the rest of the time he was Irish and disinclined toward your rehabilitation.

'Zorro was one crazed copper. LT said that since Banahan retired back to Homicide, you're the most decorated cop in the city.'

I tell my window what I tell the reporters, 'That's a misprint. All the old guys who actually worked retired.'

'So, you really work like they say?'

I glance, knowing what he means, but not where he wants to go with it.

'Rumor has it there's a bunch of these shitheads,' he nods at the crack crew on the corner, 'still alive because you don't shoot till they make you.'

'That's what they say, huh? Up here on the Northside?'

'Yep.' No tone change, no bait. 'That's what they say all over.'

This is not the first time I've had this discussion. Usually it's with uniformed patrol officers sporting tight sleeves and hard eyes, peacekeepers who think I'm putting the good guys unnecessarily in danger. 'I've been where a lot of these folks are; don't have to hate 'em to arrest 'em.'

He wants to know what I mean, like we're gonna be best friends and need to share all this shit. I just want to go back to bed and hide. We pass a busted-open section of wall and I see Annabelle Ganz and her hand, hear the whoosh of the steel mills twenty years ago and taste the metal air on my tongue.

He asks, 'That where you're from, down there in 6?'

Without thinking, I say, 'Calumet City.'

He breaks into a half smile. 'You're *from* Calumet City?'

Calumet City touches Chicago just the other side of the city's main sanitary district. Not so much a city as a switching yard for the Michigan Central, B&O, and Penn Central railroads, all shoe-horned between the Port of Chicago and the Indiana border. Picture transients, dead elm trees, bust-out strip joints, and pawnshops with no customers. Add smokestack winter all year long, and you're in Calumet City.

In its only heyday, my hometown was the Outfit's prime gambling and vice locale – 'The Strip' before the one in Vegas was named. In the '80s, when I was still there, John Belushi made it famous again as the home of Joliet Jake and Elwood Blues. Belushi got the look down, but the humor was new – there wasn't one thing funny about it I can remember.

My new partner tries again. 'Calumet City. No *shit*? That's where Monday's stinker was from; the one in the wall. Today's *Herald* said the mayor's wife owned the building. Hell, the superintendent lived in it.'

'That a fact?'

'For real. The Homicide dicks ID'd the body two nights ago, traced her from an old driver's license in her wallet.' He pauses to stare at two street–corner Nike jumpsuits standing face to face. 'She was party to some weird shit over there, *plenty* weird for a small town, hell, for a big town.' He's laughing now. 'You know her?'

The radio squawks an all–call. '1812?'

A uniform car answers, '1812.'

'1812 and all units on city–wide. Kidnapping in progress, two perpetrators, Assistant State's Attorney Richard Rhodes. 1-7-1-0 Wells, in the alley.'

Before I can say, *Jesus Christ, an ASA*, my partner pulls the mike, '1863 rolling in plainclothes,' and we light it up. U–turn, siren, and he's doing 70 eastbound on Division's narrow lanes. The neighborhood morphs from projects to yuppies in four fast blocks. We dodge a bus and a van, slip to the wrong side of the

84

yellow line and jam the brakes. *Hooooooorn*. I'm braced into the dash. We miss the truck coming at us, swerve, more brakes, gas, hand-over-hand, and we're sliding onto Wells Street.

Only the TV police hit an intersection like this. Almost a lock you'll be T-boned or kill a pedestrian. Mid-block he's doing 80, using the center stripe, screaming past pedestrians lunging for cover. We miss a bicycle and a parked Baird's Bread truck that someone else didn't. The radio squawks again. 'All units on city–wide. Suspect kidnap vehicle southbound on 1600 block of Wells. Brown Chevrolet SUV, high rate of speed, officers in pursuit.'

'Comin' our way.' He jams the brakes and turns the wheel to slide–block the street. This means the 6,000-pound SUV traveling at a 'high rate of speed' will smash my side and kill us both. The tires on my side buckle and we flip straight. An SUV grille roars up Wells at us like a train. Nowhere to go. I duck and the SUV shears off our driver's side fender to the door. We spin into parked cars, bang three and our gas tank ruptures. Sirens scream past. Gasoline replaces the air. Disoriented, I jerk the seat belt that saved me. *Stuck*. The gas ignites and takes all the air with it. Hot. Loud. The belt pops; the door won't open. Flames. I lean into my partner and kick the door. He moans in my ear. I kick with both feet. Flames fill the backseat, smoke everywhere. Can't breathe, see stars. My shoe catches the handle; the door opens and I'm out, through the flames, rolling on the pavement. The car's belching fire. *Scream* from inside. I dive back in because I don't think. My partner comes when I grab through the smoke. Too heavy, can't breathe, somehow I drag him out to pavement. Somebody slaps us with jackets; more screaming. It gets dark very quickly and everything stops.

*　*　*

Heaven has coarse linen bed sheets and perfume I've smelled before. Somewhere.

And strangely enough, a police superintendent. Could be he's God after all, like he always said. Wish I would've listened. God is holding my hand which I take to be a good sign. The crowd behind him is not so good. Over his shoulder is a very pained-looking Sonny Barrett and six strangers in suits, one of them a middle-aged, well-heeled woman. Is she the perfume? Beyond them, uniforms are holding reporters at bay. Chief Jesse lets go of my hand as soon as he notices I'm awake.

I smile. 'Miss me? I can come back from 18 anytime.'

He doesn't answer and waves Sonny and the other men out of the room. Sonny hesitates like he's thinking about it, then does what he's told. I remember the fire. 'Oh, shit, tell me the kid didn't die.'

Headshake, pride in the superintendent's face but suppressed. 'The cop you pulled out of your car ... his father was the alderman in the old First Ward, Toddy Pete Steffen.'

Wow. The old First Ward was the Chicago equivalent of Tammany Hall – guys who could fix murder trials for Outfit hitmen as notorious as Harry Aleman and some say the occasional presidential election, 1960 for sure. When he's not doing the public's business, Toddy Pete Steffen is a *big deal* insurance broker, big in the insurance biz like Alan Dorfman was before the Outfit capped him.

'Toddy Pete's very pleased with your performance, thinks you need another commendation. Personally, I'd recommend a convent. Of late, the stars do not seem to be aligned in your favor.'

I hear reporters yelling and say, 'Nice of the press to notice.'

The superintendent of police straightens a bit. 'That's not why they're here.'

THURSDAY

Chapter 6

THURSDAY, DAY 4: SUNRISE

Lake Shore Drive, heading south. I'm out of the hospital, that's the good news – tan, rested, and ready, having snuck past two groggy reporters without answering a question. The bad news is everything else Chief Jesse said. IAD is waiting on me, licking their lips. The clothes I'm wearing are ruined, including most of my Cubs hat and Julie's shirt – that's two of hers in two days – and I smell like an oil furnace.

Thursday's sun leaps out of the water, glaring dead–level across Lake Michigan. I add Ray-Bans but they only block half. All I can do is squint and hope the car in front doesn't stop. My cell vibrates but I can't answer until I can see better. When I first got to my car my cell had six '911' messages from Tracy Moens, five of which I haven't listened to, and one from Sonny Barrett that said 'Call me at 0-10 hundred.'

I know what Tracy and Sonny want to talk about. To steal a phrase just used on the radio, it's the kidnap that almost burned me to death and has the whole city sideways. Chief Jesse told me before he left my room that the person the SUV kidnappers grabbed was not just an assistant state's attorney, but the ASA heading the mayor's assassination task force.

This is big news. And whether the kidnap is tied to someone taking three shots at His Honor and almost killing his wife or not, it represents a certain brazenness not seen in this city since Al Capone. And that Outfit comparison isn't lost on anyone with both eyes open. The jazzy radio banter quits and Cameron 'Superfly' Smith says almost twenty–four hours have passed and there's been no ransom demand.

No ransom demand is not good news for Richard Rhodes. Cops are rarely cheerleaders for state's attorneys – they blame us for all courthouse failures – but I shiver for this one's situation and knock the dash twice above my radio. There aren't any prayers you can say for captives; God doesn't listen to those.

Before I report back to 18 this a.m., I'm trying to get to my locker in 6 via what the Northsiders call the 'Whiteman's Expressway.' They call it that because Lake Shore Drive's northern half runs along the Gold Coast and its yacht harbors to Evanston and leafy North Shore society beyond. Most of my trip will be on the southern half because it runs to Ghetto Central via Forty-seventh Street, Stoney Island, and Seventy-ninth Street.

The plan is to dodge the Ayatollah's pickets at 6, clean out my locker, then stop by the duplex, feed Jezebel and Bathsheba, change clothes, and tell Stella not to worry if she watched the news last night, and not to plan a wedding if she didn't. Me and traffic are crawling over a drawbridge that spans the river and the glare makes us all Ray Charles; it's now clear why so many Northsiders working downtown die in traffic accidents. My leg vibrates again, I answer this time and try not to drive into the lake or the river.

The superintendent of police says, 'Phone transfer. You're reassigned to the Intelligence Unit.'

I don't have to ask by whom. Only he can order two phone transfers in two days. To describe that as suspicious would be to understate the Virgin Mary appearing in Gerri's Palm Tavern. 'Can I ask why?'

'Front page, today's *Herald* – the task force ASA, Richard Rhodes, was in a foster home in Calumet City. Guess which one.'

I swerve up onto the sidewalk.

'As a minor he was a suspect in the 1987 murder that occurred there. No reason till now to match the name in an eighteen-year-old homicide report to *our* Richard Rhodes. The murder never cleared, hence he remains a suspect.'

Horns blare. I drop the phone and hear 'FBI,' while two-handing my Celica to a stop in Daley's $450 million Millennium Park that I've never seen before.

'Officer Black?'

I fumble the phone to my face. 'Yeah. Sorry, Chief, ah Boss. Sorry.'

'Can you hear me?'

'Yeah. Yeah, traffic. *Jesus*. Did you say Richard Rhodes was a foster . . . He was in Annabelle Ganz's home?'

'Stop at the next landline and call my office.'

'Ah, yeah. But—'

Click.

I stare at my cell like it bit my ear. *Richard Rhodes was in that home too? With me?* A face flashes, he's called Richey, he's ten or eleven. Like me, Richey's scared shitless all the time too. *Oh my God.* Daddy's favorite boy and I'm Daddy's favorite girl. The vomit gushes before I can get the door open. And keeps coming.

THURSDAY, DAY 4: 8:00 A.M.

The soapy pistol wand at Leon's RideBrite cleans hospital breakfast off my floor mats and hands. The wand's detergent doubles as mouthwash, not something I recommend. The superintendent is still waiting for my landline call. I need to run away, be somebody else. A gang-encrypted pay phone stares at me. The phone is surrounded by three street gangsters doing crack business. I pull the CPD star out of my shirt and unholster my pistol. Being here alone is not a good idea, but neither is eating soap or reliving a portion of your life that came close to killing you the first time you lived it.

The gangsters retreat twenty feet and bitch–stare me. I dial the superintendent's direct line.

'Sir, Officer Black reporting.'

'You're official at Intel and working directly for me. Understand?'

'Yes, sir.'

I understand, sort of. The Intelligence Unit is an investigative arm of the Superintendent's Office, working directly under his supervision, with citywide jurisdiction and no enforcement responsibilities. Lots of juice when an officer's carrying that star and on a mission from the boss. Lots of suspicion, too.

Chief Jesse's tone is formal, like he's speaking to a microphone. 'As of 0-600 today, the FBI is officially in. They are investigating three cases our governor in his infinite-election-month wisdom deems related. Case one: the mayor's assassination attempt. Case two: the kidnap of ASA Richard Rhodes. And case three: the discovery of Annabelle Ganz's body. The FBI incorrectly agrees with the governor that all three cases are related.'

'Sir—'

'There is no evidence to tie these three cases together other than Assistant State's Attorney Rhodes and Annabelle Ganz once lived in the same Calumet City home eighteen years ago. This is political character assassination. And your friends in the media are standing in line to help.'

'Sir—'

'Get on the highway to Joliet. You can do that, can't you?'

'Why are you mad at me?'

Silence.

I'm way out of line and know it. He doesn't know I'm in a car wash eating soap while teenage gunmen try to figure me out. He doesn't know about me and Calumet City because no one does.

'Sorry. I'm on the way to Joliet. Sir.'

'The Stateville condemned unit has a convict doing double life who says he has "urgent" information regarding ASA Richard Rhodes. This convict will only talk to you. Explain that.'

'Ah, I'd like to. Who're we talking about?'

'The *Herald*'s Tracy Moens – your friend, and teammate I believe – has called everyone in this building, *and the FBI*, to verify that you and this convict have a standing relationship. If that's true, it had better be arrest related.'

I wince at FBI – the G as we call them, and Tracy's incessant need to know.

'Sir, what convict?'

'Danny del Pasco.'

'Danny D from Canaryville? The biker?'

'You do know him.'

'And he wants to see me?'

'Only you. Why?'

I have no idea and say so. None. Zero.

'This is not a good time to bullshit me, Officer Black.'

'I'm not, Chief, sir. I've never seen Danny D. Just heard about him forever.'

Silence or the pay phone's stopped working. Then:

'The FBI's organized crime unit is out at Stateville now, attempting to coerce an interview – they believe these three cases – the mayor's assassination attempt, the ASA kidnapping, and Annabelle Ganz's body – are part of multiple kidnappings and murders dating back to 1987 in Calumet City. The FBI believes these three cases will lead them to "an extensive coverup and corruption within the state's attorney's office" and "continuing criminal activity within the Chicago Police Department"—'

'Not the Republicans or the blacks; now it's CPD or the state's attorney's office who tried to hit the mayor? Even the G's not that stupid.'

More silence makes me wish I hadn't said that, although the conclusion's hard to avoid . . . Movement – the three street gangsters are fanning but not away. I show my pistol but don't aim.

'The coming election is a time for settling old disputes—local, state, and federal. I want a call one second after the del Pasco interview's over.' The superintendent pauses for my agreement. I give it, then he adds, 'No press, no nothing. And not so much as a "hello" to the FBI.' Click.

I flash on me and Richey as foster kids. Richey on top when they made him . . . STOP IT. Until this moment I never knew Richey and Richard Rhodes were the same person. Jesus, and what if it's true? What if the FBI's right and all three cases *are* related . . . ? And what if Chief Jesse *knows* they are? What if – no way. Go to the death house in Joliet, hear Danny del Pasco, then tell Chief Jesse your story.

Can't do that. My hand crushes the phone. *You have to*; Richard Rhodes may die if you don't. No he won't; the kidnap isn't related, it's an accident, an awful coincidence. Coincidences happen; no need to tell. Not now, not ever.

Trust your friends. Tell Chief Jesse now. I feed the phone quarters, hoping it jams, hoping Chief Jesse doesn't answer. The gangsters watch. One turns away and I lose sight of his hands. The phone rings but doesn't answer. The bar across the street behind the gangsters has an Old Crow sign in the window.

No. Get outta here.

The two gangsters facing me notice my meltdown and pull the third one back. He has a cell phone as he turns, not a pistol and I don't shoot him. My Smith rises into their faces and helps them add a quick twenty feet. The one with the phone is nodding small and keeps talking to his phone. He's marking me, sure as I'm standing here. Could be because of the dead GDs at Gilbert Court, but I don't have time to know or deal with it.

Among the many things I wonder as I bail the neighborhood and try to outrun my new need to confess, is why hasn't IAD grabbed me for the alderman's charges on the GD shooting and Ruth Ann's *assault*. That worry lasts one block; I've got bigger wonders now, like how many FBI agents it takes to investigate a foster home. How many days do I have before the whole city knows my story? Before I have to publicly face the truth about Patti Black?

THURSDAY, DAY 4: 10:00 A.M.

Me and my thoughts finish thirty–seven miles of interstate at a prison town trying hard not to be. Other than a sprawling weapons arsenal, Joliet is known for one thing – the just-shut-down 1858 Penitentiary, a limestone nightmare used in every movie that needed to scare the shit out of the audience with just silence and pictures. It and its successor guard the city's flank and troubled history, brooding out there on the northern outskirts, past the visitor motels and their sticky vinyl coffee shops, past the roads that lead there and stop.

Among the criminal classes 'Joliet' still means more than prison – it's a condition, a level of punishment. Architects liked Joliet so much they copied it for most U.S. facilities of the era; Joliet didn't have running water or indoor bathrooms for the first sixty years.

Now the newer Stateville CC (1925) is the maximum-security facility. The Condemned Unit is here, except they don't call it that while the courts and the politicians try to figure out how to house prisoners they want to kill, people who deserve it, like Danny del Pasco. The other inmates who have to share this prison would know how to *house* them. Staring at the outer fence and its rolls of concertina wire, I for sure do.

The front gate on Highway 53 is a brick guard shack separating a long, uphill in/out asphalt drive. Bilingual signs bolted to the bricks explain that *all* persons give up their rights to search and seizure when they drive onto the property. By its looks, this gate is probably unmanned on most days. Today it has state police cars parked across the entry and exit.

I show my star and a photo ID. Both are checked against a clipboard list by a guard who could've been a postman in blue-black. A man and a woman approach my car from both sides – they have to be reporters. Strange that press credentials can't get them inside.

One yells, '*Patti. Patti.* Why does Danny del Pasco want you?'

The guard hands me my ID and waves me onto the road.

'Have you been charged by Internal Affairs? Is Richard Rhodes alive?'

The state police car backs out of my way. I slip through and two troopers step in behind my car, separating me from my freedom and the reporters in my mirror. *That quick* and you're no longer a citizen; you're a captive. I feel 'captive' on my skin and shiver at what it's like to face this place for real, for ten years or forever. I've been sending people here – you'd think I'd know.

I 5-mph into a shadow cast by thirty-three feet of poured concrete wall. As the wall takes more and more of the sky I focus on *captive*. Assistant State's Attorney Richard Rhodes flashes in restraints, but as a boy, not as an adult: cow-eyed and hairless and naked. No telling how bad it is for him right now, but there's no hiding from how bad it was when he was just 'Richey.'

One of two guards outside the visitors' intake building eyes my white-knuckled steering wheel and plastic expression, then points my car through to the near end of the 'staff' lot, then talks to her radio. I park without a problem, but it takes five minutes of gritted teeth and denial to piece my own walls back together. Richey as a boy is not a picture I want to carry.

The visitors' building is shut down for the day; I'm pointed next door to the staff entrance and buzzed inside by a large, mid-forties German with a smile that doesn't fit his geography or the day's precautions.

I see his name tag and think I hear Officer Leo Didier say, 'Got fifty dollars?'

'Excuse me?'

'Fifty.' He uses both hands to frame the shape of a bill. 'About so big and green.'

'Ah . . . probably not.'

'Have to take your pistol then.'

'For fifty I could keep it?'

Headshake and another honest smile. 'Nah, I just need the fifty.'

A comedian was not what I expected at the ticket booth of a horror movie. I sign in my Smith and raise both arms to be searched. Officer Didier smiles again, almost shy, and says, 'Would love to, but I'd be lying. You're juiced in, superintendent to warden. Just show me an ID,' he nods over another guard's weightlifter shoulder to his glass back door, 'and you're *behind the Wall*.'

Across a fenced internal roadway is the Wall. Beyond it are the ghosts of John Wayne Gacy and Richard Speck and a living, breathing Ralph Andrews.

Officer Didier adds, 'Careful in there. Talk fast; today's not going well.'

I don't ask but should have.

'Inside' begins with an escort across the road to the main entry, then through Gate 1 to the Guard Hall in the Admin building. I pick up the rhythm of a working building and become a cop again. The deep breaths, harsh lights, and linoleum help reduce the dungeon effect to tolerable. Not much has been spent on décor for the inmates' visitors, about like community hospitals but without the two-year-old magazines. The staff looks at me closer, though, like I'm an accident that hasn't happened yet.

My escort stops, apologizes, and says we have to backtrack back through Gate 1 to the warden's conference room. We do. Three gentlemen in dark suits are waiting. One interrupts my trip.

'Officer Black?' He offers his hand. 'Special Agent Stone, FBI, Organized Crime Unit.'

We shake. My escort watches; she knows that often these meetings don't go well.

Special Agent Stone says, 'We should talk before you see Mr. del Pasco.' He hands me a copy of an old Tracy Moens article. 'And then right after.'

'Sorry. I report to my boss; it's procedure. You can talk with him.'

'Would that be Kevin Ryan in District 18 or the super-intendent?' He adds what might be a leer with 'superintendent.'

'Pick 'em.' I don't mention the second phone transfer.

The guard waves me forward; either she's impatient or she has the same animosity for the G that most cops do. 'Sorry . . . my appointment.'

We walk through linoleum halls that smell the same as most city buildings before they open; the walls are as blank as the floors. The interview area we're using is between Gate 2 and 3 in the attorney visitation rooms. Mine is 9×14 with a glass door. A worn, wooden table sits long–ways in the center, separating two chairs. My escort points me inside and turns to leave.

I touch her shoulder. 'There a problem in here . . . today?'

She purses her lips and nods, finishes her turn, and walks down the wide hall. Alone in the room it feels, I don't know . . . odd? Like I'm the one who's guilty. I notice Tracy's Op-ed article in my hand and read while I wait.

©Tracy Moens, *Chicago Herald*
January 16, 1996

Danny del Pasco already had a name in Canaryville.

But he carved it in stone on Christmas Day, 1995. And that's hard to accomplish south and west of Comiskey where the channel workers and slaughterhouse stockmen live cramped and angry, the Irishmen who built this city but were too poor to live in it.

On that Christmas Day Danny del Pasco had been drinking just the one Harp for an hour and slowly smoking Pall Malls to his fingertips, lighting one with the other. Tobin's Corner Bar was humid with sweat and full of loud conversations. The stools on either side of Danny were empty. No one knew it yet, including Danny, but he'd kill nine people before Dallas beat the Cardinals 37–13. He said he thought it would be two dead, maybe three. But it all depended on them. Under his leather jacket he wore a sleeveless denim with *Gypsy Vikings MC* in an arch and Chicago at the bottom. He washed it in 1990, 'had to, DNA thing.'

Like Danny, Canaryville and this pub had history, Chicago's version of Hell's Kitchen and the Five Points, a neighborhood that housed and hid Irishmen who fought overseas, as well as contract killers who did, and do, the Outfit's bidding when the Italians want their hand hidden. There are good people here, poor and hardworking, who keep out of the bad business unless they're forced into it. They knew Danny, knew him all his life, just like the bad ones knew Danny. That's why the stools were empty.

By halftime the sun was down and Dallas had covered. Danny left five silver dollars stacked in a pile, walked outside into 28 degrees, added tight gloves, and waved up an '82 Bonneville. Inside he pointed the 24-year-old driver west to Cicero. Over his shoulder he was handed a second Glock that he checked, and a hand grenade. The pin was tight and he loosened it.

At the trial the family of the victims testified that Danny del Pasco walked into the house after knocking twice and dislodging their Christmas wreath, pulled the grenade's pin one-handed, and asked for $38,000. Half the room consisted of women and children, all first- or second-generation Mexican-Americans. The men didn't move. He asked again, then tossed them the grenade and started shooting.

Seven of the dead were male, ranging in age from 54 to 20, all armed with a gun, knife, or razor. The two women were both minors. It was a crystal meth deal gone awry. A matter of honor, the Gypsy Vikings said.

And here he comes, shouldered by two titanic guards, neither touching him. One looks me over, more with respect than A-male dick wagging. The other introduces himself. I decide that prison guards are not accurately portrayed in the movies or professional wrestling. The prisoner, on the other hand, is right out of Central Casting.

Danny del Pasco is a shaved-head white male of about forty, lean at 200 pounds, corded and vascular in belly chains and Aryan tattoos. The unadorned portions of his skin are a lighter shade of the worn wood that will separate us. Two tears are tattooed under his left eye–badges for prison murders. He moves with confidence, not swagger. His eyes are bright but quiet, reserved, not wary. I've seen a number of overamped thugs who have committed murder, and he is not one. This is a *stone* killer.

We sit, twenty-four inches apart. The only defense I have is to duck. The guards retreat and close the door. One stays outside, his hand hidden in the vicinity of the doorknob. Comforting, but likely too far to stop Danny D's first move if he makes it. Danny's eyes are steel blue and on me, but not a glare, not a threat. I'm game faced, showing him nothing, semi-slouching in an uncomfortable plastic chair. We're two people having coffee at Art's on Ashland, no more, no less. At least that's what I'm faking.

'So what's up, Danny?'

He smiles. It doesn't make him less threatening, but that seems to be what he's shooting for, a prison version of nice. He leans in and I force myself not to move. The guard turns the knob, hesitates, then when nothing happens steps back.

Danny whispers. I can't hear and have to lean forward. This is an old lockup trick that almost never ends well for the cop doing the leaning. I lean in anyway.

Danny whispers again. 'FBI had interesting questions this morning. Backed 'em with an offer – I talk about you and Richard Rhodes and anybody else connected to this, and maybe they can work somethin' out.'

I wait for more, but he doesn't elaborate. He adds another smile, an honest one that's hard to place in this environment.

'C'mon,' he says. 'You gotta remember. It's me, Danny.'

I stare, clueless. No way I wouldn't remember. From *somewhere*.

'Danny boy. The bat.'

I snap back. My neck and face flush.

The door jerks open. 'All right, Miss?'

DON'T FAINT. Words don't form, so I nod, then wave *thanks, no problem* until the guard believes me and leaves. Danny watches me, but it's not the snake eyes you see on the street. *Holy shit – the* Danny del Pasco and I *do* know each other. All I can say is, 'How you doing, Danny?'

'You look better than the pictures. Think I like the one in *Chicago* magazine best; Paul Elledge took that, didn't he?'

The bomb's still exploding. This is the Twilight Zone.

'Little spooked, huh?' Danny gives me a smile that bunches the two tears by his eye. 'Been a weird fuckin' week, I'd imagine.'

Long exhale, deep breath. 'Yeah.'

Danny starts talking. I hear words, but the memory has me by the neck. My first three days in the foster home. Danny D was the older boy who protected me. He scared off Richey, who immediately saw me as a punching bag. And he scared off Roland Ganz, who had worse intentions. Sixteen-year-old Danny coldcocked Roland with a baseball bat on the third day and ran when Annabelle called the cops.

'. . . so that's why.'

'I'm sorry, what?'

Danny stares and suggests I take a deep breath, which I do, and continues talking, demonstrating education he likely got inside, an offset to the tattoo tears. After four minutes it's obvious that there's no way to deny my past to Danny D if he decides to talk about it – to me or anybody else. He finishes with 'Religion's a go-rilla in here.'

We're here to talk about Richard Rhodes the ASA, and I want to say that, but Danny keeps going.

'Like *PTL* was, you know? Jim and Tammy and "send us the money." ' He bites his lip at the corner where it's scarred thick. 'You and I gotta talk about it some, or I gotta. You don't look so good; maybe you just listen.'

Not if I can help it. *PTL*, television's *Praise the Lord Club*.

'Maybe you just nod.'

Glare reflections slide across the glass in the door.

'When I ran, you was what, thirteen, fourteen, twelve? Richey ten or eleven.'

Nod.

'Roland do *PTL* to you, like he did me and Richey?'

I squeeze the table leg hard enough to break my wrist.

'See, I don't know when you got out, just that you did. You know, all the cop stuff in the papers. I knew it had to be you.' He stops and squints. 'You okay, Patti?'

'Uh-huh.'

Danny's voice is too calm for the pictures I see: Roland and Annabelle, the faces they made.

'When I heard somebody capped Roland at the house in '87, I figured it was Richey. Woulda been me if I'da stayed in that basement.'

Somebody uses my voice to say, 'It wasn't Roland, initial ID was bad. It was a friend of his ... a guy Roland worked with.'

Danny adds prison to his face. He leaves it there while he sees something unpleasant, then regroups when I mutter us back to Richey. Richard. Danny wonders out loud about any others at the foster home.

'There was another girl,' I tell him and me. 'Little Gwen. But she came after you ran.'

Danny drifts again. I don't want to ask any more but I do. 'So, Danny, about Richey—'

'Recognized him from a picture they printed – big fucking deal assistant state's attorney, or thought I did.' Danny reaches for his shirt pocket and produces a new Polaroid. He slides it halfway across the table.

It's a photo of a prison cell wall.

'Had a guard take it.' He nods at the big guard with his hand on the knob.

The wall is ordered, five rows of clippings and photos and articles. I look close. It's me. I can make out the Paul Elledge photo when I was named Officer of the Year the first time. Danny talks while I blink.

'See, I sorta pretend you're my little sister. Wish I woulda come back for you after kicking Roland's ass.' His face hardens again. 'But I got jammed up pretty quick, life of crime and all that . . .'

I stare. At the picture. At him.

'Man . . . that ain't right. Faggot motherfucker being alive . . . All this time I thought Roland was gone.' Danny D looks like who he is now. He says, *'Faggot motherfucker'* to his hands, then composes himself, folding his arms. 'Roland was an accountant or bookkeeper, somethin' like that. Worked for hospitals, mostly. Kind of a weekend missionary too . . . but that ain't news to you.' A red swastika ripples across Danny's forearm. 'Should know both him and his ol' lady better – been killing the same two people all my life.'

I remember to ask the superintendent's question. 'Who grabbed the ASA?'

107

'No idea.'

The picture of Danny's wall is still in my hand. 'Then why call me?'

'A guy hears things. Most of it bullshit in here. *Most of it.*' Danny takes a long look at me for emphasis. 'There's money out on you. And soon.'

The guard knocks on the door's glass and spreads his palm; five minutes.

'*Somebody's hunting me?* Like they did Richey?'

Danny D shrugs. 'Don't know shit about Richey-the-big-deal-ASA.' Pause and another long stare. 'You, I know about.'

I sit back like I've been shoved and take him all in, then lean forward because I've forgotten seventeen years of street smart. He leans at me and whispers, 'An Arizona-Idaho whiteboy shows up, starts buying crystal, met some people, hired himself some accomplices.' Pause. 'He puts money out, wanting your particulars. Good-sized money.' Danny's nose is five inches from mine. 'And nobody I know minds giving up cop particulars if they can.'

'You're inferring—'

'I ain't *inferring* shit. We both know about those kinda questions. Ask them with that kinda money attached and they mean what they always mean.'

'And you know this how?'

Danny rubs the Gypsy Vikings tattoo above the swastika. 'One of my visitors. A brother who knows you and me are family.'

'What kind of accomplices is this whiteboy hiring?'

Danny takes a moment to answer, weighing the words. 'Torches, for one.'

I see the white ComEd workers splashing gas in the Gilbert Court basement. The same guy that hired them wants my particulars—

'We got a minute or less,' Danny says. 'Go by our clubhouse, ask for Charlie Moth, tell him who you are and that I sent you to see Pancake. And no cop shit – you gotta guarantee no cop shit or it'll be me hunting you. And you don't want that.'

Nice even tone like we're talking groceries. I'm still processing 'torches' and having trouble. He has to mean the arsonists on Gilbert Court. And because of my connection to Annabelle Ganz, he's inferring the arson attempt wasn't just on the building, it was on the body in the basement too … or maybe *just* the body in the basement. Fear knots deep in my stomach.

'No cop shit. None.'

I mumble, 'Okay,' thinking about Annabelle Ganz. If the arson was about her, why twelve years after her murder? Clean up the evidence? Shit, this stuff goes in every direction at once. Maybe the FBI's right, maybe all three cases do intersect, all of 'em somehow with my history. Hell, the mayor's wife owned the building.

'Pancake has answers about what I'm hearing in here. Tell Charlie Moth and him what I said – you're my sister. If Pancake fucks with you, and he might, go ahead and shoot him. He's a supplier, not a brother.'

'How come you're sticking your neck out?' I nod at his surroundings.

'I like being your brother, sort of. Can't imagine you feel too good about it.'

I pat his hand for the first time and look at him differently.

'Don't be so sure. And thanks.' My smile's as honest as a little girl's. 'Both times.'

THURSDAY, DAY 4: 11:00 A.M.

Special Agent Stone is waiting outside by Officer Didier's staff entrance, between me and my pistol. Stone has two sidekicks behind him, three pairs of government-issue sunglasses like they're imitating Will Smith and Tommy Lee Jones.

'We've had an interesting half hour, Officer Black. Your friend Danny del Pasco's quite a fan.' Special Agent Stone has his own Polaroid of Danny's cell.

I smile an inch. These guys can cause an officer a great deal of heartache if they wish to – info drops to the press, unsourced accusations that light up the mayor who lights up the super-intendent, formal complaints to your Watch LT, who folds and writes a CR number for Internal Affairs to work. They can subpoena your personnel file and cause IRS audits until you're a hundred. They can also put you in prison.

Agent Stone knows I know and says, 'Let's have a cup of coffee and talk about it, see if we can help each other.'

'Sorry. Have to report to my boss first. Procedure.'

'This is a federal investigation, Officer Black. We have jurisdiction, not your boss.'

His hand lands lightly on my shoulder, like I should follow him back toward the Admin building. I don't and he stops.

'Right in here'll be fine.'

'Sorry. Got a train to catch.'

He points, 'Right in here.' His pals politely block the only path to my pistol and personal items.

Headshake as red heats my face.

Special Agent Stone closes our distance. 'We searched Mr. del Pasco's cell and believe you have information that may save the life of Assistant State's Attorney Richard Rhodes.'

'Talk to my boss.'

'I'm talking to you. About a man's life, about obstruction of justice, the federal version. It puts officers and superintendents suspected of collusion or corruption into prisons like this one.'

'Superintendents? Is that what you said?' Our noses are almost touching now. 'Fuck you and J. Edgar's prom dress.'

'This is our jurisdiction—'

'This is a *state* prison, asshole.' I wave at Officer Didier to give me my gun. 'Your jurisdiction doesn't extend beyond your fucking underwear.'

Agent Stone purses his lips and nods to himself. 'Possibly Alderman Gibbons is right; maybe we *should* take a closer look at the Gilbert Court shootings. "*Federal* violations of civil rights."—'

The outside gate should feel better, but it doesn't. I'm wondering who's trying to kill me out here and how long it'll take the FBI to mount an obstruction case over Danny D or a civil rights prosecution over the Gilbert Court shootings. They'll subpoena my personnel file, find the hazy parts, and—

One of the reporters who was here when I arrived shoves a cell phone at my window and yells 'Tracy Moens. Tracy Moens.'

Nada. The only call I'm making is Chief Jesse, and that one's not going to be easy. How do you tell a story you can't tell? And to a guy who's running you all over town tied to puppet strings? First I have to lose Tracy's stringer scrambling for his car. Tracy's burning for the Danny D angle – whatever it is. And the fact that Danny D knows nothing about Richard Rhodes being kidnapped won't matter. Danny D asked for me. Only me.

My mirror fills with the reporter's grille. Give the media two or three hours and either they or the FBI will place Danny D in *a* Calumet City foster home. From there, coincidence or not, it'll be an avalanche. The FBI will rip my personnel file, piece together my past – the runaway years on the street, the Salvation Mission, a young woman's lies of omission that made her CPD job application look presentable umpteen years ago. IAD will be next. Won't even need a hearing to get my star.

None of which helps ASA Richard Rhodes. With no ransom note and no clues, Chicago is just too huge a city; worse, it's surrounded by millions of people in other cities. If he's still alive, CPD and the FBI won't find him until his kidnappers want us to. And by then Richey will be well down the road of his second trip through hell.

I wince at that picture, make a hard left, and speed through Joliet's outskirts, feint onto the Stevenson eastbound, loop a semi, and cut back under. The reporter is buried on the on ramp. I need a landline phone and the balls to tell the truth on the off chance my confession will save a man who as a boy was forced to rape me twice. Richey flashes on top of me, scared and aroused and—

SHUT THE FUCK UP.

I see the seven digits that became my armor and count backwards. At 999,992 the picture's gone. I fluff off the exercise, but the pain in my jaw is real. I don't stop at the first ten pay phones I pass. Red light. An SUV and a trailing van fill the adjacent lane, so close and high I can't see in either vehicle's window.

Danny D's warning jumps in front of buried terrors. *Pay attention.* Any one of these vehicles could be the one with a whiteboy from Arizona or Idaho driving. And him and his 'torch' accomplices either want to grab or kill you. Grab is not fucking possible; I have a standing suicide promise before I go through that again. I feel for my pistol; it's out and under my leg and I don't remember moving it.

I run the light and turn; one block down I turn again and check the mirror for the SUV or the van. Nope. Better stop, regroup, and face the phone call. A badly flawed plan comes to mind, and I desperately want to shelve it in favor of just disappearing into the sunset.

THURSDAY, DAY 4: 11:30 A.M.

Armando's Pizza has baked-oregano air and a phone. I order a calzone for lunch that I probably won't eat and make the call from between two opposing bathroom doors. Above the phone there's a U of Wisconsin football player smiling at me through two pounds of '70s black hair. It's signed 'Gale.' The phone answers on half a ring. 'Smith.'

'Officer Black, sir. I'm on a landline if you're ready.'

'Go.'

Deep, deep breath. 'The infamous Danny del Pasco was in the same foster home as Assistant State's Attorney Richard Rhodes.'

'*Bullshit.*'

'As you said, sir, this is not a good time to bullshit the super-intendent.' Pause. 'Bottom line, Danny D has no information on the kidnap or the ASA's whereabouts.'

'Why the meeting?'

My plan was to tell my story, most of it, and say it's Danny's, but now, standing at the starting line, I can't seem to start, even as Danny. It's not a surprise; this is a story I can't mention to a mirror with no reflection or a window full of Chinatown lanterns. I couldn't say it to a priest or the police back then, and I can't say it to the dark now.

'Officer Black?'

Silence. Silence . . . Silence. Eyes closed, I plunge. 'There appears . . . was . . . extensive child abuse of a violent sexual nature in that foster home.' I'm channeling Joe Friday and realize I've now faced myself into the corner like a five-year-old. 'Danny D will deny any of this took place if he's put on record, but told me that Annabelle and Roland assaulted all four children in the household and that ASA Richard Rhodes was forced to participate . . . raping a teenage girl who was also there; the runaway you mentioned.'

I hear Chief Jesse whisper, 'Jesus,' then tell someone to run Roland and Annabelle Ganz again, get it all. He comes back to me. 'Who were the other children?'

I choke on the question. Try to speak but can't. I drop the phone, shoulder into the bathroom and the wall mirror flashes: I'm fourteen, scared shitless and alone, assaulted every day by someone. I scream, stumble back, and fall to the tile. Tears pour out of my eyes; can't breathe, suck a breath—

The door bangs open. A man. He stops mid-step.

I press back into a wall, hands on the floor.

He blurts something in Italian.

I catch three breaths, don't look at the mirror, and wobble to standing.

Italian accent, 'You'a fine?'

114

Slower breaths, slower breaths, then, 'Thought I saw a rat, but didn't. Sorry. Really, I'm sorry.' He fixes on my pistol. I say, 'Copper,' and fumble out my star. 'Chicago.'

He nods, big-time confused.

'Really, I'm okay.' I wave him out, pointing at the stalls like I'm about to use one. He nods again, embarrassed now, and exits. I use the sink and avoid the mirror. The cold water snaps me back to the superintendent of police – who may still be on the phone wondering how dead his officer is.

Outside, between the doors, I grab the dangling phone, say 'sir' four times and he answers in his street voice. 'What the fuck is going on?'

My courage fails once again. 'A domestic. I'm in a restaurant, got it stopped, but it took a minute. Sorry.'

'So? The names. Who're the two children MIA?'

'Danny D didn't remember. We'll have to try to get the names through Cal City Juvy.'

'That'll take a month, if at all.'

'Sir, there's more. The FBI braced me and threatened you. Said I was obstructing justice and you were involved in corruption or collusion.'

Long silence, then, 'They said that, huh? And the agent's name?'

'Special Agent Stone. Is there, ah . . . any news on Richard Rhodes?'

'News? Yeah, there's news. State's Attorney Richard Rhodes was found eleven minutes ago, roughly five hundred feet from the Jackson Park Yacht Club. As I'm sure you're unfamiliar with the neighborhood, that's approximately the front lawn of Mayor McQuinn's mansion.'

'Oh, shit.'

'Yes. That would be accurate. Richard Rhodes had barbed wire restraints dug all the way to the bone, three fingers severed at the tips, and appeared to have been beaten to death slowly with a blunt object, possibly a shovel. My guess is the killers wished to know something.'

Tell him the rest. Just say it . . .

'The bodyguard on the mayor and his family has been doubled. At this moment, we and the FBI are arguing at the crime scene, where they continue to accuse the department of incompetence and worse.'

'Chief, I—'

'Once again, Officer Black, why did Mr. del Pasco ask for you and only you? Think before you answer.'

I do think, but my jaw bites shut. A half–lie allows me to answer. 'He's a fan, showed me a picture of his cell – a wall that's all about me, who knows why. He says there's money out on me, but didn't know who, just that it's out there in the crystal meth crews.' I shut my eyes and add the lie, 'Probably the GDs. He used the Richard Rhodes kidnap so he could tell me in person.'

'That's it?'

Shit, that's not enough? I want to tell him about the twenty-something whiteboy from Idaho-Arizona shopping for arson accomplices and my particulars. And I want to tell him those torches probably tie me to Annabelle's crypt and that she could tie me to . . . history I don't want to remember, let alone admit. Instead, I answer, 'Yeah. That was it.'

Silence. Too long to be good, then, 'Calumet City PD has already informed us that they cannot produce the names or juvenile records of the children in the Ganz foster home even if

116

they wished to, which they don't. Unlike our mayor's political opponents and the FBI, I now believe we have only two cases here, not three, but they remain definitely *unrelated*. Case one is the assassination attempt on the mayor and the kidnap-torture-murder of his task force attorney Richard Rhodes. These two events are somehow connected to the casino license vote or the mayoral election – most likely both. Case two is the Annabelle Ganz body and the building in District 6. This case also ties to Richard Rhodes, but indirectly. His connection is eighteen years ago in a Calumet City foster home and, I still believe, completely incidental.'

I start to say that the arsonists and I are almost certainly the bridge between Richard Rhodes and the building. But don't.

'Case two has tremendous smear potential. Associating the Black Monday murder at the Ganz foster home with either the mayor's wife or me is, according to His Honor, worth several thousand votes in a close election. I believe it would be accurate to say that he is currently more worried about that than he is about avoiding another bullet.'

'Yes, sir.'

'I'll call Calumet City and tell them you're coming. Review the Black Monday murder file, all of it, everything you can find that could remotely tie me, the department, the mayor's wife, Assistant State's Attorney Rhodes, or Mr. del Pasco to case one or two. Any questions?'

There are only a few things I want to do less than go to Calumet City. One would be to look at pictures of my former foster residence and the murder that took place there.

'Is there a problem, Officer Black?'

'Huh?'

'Do you have a problem going back?'

Back? Did he say 'back'?

'Patricia, I know you have history in Calumet City – it's in your file, which I reread last night and kept away from the State's Attorney's Office, the FBI, and Internal Affairs.'

'I, ah—'

'Upon closer review, it's a file with more than one gap. These gaps likely didn't matter to anyone before, but they will now. Since this conversation has included nothing marginally believable that supports why Danny del Pasco, biker-hitman, would warn you instead of celebrate when another cop died, I have to figure that these gaps and Mr. del Pasco's history have something in common.'

Suddenly it's very cold in Armando's Pizza.

'All I know for certain is that you and Mr. del Pasco were both in foster homes in Calumet City, Illinois, in the 1980s. Best I can tell without much investigative effort, there were only twelve such homes in a town of less than thirty thousand. Since all the records have yet to be unsealed, I only have your word that you weren't in *the* foster home. But if you were, I better know every fucking thing you know and right now.'

I only have enough breath to say, 'Call you back.'

Chapter 7

THURSDAY, DAY 4: NOON

How long has Chief Jesse known? What does he know? I'm alone in my car, fingers tight on the wheel. How far can I get before they . . . 'Screw that, Patricia, you didn't kill anybody.'

Right. So my file has gaps, I fudged on my application. So what?

'Sure, just fill in a gap or two – Roland's *PTL Club*; raped every way possible and pregnant at fifteen; alcoholic–runaway life on the street for forty–nine months.'

So? I'm the only teenage alcoholic with a badge?

My knuckles are white.

'But what did you do out there? How'd you keep going, pay the rent? Tell 'em about the blackouts, the hospital stays, your baby . . . Patti Black, hero.'

I realize it's me answering myself out loud, a sure sign that I am really, truly losing it. My cell vibrates. The ID is Chief Jesse's number. Another mile and it vibrates again; this time it's Tracy Moens and I don't answer her call either. Calumet City – I'll be there in less than an hour. Seventeen years, and now I get to face it all over again. The Old Crow bottle on my keychain says what it says every Friday night when it's time to go to Chinatown: You don't have to.

I take I-80 east, hoping for traffic. There's plenty, but not enough. Each exit looks better than the last – all point to a better future drowned in Old Crow. My phone vibrates again. The caller ID registers a strange number so I answer.

It's a girl. 'Patti Black, please?' Maybe a woman trying to sound like a girl.

'This is Patti.'

'Officer Patti Black?'

'Yeah.'

She yells, '*Oh, God*. Thank heaven. Thank heaven.' Static. 'This is, is Gwen . . .'

'Who?'

'Little Gwen. Your sister. Don't you remember?'

I miss the car in the next lane by paint thickness. 'What!'

'From Calumet . . . I'm sorry, but there's no one else to call. Please help me, Patti. Please. He has my son.'

She's crying now. Sobbing. I see this blond ten-year-old huddled almost under the sofa while Annabelle and Roland hover. My eyes squeeze shut, then snap open.

'Please help me. Don't hang up.'

'Calm down, honey.' I try to pat comfort through the phone. 'Who's got your son?'

Now it's a wail. '*He* does. He has my son!'

'Who, Gwen, who?'

She's stuttering; I can't understand her. 'Calm down, okay? If we get cut off, call back. Who has your son?'

'ROLAND!' She screams it, 'ROLAND HAS MY SON.'

'*Roland Ganz?*' I say it and don't melt down. 'Roland Ganz has your boy?'

'He's here! He wants us all.'

'*What?* Gwen?' The phone's dead. I punch the Talk button. Nothing. I'm somewhere in a Will County dead zone. *Roland Ganz – this is not happening.* Horns blare. A Camaro loops me, the driver jamming his finger. The phone vibrates in my hand. Cars speed past.

'Gwen? Gwen?'

'Please don't hang up again, please—'

'I didn't, honey. Listen to me, okay?' Heartbeats hammer my chest. 'I'm out of the city on my way in. Call 911. Tell 'em the whole story; give 'em my number. Where are you?'

'Will, will they arrest me?'

'*No.* For what?' That was strange. Then I realize she'll tell my story too, whatever part she knows. Before I can balk and build the walls, I imagine her son, like my son. Fuck it, I'll lie, run, Old Crow my way though the repercussions. 'Where are you?' Silence and no static. I fake calm, 'C'mon, honey, I'm here to help.'

'I got away in Arizona, but he found us, found my boy. He'll hurt him if I don't come back. No police, Roland said so.'

'*Do not* go back. Call the police. We'll help, I'll help. Where are you?'

'Can the police kill Roland?' She sounds almost retarded, so scared her sentence has spaces that I feel in my throat. 'Can they? Would that be all right?'

'Probably, honey. But they, we, need to find you and your son first. We'll keep Roland away.'

121

'Forever, this time? They didn't before. He said no po—' And instead of telling me where she is, she cuts out again.

'Hello? Gwen?'

I punch 'Talk.' The line rings twenty times. I do it again. Ten more and a woman answers, she says it's an Exxon station on Highway 30 across from St. Margaret Mercy Hospital in Lake County, Indiana, and no, she didn't see a girl using this pay phone.

I cock to smash my cell. *Fucking Roland Ganz is not dead.*

I'd long since decided that Roland was old and had to be dead by now. He couldn't still be walking the same ground that I did. But not only is he *not dead*, he's still doing to others what he did to me. *The absolute piece-of-shit motherfucker* is still out there for real. And my Celica is heading to Calumet City, Roland's hometown, to look at pictures of his house, his furniture, his basement, his . . .

I'm doing 105 when the engine screams me conscious; both hands vise-grip the wheel, shoulders pinned into the seat. The car's starting to sail, losing its track. A truck's rear doors charge at me. I slam the brakes, skid across both lanes, slide the left shoulder spitting gravel. STEER – too much, slide across and off the other shoulder – SHIIII-IT – then back on. Hold, hold, hold! On the pavement, all four tires. Straight.

Straight and narrow. One lane.

Okay, okay . . . Deep breath, tongue over the teeth, touch the pistol. We're okay. Cruising now, just us and I-80 . . . I'm talking to me like a five-year-old. My back and shoulders relax, then my hands. I add another big breath. Be a cop. It's safer; be a cop. Work. Work has saved you. Roland's a perp, not a person.

But he's neither. Roland Ganz is a monster. *And the motherfucker is alive.*

EASY, easy does it. But . . . beating someone to death with a shovel is new – *if* he's the one who murdered Richey. And that's not the Roland I know. Knew.

Good, be a cop, not a victim. Solve the crime. Be a cop. A truck passes on the left; a road sign appears just as his trailer clears my fender: 'I-394/94, Highway 6, Indiana Border.' Homecoming in twenty–one miles. Roland's cotton underwear. Jim and Tammy Faye. Annabelle's skeleton hand. My skin flashes hot. If there is a God, she needs to take over once I'm in Calumet City. Patti Black isn't cop enough to do this one alone.

Sonny Barrett.

I punch speed dial and he answers. His voice is . . . comforting, and no one's more surprised than me.

'Patti?'

'In the flesh.' I fake a smile.

'Jesus, P, what the fuck are you into?'

The smile fades and I change hands. 'Meaning?'

'You still speak English, right?'

'Glad you missed me.'

'No shit, what the fuck's going on? We had the FBI up our ass all morning. And that was *before* the mayor found one massively fucked–up ASA on his lawn. The G's sayin' you're the prince of darkness.'

'Told you.'

Sonny shouts at someone, then says to me, 'We got bullshit here; the Ayatollah has the 'hood marching everywhere there's a sidewalk.' Sonny shouts another order, then, 'I'm your pal, you know that, right?' He doesn't wait for an answer he doesn't need. 'Meet me at Ricobene's. We gotta talk.'

123

God, do I want to. I want to say that Roland Ganz is back, but don't. 'Can't. There's this thing I—'

'You need to meet me, is what you need to do.'

I reach for bricks instead of help and the wall comes together before I can stop it, not so much second nature as my only nature. 'Can't now, I'm on special assignment, but I will. Could you go by my neighbor's, see that Stella's okay? She's supposed to be feeding the girls.'

'Patti—'

'Gotta go.' The longer I talk, the more impossible this trip will be to complete. 'Tell Cisco, hey, and to back off the nurses. I'll be in touch. And thanks.'

I button off, then hide the phone where I can't feel it vibrate. False cheer is not my specialty, nor is lying to my friends. Roland Ganz is back. And I warned no one. He has Gwen's little boy. He tried to burn Gilbert Court and his wife's body with it. It's Roland Ganz – Gwen said, '*He wants us all.*'

I picture Richey gray–black and beaten to death on the lawn, and shiver till my spine pops. Man, all this is so fucking awful it can't be true. It can't.

The sign blocking the sun reads: 'Calumet City Next Exit.'

Chapter 8

In two weeks I'll be twelve years old. I'm frightened and in a funeral home for the first time. It smells like church, the one my aunt Eilis Black took me to, but this place has hallways and small rooms, and the ceilings are much lower.

The stranger who has ahold of me is from Child Services, a silent woman with a school principal's frown and hands colder than my mother's. She has tight lace cuffs and tighter hair and won't tell me it's all going to be okay no matter how many times I ask. My parents are here too, in those brown coffin boxes. They burned to death in a car fire they caused, an afternoon DUI that killed them, my only aunt, and the driver of the other car too. No flowers separate my parents from the five empty folding chairs. No one knows or cares that I'm not in those coffins with them.

Twenty–six years ago. Calumet City. And now I'm back.

THURSDAY, DAY 4: 2:30 P.M.

The parking lot at Cal City PD is full of blue-and-whites, lots more police cars than a city this size should have. It's modern too, way different than when I lived here on the streets, after I ran from the foster home into the jungle. Finding this windowless, brown-brick reincarnation took most of the courage and all the dashboard insults I could conjure. I only drove streets I didn't know – no foster home drive-bys, no Salvation Mission visits, no State Street Sin Strip cruise by the Rondavoo and the Riptide Lounge. Just strange streets and sweat while I broke an ironclad promise that until now has saved me from drowning in an ocean of madness.

At the door, I add every ounce of cop game face I own. Be a cop not a victim.

Inside, Cal City PD is as faceless-modern as the outside and that helps. The second man who talks to me is a detective who has the Black Monday murder file and a message from my employer. 'Call the superintendent's office.' He floats thick eyebrows like he has some idea that I'm in trouble. I notice a business card on a table next to the table he points me to. 'FBI' is prominent on the card. No need to pick it up to know that it once belonged to Special Agent Stone.

Detective Barnes says, 'All of a sudden half of Illinois is hopped up over this?' and folds his arms over an evidence box like he's hatching it. I don't smell whiskey breath, but I'd bet my pension on it. He radiates Aqua Velva or Old Spice mixed with the Dutch Masters panatelas in his pocket and adds, 'Been eighteen years. Don't see why we should give a shit now.' Obviously Cal City PD is unaware that former foster child Richard Rhodes was found dead minutes ago.

'They pay me, Detective; tell me to go here – I go; go there – I go there. Same shit, different day.'

'*Hear* that.'

126

He's white, but *down, Jim*, like Sonny when he's joking. Both arms stay folded on the box, his eyes stay on my chest. 'I get off in an hour; be happy to run you by the scene, maybe catch a beer up to the Hollywood, show you around some.'

I'm happy to think 'cracker' instead of about the box, but Florida's TV ads are too refined for Detective Barnes. 'Thanks. Quicker I get to it, the better chance we have of you not working overtime.' He gets the best trailer–park smile I can remember.

'My pleasure, Officer Black,' and he slides the box to me greased with a wink and a toothpick leaving his lips. The box is just legal-size cardboard to him. And unless he's made a career of the 1987 case, successfully breaking a number of Illinois laws, he has no idea what it means to me, what it may cause when I open it. He stares while I examine the outside. It's hard to imagine that hell could fit in a box.

I feel Detective Barnes and his eyes lingering. Maybe he does know something. Or maybe he's wagging his dick for my benefit. I pretend my phone vibrates and answer. 'Patti Black. Yes, sir. No, sir.' I shrug at Detective Barnes and show him the phone. 'Could you give me a minute? It's the superintendent, sorry.'

He nods and uses the table to help himself up. 'Yell when you're ready.'

The door opens and closes behind me. I'm alone with the box. I screw on my game face so tight my lips peel. Numbness creeps into half my left hand when it removes the box's lid. Chief Jesse wants any and all information that might tie him, CPD, the mayor's wife, Richard Rhodes, or Danny del Pasco to this 1987 murder. Chief Jesse is worried about political smear; I'm worried about . . . everything.

Deep breath: Think of it as folders, edges of pages, and evidence bags. My right hand pulls a folder, dog-eared and manila, the first one. It's a contents-and-inventory list smudged with brown, just a sheet of paper, the keys to the kingdom, as it were. My eyes don't want to focus but they do.

The list says File #1 is the General Offense Report – that would be the beat car, the first cops on the scene. It has a checkmark and would contain the 'canvass' interviews of the neighborhood. File #2 is the Arrest Report; it has no checkmark. File #3 is the Homicide dicks' report; it has several checks and makes me glance at the box. File #4 – a thick one – is the transcribed interview of the one unnamed foster child found hiding in a garage a block away. Has to be Richey. File #5 is the M.E.'s Report. File #7 contains the photographs of the house. File #9 contains photographs of the crime scene.

Files #10 through 15 are evidence bags. This would be clothing or crime scene articles depicted in the photographs. If it was a head wound, the hat will be here; a chest wound, then it's the shirt.

I'm sweating now and cold. My left hand pulls File #3 – the detectives' report. Closed on the table the folder doesn't seem that frightening. After two minutes, I open it. It's written in police speak, absent any colorful description, a style akin to reading gray type on gray paper. The pages are typewriter typed, the info boxes filled in slightly out of center like the paper went in late or early. The date is half in, half out: October 19.

My son's birthday. October 19, 1987 – four years to the day after he was born.

I grab the table. *Read it. Another boy's life is at stake. One you can save.* I steady by staring at the wall. Having a child is as hard as they say, giving him away is far, far worse. Living with the decision makes the first two seem easy.

The second line of the report mentions the significance of the date: the *Wall Street Journal* dubbed October 19, 1987, 'Black Monday.' The stock market fell 508 points, 22.9 percent, double the crash in 1929.

Tracy said that too, but I don't have 1987 memories, don't want to remember.

The report mentions the next–door neighbor's call to Cal City PD, then dispatch's call to the detective, then gives the address and time of day, and the detective's approach to the scene. It lists their names and begins to lull me with the dull rhythm – I've written and read a million of these. The weather, the house exterior, the well-kept lawn, the condition of the door . . . all bland, but not enough to be benign. I remember the house.

I remember the oak leaves on the lawn, once green like the gabled roof's asphalt shingles, now the leaves would be brown, dead, and shriveled. The mottled red bricks, and an attic with one dormer window. It had curtains, thick ones tacked top and bottom; the sun and moon and streetlights only glowed at the edges. I don't have to read the report to know about the garage or the fenced backyard, or the basement.

I remember the basement. I'm glad I haven't eaten today and remember what we ate. And I'm doing great not crying or screaming. I'm doing great, remembering . . . I remember the carpet. What it smelled like, how it tasted. How Roland tasted.

I drop the page and cover my face with both hands. Try to breathe, be a cop, someone he didn't conquer, someone who will see this through to the second page – the door behind me pops and I look. It's a uniform who says, 'Sorry,' and closes the door.

Back to the page – it's stiff–armed now. And the house. This Homicide detective is describing the crime scene; this part's easy because it's not part of my life. He moves on to the victim:

```
VICTIM:
Unknown M/W, 35-45 yrs., 5'8'-5'11', 145-175 lbs.,
brown eyes, brown hair, no distinguishing marks,
scars or tattoos noted. The victim was clad in a pair
of black-colored rubber panties. No other clothing
was on the victim. A quantity of what appears to be
lipstick was applied in an irregular pattern around
the victim's lips and what appears to be a cosmetic
makeup was applied to the entire face.

INJURIES:
1) Victim sustained a single GSW to the upper right
chest (Embedded) (Fatal) Tattooing and powder burns
were noted around the entrance wound.
2) Trauma was noted to the groin area, cause or
origin unknown as of this writing. A baseball bat was
recovered six feet northeast of the body and
submitted to the crime lab for analysis.
```

The report moves through the rest of the house and carries me with it.

```
The deceased was lying on the dining room floor,
approximately 15 feet southeast of the basement
stairway with his head facing northeast and his feet
```

facing southwest. The body was encircled by a white powdery detergent-like substance in a heart-like pattern. There were four piles approximately three feet to the left of the body also made from a powdery detergent-like substance. Two feet north of the four piles was an empty box of Tide.

There were no apparent signs of a struggle.

A tickertape and 1929 stock certificate collection cut up into confetti-sized pieces littered the 1st floor. In the kitchen, the cabinets are divided into shelves. Under one shelf is the name 'Gwen' printed on a piece of masking tape and under another shelf is the name 'Richard,' also printed on a piece of masking tape. There is cat and dog food on these shelves. No pets were on the premises. Further inspection of the premises failed to reveal the presence of any items associated with pets such as bowls, collars, leads, etc.

There were no items of clothing recovered from the closet in the largest bedroom located on south end of the 1st floor, designated as Bedroom #1 in the diagram of the scene. Two dressers were located on the south wall. All drawers were empty.

There are two bedrooms located on the second floor of the home. The first bedroom is located at the top of the stairs and will hereinafter be referred to as Bedroom #2. It has no door. The floor is wood. The single window on the north wall has heavy curtains. There are seventeen framed religious pictures, each measuring 11 × 14, hanging on the walls: five on the east wall, five on the west wall, five on the north wall and two on the south wall where the entrance door and a closet are located. An inspection of the closet revealed boy's clothing, slacks hung on hangers were all on the left side of the closet and boy's shirts were all hung on hangers on the right side of the closet. A single dormitory-style bed is located against the west wall. There is a wooden desk-dresser against the south wall with a baseball glove on top of the desk. No other items were noted in the room.

The report continues to Bedroom #3 saying it has no door and is a repeat of Bedroom #2 except for:

An inspection of the closet revealed girl's clothing. A single dress lying on the floor. A dormitory-style bed is located against the north wall and a wooden desk-dresser is situated at the south wall. The mirror above the dresser has what appears to be smudged 'kisses' on it, made with what appears to be lipstick, either made by pressing one's lips against the mirror or possibly hand drawn.

Page 3 of the report goes to the attic, I don't want to read that and don't. Page 4 goes to the basement. I don't want to read that either. I know what's in the basement.

I pull the M.E.'s report. Cause of death is the gunshot wound. Time: approximately 4:00 p.m. The groin was smashed postmortem, either by the repeated stomps of a heavy boot or by the baseball bat found at the scene. The victim's box in the M.E.'s Report is somewhat of a shock:

ROLAND A. GANZ.

And now I remember. The night I heard about the murder ... I'm four years and one day past motherhood, four years and one day out of Roland's hands. I'm living on the street, drinking myself into Old Crow oblivion nightly. It was the night after my son's birthday – I'm drunk in the Riptide Lounge, sharing a back booth with two sixteen-year-old junkie prostitutes. I remember standing and cheering, twirling like a top, and being thrown out into the alley ...

VOID is written at the bottom of the page. M.E. page 2 is a duplicate of page 1, except the box for the victim's name is corrected to read: BURTON E. OTTSON.

I jump back to the dicks' report, skipping to page 5. The victim was misidentified for three days as Roland Ganz, then correctly ID'd as Burton E. Ottson, age forty-one, proprietor of Burt's Big & Tall, a Calumet City clothing store. I remember unscrambling that the victim was Ottson, not Roland Ganz, but it was a year later, after I was sober, after I'd run away from the Salvation Mission. Somehow Roland's 'death,' then celebrating on the bar table and being thrown into the alley had led to the Mission – sick, weird bastards too, but no sex, just piles of religion. I sobered up there, faced where I was, and ran as soon as I could.

I found my first job the day after I ran from the Mission – animal control officer trainee in South Holland. And I liked it, but they fired me for driving the animals I caught into the better neighborhoods and setting them free. From there I took the CPD exam, left those 'gaps' in my history, and didn't look back. Until today.

Take a breath. And another. One of my hands has stopped trembling. The dick's file has Burton E. Ottson's history:

Relationship to foster home: None direct.

Relationship to Roland and/or Annabelle Ganz: Attended same church – Redeemer Methodist, same stockbroker – 1st National Bank of Calumet City. Both men had given money to The PTL Club in 1987, as well as the Republican National Committee, and the local mayoral candidate. Both had taken separate trips to Branson, Missouri.

A note in the margin is dated 6.5.03 but has no initials: *January 2003, Jim Bakker opens religio–based radio show in Branson, the Studio City café*. I blink, then shut my eyes again, seeing Reverend Jim and Tammy Faye on the TV, Roland pretending to preach to me while he ...

The page flutters to the floor. I need to get the fuck out of here.

Seventeen years of cop intercedes. *Wait: Why was someone working this file in 2003?* That little puzzle helps; so does the sound of Little Gwen's voice still in my ear.

The next page is more history: Both Ganz and Ottson filed extensions on their 1986 federal income taxes. Neither had a criminal record. No pornography was found in either residence. There's another margin note but in different ink – no date or initials: *Ganz and Ottson signatories on an assumed-name safety deposit box (emptied October 20, 1987) at the Grand River S&L in Berwyn. Grand River failed following year.*

So?

Next paragraph. Ottson's bank accounts were interesting. He'd given half his 1987 salary to PTL – I'm starting to sweat again, but it quickly registers that I don't know Ottson, have never seen him; he never touched me. I hear the wall clock tick for the first time and keep reading. Ottson's checks bought 'life partnerships' to PTL's Heritage USA pentecostal resort in South Carolina. There's another note dated February 1989: *Jim Bakker stepped down from PTL re Jessica Hahn. 3/19/87.* Reverend Bakker's sex scandal.

A search of Ottson's lake cottage produced exactly one hundred photos of Tammy Faye – all signed and inscribed to him. The handwriting was different on several. I flash on page 2 of the detective's report and flip back to it. *'Male Caucasian clad in black-colored rubber panties. Single GSW to the upper right chest. Tattooing and powder burns around the entrance wound. Lipstick applied in an irregular pattern. Makeup applied to the entire face. Body encircled by a white powdery detergent-like substance in a heart–like pattern. Trauma to the groin area. A baseball bat recovered six feet northeast of the body.'*

There was lipstick on the mirror; the face is smeared with it too . . . Are we making a Tammy Faye?

Man, I gotta go; this is gonna kill me. It is, I know it.

A minute of blank turns into five. I roll my shoulders, look everywhere but at the file, say fuck it, and press on. The numbness from my hand has moved to my head and lungs. I feel better.

There's a signed statement from a neighbor.

'The foster family watched PTL with the father every day. EVERY day - he was a good, God-fearing man. Same with Wall Street Week every Friday at 7:30, but Annabelle, God bless her, was never home for that - she and I went to vespers, it was a special time just for the father and the children.'

I drop the pages; *enough*. A paperclip and a loose card fall out. It has a shop name and a Tarot symbol. It says, 'Tom, re: October 19. It's a Roman Empire holiday honoring the god, Mars; it celebrates the Armilustrium; when the weapons of the soldiers were purified and stored.'

Faint memory. Have I heard that before? The door opens again; it's Detective Barnes.

'We done?'

I fake a human being's calm. 'Not quite. Few more minutes, I'll yell at ya.'

'Better yell at your superintendent too. His office just called up front.' Barnes's grin is either a leer or his toothpick's heavy. He shuts the door.

I stand, hoping my knees hold, thinking I'll need to pace. And I do as I turn on my phone and punch Chief Jesse's number, no idea what I'll say or what he'll ask.

He answers, 'Smith.'

'Hi. It's me.'

'I can see that.'

'Sorry that I hung up. I"—'

'How much trouble are we in, Patricia?'

He only uses my name like that when he's being fatherly. It doesn't last long, but it feels like fortress safety. I'd hug him unconscious if he were here. 'Oh, I don't know. Not much, so far.'

'TAC officers don't hang up on the superintendent of police in the normal course of their day.'

'Yes sir, I'm sure that's true. I mean, I know that's true. Sir.'

'Let's have it, the story on Mr. del Pasco and his relationship to you.'

Deep breath. 'Not really ... ready to report. Sir.' I can see Chief Jesse nodding through the phone. 'But I will, if you just give me a day or so to prepare.'

'A day or so?'

'Sir, I'm in Calumet City reviewing the '87 homicide file right now. So far there's nothing in it that matters. But there's a lot to look at and I plan on staying as late as they let me. If I could get some sleep after, then write it up—'

'And bring it to my desk tomorrow morning by 0–9:45. Is that what you want?'

I lean into the wall. It's a reprieve, not a pardon, but it's something. 'Oh, yeah, that would be golden. Sir.'

'0-9:45. IAD wanted you today. I pushed them off until 0-10:30 tomorrow. The FBI was not as generous and made a formal complaint to me, the State's Attorney's Office, and the mayor.'

'Special Agent Stone?'

'Special Agent Stone. He's asked the U.S. Attorney to charge you with obstruction.'

'Danny D knew nothing about the ASA kidnap. The union will eat the G's eyeballs, Chief. Sir.'

'Maybe so.' Chief Jesse doesn't sound all that confident. 'Read that file carefully, Officer Black. Write two reports – one about it and one about you. Understood?'

Big swallow. 'Yes, sir.'

Click.

There's a whole box to look at, including all the history on Roland and Annabelle. I'm not up to reading it, not here, and take the pages out to a secretary for copies. She does them while I wait, smiles like she knows me, and asks how's it going.

How's it going? It's like going to hell in house shoes.

Back in the room I stuff the copies under my shirt, then skim the evidence summary on why the teenage boy was considered the prime suspect. His name is right there, Richard Rhodes, but with no middle initial. What I read seems too flimsy to juice a grand jury, let alone an ASA looking to try a winner.

And that's strange, given what Chief Jesse said about Richard Rhodes still being a suspect after eighteen years. The photograph file is next and hasn't gone away in the last hour. I reach for the tab, but my fingers slip off. My hand hesitates, any reason not to open it is a good one, then I use both and the folder slides out with no effort. Right there. Flat in front of me.

You could leave. Get another job. Let Roland own you again. Let him . . . preach . . . to Gwen's little boy – I grit my teeth and open a vampire's coffin not a folder.

The first photo is an 8 × 10, face–on from directly above the corpse, a harsh black–and–white like a million others I've seen and not much different than what's on the TV shows. Same with the second one shot in color – neither shows much of the room and I don't hurt yet. I focus on the corpse, a middle–aged guy shot to death. He's painted like a clown. The next two glossies pull back and away, showing the white heart on the floor. Something clicks deep in my stomach. And my hand numbs again.

The next photo is from the left and I recognize the chair, the upholstery pattern, the—

I realize it's not the chair, not the carpet I recognize. It's the death scene itself. I've seen it . . . before. Live. No way. I splash two of the remaining photos – *see, never seen that, never seen that either*. But I have, I've seen it. All of it; every bloody, twisted inch.

No. No way. I didn't live there then. I was four years gone. How . . . ?

I push the photos away like distance will help. We ain't going there, sister. No fucking way we're going there. I stare at the wall and feel the tears on my cheek. All I see is white. Bright white. Everything blurs; then my feet are running. I'm sucking for hothouse air that isn't there.

Blackout drunk – three;

The stock market crash – two;

My son's birthday – one.

Oh, my God. I've known all this time.

Patti Black. Murderer.

Chapter 9

THURSDAY, DAY 4: 6:00 P.M.

Old Crow. Jack Daniel's.

Tony's Liquor store. The parking lot's half full, same as the Whiskey Barrel lot I escaped five blocks back. Both hands are fists. My rearview mirror wants me to take a good look – the Old Crow sign in my windshield says I don't have to, Tony's got my answers inside. My .38's in my lap; I'm either gonna shoot myself, or the sign, or the next voice that speaks. This is . . . not possible. My fish. The strays I saved. The people I helped.

It can't come to this? I'm not a killer.

No? Look in the fucking mirror – *long enough to SEE. Look in the liquor store window, asshole.* Patti Black. Murderer. She walked into that house blackout drunk on her son's birthday, shot a complete stranger, and beat the rest of him to death with Richey's bat.

I jam the ignition, hit the gas without looking, and don't care if the curb breaks the axles. I'm doing 65 when I blast through the first light and hit 80 by the second. The on ramp to I-94 is bumper-to-bumper; I veer to the shoulder doing 100. Patti Black painted his face and drew the heart on the floor. She's just as crazy as Roland; just as fucking dangerous. Cars blur. Patti Black, murderer.

Somehow I don't die in the Dan Ryan's traffic, a coughing metal congestion buffer between new reality and crumbled fiction. Numbness fills my car and pins my shoulders to the seat. Two hands that belong to someone else steer through dusky headlights to Wrigley Field. Horns push me up the street to the L7. I feel a spit line caked on my lips; I'm in the Twilight Zone again, only this time it's real. Then I'm at the bar ordering a double Old Crow, neat. The glass is in my fingers and feather light and I can taste the bite as the whiskey approaches my lips.

'Oh, damn. Sorry.'

The Old Crow sloshes the bar and my arm. The channel changes and I'm not in the Twilight Zone. Julie McCoy is on the stool next to me, waving at the bartender for a bar towel.

''Nother bad day?'

'Huh?'

Julie pats my shoulder and straightens my cap. The bartender arrives, does the wipe–up, and reaches for more Old Crow to pour my refill. Julie shakes her head and says, 'Two waters, no ice,' then looks at me. 'Eighteen years is a long time sober. Whatever today was, it'll be different tomorrow.'

She nods at the autographed motorcycle wreck that spans the back bar. All I can do is keep my teeth together.

'Cello was everything I had, every day since I could remember, all I worked for and wanted to do. And I threw it away riding a Ducati, showing off for a French girl whose name I can't remember.'

The bar audience laughs at a joke from the stage. How'd I get here? A girl comedian with a saxophone is pointing at her head and hips. Julie wraps my arm through hers. There's a business card between her clear–lacquer fingernails. The rectangle reads *Confidential Investigations* and has a Chicago phone number. The name at the bottom is Harold J. J. Tyree.

'This clown's been by twice.'

I'm coming to in a manner of speaking and touch the bar hoping to make sure it's there. My clothes smell; my left hand's attached to my arm. The mirror has the same bleary image that all of them do. The bartender brings the waters and looks at me semi-sideways, then at Julie and says hello to someone beyond her. My neck hurts. I remember to breathe.

Julie wags the business card. 'Been by twice. You hear me?'

'Ah, yeah,' I blink her into focus. 'And he said . . . ?'

'That you and he should talk. About R and A and Calumet City.'

I look at the card again, concentrating this time. 'How did, ah, Harold know I was here?'

Julie shrugs. 'Drink your water. There's something I want to show you.'

Outside, night has come to the Northside; the air's cool. Julie talks about Saturday's rugby match against BASH, something that may have been hugely important to the old me. The new me is using more sidewalk than necessary. Julie seems to notice but she doesn't comment. She keeps talking about BASH.

I've seen this before, EMTs when they see victims falling into the well. Once they're shocked–out, many don't come back the same. Julie's hand grabs my arm and pulls me into a left turn . . . like we're on the field and I've been coldcocked but still have to play. Okay, sure; I've been here before – muddy, dazed, climbing out of the fog.

And it is foggy. She pulls me again, this time back from a car passing. It all seems so normal, being led around by my sleeve. She says, 'Another block,' and by the fifth one I begin to un-zombie. Three more blocks of crisp fall evening and she stops us at a two–story wall mural. It depicts a man with a book. Only one of the three lights there to illuminate him is lit. Julie tilts her considerable head and smiles.

'Carl Sandburg.'

I do a 360 before looking at Carl; my personal safety concerns are returning too. 'And he is . . . ?'

'He's a man who saw hell and decided not to enter. Thought you should know there's a choice.'

Maybe for him. Now she's looking at me looking at the painted bricks. I have the strong sensation that Julie wants to kiss me, so I don't look at her. We covered this once before. The man on the bricks doesn't do anything, but I keep staring. Julie puts one arm around my shoulders, and it's like mom again, like guys do when they allow their friends the rare proximity.

'Want to talk about it?'

'Huh?' I was lost in the guy who chose not to go to hell, wondering how and why he got to choose. I ask the big blond with her arm around me.

'You'll know why tomorrow, if you'll give it till then.'

Now it's my turn to stare. *Cop-stare* would be more accurate.

Julie smiles and unwraps her arm. 'See? You're already on the way.'

So we stand there, her, me, and Carl on the wall, while Chicago drives by enjoying 60 degrees and no horns. The maple trees rustle and I smell the lake. The Cubs are only two back of Houston. My fish love me. Julie doesn't know who I am, but she loves me.

'Yes I do.'

'Huh?'

Julie just smiles. 'Need to get back to work. You coming?'

'In a minute. Might talk to Carl awhile.'

Julie checks me a last time, kisses my cheek, and heads back. Carl doesn't watch her ass and I like him even better. My hand's in my pocket with the edge of Harold J. J. Tyree's business card. Jolt – Little Gwen's little boy. Focus on that, do something about the horrible here–and–now, the other shit can drown you later.

I pull out the business card and my phone follows. Harold's number requires two tries to dial. His answering machine says leave a message. I leave my cell number and call Sonny Barrett. He doesn't sound as good as last time.

'All fucking day, Patti. All day. The G and IAD have lost their fucking minds.'

'The hit on the mayor?'

'The whole fuckin' show. The hit on the mayor, the ASA dead on his lawn, and now all that foster-home kiddie-voodoo-murder bullshit in Calumet City tied to his wife's real estate. This show even page-2s the Ayatollah and his fucking freedom riders. Hell, the FBI's making a miniseries out of it; they got one spokesman saying the hit and the ASA are about the Outfit and the casino license – which makes sense to me; and a U.S. Attorney saying it's the cops running some kinda twenty–year coverup that's coming apart. *Us*. Like we buried that bitch in the wall. Can you fucking believe that?'

'Us, like CPD?'

'Us, like you, me, Cisco – even the superintendent, anyone who's been with you since you rolled into Chicago.'

Another ugly memory flash – Internal Affairs and the FBI tomorrow after Chief Jesse. And Chief Jesse's reports I can't write. Patti Black, murderer.

Carl seems to have turned away from me. 'Sonny, I need a favor.'

Silence, other than a background TV describing the Richard Rhodes death scene.

'Sonny?'

'I'm here. Just taking a good look at the wife and kids I'll never have.'

Words exit my mouth that shouldn't. 'Danny del Pasco says there's money out on me, same guys who tried to torch Gilbert Court and the body in the wall.' My eyes close tight. Hide in the dark; that's what I did in Calumet City. Deep breath. 'I need to find those guys fast. There's a Gypsy Viking who might help. Then a meth-lab rat who may have the names and faces.'

'This has been reported to your . . . superiors?'

'Nope.'

'And why's that, considering every boss in this city wants to brace these Gilbert Court assholes?'

'All I want is backup, Sonny. The less you know, the better.'

'That's true in the movies.'

More silence and background TV. Carl's turned his back completely. Cars pass slower since I mentioned the money out on me. In a *very strange* way I feel better – survival instincts might keep me out of the liquor stores tonight, focus me on a mission to stay alive that finds Little Gwen's son; will her to call back.

'I know I'm asking a lot. But I need it or I wouldn't.' Nothing but TV answers. I frown and answer his silence. 'That it? That's where we are?'

Sonny grumbles, 'You owe me forever.'

'Naked pictures at a minimum. 111th and Cottage, 0-700.'

'That's their fucking clubhouse, Patti. Two of us ain't enough.'

'7:00 a.m., I'll bring the pictures,' and hang up before he can come to his senses.

Or I can come to mine. *Naked pictures* was a very strange thing to say and so's calling a guy for help that I'm not sure I trust anymore. An SUV cruises too slow and draws horns. It's colorless in the dark and then quickly gone. Headlights wash me and Carl. The hair stiffens on my neck. My hand's on the pistol and . . . And what? The SUV's headlights pass and I'm alone again.

The G drives SUVs – they have budgets to match NASA's. IAD drives Fords. A Chevy SUV kidnapped Richard Rhodes and put me in the hospital—

Calm down. Detroit only makes three SUVs a minute. Couldn't Roland Ganz have been the driver? The ComEd workers were young, but they're the accomplices . . .

Somehow it's all Roland now. He's everywhere. Admit it.

No. Walk away. Now.

I turn and start back toward the L7. I'll fake a report or just fall asleep and trust that Carl wasn't loaded when he decided tomorrow would be better. Four SUVs pass. I watch every one and wonder how long I've known who I am. The breeze shifts back to the lake. The last twenty–four hours have been a whirlpool without a bottom. I shortcut across alley asphalt between two three-flats.

Blinding headlights.

An SUV roars down the alley. I stumble back, then sprint.

The alley's narrow. Trash cans bang off the SUV's bumper. Nowhere to go. Doorway, *shit*, runnnnnnnn. Telephone pole. Hit that and they're dead too. I jump behind the pole and the SUV roars past, locks the brakes, and skids in the water. The doors pop. I yell, 'POLICE, ASSHOLE.' The shapes are fifteen yards away and probably can't see my pistol two–handed at them. 'DROP. DO IT NOW.'

The shape shadows hesitate, then jump back into the SUV. It guns down the alley. My heart pounds. I duck and spin to a trash can rolling behind me. Three floors up, a woman pops out her window. It's too dark for her to see me. I hold breath I don't have, waiting for a second pass, or more GD gangsters, or more SUVs.

Headlights again; opposite direction.

Only the pole between me and them. Still nowhere to run. The headlights get halfway to me and stop; they high–beam to brights that don't quite reach. I can't see anything but glare. *Run. Dumbshit.* And I do, to the alley's T, go right, see an open door-way, and pass it for the next one. A long, narrow sidewalk leads to the street. Engine noise, getting louder. I crouch quick and peek. Lights splash the T's dead end. I check the sidewalk escape again. The lights hesitate at the T, then go left, pick up speed, and make a right onto that street.

I wait for the footfalls. A breeze flutters through the alley, carrying distant bass beats and fried potatoes. My heart's thump-ing. The G and IAD don't run down their suspects . . . *Shit, Julie!* I run my escape sidewalk to the street. Headlights pass as I approach; it's a Corvette. I sprint seven blocks to the L7. Julie's out front with a well–dressed woman who's playing with her own hair.

147

I pant, 'Sorry,' smile at the debutante and hide my Smith too late. Julie looks past my shoulder at where I came from. I add, 'Got a little weird back there. Better take her inside. And keep your eyes open.'

Julie cuts back to me and the Smith.

'Now would be good.' I wink trying to look a lot less spooked than I am, and backpedal ten feet to my car I could only have found by accident. 'Call you tomorrow. Remember, eyes open, and thanks for Carl.'

The debutante isn't playing with her hair anymore. I keep the Smith tight to my thigh and rescan the street. The debutante follows my eyes; she's scared and I don't blame her.

FRIDAY

Chapter 10

FRIDAY, DAY 5: DAWN, 6:00 A.M.

Jolt. Upright and awake, and into an upholstered roof.

I'm in a straitjacket. I fight it off and rip at manacles on my wrists that aren't there. Suddenly I'm not in the crypt with Annabelle and Burton Ottson. The straitjacket is my all–weather car cover. Dawn lights the sky far to the east. I wince at the pain in a sleep-twisted knee. I'm in a parking lot, in the backseat of my Toyota. I fast-glance it in every direction. A leaf blows across my windshield, then another. District 6; I'm at the office, my old office. Headlights pass slow on Halsted. *Okay, okay*.

I remember now – a whole night in the backseat of a Celica. With murdered ghosts and a nest of snakes wrapped around my neck. *What am I doing here?* Plan B. Plan B. *Right, right*. Plan B. You figured your car would be more comfortable in a space it knew. And taking a run at its owner in a cop parking lot would be suicide. I scan the lot for meth-jacked arsonists who wouldn't understand that in the same terms as standard criminals.

My face is wet; I revisit the dream visions of pompadoured evangelists promising hell and penitentiary cells offering the same. God hates you, Patti Black. You're a murderer; go to a liquor store.

Good idea. I sneak a glance at my wrist. Elvis has his hands straight up and down: daylight in an hour. My heart eases to regular speed. I palm my .38 and rub one eye at a time. Need to roll before daylight brings out the alderman's pickets and the inevitable confrontation with second-watch LT Kit Carson; he'll be all over me because his bosses and the media are all over him. Don't want to explain the last three days and the new me to my old TAC crew either.

I ease out of the backseat and 360, then remember that I wrote neither report promised to the superintendent. And today is FBI day, IAD too. Today is also Gypsy Viking day, first thing, with Sonny – find the accomplices; they lead you to Gwen's little boy. Deep breath. And Roland Ganz.

Driving south the ghetto looks the same after three days of being North. I'm not the same and never will be. The PI, Harold J. J. Tyree, has a message on my cell. I play it twice; both times it sounds like a trap, like the SUV in the alley looked. No messages from Gwen and that stiffens my neck. I check the phone again, willing it to make her call. When I was in Animal Control in South Holland I could sometimes will a couple into adopting a puppy before we closed on Thursday, before the killers got there on Friday. I worked Sundays instead of Fridays, never Fridays.

Today's a Friday, isn't it? I should be in Chinatown, watching the window for . . . not pulling into 104th and Western to buy coffee. The coffee tastes bitter and smells the same. The donut is old enough that the sugar has trouble melting. A Harley rumbles past and I check Elvis again: 6:48 a.m., not a great time to visit an outlaw biker clubhouse. Whoever's awake has probably been up all night. Whoever isn't, will be unhappy about getting up.

Coffee down, I roll south into Pullman, a gothic red–brick wedge of the far Southside where they used to build the fancy train cars. When the railroad business tanked, the neighborhood died. The local street gangsters moved in and burned down half the historic buildings. A block ahead on Cottage Grove Sonny's car idles at the corner. I stop broadside, drop the passenger window, and speak to a large, unshaven Irishman who does not seem happy with his situation.

'Hi, Sarge.'

'This is fucking stupid, you know that.'

'Yeah. I know.'

'And we're doing it anyway?'

Small smile. 'I have to do the door alone.'

Sonny shakes his head and looks away. Ten seconds pass and he says, 'Stay outside, no matter what. Dial my number now and leave your cell on in your pocket. If I hear gunfire I'll figure it ain't going well.'

I float another small smile and say, 'Thanks.'

He flips me the bird. We tandem out of semi-civilization and into railroad–warehouse no-man's-land, home to the Gypsy Vikings and Charlie Moth, psychopath, career felon.

For the record, Chicago has two other outlaw biker gangs: the Hells Angels and the Chicago Outlaws. Both are part of nation-wide – *shit* – worldwide criminal organizations. Both have been tried and convicted on every major felony known to mankind from slavery to mass murder. Grading on that scale, the Gypsy Vikings differ only in their colors and their absolute willingness to die for their territory right alongside any adversary dumb enough to try to take it.

As I weave around badly patched asphalt and wavy roadway not designed for the machinery it traffics, I can feel the weight of Sonny's advice: An approach like this is either made with big firepower backing a calm request, or a tidal wave of bullets, then the calm request.

Like most bad ideas and good advice, both tend to carry more weight the closer one gets. The bad idea in question is two-story brick – an old armory set back way off the street on what will someday be a superfund cleanup site. The building has lime-stone-block trim at the corners, painted flat black. Sheets of rusted steel plates cover the windows bleeding orange streaks onto the bricks. The arched double door facing me must be the entry; together the doors are eight feet wide at the bottom and barricaded with bolted cross-members.

Between me and the doors is a twelve–foot chain–link fence topped with concertina wire, then seventy feet of oil-stained gravel stacked with dead cars, scrap iron piles, rusted 55-gallon drums, and close to thirty motorcycles. The bikes aren't shiny like the concertina wire, but they're well tended. A half-open freight door to their right has a ten-foot Nazi flag painted on it. The flag's the cleanest thing here.

I've seen the movies where the girl in the hot pants visits the biker clubhouse. I'm twenty feet through the open fence gate when I see the first rottweiler.

Dusty black – and huge. And already moving at me. I draw; the chain tightens at his neck – thank you, God – taut to a point somewhere beyond the freight door. He must weigh 130, as much as me. That fast and there's another two, same size and snarling. At that same instant I realize there's no closable gate in the fence I passed through, just the framed opening. If I run, it's just me and the three dogs if some mental patient lets them loose.

Danny D definitely didn't mention shooting a dog; a length of chain rattles out and I stumble back. The nearest rot feels the additional lead and roars teeth and saliva at my face. I brace to fire; the chain snaps tight, suspending his huge head three feet from mine. The two other rots lunge – I wheel, start to squeeze – their leads jerk them chest-up and clawing the air between us. Three mouths try to rip me apart.

A mammoth upper body steps in behind the charge. SHOT-GUN. It's butted hip–high on dirty jeans, a finger tight on the trigger. TWELVE-GAUGE PUMP. He's naked to the waist, save for the tattoos and Appalachian beard, and yells over the dogs and their saliva,

'Wouldn't move, bitch,' then nods to my feet. 'Forward or back and you won't be doin' no man no damn good.'

I'm only thinking about dog teeth and shotguns; and won't survive either if—

The rots quit barking. Heavy bass booms the air. The guy glances into the building, then back at me, and yells, 'Drop the pistol.' His hands might be shaking and not because he's afraid.

'Police. CPD.' Unless his shotgun is on full choke or has deer slugs, I still have a chance at fifty feet.

'Drop the piece or wear the beast.'

Two men step out behind him, both smaller and wearing Gypsy Vikings colors, one pushing 200 pounds. He has a fourth rottweiler, this one on a leather lead wrapped to his forearm; his partner has a pistol out and cocked. The rots go death still on his command. I show my left hand, then lift the star out of my shirt. The men fan apart; the one with the rot on the leather

155

lead steps at me and says, 'We ain't fuckin' old women today.'

I check his partner with the pistol, then back to the mountain man with the shotgun, then back to him. 'Charlie Moth. Just want to talk.'

'Never heard of him.' His denim colors cover parts of swastikas on both pecs. His rottweiler is twenty feet away, straining to get closer.

I hope Sonny can see the Viking on the left with the pistol. 'Danny D wants me to talk to Charlie Moth. I just came from Stateville.'

'In your fucking dreams, cunt.'

I cock my Smith. 'That dog won't save you, hoss.'

Above the colors, his head is shaved and his ears are pinned flat. We're close enough now that the dog might save him and he knows it. 'Danny D don't send cop bitches here.'

'I'm his sister.'

'Charlie Moth ain't got no sister.' He tightens up on the 100-pound rot by crooking his arm. 'You gonna die, bitch, right where you fucking stand.' He probably figures an HBT shooter is aiming at his heart, half a squeeze from good-bye. 'We got us shooters too.'

And I'm sure he does. And I'm sure they're awake by now, crystal–meth paranoid and preparing for Ruby Ridge II. 'I'm *Danny D's* sister, asshole. And just want to talk to Charlie Moth, that's it. Whatever else you're doin' is whatever you're doin'.'

'Gimme the gun.'

Headshake. 'You know it doesn't work like that.'

He stares. 'Danny D's sister?'

I nod. 'Calumet City.' Then reach for, and card–flip the

photograph of Danny D's cell wall. The rot lunges for it. The third Viking points his pistol at my head. The one talking to me gathers up his rot closer still, steps toward me, and picks up the picture. He doesn't look at it long enough to read the clippings behind Danny's shoulder or the signature on the back. He does see the lightning bolts and the two tears in blue ink. He says, 'There's a trip wire six inches from your shoe. Don't move much or half a you's in Indiana.'

Every part of me wants to look. But there's four dogs and two guns, so I watch them instead. My host turns and walks back inside. His associates don't, they still have the guns and the dogs and zealot eyes. I think 'zealot' because pointing a firearm at a police officer will usually end badly and they don't care.

The land mine at my feet is affecting my balance. How do the dogs miss it if they're turned loose? I glance for the trip wire; eyes down like a rookie, searching the gravel and debris. *Commotion*. I look up, Vikings stream out, lots more, maybe twenty. Another bearded Appalachian steps through – this one fully dressed. He has a Schlitz tallboy in his hand and a machine pistol, possibly an M11, in his belt. If it's full-auto, it's a federal felony. He's close to 6-6, maybe 350. I'm sure my .38 will only slow him.

He stops at thirty feet. 'Who the fuck are you?'

'I just told your girlfriend. I'm Danny D's sister, just came from Joliet to—'

'You're that fuckin' bitch cop Patti Black, ain't you?' He unchains the closest rottweiler, grabs it ten links above the collar, and comes at me. 'I seen you on TV, all hero'd up.'

I don't want to kill the dog . . . I *do* want to believe that this bearded monster knows about the trip wire. Thankfully,

157

this guy's eyes aren't cue balls like the first three; his are droopy but on fire like they bled all night. He lets his dog strain toward me and the trip wire.

I start to step back but stop in time. 'Ah, maybe we ought to—'

'*Maybe* we get married, you and me, I ass fuck you to death.'

This bad idea isn't improving with time. If I had another lead, somewhere else to go, I would. But I don't, so I say, 'Fine' and aim at his balls. 'You feel like fucking after six of these, I'm all for it.'

He starts for the M11.

'Don't. I'm past believing this'll work out.'

He stops, then uses the other hand to drink the beer. 'I'm Charlie Moth.'

I don't know why I'm surprised. 'We gonna talk, Charlie?'

''At's all I'm doing.' Charlie might really be from Appalachia. 'If we was fightin', she'd already be over.' He tosses the beer can in the general direction of my feet.

I wide-eye it to the ground. It and I don't explode. Deep breath. 'Well ... Danny D said your chemist, Pancake, knew stuff I need to know. He told me to tell you to arrange a meeting, today, now.'

'Did he? Danny D told you to *tell* me? So you did; now haul your skinny ass back to Joliet and tell Danny to fuck himself.' No part of Charlie Moth looks scared or interested in helping me.

'Sure. Okay. Want to be clear, though. On what you said. My brother will wanna know that he's doing double life for you guys and you're pimping him.' I glance at the guy with the shotgun;

he doesn't look like he's all that comfortable with pimping Danny D. 'He'll wanna know that.'

Charlie Moth says, 'Who's gonna tell him?'

'Just about everybody, Charlie, after you and his sister die in this shoot-out.'

Actually, dying right now, today, wouldn't be bad, solve a lot of my problems. And Charlie seems to notice. His associates too, and they don't look like guys who want to end up in Joliet over this and have to explain it to my brother.

'Cut the bitch some room, Charlie. She may be Danny's sister. *Shit*, he may've sent her.'

Charlie Moth doesn't bother to look over his shoulder. 'You wanna take a Chicago cop to a dope lab, go ahead. I don't know about any; won't be doing two dimes for conspiracy whether Danny fucking del Pasco thinks it's a good idea or not.'

I say, 'Don't take me. I'll meet Pancake. Pick a corner; we'll do it there.'

Charlie looks like I've given him an out, then looks at his dog, then looks at me. 'Western and Ninety-fifth. Four o'clock.' He drapes one hand on the M11 and points with the other. 'This shit goes bad, bitch, your family'll be dead before the trial. Believe that.'

All the men and all the dogs walk back inside without looking at me again. It's as if my future and theirs no longer intersect, like my star didn't matter ten minutes ago and doesn't matter now. I exhale big and mount another glance for the trip wire. And there it is, two feet from the Schlitz can, silvery and tight, and just where they said it was.

Whoever said that crystal meth could make *anything* worse was not lying.

* * *

Not counting the Penn Central tracks, 103rd and Beverly is a five–way corner. It's busy and loud at 8:00 a.m. Sonny Barrett is sitting behind the wheel of his Ford; I'm listening from the sidewalk, arms folded to his passenger window but eyeing the traffic. He's only an hour into his day and Sonny's already full–up on mystery. He wants an explanation. Several in fact: Calumet City, the mayor, the mayor's wife, and dead Assistant State's Attorney Richard Rhodes.

'Cut the bullshit. Tell me.'

'Can't.'

Sonny palms his salt-and-pepper stubble and curves the mirror down so he can see his reflection. 'Nope. It's me.'

'Sonny, look—'

'At what, ghosts?' He slaps the passenger headrest near my hands. 'I'm callin' bullshit here. You're up to your ass in somethin' that's gonna eat you, me, and everybody else we know. *You owe us, Patti.* These guys got families. And you know IAD and the G's gonna fuck 'em up. You know that.'

He's right, but I can't. I know what I did years ago, but I don't know where or why or how it fits now.

'Talk to me, damn it, I ain't got the fucking day.'

'Sonny—' My throat chokes off the words. 'Sonny, this has zip to do with you guys, okay? Or the superintendent. No matter what you hear, it doesn't.' A tear runs down my cheek and I look away too late. 'If I go down for this, it'll be alone. I promise. Nobody goes with me.'

Hard-ass Sonny Barrett exits his Ford to a *hooooooorn* and a panel truck's near miss, then loops his front bumper to stand close enough to touch me but doesn't. I concentrate on his thick

160

shoulder, not his eyes. Mine are watery. This is not my game face; I'm having trouble finding it since becoming the new me.

Sonny has good teeth he bought in a fistfight and shows them. 'We friends, right?'

I reset my semi-charred Cubs cap. 'Yup.'

'Then it's simple. You talk, I listen. Then we do what we gotta. How fucking hard is that?'

I'd like nothing better than to hand this to someone who would face it for me. But all I can say is, 'Sorry.'

Sonny closes one eye, then cocks his head into street sergeant. Like all sergeants, he's not a fan of opposition to simple solutions: Face it, defeat it, go home, repeat same tomorrow. Either I give him a better answer or—

'Sonny, this isn't a trip you or Eric or Cisco can take.' My feet want to step back; lies need distance. 'No telling what the FBI knows.'

'Knows about what?'

I shrug with a wince that adds nothing but *poor-little-me*. 'Or what they'll pull.'

Sonny grabs my shoulder and keeps a handful of my jacket. 'Like what?'

I don't like being grabbed and he knows it. Today, that isn't stopping him. This is phase 2 of his frustration index. Phase 3 is both hands and your back hitting a wall. I doubt he'll do that to me, but then he's never done phase 2 before.

'Knows about what? Answer me.'

'Calumet City.' There, I said it.

'So?'

'The G was at Cal City PD before they braced me at Stateville.'

161

'So?' His other hand brushes my waist.

There's no way to answer. Sonny watches me breathe harder, sees that I'm fighting but just can't get there. Just can't. He exhales in my face, lets go of my shoulder, and pushes away. His teeth grind. He stares until it's obvious I'm not answering, snarls, and pivots toward the street like he intends to talk to the passing cars . . . then throws up his hands and turns back.

His eyes are narrow now, the way they get before he fights, and he starts to nod, building to something. Three, two, one, then:

'The G says you and Chief Jesse are makin' babies . . .' He swallows after he says it, like his throat hurts. *'Like it's some of their fucking business.'* Sonny looks away again, then back. 'The G thinks both of you were/are hooked up with Danny D, into bad shit that goes way back.'

Sonny stops talking so I can confess.

I don't.

He reddens the rest of the way while he waits. The cords show white in his neck and he growls, 'They wanted all of us – me, Eric Jackson, Cisco – to bust you for the story. Trap you into talking. They got you doing felonies with the superintendent, felonies that somehow murdered the ASA – the G sent suits to Cisco's fucking hospital, you believe that?' Sonny shakes his head hard enough to sprain his neck. 'They say they got you and Chief Jesse put together with the mayor and his fucking wife – *her motherfucking building* – and Richard Rhodes and who-knows-what-else. And since we worked with you for seventeen years, there's no way we don't know, no way we didn't cover it up.'

Sonny's face is twisted into emotions I haven't seen in it before. It's awful to see people you care about suffering for your sins. It's worse to let them. Worse for them, worse for you too – except *you* deserve it, usually in the biggest possible way.

'Gotta go, Sonny. Have to.'

His hands ball as he leans at me, a huge man stripped to powerless. 'For chrissake, Patti—'

I put three feet between us, hoping space calms him. 'Sorry. Nine o'clock. Me and the superintendent, then IAD, then the FBI.'

Sonny glares, then exhales in a rare surrender. He spits sideways, frowns me up and down, and turns away to tell the passing traffic, 'At least pretty up for the trip to Metro.'

Metro is the Metropolitan Correctional Center, the G's own prison, a twenty–seven–floor high–rise downtown on Van Buren. That's where city cops go when the U.S. Attorney makes charges they think will stick. Sonny waits a beat to see if I'll fold, then walks back around his Ford, mindful of the traffic this time. At the driver's door he spits again and tells the inside of his car, 'I'll meet you for the meth chemist at four o'clock, if you ain't in federal handcuffs.'

I'm surprised, like I was the third day in junior high when a boy asked me to a school dance – *Jesus, where'd twelve years old come from?* Sonny fires up his Ford and I wonder if I'd step into this disaster for my friends. I'd like to think I would, that big parts of the old me weren't a lie. Sonny pulls into traffic, and like that one good day in junior high, I wish I were with him. Or he was with me.

More than anything, I wish I were somebody else.

I'm not going to 'pretty up' as suggested, but since I'm only three miles from my duplex, 'clean' would be reasonable after a night in the car. Stella agrees when I arrive but has customers coming and can't do anything but mention my never–ending wardrobe failings. While I'm checking my phone, hoping Gwen has called, Stella adds that the black man has been by again.

The who?

The same man who was here before. Have I lost my mind, having a black boyfriend?

'Stell, honey, hold it a sec. What do you mean, *before*?'

Stella harrumphs and cocks her head on shoulders that are mostly padding. '*Before*. Jesus, God, are you drinking again?'

I check every room, then she and I count back Home Shopping Network days until we determine that 'before' is the day of my B&E.

Chapter 11

FRIDAY, DAY 5: 8:50 A.M.

Black man at my duplex. Private eye Harold J. J. Tyree's voice mail sounded black.

Idaho-Arizona whiteboy. White ComEd 'torches.' Those three crews fit, but how? All with Roland Ganz?

Roland Ganz has Gwen's little boy. And now's he's probably got her too. *He wants us all* – Goddammit, why didn't she call back? Like Richard Rhodes, this city's too big to find anyone without clues. Unless they throw them on the mayor's lawn.

Shiver.

My Celica's not steering well. I change lanes and eye the asshole with the horn, then push a clean shirtsleeve up my arm. The shower at my duplex felt good but not clean. The jeans and flannel shirt are mine. Jez and Bathsheba looked happy. Cubs won and the Sox lost. I'm sober.

As good thoughts go, that's as good as I can think.

I'm almost downtown, hoping for the courage to be Joan of Arc when I get there. This isn't as easy as it looked in the movie, probably because when they turned on the houselights I got to go home. Two squads scream past. They're westbound on Thirty-fifth and leading a fire engine. I can see the driver's eyes. I could see Joan's eyes too, as the flames leapt up her clothes. She faced burning at the stake without folding – there's comfort in that – and the fact that they rarely burn anyone in Illinois anymore. But my real comfort is that I don't believe I'll go through with this. Prison sounds better. Swallowing my pistol sounds . . . about the same.

More fire engines scream west; maybe they need me there instead? Each block east finishes faster than the last. All my lights are green. And there it is, five stories on ten acres. Head-quarters, the new building at Thirty-fifth and Michigan, now close enough to USCF Comiskey to catch a home run if the White Sox could hit one. CPD headquarters is a new building in a bad neighborhood, a new building that looks a bunch newer than it acts.

I park on the street. IAD offices here too, the grand inquisitors with their rule books and unfired revolvers. Every cop who crosses this threshold feels their presence, an insult in my opinion, to the stars that ring the first-floor lobby. Stars of cops who died on the line. That's how I felt yesterday, before I knew who I was. Now I know why we need IAD.

Instead of facing the elevator bank, I walk the wall-mounted stars and realize how proud I am – was – to be part of these people, how much it meant to me. It's the first time I've done it this year. Bobby Grapes dead on Thirty-eighth Street, saving two black kids from a dad with a shotgun; John Sharpe, dead on Wilson Avenue – I went through the academy with John, finished my first full year sober with him on a park bench argu-ing about the Cubs. He died fourteen months into his new uniform and the shortest haircut he'd ever had. Carl Medrano, dead on a cracked sidewalk three doors down from a liquor store holdup in Cicero.

Every one of these guys is better than me. Every one of them.

Especially these two, George Pulaski and Irish Mike Constance. Irish Mike was Greek and should have been a counselor or a priest. The GDs shot him twice, once in '85 when he was a rookie and once in '97 before they killed him and George on Gilbert Court two years ago, lured there by a little girl who said her brother was trapped in a basement.

I remember the funerals too; the nervous feet, the blowing leaves, bagpipes just beyond the hill, and the crows on the tombstones. It's always winter at a cop's funeral and there's nowhere to put the anger. All you can do is hold on and don't betray your friends. Ever. I try to remember that as I pass the wintry mural that covers the lobby's south wall and hides the elevators.

Superintendent Smith's office is on the fifth floor. The secretary staring at me, not at my clothes, is the superintendent's; she makes no bones about how she feels. Gertruda Parsons thinks I am now, and always have been, radioactive for her boss. Her 'good morning' was not meant to be comforting, nor was her request for the reports I don't have. She is a gatekeeper, a vigilant one with mouse-brown hair and a bull matron's posture. On the street she would be formidable; in here, surrounded by wood paneling and the power of office, she is often the last career light a ranking officer sees.

'Please sit over there.' Her eyes cut me to the distant corner, the table by the kitchen if this were a restaurant. 'The superintendent will see you shortly.'

The corner has a lamp but I don't turn it on, don't wish to

illuminate how nervous I am. The best role I could play would be TAC cop, which I no longer am, running in fresh off the street to— *Bullshit*. Everyone in this building knows why I'm here.

'Superintendent Smith will see you now.'

Gertruda Parsons stands sideways to the internal corridor and nods left. We walk down the deep-pile blue carpet without speaking. At an open door she raps the jamb and says, 'Officer Black.' Chief Jesse is without coat and standing, a phone tight to one ear. Downtown's money and power fills the window behind him. I can smell the bleach in his shirt, see the veins in his neck, and the job's weight under his eyes. He points me inside without smiling, but not at upholstered furniture to sit; for sure he knows there are no reports. I check my sneakers; they look shabbier in here, as do my jeans. I remove the charred Cubs hat, wishing I'd done that in the waiting room, and have never wanted a father more than I do now.

Chief Jesse booms: 'That-will-not-happen.'

Nothing rattles; this office was built to be heavy. Everything in here is dark and polished and regimented and Chief Jesse looks out of place.

'No. That's final,' he tells the phone.

His shoulders roll while he listens, the other hand is a fist on his desk, the weight of his right side jammed on the knuckles. They're white and the color is traveling up his arm past the rolled cuff.

'No. Pat Camden at News Affairs. *Only* News Affairs.'

He listens again and I recheck the view from the top, if five floors can be called the top, while lost in nerves I try to hide from him and me.

'Why?' Chief Jesse is no longer on the phone. He's staring bullets at me.

I mount the best explanation I have: 'Huh?'

'Why?'

'Um, I ah, don't have an answer, sir.'

'You don't have a job either.'

This is not that big a surprise, but I try to look it. Worse, his 'why' could be about a number of things, not just the phantom reports.

'There's substantial interest in this, in you. Many of your friends, including me and the mayor – not that he's your friend – have a serious interest in putting this to rest. You are aware of that, correct?'

'Yes, sir.'

'Are you willing to report orally, or is that out of the question?'

'No, sir.'

'No, sir, what?'

'I can . . . can report orally. Sir.'

'Well, do it, for chrissake.'

I tell him that Calumet City PD's 1987 homicide file has nothing in it that focuses attention on Mayor McQuinn, CPD, the superintendent, Danny del Pasco, or . . . I want to add 'me,' but don't. I explain that the file is, however, loaded with Richard Rhodes detail as a murder suspect.

'Did he do it?'

'Doesn't look like the local prosecutors thought much of it, sir.'

'Good news for Mayor McQuinn. Richard Rhodes was his boy before he switched sides to the governor.'

'Sir, is the State's Attorney's task force—?'

'They're chasing the Outfit and the casino license.' His eyes stop melting me and wander to the window. He hesitates in the face of the city he polices, then tells it: 'Something's seriously wrong in this entire combination, and our mayor hasn't shared it with me.'

I leap at the possibility that this isn't all about me and Calumet City. 'Wrong enough, sir, that the Outfit would kill the ASA and try for Mayor McQuinn?'

'You have trouble with his name, don't you?'

I stutter, surprised, and say, 'Rhodes.'

The superintendent returns from the window angry and distant and tells me to finish my *oral* report. I finish the part that avoids all the instances in which I have underperformed his expectations and mine. But at each sentence break I just want to blurt what I'm afraid I did blackout drunk on my son's birthday. And if Little Gwen's call isn't fear fantasy, what kind of monster could be out there now?

Instead, I move on to Danny del Pasco, explaining that while he has said he does not intend to talk to the FBI unless he's given a full pardon and set free, he did talk to me. The superintendent already knows this, from me, from the FBI, and from the State's Attorney's task force briefing he has to be part of. I'm stalling, and he knows that too; he was a street cop before he was a suit.

'Cut to it. What's your *direct* connection to Mr. del Pasco?'

I stare.

'Your job, your career, is on the line right now. The whole thing, everything you care about other than rugby and those two goldfish.'

No words form that begin a sentence and lead to the answer

he wants. Just cow eyes I'm ashamed of and glad I can't see. He inhales; his jaw muscles roll and he glances at his watch. 'IAD first, then the FBI. You have, to state your situation correctly, no chance of surviving today. None.'

My lips tremble. Patti Black, gunfighter, little girl lost.

'Who's representing you from the union?'

Shrug and headshake.

He leans across the desk at me as his voice fills the office. *'You don't have a lawyer?'*

I try to read the thread count in his carpet and wish I could talk, say something, anything. Funny that he keeps it so hot in here, being that he's a big man. He's talking again but it must be to Gertruda since the words kind of float.

'Sorry, sir, what was that?'

His neck is fiery red, as is his face. And he sits down. I want to sit down too but don't. He looks at his desk. I take up space, saying nothing, looking out his windows, deciding zero. I don't know why he hasn't thrown me out. Previous to the last three days this would have been the oddest of moments, an impossibility of insubordination. But now it's just one of many impossibilities that seem to flow together like a river, all connected in a big, grand indecipherable gush.

There, that was a thought. I'm thinking, making unspoken sentences – I hope to God they're unspoken.

'You can't do the FBI without a lawyer. Tell them and the U.S. Attorney you had no idea what the meeting was about. She can reschedule or go fuck herself.'

'Yes, sir.'

The U.S. Attorney for the Northern District of Illinois is Helen Holden. For the last nine years she's been the archenemy of the Chicago Police Department. A graduate of leafy, lakefront Northwestern, Helen is as tight with the Republican governor as one can be and not share turkey dinners on all the holidays. A very well-connected CPD deputy super from the last administration is in federal prison because of her. And of course, his own malfeasance.

The advice on handling Ms. Holden sounds almost friendly, fatherly.

'IAD's different,' Superintendent Smith says.

'Yes, sir.'

'Tell me what you're hiding and I might, *might*, be able to save you.'

Both my hands are trembling and I clench them white behind my back. He glares until I spend the last of his patience and friendship, then waves me out of his office with a disgusted flip of his hand.

The pre-IAD bathroom spruce-up doesn't help. The woman who steps out of the second stall looks at me but doesn't speak; she checks her lipstick in a mirror I don't want to test, glances at me again, and leaves.

Ten o'clock sharp and Internal Affairs begins in a windowless fifth-floor conference room under office lighting that's tucked into a drop-down ceiling. Most street cops believe IAD hides cameras up there, legal or not. I figure IAD would rather show you the camera, let you know you were being recorded, but I check the fixtures anyway.

The detective across the table from me is more deferential than expected. He's thumbing through my file, the record of arrests, commendations, citations, and letters of appreciation from mostly black, mostly ghetto citizens. He smiles at the Paul Elledge magazine cover and shows it to me, then eases it back into the folder.

'Officer of the Year. Twice. That's never been done before.'

I smile and don't answer. I know better than to start saying 'yes' to the easy pitches. He notices and continues to look at pages that aren't fearful to me, not that they can't be criticized if you're looking to do that, but spending his time on this stuff would be a blessing I can't hope to get.

'You've been in District 6 for . . . seventeen years?'

Nod.

He grins over the pages. 'You can speak, Officer Black, it's within reason.'

I don't.

He continues to check me out with a bland expression, then returns to the file, rustling through pages he doesn't read. The new CRs are next to his left hand and he glances at their top page. Those would be the two CRs filed by Watch Lt Kit Carson. Under them would be the criminal complaints filed by Alderman Leslie Gibbons.

The detective taps a mechanical pencil on the CRs then returns to page 1 of my personnel file, sits back as if confused, and says, 'We're missing significant information.' He looks at me after he says it, like I'm guilty of not providing.

Which I am. He wants me to ask, *What information?* But I don't; I stone-face him and force my hands calm.

'We're missing significant information, Officer Black.' He adds emphasis, like it's possible I didn't hear him in a ten-by-ten room. 'Where were you born?'

Some questions you have to answer . . . and that's how they do it. You begin by answering questions that can't hurt and stop answering when they can. That's the spot where they slide out the dental drill, turn on the motor, and say, Open wide, honey.

I check my watch, look at him, and tap the plastic lens.

He's unmoved and asks me again.

'You can read and I've got a case, then the FBI interview. If we're covering the CR numbers or the alderman's complaints, let's.'

'I'd like to cover those, plan to, but it strikes me as interesting that a significant portion of your file is incomplete. It's—'

'Save that for Records; I'm here to answer the CRs and—'

'You're here to answer whatever I ask.'

He looks no less friendly, put off, or blustered. Just matter-of-fact, other than the pencil still tapping, now between two fingers like a seesaw. There's a wedding band on the widow finger and a button missing on his jacket cuff.

He stops tapping. 'All right, have it your way, we'll start with the CRs. Tell me your version. We have Lieutenant Carson's.'

'Which CR?'

'Gilbert Court.'

There is a god. We can talk about the shooting three ways from Sunday and I can't go to hell or prison unless they make a violation of civil rights prosecution out of two Gangster Disciples trying to murder policemen. But instead of burning an hour of IAD time retelling the story, I get angry, because I get angry when I'm scared. 'Maybe you *can't* read.' I glance at my personnel file that for sure has my birthplace and date in it. 'I wrote reports after the interviews. It's all there.'

He nods, again without expression, and clicks his pencil. 'Tell me or refuse to tell me. Simple – one or the other.'

So I tell him about Gilbert Court. For thirty minutes. He nods a lot, but always small and occasionally looks at me. I get the feeling he's bored. His pencil never stops tapping, slow though, *tip-tap*, *tiptap*. When I finish he says,

'The building across the alley? Have you been in it before?'

'No.'

'Not in seventeen years?'

I feel my heart rate change but don't move in my chair. 'No.'

'And the woman,' he looks at the CR numbers, 'Annabelle Ganz?'

I shrug.

'Sorry, Officer Black, I didn't hear your answer?' He's looking at the spot where his pencil will record my answer.

'Didn't hear a question.'

He nods. 'Do you know or did you know Annabelle Ganz?'

Pause. 'No.'

He looks up from the pages. 'You don't?'

None of this is relevant to the CR numbers. I shrug small with pursed lips, then a headshake. Too many movements if he's paying attention. And he is; he keeps staring at me.

'You don't know Annabelle Ganz?'

'Nope.' No pause. Just the lie, as big a lie as a girl can tell.

'You're aware that Superintendent Smith lived in that building?' Before there's time to answer he adds, 'You just met with him, didn't you, before coming here?'

'Yes to both.'

He writes that down, but with too many words. 'Are you acquainted with the mayor's wife?'

'No.'

'Never met her?'

175

Now I can shift in my chair. 'Met her, yeah, but don't know her.'

'How did you meet, and where?'

I frown and check my watch again. 'Who gives a shit? I'm not a politician; I don't care who wins the election. Let's cover the CR numbers or call it a day.'

'Tell me or refuse to tell me.'

'I don't remember. Could've been at both Officer of the Year awards. Maybe a third time when the *Herald* wrote us up for the dogs in the river.'

'That was you alone, not *us*, who saved the dogs in the river.'

'Whatever.'

He checks a page, then checks it again and wrinkles his forehead. 'And your relationship with the mayor's wife?'

'None. I told you.'

'None?'

He's pissing me off and knows that too. So I don't answer. Fuck him.

'Officer Black . . . ? Are you refusing to answer?'

'Yeah, I'm refusing. Happy? You got something to cover that matters, ask it.'

He blinks and tries to read my face. 'This does matter, Officer Black.'

The door opens behind me and neither of us bothers to look. A larger version of the seated detective loops behind him and sits on my right six inches from my elbow. There's no introduction other than the glance we share. He has a spiral notebook and a manila file under it with the title tag hidden. The first detective pushes a note to the new guy, who cranes to read it, shows nothing, then resumes his military posture at my elbow. The first detective continues talking as if we're still alone.

'Danny del Pasco—'

'There's no CR number on Danny del Pasco or the mayor's wife.'

'Danny del Pasco—'

'I'm not lying to you. Focus this shit on something that matters, something in those CR numbers, or I'm back to work. I told you—'

'In my experience, Officer Black,' the new guy's voice is deep and condescending, 'and likely yours, when someone says "I'm not lying" they most often are.'

We share that special look. I say, 'Try me.'

He removes a printed form from his file instead, dates and initials the form, then pushes it to the first detective, who witnesses. It's a notification waiver, one an idiot would sign or a cop who had no fear of talking without an attorney present. This one is called a Criminal Rights Waiver. The first detective pushes it along to me. The new guy explains.

'Please read the waiver of rights, then sign and date it at the bottom, there.' He points at two boxes that I can check, one that is the beginning of a walk to the gas chamber when Illinois reopens it.

'Bye.' I check the box that says 'Do not waive,' sign the bottom, and stand. 'I'll be going by the union; they'll arrange for an attorney and we'll do this again.'

'We're not finished, Officer Black.'

'Fuck both of you.'

As I turn just outside the door I hear one of them say, 'If she takes a deal from the U.S. Attorney, we'll never get her back.'

Chapter 12

FRIDAY, DAY 5: AFTERNOON

Two Augusts ago a gentleman felon from Mississippi tried to blow up Alexander Calder's 53-foot red flamingo. Had he not been stopped, his 5,000-pound fertilizer bomb would have leveled the whole block. Other than the Calder sculpture the block consists of two skyscrapers that resemble a reduced version of the World Trade Center in New York. The less imposing of the two structures is the thirty-floor Dirksen Federal Building. It houses the federal courts, the FBI, and all thirty-one Assistant U.S. Attorneys for the Northern District of Illinois. They're on the fifth floor overlooking the Berghoff Restaurant.

Helen Holden, *the* U.S. Attorney, took the bomb personally.

Helen tends to take a number of things personally, rarely granting absolution to those she dislikes. And she absolutely hates the superintendent. Rumor has it that he and her had it out when he was chief of detectives and she was lawyering RICO cases for the feds, but not the big ones. Chief Jesse won and rose quickly to the top of his chosen profession; Helen spent eight years out in Rockford prosecuting guys who willfully removed their mattress tags.

As I'm passing the Berghoff, the sidewalk crowds up with coats-and-ties and I can't help but consider the geography's co-incidence. Last Monday when I was here, I assumed that Chief Jesse had come from a dinner meeting, stepping out to his car after shaking hands and saying good-bye to his—

My feet stop. What if the meeting wasn't at the Berghoff? What if it was next door where I'm headed? A nighttime meeting at the Everett Dirksen Federal Building? The courts would be closed, the post office would be closed. Getting in and out of that building at night would require an M16 no matter who you were, *or* an escorted hall pass from the FBI.

Chief Jesse's car was pointed toward State, away from the Federal Building. Inside, the car was clean leather and a ... cigarette trace? Odor that lingered, and he doesn't smoke. Or was it a cigar? *And perfume*, there was perfume, wasn't there? A woman bumps me with her briefcase and I snap back to today, looking for an SUV. Adams Street is buses and cabs.

Heat fills my face. *Chief Jesse has done nothing but protect you, and this is how you repay him?* Above me the Dirksen Federal Building agrees, the ninth floor seems to be grinning. My next appointment has a suite of offices on nine.

To get there I have to actually go in, then successfully navigate the lobby, a process not unlike being slowly digested. Visit one of the G's buildings where it houses its own and you get a real sense of its mind-set – the 'us or them' fortress mentality is as strong as prison. And prison is what I'm thinking about in the elevator with my VISITOR badge and empty holster. My escort punches 9 and says, 'Photos first' and nothing else.

The FBI has one agent assigned full-time to investigate the Chicago Police Department. Full-time, big budget, it's all he

179

does. And when you come to visit, voluntarily or by subpoena, they drop you into a room designed for crook shots – 'Face the video. Feet on those spots, profile, face.' Mind games before your interview. And they don't answer your questions.

Their interrogation room looks a lot like IAD's but larger. I get the feeling that I'm a bigger fish here and it's not a good feeling. Special Agent Stone shares a ten-foot oval table with two black suits. The remaining chairs are empty; one has a small stack of folders in front of it, a coffee cup, and a roll of LifeSavers.

Special Agent Stone says, 'Are we waiting on your attorney?'

I stare at him in lieu of answering.

He flat–lines a smile. 'Then we'll begin as soon as—'

The door opens and a tall, attractive woman in a severe suit enters. All three men rise and she pats the air down before they can stand. She offers me her hand, 'Jo Ann Merica, Assistant U.S. Attorney,' and her card. 'You're not represented, Officer Black?'

I examine her card and tell it, 'Nope.'

'Well then, let's begin.' Her smile is more of a reflex and only marginally brighter than Agent Stone's. 'You are currently a tactical officer in District 18 or on loan to the Superintendent's Intelligence Unit?' The smile adds a lacquered inch. 'We're having trouble keeping up with you lately.'

I don't feel the levity. 'What's this about, counselor? Why am I here?'

'Excuse me?'

I stare; Assistant U.S. Attorney Jo Ann Merica does too. The FBI agents join her. She glances at her papers, then uses one perfect, pearlized fingernail to flick the LifeSavers across the table. We watch them roll until they reach my hands.

Cute. Actually Evergreen sounds good, so I open the roll and pop two while they all watch. Then we stare again. Finally Jo Ann Merica says, 'I intend to charge you with obstruction of justice and complicity in the death of Assistant State's Attorney Richard Rhodes.'

'*Really?*' My jaw snaps a LifeSaver. Everyone hears it as punctuation.

'Really.' Jo Ann Merica has 32-degree eyes under long lashes and confidence she earned. 'I can wait while you call the union.'

'I'm not interested in waiting, Jo Ann, or talking.'

She opens a second folder without any flourish, checks her watch, then Agent Stone, and says, 'We have incontrovertible evidence of organized crime within the Chicago Police Department.' She shows me a page clipped between two fingertips. 'The old First Ward and the mayor's office. Long-standing racketeering that I will prosecute under the RICO statutes. You can be a target or a witness. It's up to you.'

I can't read the page from this distance and don't try, although I'd love to. It's not blank, but could be evidence against her dry cleaner. 'Or I can be neither.'

Jo Ann's hundred-dollar haircut barely moves. 'Sorry. You're in too deep.' She pauses for my benefit. 'As are your friends. Some of whom have already come forward. You can guess which side they picked.'

I pretend she didn't say that and smirk. 'Uh-huh.'

'I strongly suggest you engage an attorney. She'll help you—'

'Tell you what, Jo Ann. It's the same thing I told Agent Stone at Joliet. I work for the superintendent. If you've got a beef, talk to him.'

'We're here, Officer Black, to talk *about* him.'

I stand to leave. 'Not with me.' One of the FBI suits stands as if he intends to block the door. No one but me watches him do it.

Jo Ann Merica says, 'You can corroborate what we've already been told, then wear a wire, or go to prison. Your days as "Patti Black, Officer of the Year" are over.'

'Am I under arrest? If not, I'm leaving.'

'Up to you. But know this, that missing file in Calumet City will turn up, and when it does, *everyone* in it will be going to prison.'

I take my first real breath after I'm outside in front of Calder's flamingo. Two very bad echoes are still with me: 'About *him*' and 'Missing file.' Chief Jesse as a RICO target. *Jesus Christ*. That's gotta be bullshit.

Doesn't it?

I'm turning red again, ashamed again, and walk into an army of pigeons without seeing one. They explode; I stand at their center, thinking: Chief Jesse's somehow in this? It's not just a coincidence, his connection to Gilbert Court? And 'the mayor's office' too? Even if it were possible, and it isn't, why tape me up with a wire – I don't know shit about anything but Calumet City.

That's the other echo. The 'missing file.' It can't be the Calumet City police file; Agent Stone's card was there on the table when I arrived . . . he had to have seen everything I saw. *Shiver*. The pigeons settle and it hits me – the 'missing file' has to be the foster home file from Calumet City Juvenile Services. Someone has pilfered it.

Jo Ann Merica and the G don't have it – how fabulous is that?

Internal Affairs doesn't either or we would've already covered every sentence that included my name. Who's got it, then? Could be lost; shit, I left twenty-three years ago and it's been eighteen since the Black Monday murder. Back then computers were . . . fruit crates compared to now. It could easily be lost.

Or it could be sitting in a file cabinet. But why?

A shoeshine boy looks at my feet, then me, like he could help gym shoes. Behind him his ghetto blaster is playing Muddy Waters instead of 50 Cent. A bus passes with a movie ad covering the entire right side. Denzel Washington has a pistol pointed at his ear and a briefcase at his feet. He's standing behind the title, *Shakedown*.

I flash on the most recent margin notes in the Cal City PD file about Jim Bakker's new radio show in Branson. And for the very first time I see the striking resemblance between Mr. Washington's situation and Assistant State's Attorney Richard Rhodes. Whoever made those notes knew where Richard Rhodes spent his childhood.

But if it's a shakedown, why kill him?

It's 4:55 – still no call from Little Gwen – my back's against Sonny's driver-side fender at the redeveloped corner of 95th and Western. The corner's busy and has been for the whole hour we've been waiting, Sonny inside his car. Truck wakes make the only breeze and keep the noise constant; the exhaust odor too. My fingertips drum Sonny's fender. This meeting – if Pancake shows – is about the bad guys, guys who want to do to me what they already did to Richard Rhodes, bad guys who can lead me to Little Gwen and her boy if they're still alive . . . if I didn't somehow dream her call.

I'm anxious – about the meeting, about Gwen being a delusion, and about Sonny, but I'm not in jail – city or federal – and I'm big happy about that. So was Sonny when I got here, although he'd already heard that IAD planned on having me back in tomorrow. It was news to me, but not a surprise. IAD sucks, but the FBI will be the final hammer and I'm doing pretty good thinking about Pancake instead of them.

Sonny yells out his window, showing me his watch, 'Pushing five o'clock, P. I ain't waitin' another hour.'

Neither of us knows what to say and that's the real reason I'm outside leaning against his fender and he's not. 'Afraid you'll miss *Barney Miller*?'

A rail thin, pasty white man is checking me out from across the street. He's alone and not walking happy. I wave at him and tell Sonny out of the corner of my mouth, 'Be cool, he'll have cover.'

'Duh.'

I shove off the fender to jog through the traffic. The guy stops cold. Then looks over his shoulder like he wants to run but doesn't. I watch his hands, not his face, then look behind him on the 50-50 chance he's as fucked up as his business partners. He steps behind a parking meter, keeping it between us, and says, 'That's good' when I get to his side of the street.

We're twenty feet apart. 'I'm not contagious, Pancake.'

His head swivels, but like a lizard's, clicking in stutter–frame motion. The railroad cap resting on his sunglasses is a size too big and follows late each time. The threat of Charlie Moth looms between us.

'Cops lie. You're all contagious.'

I can barely hear him and step closer; he backtracks. I try

again and his combat boots tangle or he'd be gone. 'Be cool, okay? Danny D said you could help me.' I open my coat. 'Nobody's on the job.'

He's hiding as much face under the cap as possible and keeps rotating his head sixty degrees either side of mine.

'Danny D said there's money out on me and you know who and why. Tell me and I owe you one.'

'Uh-huh. A whiteboy, from Arizona or Idaho, might be hiring partners.' Pancake jerks a look over his shoulder then back and steadies with a hand on the meter. 'Torches, maybe others. Payin' for your work schedule too, phone numbers, home address, friends' names, everythin' and anythin'.'

Pancake looks behind him again, adds the other hand to the meter and speed to his speech.

'Buyin' crystal and talking shit about you right after that nigger shoot–out Monday – where and when you work, says he has top dollar to pay.'

'What's his name? How's he look?'

'How's he look? How's he look? Young, white, I never seen him. Idaho Joe.'

Involuntary exhale. Can't be Roland. But since Pancake's never seen this young whiteboy Idaho Joe, this ID is *at least* secondhand. Add dope and fear and no telling how far off we are. If an SUV hadn't tried to paste me in the alley by Julie's I'd be willing to believe Danny D was wrong.

'Let's say you had stuff to sell about me, how do you find Idaho Joe?'

Pancake scrunches up in his coat and railroad cap, but his sunglasses stay on me and the street beyond. He answers through a hand bleached by chemicals and industrial soap. 'Idaho Joe calls a bar. Up in the twenties, just north of the niggers on State . . . by Twenty-sixth Street, calls it twice a day.'

I know the bar, the Cassarane, it's the first white club north of the Harold Ickes Homes housing project. The bar's in the urban–renewal DMZ between the worst ghetto in the city and Chinatown.

Pancake starts backing up and adds, 'And he's real interested in your kid. Johnny Somebody . . . like that farm guy from Indiana.'

'What? What'd you say?'

He resets his sunglasses and jumps back another step. 'You know, like the singer – Cougar, Johnny Cougar – Idaho Joe's got a thing for your kid, even more than you. Same money on him for his numbers, addresses . . .'

What? I lunge and he's already running. Fast. We sprint a block, but I can't catch him. At Ninety-sixth Sonny's Ford tries to clip him but Pancake leaps a hedge into the packed parking lot of the Evergreen Plaza and disappears. I stop between cars, blinking at the sea of cars, breathing much harder than a one-block sprint.

Sonny pulls up and yells, 'C'mon.'

'My son,' I pant a gasp. 'He's after my son.'

'You don't have a son. Get in the car.'

These pieces–of–shit are after my son . . .

'Yo, Patti. Get in the fucking car. We'll run the lot.'

I don't get in. Sonny cranes his neck from the driver's seat. My hand grabs the passenger door for support. *My son. The devil is after my son. They know his name.*

'Get in the damn car, will you?'

And then I'm in it and we're cruising the lot; cars, trucks,

186

people but no railroad cap, no sprinters. Sonny says, 'A kid? Whose kid?'

'Huh? Ah, no, yeah.' I'm too stunned to lie. 'Mine.'

'No way. That'd mean you had a date.' He's laughing because I have to be joking.

'No it doesn't.'

He stares, then slows the car and stops as twenty years of cop kicks in; he knows what 'kid and no date' means and says, 'For real?'

I look out the window, seeing my son's face, the face that shares my pillow. Now it's tied to this sewer instead of the big suburban house and happy family I decided Johnny has, tied to this sewer instead of trees with leaves that don't fall and pets that don't die. Now he's here, with me, and crystal meth, and the Gypsy Vikings MC.

'Patti.' Sonny semi–winces as I turn. 'Jesus, P, I didn't know.'

My voice is monotone. It fits the prim schoolgirl now sitting in Sonny's front seat and she speaks before I realize that's what I'm doing. 'Nobody does. It was a rape . . . years of 'em.' I feel Sonny staring at a terrified teenager, numb and alone, looking at the edge of Roland's attic curtains. *PTL* is over, we're done in the basement, for tonight.

A ghost tells my ear, 'But it's different now. Pancake said so.'

I jerk past Sonny's stare to see who spoke. I see Chief Jesse and all his years of mentoring. And the ghost says it again and this time it's a little boy's voice, my boy and he's scared, scared and wet and humiliated like I was. Shame crawls up my shoulders to Roland's hands. A titanic rush of rage slams me back in the seat. My eyes squeeze shut and I blurt, *'One million, 999—'* The rush is Chinatown, the poison that can never ever be allowed out in the light. But I'm not me any longer so I can't stop it. I'm a killer and don't want to stop it. This new person doesn't feel beat shitless and violated; she doesn't need to count anymore; she feels like . . . like—

'Patti?' I look up and this time Sonny does wince. 'You okay, babe?'

I say, 'Fine,' but the skin seems too tight around my mouth.

'You don't look fine.'

'We'll grab my car' – my monotone's gone and I'm no longer anxious about Sonny's inconsistencies – 'then go by the Cassarane Bar when it opens. When Idaho Joe calls in, we'll—'

Sonny gets a radio call, answers the dispatch, then me. 'I gotta do this. Roll with me, then we'll do the bar. We gotta talk about this. About you . . . and your kid.'

'Can't. The Cassarane doesn't open till seven p.m.; I've got stops to make—' I jump out before he can effect a kidnap; he has that look, or some kind of look.

'Where, what stops?'

I lie, 'Chief Jesse. Call you after and we'll hit the bar.'

Sonny frowns. 'You lying, Patti?'

'Keep what I said between us, okay?'

'Wait a minute. C'mon, we gotta talk—'

'Between us, okay?'

Sonny's radio squawks. He shows teeth, then surrenders for the second time in one day. 'Don't do nothing stupid.'

'Roger that.' I kiss my fingers and pat his car, two things I haven't done before. He guns it south and hits the siren. I'm headed north. To a building in Evanston I visit on my son's birthday. Until today I never had the courage to go inside, but all that's different now. So different that I'm not sure I've ever met the girl inside my flannel shirt. She's not the same kind of afraid she was all day, not the same kind of ghost.

An SUV passes and slows.

I palm my Smith and hope the motherfucker stops. Little Gwen's call wasn't a delusion. Roland Ganz, the man who killed me, raped me, murdered me as a teenager, wants our son.

He's always wanted our son. So he can preach to John the way he preached to me.

Chapter 13

FRIDAY, DAY 5: 6:00 P.M.

For seven miles of city I've been wondering, How do you erase a disease?

A monster that was dead and now isn't; a man who you decided *had to be dead*, so you could go on living. And how twisted is Roland Ganz after eighteen more years to putrefy under his bookkeeper's suit? How many children since me? Children I did nothing to save.

A picture forms on the inside of my windshield, a picture that until today I only allowed out in Chinatown. Still six feet tall, thick-lipped, and wearing cotton underwear too full in the front. Blotchy-hot skin, his breath wet and musty with dinner, syrup voice, and long, demanding fingers. He's somewhere close, breathing in Chicago's coming night, just the TV on, kneading his cotton briefs, reading scripture to Little Gwen's son—

Roland Ganz did things to me that I can't describe. He did them so often and so many ways that I stopped fighting and went to the basement or attic on command. I wore what I was told, did and said what I was told, and slowly lost all touch with anything but Roland's and Annabelle's wishes. Their home was a violent frozen wasteland, not unlike the river of Old Crow that followed my stumbling, confused escape. The two journeys lasted eight years and neither taught me anything other than how horrible humans can be to one another and that there is no bottom to the bottom.

I two-hand the steering wheel; he's behind the SUV that missed me near the L7 and the B&E at my duplex. He *did* do Gilbert Court, murdered Annabelle and left her there, and he did beat Richey to death. The fucking monster is back. A shiver shakes me to the seat.

Victims shiver; you're a cop with a gun.

And Roland hit the mayor – Bullshit; no way. That takes big –city juice and Roland Ganz is an aging monster, not an Outfit assassin. I focus on Kennedy Expressway traffic. He's got nothing to do with the assassination attempt, but that fucking monster *is* after our son. I feel that so deep it has to be true. I steer past downtown to Armitage. The exit's slow, short, and crowded. Once a year, just like today, I take this exit. Seven miles north it will lead to Howard Street, where I make a right, three miles from the front door of Le Bassinet.

Le Bassinet is an adoption agency. I gave them my baby so Annabelle and Roland couldn't have him. Twenty-three years ago I made them promise Roland couldn't have my baby. Now they have to tell me who my son is so I can save him. They will not want to do this, nor will they be inclined to believe me. They will, in fact, use all heroic efforts to stop me. It's their job to protect the new lives from the old, no matter what version of 'emergency' they're told.

Ashland changes to Clark Street at 5900 north. I'm passing through the cheap, bright colors of a Mexican neighborhood flooded with latchkey children and loud music. The storefronts have hand-painted windows – Super Mercado and Taquería. Brown men in T-shirts tote white grocery bags. Pinched car lots offer them $400 cars and promises in Spanish. I've driven this street seventeen times and have no memory of it until today. I was always in a trance, edging closer to my son, reliving his most recent year.

I've imagined each of these years. During high school I made him a football player with muddy elbows and tousled hair. He was a B student who could have done better and still has the girlfriend he's adored since they were sophomores, and a younger sister he helps with her homework. John was born in the fall and I've made fall his favorite season; his mother loves it too and used to rake and burn the leaves with him every Saturday when the city would still allow it. They'd stand there, leaning on their rakes, mother and son, dressed in crewneck sweaters and crisp fall air, only the sweet smoke from the oak leaves separating their smiles.

Halloween was big in the suburbs, two nights instead of one, and it wasn't scary.

Each year that I've made this drive, my vision of John got a year older, still boyish – I think he'll always be – but more mature. Four years ago I settled him on Northwestern to be close to home and because it was the best university in Illinois. In my dream he graduated this May, with the mortarboard hat and gown. There were joyous pictures of John and his family, a day they'd all worked for him to have. At night sometimes, I can feel the warmth of his cheek on mine.

Because he doesn't know me, he'll never have to know about his real father, what he was. He'll never have to wonder, like I

192

have, if any of that sickness was passed on. He'll never have to read the papers or check the arrest sheets to see if one of our young, current deviants matches Roland Ganz's old MO. And John won't ever have to apologize – to the mirror or anyone else – because his mom was what she was. Me.

I catch the light at Howard Street, Chicago's border with Evanston. At Howard these two cities are identical. The farther north you travel the more they differ. I know only two things about Evanston – there's an elm tree across from Le Bassinet's small parking lot; and from under that tree – staring at Le Bassinet's arched front door – Evanston seems safe and clean and the best place for John to have grown up. It is so far from Calumet City that maps could not connect the two.

But now I have to walk through those doors and risk poisoning John's past and maybe his future to save him. My career as a police officer will end shortly after that conversation too, giving IAD and the FBI all the admissions they require for the first half of their charges. No more commendations and citations and pats on the back from the boys I work with. No more appreciation from the civilians I assist, only lawyers and courthouses . . . and maybe prison. And I deserve it.

After I save my son, I will kill Roland Ganz. I won't be blackout drunk; I won't ask for strength or forgiveness. I never named Roland Ganz and he will not tell the world that he is John's father. Roland and I will end us and his threat to John wherever it is that we meet.

Inside, Le Bassinet looks nothing like I imagined. A gingham-draped baby grand piano takes up most of the tiny lobby; to the piano's left a fireplace mantel is lined with baby pictures. The wood floor has a throw rug and two cozy chairs. I smell cinnamon and see a receptionist smiling from a bolt–hole cubicle. She has an eighteen–inch fir tree on her counter and gray hair tied with a ribbon. The walls around her are limestone and quiet, but not churchy. Bing Crosby's crooning floats out of a hallway lined with more photographs.

'Ah, hi. Do you have a post–adoption department . . . or anything?'

She doesn't react like I expected, given my clothes, Southside accent, and a request that must almost always come from women or men who long-ago abdicated their responsibilities. Instead, she smiles wide like grandmothers on TV, holds a finger up between us, and reaches for her phone. Sweat forms under my shirt. She lowers the phone and says, 'Ms. Meery will be right with you.'

The woman who greets, then seats me in her office is exactly what I fantasized. I wanted her to have kind eyes and slow hands, and she does. I also wanted her to have a keen sense of honesty and the strength to challenge if honesty wasn't present. I wanted her to have placed John with the right family. All these years I was too self-conscious to leave my car, choosing instead to sit and hope. I don't feel self-conscious now; I'm afraid in a very different way. I'm also very, very angry.

'My name's Patti Black.' *Bury the anger, hide it*. 'I gave you my son on October 19, twenty–three years ago. I have to find him; he's in . . . serious jeopardy.'

Ms. Meery nods small and keeps her hands folded.

'I'm a Chicago cop, Ms. Meery. We have information that John – that's my son – may be the target of a kidnap-murder attempt.'

Ms. Meery's eyes widen. 'My goodness. But we haven't been contacted by the police.'

I cut my eyes and wish I hadn't. 'It involves a city and federal investigation that can't be made public until the perpetrators are caught. You may have seen some of it in the papers earlier in the week.'

'*My, my*. I'll get the director.'

I raise my hand. Hers hesitates above her phone, but her eyes stay with me. This is it, if I can do it, the end of my career, the beginning of my trip to prison. Deep breath . . . I tell Ms. Meery my story, the parts that I can say out loud, alternating between telling it to my shoes and my hands and the walls and the back of my eyelids. It's a whisper in some places and broken sentences in others.

I open my eyes and Ms. Meery hasn't left the confinement of the small desk that separates us. I pause to breathe, to force myself to continue, and catch her expression, one I've seen on relatives of children who aren't coming home. She's trying hard to hear but not touch, and I don't blame her. When my story's finished, I can't look at her. My cheeks have silent tears but I don't wipe them. I sit straight and breathe deep until they stop. It's important that Ms. Meery believe I'm not crazy; vital that she participate in this felony, one that could, and likely will, end her career here, one that may send her to prison when I kill Roland Ganz.

The silence between us lasts until I break it with a glance. The glance carries no hate, although hate is there in equal parts with shame and fear. Ms. Meery is far back in a chair that now seems too big for her, like she's been hit once and might be again. I can't change what I said or how it sounded; I can just try to look 'okay' and know that I don't.

'I'm so, so sorry,' says Ms. Meery.

Calm, benign, not crazy . . . 'Yeah, well, there it is.'

'If it was a closed adoption, we just can't . . .' Ms. Meery smiles an honest smile that doesn't remove the helplessness from her eyes. 'And I think you know that.'

'Know what?'

'I'm so sorry for what happened, but Illinois law does not allow—'

'John's in danger. *Real* danger. No "law" is going to protect him from—'

'I could check with the legal department. Possibly the courts could . . .'

'Court won't work.' My voice has too much timbre, too much street. I should've flashed my star when I said I was a cop. 'We gotta do it now.'

Ms. Meery eases her chair away from the desk, away from my tone more than my words. I lean closer, too close, like a crazy, desperate person would. 'Listen to me, okay? My story . . . I've never told anyone else. It's probably not new to you, but—'

'It's not new . . . Officer Black . . . Patti.' Ms. Meery smiles sad and tiny and doesn't get any closer. 'Other than the current threat, of course. We hear threats, frightening ones from time to time, but to my knowledge they never—'

A woman appears at the door on my left, acting familiar, like she might've been listening in the hall. She's twenty years older than Ms. Meery and smiles as she takes a seat beside me. Her clothes are expensive, her demeanor aristocratic but not pushy, and she leaves her glasses on her chest dangling from a silver chain. Ms. Meery introduces her as her superior, Mrs. Trousdale, the agency's codirector. We shake and I start into the story again.

It's no easier the second time. Mrs. Trousdale stops me with a knowing smile and covers my hands with hers. 'I know, dear, I know.'

I smile, knowing she doesn't, but happy that it's going well.

'It's just that we can't.' The smile suddenly looks like Prozac. 'As a police officer,' she glances at Ms. Meery, 'I'm sure you understand.'

My hands free themselves. Ms. Meery has the better smile of the two but no words. I press too hard, 'They're going to *kill* John, Mrs. Trousdale. That's worse than whatever secrets you and I may not want John to know. Dead's forever.'

'We're very sorry.' And Mrs. Trousdale rises to leave. I grab her wrist. She tugs, but I don't let go. 'Please, Officer Black, you're hurting me.'

I stand, adding grip that rolls the muscle in my forearm. 'Roland Ganz is going to kill John. After he does his same God and semen fantasies to him that he did to me. I'm not gonna let that happen, and you aren't either.'

Mrs. Trousdale tries to stretch away, lengthening her arm to the shoulder. Ms. Meery rises to help, 'Please, Patti, Officer Black—'

Mrs. Trousdale tugs again. When that doesn't free her wrist, she yells, '*Donna! Donna, 911.*'

Ms. Meery pats at me. 'Let her go; we'll talk more, you and I.'

I don't, then do, and Mrs. Trousdale stumbles backward into the door, holding her wrist. Ms. Meery waves her out before Mrs. Trousdale can say what's on her face. My pistol's visible on my belt, but so is my star. Neither look believable or promising if all you see are polite detectives or pressed uniforms. Ms. Meery is staring at the pistol.

197

'I'm a TAC officer, should've said so; this is plainclothes for the ghetto. I don't want to hurt your boss – I'm not *going* to hurt her – I just want to find John. Right now. Today.'

Ms. Meery pats again at the air, trying to get me into a chair. 'Please. Please.'

The Evanston police are likely on their way. I need to make a decision. Now.

Ms. Meery adds, 'I know who you are, I do. The *Herald* article on Tuesday. Quite flattering, even if the picture wasn't.' She smiles scared and through her eyebrows. 'I'll try to help. But it won't be till tomorrow, first thing. And you can't say anything to anyone. I'll lose my job.'

'No.' I'm standing again. 'Get up. Gotta be now.'

'The records vault is already locked. No one here has a key—'

'*Bullshit.*' My hand is very close to the Smith.

Ms. Meery shies. 'It's the truth.'

I ghetto–stare her, know I'm already out of time and don't lie. 'If I trust you and this is bullshit, my son will die. Understand? I'll be a step or three beyond crazy and you'll be . . .'

She nods as small as possible and says, 'The security on the records vault is, is . . . like a bank. Our codirector takes the keys to the outer doors. She and Pinkerton have the only combination that supersedes the time lock.'

I stare till I decide to believe her. 'What's your codirector's name?'

'Mrs. Elliot. Marjorie Elliot.'

'What time in the morning?'

Ms. Meery shies again. 'Nine?'

'This is the most, *the only* important thing I'm going to do before that story I told you falls in on me. You need to decide right now if you're lying. And trust me, it'll be better 'cause I'll walk down the hall and your boss will be the one who faces this.'

No hesitation, no eye shift. I believe her when she says she's going to help. 'Please, Officer . . . Patti, fourteen hours until it opens, two more to be safe, three at the latest. Call me first.' She trembles me a card with her direct number on it. 'Better go, I believe Mrs. Trousdale will call the police if Donna already hasn't.'

'Where's the vault?'

Ms. Meery shakes her head. 'You can't. It's locked. Three doors, I think.'

'Where?'

'In the basement.'

'Any outside doors to the basement?'

Ms. Meery shakes her head. 'You can't. No one can get in till tomorrow.'

I hear the words and stop long enough to think she may be right. For sure she's right about her boss calling the cops. 'Okay.' I start to ghetto–stare her again and stop. We share the moment until I speak. 'Thanks. You'll be in danger for doing this. I'll do what I can to help, but . . . I'm saving my son. First, I'm saving my son.'

The two secretaries in the outer office are talking near an open back door and staring at the hall as I make the too-fast exit. They hug the doorframe but don't look away, a guarantee that the cops are en route and that Mrs. Trousdale has left the building. As much as I want to see the basement, I need freedom and time more.

* * *

I beat the Evanston blue-and-whites by less than a minute. They fly past as I make the light at Church Street. I'm too calm, too cold to be okay – a stranger knows my story; I know my story; I'm changing into someone I don't know. The blue-and-whites keep going in my mirror. My phone vibrates. I mash the gas and answer. It's the PI, Harold J. J. Tyree.

Harold says he and I have to talk, right now.

'About what, Harold?'

'Oh, you know, baby.' Harold's using a sweet-pimp voice. 'You know.'

I loop three civilians doing the speed limit. 'I don't know shit, Harold, other than you came by the L7, and not long after that an SUV tried to pin me in an alley.'

'Baby, I don't know nothin' about that.'

'Uh-huh.' Mirror check. 'So what do you want?'

'You know.'

'Harold, I'm driving a slow car at high speed and need to concentrate. Tell me what I know or bother another white broad.'

'Annabelle and Roland.'

My jaw clamps and I check the mirror; Harold has just been called up to the majors. 'Meet me on the corner Forty-fourth and Halsted in an hour, by the Amphitheater, standing alone, hands out of your pockets.'

'Why there? We can do it—'

'We can do it where I say or fuck you. Amphitheater in an hour. *Alone*, Harold, or I'll make sure that neighborhood makes you Rodney King.'

Harold agrees.

I adrenaline-dial Sonny, now positive that Harold J. J. Tyree did the B&E on my duplex and has high hopes of setting me up for another rundown/kidnap attempt. He and Roland and whiteboy Idaho Joe will grab me because they think I know how to find John. They get two for one, mother and son.

But these pieces of shit are wrong. Through Harold, I will find and kill Roland Ganz before the FBI decides to arrest me for no–showing their interview, before I'm put in prison for the Black Monday murder in Calumet City. My son will never know any of this happened.

Sonny answers, 'You hear?'

'Huh?'

'Chief Jesse. Heart attack after dinner. He's in ICU at Mercy Hospital.'

I'm afraid to breathe. 'He's . . . gonna make it?'

'Don't go over, you can't see him.'

'*Will he make it?*'

'No tellin'. Had your file in his lap, P.' Long pause, then, 'IAD and the G plan on taking a bunch more of your time the next few days.'

That's a polite way of saying that confinement is likely, arrest almost a given. Once that happens, anyone who helps me is toast, on their pension at a minimum. I want and need help but can't ask Sonny for it – the Gypsy Vikings backup was already way past what's fair. 'Sonny, there's a PI named Harold J. J. Tyree. If I'm dead or missing tomorrow, here's his number. At the very least, beat the shit out of him.'

Silence, then, 'Want help?'

'Got some.' Like a divine vision, I see Tracy Moens just a cell phone call away, plain as if she were standing next to me. 'I'll be in touch, and thanks for being my—'

'I went by the Cassarane, left my number at the bar for Idaho Joe.'

That feels like a kiss on the lips I haven't had in the longest time, and again it's coming from the strangest place. I'm glad Sonny can't see me blushing. 'Sonny, you need to stay out of this now, okay? I'm about to be in shit that won't wash off.'

'That's news?'

'This is different. My history won't stay hidden past the weekend.'

Sonny's voice changes, not weird, but sorta. 'The Cassarane already has my number. If Idaho Joe calls, I'll call. Keep your head down, P. Me and Eric and Cisco are rootin' for you, know that.' Pause. 'The whole crew, no matter what.'

I want to believe it and the tears in both eyes are proof. 'Bye.'

FRIDAY, DAY 5: 7:45 P.M.

In person, Tracy Moens is definitely surprised when we meet on my side of the river and I make the offer— 'You get pieces of the story now, the whole thing when it's over.' She has the look of a sleek, great white shark that's just seen more dinner that it thought possible, turning on a dime the way they do on the Discovery Channel, so fast the 3,000-pound fish seems to be going two directions at once.

'*Deal.*'

'You could die doing this, Tracy; if not, either part of the plan could put you in prison.'

Tracy takes a half-step back, not a full one. 'What are the odds ... on dying?'

From the shadows I eye the traffic as it passes. So many SUVs are on the street that there's no chance of IDing *the* SUV unless the kidnappers put a sign on it. 'Worse than if you stay out of it altogether.'

'But then I don't get the story.'

'Yup. There's the price of safety.' I dislike Miss All-Everything sufficiently to involve her in this. That and I don't expect her to betray me unless it *is* life-or-death. Reporters are just as ravenous as Hollywood portrays them, almost as crazy as skydivers. Tracy sees a book contract and a new town house in Lincoln Park; I see a gunfight, prison, and maybe a cemetery.

Fifteen minutes later the headlights of Tracy's red Jaguar are tailing me.

I make a right and her Jaguar follows. We're just west of the Deuce, the 2nd District – the only place in this city more violent than where I work – rolling Halsted's cramped four lanes through light rain, wind, and dark. Thunder booms and rattles my car windows. We pass brick storefronts and klieg-lit gas stations fenced with concertina wire. The fences are fronted by street-gangster lookouts who nervous-eye the darkening sky instead of two cars driven by white women.

This drive into the city's dark heart is the first of Tracy's required 'two parts.' She has simple instructions for part one: 'Do not exit your vehicle no matter what you see. If it goes bad, just call it in as 911 – officer involved.'

As we approach Forty-fourth from the south, the neighborhood changes to poor white people, empty warehouses, and prairies, Denny Banahan's tag for gaping holes of used-to-be buildings. A black man waits under the corner streetlight. He's exposed to the rain, backed by a thirty-foot-high, faded brick wall. His black Nike jumpsuit shines wet across narrow shoulders. An Afro glistens where it bubbles out from under a Sox cap. His oversize hand hides only part of a cell phone and he seems nervous at the outer edge of Canaryville. If he's alone like I told him, he should be nervous.

He stares when he sees my car. I stop at the opposite curb, push open the driver's door, and yell, 'Haul ass, Harold.'

Harold J. J. Tyree pimp rolls across Halsted, checking everything he can and still look unafraid. As he passes the center stripe I get out, pistol drawn, and point him over the hood. He balks.

'On the hood, Harold. *Now.*'

'Man—'

'*Now.* Asshole.' I two–hand the Smith and step so he's sandwiched between me and the hood. '*Move.*'

Harold does. I pat him. Up close he smells like baby powder and Jheri curl. There's a .32 hidden inside his right ankle.

'That's a felony.'

'Got a permit.'

'Sure you do. I find a tracker on your person, it's gonna kill you.' My voice sounds like a stranger's.

'Nah, man, no tracker.'

I grab his cell and make sure it's off, then check Tracy parked behind us. 'Stand on the sidewalk.'

Harold steps to the curb. I slide into the driver's seat and drape the Smith behind the passenger's headrest. 'Get in. Hands on the dash. Take 'em off and I shoot you.'

'Shit, lady—'

'In or out, Harold.'

He gets in after checking Halsted again. I have to gun–barrel the back of his head before his hands reach for the dash. '*Easy, man*, easy.'

'Keep 'em there.' I wedge the barrel tight to the base of his head, then make a right on Pershing. Harold shies to the window.

'Where we goin'?'

I press Harold's cheek into the window, positive Harold is the best chance Patti Black has to kill Roland Ganz. And tonight, that's my best chance at saving my son. I make the right onto the Dan Ryan and Tracy's headlights make it with us.

Harold sneaks a look at me and says, 'We can do our talkin' here, baby. Ain't no reason to go south.'

I consider Harold and his Afro, then his big hands again, and consider blowing his teeth into the window. The new me thinks that's reasonable. Harold must sense this and asks again where we're going. He won't like my answer any better than I do.

'Calumet City.'

Chapter 14

FRIDAY, DAY 5: 9:00 P.M.

It's raining harder. Harold J. J. Tyree has a gun pointed at his ear and a very dangerous white woman in the driver's seat of a car he doesn't own. But he doesn't act the right kind of nervous. We're four miles down the Dan Ryan and Harold hasn't tried to explain why we needed to talk.

I have two good ideas why he hasn't explained, and quick–check for an SUV in the smeary headlights behind us. We're bracketed by three, but none the right color. I check Harold again; he doesn't have the look of a man who's going where I'm going. That's unfortunate – for both of us. It's important Harold and I get on the same page before we discuss Idaho Joe.

I jerk the wheel and us onto the Seventy–fifth Street off ramp. Now we're in my part of the ghetto. If an Idaho whiteboy driving an SUV follows us in here, he'll be the corpse, not the killer. I steer us right, then left, and onto a dead side street that instantly becomes more canyon than street. Gutted burnouts block the night sky on both sides. I brake at sudden, complete dark. Only bold, first–floor graffiti reflects in our headlights. Ten years of slow urban rot litters the street; we're in a seven-story Gangster Disciple graveyard, a place to rape, rob, and murder anyone who doesn't know better. Tracy's Jag parks too far back.

I shove Harold with the pistol and say, 'Out.'

Harold exits, but not far, and glances his surroundings. We're facing each other in the misty dark of Tracy's headlights, him and the new me – two people with limited futures.

'You know a lot about my situation, Harold.'

He nods.

'How's that?'

Harold shakes his head. Thunder booms over the hollowed buildings and punches us with wet stench. The rain's our angel too; gangsters don't like the rain. There's only a small chance Harold doesn't know this.

'Been by my crib, Harold? Daylight B&E? You and me have to cover that.'

Harold's expression is as professionally blank as he can make it.

'What were you looking for? How'd you and Idaho Joe find me?'

His Afro sifts Tracy's headlights as he shakes it. 'Not me, baby.'

I nod again, red coming to my face. I aim at his foot. He doesn't notice. Lines I couldn't feel last week bunch at my eyes and harden my mouth. I don't feel great about shooting him, now that I'm about to. He seems more interested in the car illuminating his back.

'My girlfriend.' I angle my head at the headlights. 'You see the movie *Monster*? Aileen Wuornos. Badass number, that lady. Killed ten or twenty. My girlfriend's like that.'

I get Harold to nod.

'Her medication's in my pocket; I don't give it to her, she rips you to fucking pieces. The Stones and GDs sell you as tacos.'

Harold stops nodding and stares. 'Baby, you ain't the first *bull*dyke to threaten me.'

'Any of 'em shoot you?'

A sharp flash cracks deep in our canyon. Harold flinches and so do I. Lightning drills into the lake and shows us the gutted buildings. Thunder booms and five loose bricks shake to the street. Harold jerks to the noise, then regroups as his Afro begins to wilt.

'This is a bad place to be, Harold, alone, shot in the foot, beat sideways by my psycho girlfriend. Your track suit'll be in an evidence bag fifteen minutes after I leave.'

'I been in the ghetto before, baby. Know these boys. Speak the language, you know?'

We stare at each other until my lips curl over my teeth. Lightning flashes again and I cock the pistol. Harold notices. I aim at his intestines so I won't miss. 'Your client is trying to kill me and my kid.'

'*Say what?*'

'Trying to kill me and my son.' More thunder, and I add volume to compete. 'You and me don't need the Ayatollah, Harold. All that civil rights shit was last week.'

Harold pops up both hands. 'Whoa, baby. Ease up. I ain't into nothin' like that.'

'Idaho Joe is.' Harold is about to be shot, not pardoned. Tracy will be the ASA's witness. 'Last chance, how do you know what you know?'

Harold says, 'Patti Black, hero cop of the ghet-*to*.'

'She's dead.' I step back and aim at his head.

'*Don't. Don't.*' Harold stumbles backward into my fender and it keeps him from falling. 'Cal City Juvy. I got a guy at Cal City Juvy.'

An inch of deep frown grooves my new face. *What a surprise*. Calumet City Juvenile. The records sealed forever to protect the abused and innocent. Without permission my finger tightens on the trigger.

'Wanna die, Harold?'

'No way, baby. Fuck no.' Harold's hands are up and between us. 'The guy, he's workin' with me on this; got all kinda files he stole.'

I think about John, about what's in that file, absolutely certain it's the one Assistant U.S. Attorney Jo Ann Merica is hunting. 'This would be a really bad time to lie, Harold.'

Harold has his hands on the dash again and he's still alive. We're south of the ghetto on the Dan Ryan where it becomes the Bishop Louis Henry Ford Freeway and acts as a dam between the Chicago Sanitary District and the Port of Chicago. The Port is a fifteen-square-mile, rat-infested inland anchorage that connects Chicago to the Great Lakes' steel, zinc, and lead traffic via the Calumet River.

Pretty it isn't, even in the dark.

But it's not actually dark; it never is in the steel towns. The tops of the 200-foot brick chimneys in the distance are capped in fire, the 'Smokestack Lightnin'' Howlin' Wolf made famous. They blotch-light the distended sky in an odd pattern off to the southeast. I can taste the metal in the air; it tastes like it used to, like the blood did by the stockyards when Chicago was still 'hog butcher to the world.' But this smell is different, burnt ore and fuel oil, and it stings.

If you've been here before, that's how you know Calumet City and Gary are close. On the days when the wind was out of the south and east, it was all I could smell, in the basement or the attic, no matter what was in my face.

The memories shrink my Celica around me. Harold starts to say something and glances at me, then quickly away. If the new me has a reflection, I haven't seen it, but I can imagine. We take the exit ramp at Dolton. It drops down to State Street before State becomes what's left of the infamous Sin Strip. We roll mostly dark and deserted with Tracy behind us until we hit the first set of railroad tracks. Harold says turn south and I do, away from the warehouses and occasional damp hooker sheltering under an eave and wagging her purse.

The neighborhood we enter becomes low bungalows from the 1940s and '50s. Rain obscures their condition. Cars line both sides of a street that's dark other than our headlights and the low glow of curtained windows in the houses. I park us in the only driveway we pass, two concrete tire paths separated by mud and oil-dead grass. I phone Tracy and tell her to stay in her Jaguar with the engine running.

The porch is dry. Most of Harold J. J. Tyree is not. He knocks; a dim porch light blinks on and I step behind him with the Smith in his back. The door opens. I crouch deep and rugby-shove Harold inside. He stumbles through; I follow and kick the door closed behind us. The big, middle-aged white man regaining his balance and staring at me is only semi-surprised at my pistol.

'Sit down.' I gunpoint him at a concave sofa. 'Anyone else here?'

210

He hesitates and I palm–heel him hard in the chest. '*Down.*' He sits, involuntarily, and Harold follows. 'Who else is here?'

Headshake and he frowns at his musty living room, one that looks like he moved into it when his mother died, one that isn't much different than Annabelle and Roland's. The walls are faded paper, small flowers stained with wavy lines of nicotine. I taste undisturbed dust. Four lamps are on and hooded. The old furniture under them sucks up what light escapes the lampshades. Either he hasn't redecorated his mother's house or he has the tastes of an old white woman.

'Your mother here?'

His eyes harden and he shakes his head again.

'You know who I am?'

He glances at Harold, then back to me, and shrugs, not as scared of my condition or pistol as I would be. We do two minutes of gunpoint interrogation that doesn't go well. I feel myself edging closer to stepping off the cliff – my son is not going to die.

The bungalow's owner tells me his name is DeLay and disagrees that he's working for or with Roland Ganz; Mr. DeLay says he's a career civil servant, an ex-prison guard at the Joliet death house, and currently a juvenile services caseworker. Harold nods his Afro. Both men insist they have never seen, heard, or spoken to a white man or boy named Idaho Joe.

I try cop-bracing them three different ways, but the longer I listen to their bullshit, the more I suspect that these two have turned against an employer or client they won't name and are now blackmailing him or ransoming him their info – a felony that may actually save them from me.

'Wearing me out, fellas. I am gonna shoot you – right here on your fucking sofa – unless I'm *first*, told the name and where-abouts of your client; *second*, given the entire file on the foster home and its four kids; and *third*, a list of everyone who's seen it.'

DeLay says, 'Don't know what you're talking about. But if you use that,' he sneers at my Smith, 'I know you're going to Stateville. Know that for a fact.'

I nod at him, guessing some of his barrel chest and thick wrists are muscle. 'Harold here seems to think you have the file.'

'Maybe you should be at his house, threatening him.'

'First shot's in your foot.'

DeLay reaches for a cigarette or a weapon I can't see. Harold jerks away. I hit Mr. DeLay as hard as I can on the temple and his oversize head snaps sideways.

'*Owwww!*' He grabs at his ear and his right leg kicks me in the shin.

The pain shoots to my hip and I go to a knee, then stumble up quick and unsteady. 'I ain't fucking around, Mr. DeLay. Give me the file. Now.'

His nose dribbles blood on his cowboy shirt. When he notices the stain, his eyes flash and he tucks a scuffed brogue back to push the remainder of him up to standing. No chance I can out-fight him with just my hands, let alone him and Harold together. As he straightens, I kick him in the abdomen. The kick knocks him back into the sofa. Harold twists sideways to avoid 240 pounds falling. DeLay is gasping when he lands, both arms wrapped to his intestines. I don't think I want to shoot these guys, but the new me will probably kill them if she's given the opportunity.

I kick Mr. DeLay in the shin instead. He yells, '*Shit*,' and rolls onto Harold's legs, trying to protect abdomen and shin. 'Quit it, for chrissake.'

'Give me the file.' I kick DeLay again, this time in the hand covering the shin.

'*Owwwww.*'

I jam the gun barrel hard next to his bleeding ear and fire. He slams backward from the noise, screams, and grabs his ear.

'The file.'

'*Dining room. Under the boxes.* Under the boxes.'

I catch Harold moving, his arm now ends buried between a cushion and the sofa's arm. I aim before he can. 'Slowly, Harold. Very slowly.'

The large black hand comes out with a small black pistol.

'You're close to dying, Harold. Don't fuck this up for us. Drop it on the floor.'

He doesn't.

'Drop it on the floor, Harold. Or I put out your eye.'

The pistol bounces on the carpet. I step his way and kick the pistol across the room. 'Hands on top of your head, Harold.' He does and I back into the dining room to retrieve the file. It's only an inch thick, not much for all the hell it represents. Both men stare at me, DeLay with his face contorted, waiting for a mistake that will save their meal ticket, but neither willing to die for it.

'So far, I figure you two are facing three to five in Stateville for the file and the blackmail. My brother's there doing double life. You read the file, right? Nine murders?'

No answer.

'Maybe you missed it. My brother's Danny del Pasco. I'm his favorite sister. Make trouble for me or testify against me or my

213

son *for any reason*, I pull the pin on the file and your blackmail adventure – hello Danny D.'

We share the moment. I ask if there's questions. There aren't any and I cock the Smith. 'Who's your client? Last time I ask before one of you dies. Where is he and how do you get paid?'

Harold looks at his bleeding, half–deaf partner, thinks about my pistol and how I look, and rolls without the major fight PIs put up in Fantasyland; he explains that he's not the PI who caught the case, just an operative picking up a few bucks. Harold thinks the *real* PI has plenty of info on the client.

'Good, we'll go see him now.'

'Uh, he's in Arizona, Phoenix, I think, Delmont Chukut.' Harold spells both first and last, and produces an area code 602 number. DeLay coughs still scrunched and holding his abdomen and says he has a partner in this too, a Cal City cop who has to be paid, the detective I met Wednesday. DeLay wants to know what to tell Detective Barnes.

That's a good question, since Detective Barnes can cause me major problems and quickly. Luckily, Calumet City policemen have a reputation, at least those from the past, and understand two things with absolute clarity: death by gunshot and federal prison. I go with the former.

'Tell Detective Barnes there's thirteen thousand five hundred cops in Chicago. Out of them, somewhere between ten and fifty will come out here and kill him if anything happens to me. Then there's my girlfriend.' I cut a glance at Harold. 'Harold can tell you about her.'

Harold and DeLay share a glance, a strange one, and I ask. They don't explain. I sort of see the explanation but don't, like

I'm in the window in Chinatown and can't quite see the reflection . . .

Roland Ganz has to be the PI – the Juvenile file will show me what Roland and his employees know, but I'm really no closer to saving my son than the 602 phone number. I ask again. Neither man explains; I step to the side and roundhouse Juvenile Caseworker DeLay, this time two–handed with the pistol. The blow knocks him half off the couch. I land screaming in his face. *'Someone's trying to kill my kid!'*

The hammer's still back on the .38, but now my fingers are slippery in DeLay's blood. His eyes are baseballs and he's mumbling. Harold bolts for the door. I fan and fire, splintering the doorjamb. Harold drops to the wood floor and covers his head. I scream at DeLay from six inches. *'Trying to kill my son!'*

DeLay ducks to nowhere. 'The PI! The PI's got an angle.' DeLay peeps at Harold, 'But we can't figure it.'

'Why the fuck not?'

DeLay coughs blood.

I roundhouse him but miss. *'Why the fuck not?'*

'Don't know—'

The door opens and I almost kill Tracy Moens. Harold shies like she's Godzilla. Tracy's not used to that and looks at Harold, then the doorjamb above him, then the gun in my bloody hand and the big bloody white man spread on and off the couch.

'Jesus.' She swallows a grimace. 'He . . . ah, dead?'

I glare at DeLay. 'In a minute,' then step back and retrieve Harold's gun. 'I'm gonna kill one of you. Whoever explains the who and why of Arizona isn't him.'

Tracy freezes. Not a word from white or black. Harold knows the most about me and isn't bleeding and figures he's got the most room. Harold knows what I have to lose for this behavior, but he seems confused, and should be. He doesn't know the new me.

Tracy whispers, 'We okay, Patti?'

'Sure. Fine.' I tell Harold: 'Whoever explains isn't dead.'

Tracy touches my arm as gently as she has ever touched anything in her life. When she feels my bicep respond, she grips and tugs. 'C'mon. We need to go. Really.'

We will, right after one of these two talks.

'Patti.' Tracy sees the file and tugs harder, then leans to me and whispers, 'The gunshots. You have the file. We can always come back.'

She's right, for all three reasons, but that doesn't matter. I want the answers now, even if these two don't have any. I aim, Harold cringes but doesn't confess. Maybe he doesn't know more; I for sure wouldn't tell him shit if he worked for me.

I hear myself think that and blink. Getting arrested by Cal City cops won't help. Reality competes with rage. 'You two like Chinese food?'

Both men act confused. Like they've never heard the term.

'Been in Chinatown this week, Harold?' Louder still, 'Been there to meet anybody since you caught this case?'

Harold pushes back as far as the doorjamb will allow. Tracy grips harder and I knock her hand away. '*Answer me*, Harold. Chinatown. When was the last time you were there? The last time.' I step into him. 'You been there this week, right? After you broke into my house, *you fucking asshole*.'

Harold flinches and crabs backwards until the wall stops him. '*ANSWER ME*.'

My gun's in his face. I want to kill Harold, blow his fucking

216

face all over the oak planks and shadows, then he can go to Chinatown with me. Every fucking Friday. We'll face twenty-three years of hell together.

'Patti!' Tracy's yelling my name. 'Patti!'

'Ready, Harold?'

'They don't know! Patti, they don't know!'

SATURDAY

Chapter 15

SATURDAY, DAY 6: 1:00 A.M.

We're past the witching hour. I'm naked under a borrowed bathrobe, and exhausted. The hair dryer trembling in my hand is Tracy's.

She led me here, skirting the lake and worsening weather to her town house in Lincoln Park, testimony to Tracy's nerve after she met the real me in Calumet City. I left both men alive but it was an accident not a decision . . . John's mother is not okay.

Tracy's ten-speed Style Pro requires Stella's beauty school education, so I give up. Driving here I had the same success reaching the Arizona PI, Delmont Chukut. My hand's bruised from smashing the phone into the dash.

The three calls produced nothing but voice mail. The last two were easier than the first; I wasn't prepared to hear Roland's voice next to my ear again and luckily didn't have to. The voice mail recording wasn't Roland, so now it's possible that Roland isn't the PI; not likely, but possible. And if Roland isn't masquerading as Delmont Chukut, then this PI is a stupid man with very serious problems if he's unarmed when I find him. I haven't yet figured out how to do that, but will shortly.

Tracy's testing the space between us. 'I called Julie while you were in the shower,' seeing which Patti Black is in her house. 'Julie thinks BASH will be postponed till tomorrow.'

Lightning cracks. Rain sheets against the windows behind Tracy. Her windows are separated by a fireplace mantle lined with rugby trophies. Tracy's talking about rugby. That means today is Saturday and *tomorrow* is Sunday – *son of a bitch* – Ms. Meery at Le Bassinet knew it was Friday when I was there. She also knew they'd be closed until Monday, two facts I missed while living on no sleep and less food. Plenty of time to get me arrested before I hurt any of her coworkers. I lurch toward the door and stumble.

Tracy yells, 'Hey.'

The knob won't turn; the lock won't work.

'You'll need a hat. Pants, you know, shoes and stuff.'

I see bare feet beneath my two hands struggling with the knob. The weight of my options – all the mistakes and lies and— My knees go weak. Suddenly I'm sitting, tears on my cheeks, the rage and fear defeated into exhausted mush. I lean into the door, stare at nothing, and one shoulder rolls slow to the floor. The doormat feels good. I curl up as small as I can, like I used to after the basement, and disappear.

SATURDAY, DAY 6: 9:00 A.M.

Thunder blows me and a blanket off the floor. I'm standing before I know how and wobble into a stairway post. Murky daylight surrounds a two-story fireplace, its monumental windows streaked with rain. Tracy's on the rug, papers fanned in stacks. She has a coffee cup near her mouth and a startled expression. 'Hi?'

I blink until I'm stable. *'Jesus.'*

Tracy stares, does the hair move I hate and guys love, smiles, and asks if I want coffee.

'What time is it?'

She rolls her wrist. '9:15.'

'In the morning?'

Her face adds apprehension I remember from last night. My phone's on the sofa. I grab it and I punch–dial Le Bassinet, don't know the number, and switch to 411. 'C'mon. C'mon.' They have the number. I dial again. It's a recording – *closed, reopening Monday at 9:00 a.m.*

'Goddammit!' I cock to slam the phone and . . . there's another way to save John: *Marjorie Elliot*. That was the codirector's name, the one with the keys . . . A new operator can't find Marjorie Elliot in the city or in the suburbs. I tell her, 'Try a Mrs. Trousdale. How many Trousdales in Evanston?'

'None.'

'How about anywhere in the suburbs?'

Pause . . . then: 'Possibly eighty–five, ninety.' Another pause, and she adds: 'More than that in the city.'

Too many. Too many. 'Any unlisted?'

'No. I'm sorry.'

I growl 'Thanks' through bit teeth and click off.

My head starts to throb. The tops of my feet don't offer a solution, nor does the ceiling. I have to find one of these women – then it will be a kidnap and death threat. Ten years minimum if no one gets hurt.

Tracy eyes me, then returns to a ring of papers surrounding her on the floor. 'Try a coffee, we'll figure it out. I have ideas.'

'Get me on the Internet.'

Tracy points left without comment, toward a hutch with a flat-screen monitor and a backwards chair. I google 'Le Bassinet Trousdale Elliot Evanston.' Fifteen minutes of reading about them and their mission produces nothing on where they live. My face is hot. I need a break, help, something.

'Coffee in the kitchen. Bagels too.'

Fuck bagels, I want to smash her fucking keyboard. And the monitor. My nails dig into the robe. Tracy isn't paying attention or criticizing, which is real good 'cause ... Then her on the floor with the papers makes a picture – she's been up all night while I slept, poring over the Juvenile file and her files, and whatever other resources she has to help me. My fists ease open and for the very first time this century, or last, I'm forced to admit that Miss All-Everything may have a redeeming quality.

Her kitchen changes that. It has two redeeming qualities, both are goldfish. And her kitchen smells like a bakery ... strange what calms you down, and I watch the goldfish until I'm someone I know. The coffeemaker by the Star Trek oven is one of those incomprehensible models that most restaurants can't afford. New frustration starts to boil, but there's coffee left and I pour it into a mug stamped BITCH in blood-red capital letters. I need milk; her refrigerator has three stainless-steel doors, the first one's a freezer that contains only ice and three bottles of Grey Goose vodka. There's very little food behind doors two and three, but there is milk.

Her onion bagels are Northside fresh, still warm, and I eat two, looking around without really seeing past my own poison and the two happy goldfish. Above the fridge are photos, like the ones on my mirror. I'm in hers too, as is Julie, and several men who could be movie stars. They must be from foreign

224

countries or I'd know their names. In here I don't seem to hate her as much. Must be the goldfish. Or maybe a kitchen makes you human. I resist the urge to check her laundry to prove it.

The stove has chef-size salt and pepper shakers, pepper is Mike Tyson; salt is . . . I have to pick it up to read: my old friend Carl Sandburg. To the stove's left a book page is framed on the brick wall. The frame is nicked and scratched, either well traveled or hated by the cleaning lady.

'Patti?' Tracy's voice from the living room. 'Bring the coffee with you.'

On closer inspection the page is from Hamlet. I know this only because it says so at the bottom. Part of the first line reads, 'This above all, to thine own self be true . . .'

I wonder how well that worked for Mr. Hamlet and grab the coffee.

While I pour coffee into Tracy's cup, I eye my foster–home history on the floor. Tracy says, 'I've called the PI in Arizona every two hours. No answer. Nobody home at Arizona's state and city offices either, probably closed till Monday. I called a reporter I know on the *Phoenix Sun*. He's running Mr. Delmont Chukut, private eye.'

Thunder hammers Tracy's town house. We both balance our coffee to keep it off the papers and the rug. I scan the room instead of the papers; a grown–up lives here. On the low table to my right is a copy of her one and only book, a best seller that bought this place, *A Killing Condition*, nonfiction about a forty-year series of ritual homicides that had the city scared inside-out five years ago.

'Nice place.'

Tracy shows me a page from the file stacks. 'There were four of you in the foster home?'

Four. Counting Little Gwen. Her face turns me to the wall. Roland Ganz has her too; she and her son are in as bad a situation as imagination will allow. And my John is next. A hand rushes to my mouth to keep it shut; my abs flex tight and so do my eyes. When they open, Tracy's prepping for another meltdown. I land my bare feet right next to her and grab at a stack. 'What's in that file about John?'

'Wait!' She swats at my arm. 'Don't mix 'em up.'

'What's in here?'

'Easy. Easy . . . easy.' She locates a page she's kept separate and hands it up to me. John's birth certificate kicks me in the stomach. It's a copy from the South Holland hospital I ran to; the hospital where I hid from Roland and contacted Le Bassinet. I frantically search for a mention of Le Bassinet. Not here; I check again and exhale when I find nothing. This is a match to the copy I have at home.

Panic jolt. But if John's birth certificate is in *this* file – the Juvenile file – then at the very least Roland finally knows the hospital where I gave birth . . . and—

Heartbeats. Heartbeats. So what?

I stare at the birth certificate, try to see Roland connecting the dots. If Harold and DeLay had reported the entire file, then Roland and/or the PI in Arizona – *assuming* they aren't the same person – would've already been to the South Holland hospital; they would've snuck or bribed into the hospital's files, found papers that *do* mention Le Bassinet, then gone to Evanston. Gulp. Le Bassinet would've been a bloodbath.

And as of late last Friday when I was there, it wasn't.

Another exhale. *But why not?*

Because the dots won't connect, that's why. Harold and DeLay might not have reported the entire file to Arizona PI Delmont Chukut – hoping to extract more money. Or they *have* reported the entire file, but Chukut hasn't made the bridge from hospital to adoption agency. My shoulders relax. For three seconds.

Or what if Chukut *does* know about Le Bassinet?

But no one's been to Le Bassinet . . . so if Chukut knows, then *he* didn't tell *his* client, Roland Ganz, 'cause Roland would've marched into Le Bassinet with a chainsaw. Delmont Chukut could be running a game, too, just like Harold Tyree and DeLay, blackmail or info ransom, *Chukut's* target would be upstream to the top direct to Roland Ganz.

Tracy says, 'Earth to Patti.'

Lots of possibilities. Two levels of crooked operators in the same chain; happens all the time in the sewer. I check a number-less clock embedded in Tracy's wall. Less than forty-eight hours until Le Bassinet opens. Assuming no one blows the vault, John will be safe until then. *Swallow*, I think. But Gwen and her boy won't; they'll have Roland's full focus . . . in some overheated basement. Poison rushes up my throat and I run to a door that just happens to be the bathroom.

The storm hasn't slowed and when I return, Tracy hasn't moved. Being a rugby girl and a reporter, she's seen strange behavior, some of it no doubt in her own house. I apologize and she chuckles to make us both comfortable. She actually looks sympathetic and not the fake brand I see on her face whenever she wants something. Although I know she wants something. We made a deal – my son's life for mine.

'Ready to talk?'

'Got a bucket?'

'We'll start slow.' She shuffles papers. 'Danny del Pasco left and you stayed . . . four years more?'

I sit on the floor across from her. 'Four years, ten months. My parents died in '79; I ran in early '84.'

'Richard Rhodes . . . he was eight or nine, you're—'

We're two questions into this and I want her to shut up. 'I was twelve when I went in, sixteen when I ran.'

'The other girl, Gwen . . . Smith?'

I don't answer.

'The one who called you.'

I know who she is. 'Gwen didn't know her last name. She came just before I ran the second time . . . from the hospital . . . after the baby.'

Tracy looks up at me and my tone. 'This says she was eight when she arrived in '84. Richard Rhodes would've been what, twelve or thirteen?'

I don't care and don't answer.

Tracy says, 'Hey. We're partners, remember? No different than your TAC unit.' Auburn eyebrows float punctuation. 'I'm sticking my damn neck out – physically and legally – to help find your son.' Pause. 'Before Roland Ganz does. In return, you answer the questions as agreed.'

We share a short, violent silence interrupted by Tracy's cell phone.

She flips, frowns at the screen and says it's her assistant, finally returning a middle-of-the-night call on her day off. Tracy tells the assistant it's no longer her day off, haul ass downtown and run Arizona PI Delmont Chukut's name,

PI number, phone number, his any and everything.

Tracy closes her phone and stares at me again. I'm guessing her assistant will use whatever newspapers use to chase stories, resources that are light-years better than what I currently have. Even without the newspaper Tracy has resources most spies and collection agencies would kill for. 'Harold Tyree and Caseworker DeLay were freelancing, weren't they?'

That's a surprise. Tracy's reading me better than I'd have thought possible; that and she's likely suspicious of all living things. Tracy shows me the phone she just used. 'And you're telling me, right? Because we're partners.'

I shrug. 'Find something your client wants, tell him half, ask for more money. Always follow the money.'

She glances at the papers in her hand, then back to me. '*If* PI Delmont Chukut is actually Roland in disguise, then Roland/Chukut hires Harold Tyree and Caseworker DeLay to find you and your son in Chicago; Roland/Chukut also hires the Gilbert Court arsonists to clean up his past because . . .' Her eyes go distant, then sharp again. 'Because Roland's stepping back into the light after being missing for eighteen years.' She nods. 'But Tyree and DeLay in Calumet City decide that ransoming the information is more profitable and—'

'Nah.' She's correct, but my instant reaction is defense, hide from the light. 'Why would Roland publicly murder Richard Rhodes if he's cleaning up his past?'

Tracy bites her lower lip, a move I've seen make young men cover their pants. 'Leaving a State's Attorney's body by the mayor's lawn is not "clean–up." Maybe the obvious was right: Richard Rhodes is part of the casino license and the election. The timing with Annabelle's body is just a coincidence.'

I check the clock, wishing it had numbers, wishing it would move faster or stop altogether, then change my mind about defense. Maybe Miss All–Everything will hit an angle I haven't thought of. 'No, you're right. Roland's cleaning up his past; he's got something at stake. And if he doesn't have something at stake, then something's chasing him too.'

Tracy brightens. 'Then let's go with that.' She likes child sex and murder better than casinos and elections. Her enthusiasm falters and she looks at her papers. 'But why clean up now?' She shuts her eyes and adds her facts out loud. 'The mayor's wife sold the building to a limited partnership owned by Roland Ganz, right? And in this same building is buried Annabelle Ganz.'

'Roland Ganz also owned that building? *Bullshit*.'

Tracy smiles and lets her eyelashes filter the praise. 'We ran his and Annabelle's tax returns. Roland had K-1s from three limited partnerships, all with corporate general partners. One of those LPs owned Gilbert Court from 1976 to 1983, then transferred it to a blind trust run by LaSalle Bank downtown.'

'For real? He owned it?'

Tracy points to a stack of papers. 'Hard to figure him investing in the ghetto, though. Or having the money.'

Roland worked with numbers and adding machines, but I have no idea how he would've gotten the money. I know even less about tax dodges, other than they were popular in the '80s with everyone from cops to cocktail waitresses.

'When I came on in '88 that neighborhood was mixed, teetering. Still mostly white and not that poor yet. It had storefronts and streetlights and—'

Tracy riffles the file again. 'Roland was an accountant, right? Hospitals. He disappears in 1987, and let's guess that the Gilbert

230

Court building is where he went. Gilbert Court's only ten miles from Calumet City, but it's ten miles into a metropolis of three million, all he'd need in civilized geography.'

I finish her thought like we're married. 'And if he's part of Annabelle's murder in '93, then he's living there on Gilbert Court for six years while I was working the district.'

'*Possibly* living there. Using the place at least. But what's he do all day?'

I picture Roland in my district doing something all day. My stomach tries to roll but the muscles stop it. I see him, like I saw him at the home sometimes, bent over his desk, adding machine tape curled on the floor . . . 'Storefront accountant. There were two on Halsted by the Jewel, Jackson Hewitt Tax Service and Flannigan's.'

Tracy points. 'Hand me the phone book.'

'Those places are toast at least ten years, probably longer.'

Tracy circles a date in the papers. 'When did Superintendent Smith move out of the building?'

I balk. We're not discussing Chief Jesse as part of this case.

Tracy notices. 'You want to find your son, right? Then we have to look everywhere we have to look.'

We stare at each other again, not unlike how we do on the field. I relent, because it's my son; I'm choosing John over a fatherly friend and mentor who's been nothing but good to me.

'He said in the '70s.'

Tracy scribbles notes with a double underline. I can't read upside down and ask. 'What?'

'When were you born?'

'December 1967.'

'And your son was born in . . . 1983?'

231

'October.'

'*Damn*.' She frowns and tosses her pencil. 'It's in here, and it's there on Gilbert Court, *I know it*. We're wearing blinders.'

Thunder tumbles overhead, but less threatening than an hour ago. The windows are still opaque with water. I see it as camouflage, not fall tornadoes, and stand up. 'C'mon. We'll go down there, run the neighborhood for his footprints.'

Tracy fish-eyes her windows, then me, then looks at the papers.

Waiting on the weather isn't an option for me. 'Could be some of my folks in 6 remember something. You can think while I drive.'

'Ah . . .' Tracy does not look excited. 'From what I read and hear, the local citizens aren't too happy with you.'

I avoid the know-it-all, Northside liberal bullshit stamped in her face, then take the stairs two at a time toward my clothes. This partnership may not be the best idea I've had.

Upstairs, I call Mercy Hospital while Tracy searches for dry clothes that fit me. According to a nurse Chief Jesse remains critical. She isn't encouraging or a fountain of detail, but he's alive. And FBI or not, I'm going by today.

'Going by' will be trouble, like Sonny said, now that the First Deputy Superintendent, James Colin Braith, is the acting boss. He lacks Chief Jesse's affection for me, or TAC officers in general, often commenting that we are not now, and never have been, his idea of the police. He won't know about my Intelligence Unit mission for Chief Jesse and the reports I haven't filed, but as soon as the first deputy's head clears he'll be calling. I won't have answers, but that won't stop him from calling.

SATURDAY, DAY 6: NOON

Tracy and I don't say much on the way uptown. We take my car, me in a pair of Tracy's Levi's, a New Zealand All Blacks sweatshirt, and a rain jacket that could make my house payment but doesn't hide my Smith. From Lincoln Park to the ghetto without traffic the drive takes twenty minutes. Just twenty minutes, but once here, everything changes, the air, the rhythm, your heart rate – even mine after seventeen years.

Halsted's full of paper and cardboard debris. The rain quits when we park, the chill doesn't. People wander out, tentative on God's plans, but out and looking. It's weekend lunchtime in shit city and we're just below Eighty-second Street – two white girls on foot who aren't whoring for a street crew. We don't stand out any more than a pile of hundred-dollar bills. Tracy's nervous and should be, moving between the hooded jackets, silent, hard eyes and an occasional 'Hey, Patti; what up, Pep.'

She asks about 'Pep.'

I explain that 'Pepper' is my street name – Angie Dickinson was Pepper in a '70s cop show. A Blackstone Ranger tagged me with it a decade ago; I'm the only cop in 6 with a street name other than Denny Banahan's 'Zorro.' Some of the bosses didn't see Pepper as funny; within a month the street name bought me my first IAD appointment.

Two Gangster Disciples eye us from the east side of Halsted. Tracy hasn't left my side since the first GD brushed her much harder than acceptable. When he recognized me he quit, but showed no fear and gave no ground. He and I both know I'm out of line; he doesn't know why, or if I'm doing it on purpose –

233

trolling for felons – he just knows I'm alone right this instant. Alone gives him an edge if he wants it.

Tracy semi-whispers, 'Did you see his eyes?' She waits until he's ten feet behind us, checks him over her shoulder, adding, 'This could get old after a day or two.'

Just ahead of us the GD's nine partners are blocking her section of sidewalk. I jerk her to my other side and hard-eye the men. Weakness down here is considered an invitation. Their stance is a street challenge. Since you can't run or call the milk-man, there's only one speed; it becomes instinct, not unlike theirs, and I square up already yelling:

'Is this fuck with Pepper day? Did I miss the flyer?'

Five of the nine street mumble to save their dicks. One I don't know (do I?) looks like he might take it further. I *do not* want this, but his hand's moving to his back. We've gone from street challenge to full threat. How it often happens. Your mind's on something else, you're not ghetto ready, and then you or your partner is dead. I draw, aim, and a GD ducks quick to his left.

'*Back the fuck up, Jim.* We ain't gonna wrestle.'

'Yeah. Yeah. Bitch shot Robert and Carlos.'

Three down the line I hear, 'Gone shoot us too, ain't you? Pep like to pop.'

The one eyeing me keeps doing it. Still can't see his hand. Any one of his nine partners can shoot me and I'd never see the gun. Ten against one. 'Put your *motherfucking* hands on the wall. *NOW.*'

He does. I street-glare the others, then toss my cuffs to the one on his left. 'Cuff him. Tight.'

'Aw, bitch, I ain't gotta—'

'Wanna go too? *Cuff the motherfucker.*'

234

He does. I shove the prisoner into the wall, lean a hand into the middle of his back, and aim my Smith at his partners. They move ten feet. *'Get the fuck back.'* They slow-stroll forty more. Nothing about this is good. I whisper to Tracy, 'Call 911, get us the cavalry.' My prisoner twists when he hears we're alone, not doing decoy. I lurch back so he can't head butt me.

'Face the motherfucking wall.'

He checks his homeys, then my Smith now in his face and me behind it. I sidestep to block him from one exit. Something's wrong here. He's ready to charge or bolt. Now he looks familiar.

'Face the fucking wall.'

Tracy steps into my vision, trying to find a place to stand that's less threatening than all the places there are to stand. Her phone's out and by her face. My prisoner eyes her and I twist him back, slammed face-first into the wall. 'Do-Not-Move.' I jam the Smith into the back of his neck. 'It's cocked. Move and you die.'

He doesn't and I start to pat him. I don't want to; I want to watch his partners. God smiles from the southbound lane of Halsted, a blue-and-white stops fast. I finish patting by the time the driver is out. It's one of Kit Carson's giant 'bodyguards,' pistol drawn. He eyes the nine GDs forty feet away, then smiles at me. 'As I live and breathe, the hardest–working cop in show business returns. How you doin', P?'

'Got this *bad* motherfucker here.' I jerk my GD around; he has no ID, but smells like cordite. Kit's bodyguard stops smiling. He faces the other GDs so they can see his weapon, then leans into the prisoner. 'You from Englewood, asshole? How come you over here?'

The prisoner mumbles and checks his homeys again.

Kit's bodyguard tells his collar mike to send backup, then tells me: 'That there is possibly Wardell Scurr. There's a rumor Wardell's in 6 looking for someone in par-tic-u-lar.'

Wardell doesn't blink or seem to know who he's looking for, if anyone. His partners start disappearing quickly. *Not good.* I scan the street for a gunship drive-by.

'Lucky for you, P, this felon's big news.' Kit's bodyguard threads one hand through Wardell's cuffs and changes the subject, sort of. 'Lieutenant Carson says you in deep shit, Officer.'

'Yeah, well, he'd say that.'

Two marked cars squeal to a stop and a Crown Vic loops them both. A uniform sergeant bails, hard-eyeing Tracy as he passes, passes me without speaking, and stops only when his chest hits Wardell's.

'You looking for me, nigger?' The sergeant is about to go all-the-way off. I've seen this before, usually after funerals. '*Me?*'

Wardell and the sergeant are the same size and Wardell glares back at him, eyeball to eyeball.

'Uncuff him. Me and Wardell the motherfucking nigger assassin gonna throw down.' The sergeant shoves Wardell hard into the wall. 'Give him a gun. *Hey,*' the sergeant yells at the other GDs, 'one you nigger pimps give him a gun. I'm gonna kill your bitch right here.'

I step between them and the sergeant shoves me four feet. I come back low and up between them again. '*Sarge, Sarge,* hey man, c'mon.' He grabs me again and I grab two handfuls of his shirt so he can't throw me. 'Please. Sarge. Chill, c'mon.'

'Wardell, you pimp motherfucker.' The sergeant's spit splatters my forehead. 'You dying, nigger. Know that. To–DAY is your fucking day.'

236

Squad cars squeal-stop all over Halsted; two TAC cars join them. Uniforms climb all over their sergeant, pulling him back and me with them. I catch a glimpse of Tracy trying to be a reporter and not die. The sergeant lets go. I fall. Sonny Barrett in a new snap-brim cap and Cisco's cologne grabs me. He's clean shaven, strong enough to hold my 130 pounds one-handed, and says, 'Remember this banger? From Art's?'

That's it. I see Wardell in the booth, plain as day, and turning toward me.

Sonny pulls me to his side, staring bullets at Wardell. 'They shot Bristol.' Bristol is the sergeant's younger brother, a rookie patrolman in 7. 'Wardell killed him four hours ago.'

Chapter 16

SATURDAY, DAY 6: 1:00 P.M.

The arrest is over but Halsted Street still vibrates, uneasy with the cease-fire.

Tracy's on her cell phone; she's uneasy too. Sonny Barrett and I share his dented fender, both facing the street sans our usual banter. Cars pass and the people stare. Three blocks south the pickets are shouting in front of 6. After a long silence Sonny spits in Tracy's general direction and says it again, because I just blinked the first time.

'Wardell Scurr is Robert's cousin, the GD we smoked on Monday.'

I heard Sonny the first time. I'm thinking about Bristol's wife and his parents, his kids if he had any; I'm thinking about the circle that never stops – about Ruth Ann on her porch when she hears her family has killed a cop, thinking about how it always seems to come down to them and us. I'm thinking that the way this is going, it's gonna be a bad week to be white, black, or blue in this city.

'GDs had both funerals yesterday. Big turnout over at Oakwoods. Fucking Alderman Gibbons was there, you believe that? For fucking street gangsters. Gave a sermon; you can guess who was the devil.'

I look up at a very tired, angry man, frustrated to his limits with problems he can't solve but trying to hide it. I haven't thought of him this way before – the trying-to-hide-it part – and once again find that strange. The snap-brim cap, shave, and cologne are stranger still.

'What'd he say?'

'TV shit. How it's the mayor's fault.' He pauses and stares at Tracy's presence in the ghetto, then turns, back to me. 'Chief Jesse may have been onto something, there.'

Tracy begins to walk our way and I wave her off.

Sonny notices and hits me with a list: '*A,* you don't work down here anymore and half the suits in this district are trying to put you in prison; *B,* you got the Pink Panther with you; *C,* you do a street stop on a cop killer with no backup. So other than losing your fucking mind, what's new?'

I debate two strange, conflicting feelings and decide to go with the safest one. 'I need you to know something, okay?'

Sonny checks my jeans and sweatshirt, then my face. It's what he usually does while he waits for a confession or LT orders he thinks are stupid.

'I'm, ah, not as good as you maybe thought and I'm not as bad as you're gonna think.'

Sonny shakes his head and loses the snap-brim cap into his hands; an affectation he hasn't mastered yet. 'Chicks love riddles, don't they.'

It's an honest statement, and coming from him it could be a compliment. His usual opinions on women are far less flattering. The comment, new cap, and cologne still make me wonder, but I don't ask. I want to, not sure why, but I want to.

'Any calls from Idaho Joe?'

'Nah.' Sonny looks at a Chevy looking at us. 'Gotta figure that means your bad guys already know what they need to know.' When he looks back he makes sure I get it – that my ass is tight in their sights, whoever they are.

'Anything out on me from Evanston?'

Sonny exhales through his teeth. 'What the fuck did you do in Evanston?'

'Went by . . . a place . . . that knows about me. And my son.' Deep breath. 'An adoption agency that might know how to find him. We had an argument; maybe the agency called the cops.' I grimace and glance at Halsted returning to ghetto normal. 'Actually, they did call the cops. Know my name too.'

'Nice. Anybody . . . injured?'

Headshake. 'If paper was coming, you'd already have it.'

Sonny spits. 'Don't be so sure. Like I said yesterday, everybody you know is radioactive. No tellin' what they ain't telling me, us, the crew.'

Tracy comes to us without being invited, hand extended and hair moving. 'Hi, Tracy Moens.'

'Sonny Barrett.' His baritone raises her eyebrows and she checks her hand when she gets it back. His star says sergeant and she reads it, then his size, then his face.

'You're Patti's boss?'

'Was.'

'I'd like to ask a few questions about today, so if you don't—'

'I do mind.' Sonny pushes off the fender, turns his back on the best-looking woman ever to speak to him, and says to me, 'Remember, P, Kit Carson's sleeping in your locker.' He pauses,

240

checks Tracy behind him, and says, 'Too much coincidence – us running Farrakhan and Gibbons on the QT, then this. I'm bettin' Wardell Scurr wasn't in 6 for Bristol's brother. I'm bettin' he was here for you, like he was in Art's for you.'

'Why me? Shit, I didn't shoot his people.'

'Your warrant. You put it together; you're the one on the six o'clock news.'

'Aw, man . . .'

'Something's following you, P.' Sonny stares like he's trying to read me. 'It's mixed up, fucked up, and gettin' closer. You need to tell me what it is. Now.'

'I told you what I can.'

Sonny's eyes narrow while he waits. His face and neck add red. 'You about to piss me off, lady, one of the few fucking friends you still got.'

I stare until he turns on his heel. Tracy and I watch him leave, then it's just me and her. And Halsted Street. And the ghetto. She tries for butch that's real on the rugby pitch but not here. 'Wouldn't say he's cute, but there is that *je ne sais quoi*. You and him . . . ?'

My eyes roll.

'I called in a story on the arrest. They said the patrolman, Bristol . . .'

'Posner. Bristol Posner was a person.'

'. . . Posner was shot five times at a stoplight. Never saw it coming. I'd like to get whatever personal—'

'*He was a fucking person, Tracy.* A fucking human being, not a story. I knew him. Watched him buy coffee for ragmen and homeless crack whores. A person, okay?'

My hands are trembling; my tolerance for this shit has

241

dissolved in the last six days. I am, and I'm quite certain of this, losing my memory of the old me, the girl who almost was. Reflected in Tracy's face I see the new me, the deranged, driven, win-this-at-all-costs me.

Tracy says, 'Look, Patti, I—'

'We're down here to run Roland's footprints. *Do not* fuck with those cops for bracing Wardell Scurr. Cut them one fucking break, okay? They, you, me, and these people,' my hand sweeps at the street, 'don't need more gasoline right now.'

Tracy licks ghetto air off her lips, thinks about it, and either because she does the right thing or doesn't want to lose the thread to her Pulitzer, calls the *Herald* and kills the story. She watches me trying to decompress from confrontation to ... something less, no idea how close she came to being left here as food, and says, 'You owe me.'

I turn back toward the storefronts and questions that need to be asked about Roland Ganz and mumble, 'Get in line, honey.'

Tracy's showing the wear of no sleep and constant threat. I'm wrapping tighter and tighter. By 3:30, we've put the same description to everyone on two blocks either side of the old tax service offices: 'Middle-aged white male; a tax man named Roland with a wife, Annabelle, and a blond daughter, Gwen. The daughter would've been eleven when she moved here and sixteen or so when she left.'

We ask thirty people in and out of the storefronts. When we get an answer, it's the same: 'Nope.' I can keep asking and hearing 'Nope,' or hole up, grit my teeth, and wait for Tracy's contacts to turn up Delmont Chukut. And hope it's before Le

Bassinet opens. But I can't 'hole up,' I have to do something . . . I'll go by Chief Jesse's hospital—

A block farther south and across the street two men and five women exit a storefront. All wear white shirts and dark pants. The last man out is the African preacher from Ruth Ann's steps. He hesitates with his flock, then turns and they all walk the other way. The storefront, not him, hooks me . . . I drive this block every other day, but suddenly we're back seventeen years ago when I first came on. Back then that storefront was an evangelical mission and clinic I used to avoid. The doors reminded me of the Salvation Mission, and those memories weren't what I was looking to remember.

Now the storefront houses the Lazarus Temple. The temple has an inch-thick steeple cut out of plywood that's been repainted every time another denomination of one starts a new church. Out front there's a lawn table with one empty chair and paper flyers about right-and-wrong and Africa. I've arrested at least ten felons on this block but never been inside.

We pass the lawn table and step inside. The low ceiling is white, as are the walls and all the benches. A center aisle separates the benches into two groups aligned in perfect rows. An older woman sweeps a floor that's already hospital clean. She stands out like she's on fire, wearing a long African–print robe that stops above narrow ankles and shows her gym shoes. Her head is wrapped up high and colorful like the Jamaican women on the Travel Channel. She watches me approach and I see recognition in her eyes before I can ask about Roland and family.

'My sister, she lives by them boys you kilt. Woulda burned up too and that's a fact.'

'She's okay, your sister?'

'She fine. She fine. Old woman can't quit smellin' that gas-o-line.'

I smile and ask about Roland and his family. She sweeps so she doesn't have to answer, then raises her chin slowly above the broom's handle, eyes narrowed down a nose broken more than once.

'Somethin' bad wrong with that mother. A God-fearing woman, but . . . Finding her in that wall, *Jesus, Mary, and Joseph*,' her right hand makes the sign of the cross, 'scare my sister *right* back to church.'

'You *knew* Annabelle Ganz?'

A very small, very stern nod and a glance at Tracy sitting on the nearest bench talking to her cell phone. 'But their names wasn't Ganz. Husband was the church and clinic's bookkeeper, right here in this room. Never said nothin' bad to me, but that wife . . .' The woman shifts the broom and sweeps farther into the aisle, making Tracy scoot. 'And the girl,' her broom stops and she turns back to me, 'prettiest little white girl you ever see. Played with her every day, taught her to sing, I did. Lord, Lord,' the woman's smiling now, teeth no better than gray against her faded skin, 'stood her right there, pretending she was a preachin'. Child was a ray a light.'

Tracy perks up and starts to stand, waving her phone at me; I gesture for her to wait.

The old woman speaks to the worn linoleum she cleans every day. 'Then, *poof*, that ray a light was gone. Off to Idaho or Utah somewheres.'

'Idaho or Utah?' *Idaho* can't be a coincidence.

'Don't recall. Mormons, I think. Utah. My little white girl and her daddy . . . had to be with her daddy 'cause her mama still here. In the basement.' She raises both wisps of eyebrow and makes the sign of the cross again. 'Thought they had the gift, was what it was.'

'The gift?'

'Preachin'.'

I flash on Roland and our PTL Club ... sessions. My knees weaken but hold, I'm getting better at reliving hell. The old woman searches my face like I'm not doing as well as I think.

'Ever hear back from them? Anywhere in Idaho or Utah?'

Slow headshake. 'Not a word, an' that little girl was like mine.'

Tracy, still on her phone, walks away to finish.

'Fine-lookin' red-haired woman. She the PO-lice?'

I fake a smile. 'A friend, and thanks for your help.'

'Fine-lookin' woman.' She nods to her comment, then points the broom handle at me. 'You don't let them hoodlums shut you down, no how. We know you right. Gots to have heart to be right. You keep on goin', girl.'

It's the nicest thing anyone's said to me in forty-eight hours. I kiss her cheek and she doesn't flinch.

Outside, it's different. The war's still on, and the folks passing by hold much harsher opinions of me. Mormons? Years ago and only a maybe – it's a long shot to nowhere. I check my watch, gotta do something – Tracy steps closer but not close, she's pushing her hair back and the phone into her pocket. Her back's to the street, something that's probably acceptable north of the river. 'That was my assistant. The Arizona PI is real.'

Bingo. I have to stop my hands from grabbing at her.

'We're running him now and something called the "Pentecostal Ranch."'

'What else?' I grab her. *That's it?*

She dodges my hands and backs away, suddenly edgy as hell. 'Yeah, well ... we just got it. Give me an hour or two at the office, my assistant and I can unpack him. Maybe you could have CPD run him too.'

Pause while I try to decipher her tone. 'Maybe.'

'Good. Good. Then let's go. Drop me by a cab. I'll call you.'

All of a sudden we're divorced.

And she's keeping space between her and me that ten minutes ago she didn't think she needed.

Chapter 17

SATURDAY, DAY 6: 5:00 P.M.

In the car Tracy repeated that she'd need two hours to run the Pentecostal Ranch and Delmont Chukut, then made a series of calls that kept her face to the window and her mouth from talking to me. I dropped her at the Herald Building in the Loop and watched her disappear behind twenty of her fellow workers calling it a day, and I wondered.

Wonder and wait. Bullshit, I need to *do something*. I butch up and call Sonny, stammering like I'd been caught shoplifting, asking his voice mail to run Delmont Chukut.

What is happening to me?

My car doesn't answer and drives me to Chief Jesse's hospital.

From Twenty-sixth Street, Mercy Hospital is a series of bigwindowed cubes stacked all over each other and busy. It dominates a three- and four-story brick neighborhood, parts of which have been there since the Chicago fire. The late afternoon wind is off the lake and smells cold, either more rain or winter's coming early.

Walking a full parking lot I see uniforms outside who don't know me and a reporter who does. Him, I beat to the elevator, take it two floors higher than ICU with a silent Hispanic family and their rosaries, then the stairs back down. A nurse who doesn't squint under the bright lights points me toward ICU if I can follow the signs. My route through the maze is three turns and two sets of double doors. The closer I get to ICU, the less activity that overflows into the shiny linoleum hallway. People are crying in the rooms I pass.

The cluster of cops in ICU's waiting room is 80 percent street and 20 percent rank, about as high a compliment as could be paid to any major–city superintendent. He should live just to hear this. That, and I can't imagine my world without him.

Really? Well, the new you better get used to that. Now I wish I hadn't come, hadn't been so selfish. I walk past the waiting room's opening and look away. Chief Jesse doesn't need soon-to-be killers as friends. *Soon-to-be?* That's a lie, isn't it, if you count Roland's buddy back in Calumet City? And pretty much God, the FBI, and the State's Attorney will.

Add Roland fucking Ganz to the charges. Murder One if I can find him before he finds me and John. And then you'll have become all the things you hate. Full circle. You can't go home again, because you never leave. I bump a nurse who has to pirouette to stay standing. 'Sorry.' My hands help at her shoulders. 'Sorry.'

She regains her balance and says, 'Are you all right . . . miss?'

'Yeah, ah . . . fine. Fine.'

She passes and I exhale and see the double door to ICU. 'DO NOT ENTER' is most of the message. I pretend I can't read, pull my star out around my neck, wedge one of the doors open in the wrong direction, and slide through.

Inside, ICU at its core is a nurse–doctor station surrounded by rooms with darkened picture windows. Behind each one is a life-and-death drama running right at the edge. The visiting rules are no more than two family members at a time, and only when the ICU docs or nurses say okay. They are the Special Forces of the hospital, so even though the death rate in here is second only to the Emergency Room, it's where you want to be.

I make twenty feet before I'm stopped. She's mid-thirties, pretty, but serious. 'Excuse me. You're here to see the superintendent?'

It sounds as if he's no longer here and that stops me. But the waiting room is full. If he were d . . . they wouldn't be . . . 'Yeah. The superintendent.' I can't stop the grimace, waiting for the punch to land.

She adjusts slightly. 'He's stable. Still critical but stable.' Her palm presses against my shoulder. 'You'll have to wait outside.'

'Can I see him, just for a sec?'

'No. Please. Wait outside with the others.' She presses harder, polite, but harder.

A youngish black doctor is coming at us from behind her. He has that look they get on TV when the star's life is in the balance and they're losing. At and over her shoulder he says, 'You're Patti Black, aren't you?'

'I am.'

'C'mon.' He reaches past the nurse, thanks her, and pulls me even with him as we walk. He's silent, looking into the rooms we pass, each with monitors of red pin lights and green heart beats – *Star Trek* with consequences. At the fifth room we stop and there he is, Chief Jesse, in the dark, alone, with all the wires and tubes and monitors and—

'He's in a coma, has been. The damage was survivable, but he

249

hasn't responded well. If he wants to live, he might. Sometimes they can't make up their minds.'

I'm staring at the doctor, who's staring at Chief Jesse. I'm crying; the glass between Chief Jesse and me is like at the morgue when the family member comes to do the ID. The doctor takes my arm and me into the room and puts my hand on Chief Jesse's. The warmth is like . . . like flowers and I'm smiling, a schoolgirl who doesn't know better. I grab his hand with both of mine and hold it to my face, then lace my fingers between his and beg God for one more favor. Just one more.

'He asked for you.'

The words shoot up my arms. At first I thought God said it, a rush I've never quite felt before. I swallow the adrenaline and implications and answer, not positive God *didn't* say it.

'Me?'

'He spiked yesterday. Was conscious for twelve minutes, knew where he was . . . and asked for you.'

I'm too choked up to say anything.

The doctor turns to me after maybe a minute. 'I grew up in the Dime.'

That's a surprise. 'For real?' The Dime is a GD tag for four of the streets the GD run: Drexel, Ingleside, Maryland, and Ellis. Dell's – the cop bar where Sonny braced Kit Carson – is on Maryland and Seventy–ninth. Not many doctors have lived in, heard of, or walked by the Dime.

'Had a dog, squad car hit him, and—'

'Elfego Baca.' I smile through the tears. 'Packy Rodgers hit him on Drexel, broke his back.'

'And they were about to shoot him, to put him out. You gathered him up, and me, took us to the hospital with your siren, asked an ER doctor to save his life. Paid for it and the follow-up too. A lot, I imagine, for a uniform cop in 1989.' His eyes are proud. 'Baca lived another nine years. Got me to medical school. Saw it as magic, what doctors could do.' He nods at our surroundings. 'And parents in the Dime who thought this and me were possible.'

I squeeze Chief Jesse's hand, hoping he heard that, heard that he and I sowed seeds that bloomed into one of those 'little victories.' Chief Jesse was a sergeant then and driving the car Elfego Baca bled all over. We both got CR numbers and a day's suspension from the Watch LT.

The doctor coughs, glances past his shoulder, and his tone drops. 'The FBI and whatever you call your Internal Affairs people believe you and the superintendent are involved in the mayor's assassination attempt.'

Huh? How could this doctor know that?

He reads my face. 'They wanted to ask questions. Afraid the superintendent was dying. I allowed it, knowing he couldn't answer, and stayed in the room during the questioning.'

All I can muster is blank surprise and a great deal of curiosity.

'The questions were about you and Calumet City. A foster home there and a 1987 murder. Sounded as if they believe that Assistant State's Attorney Richard Rhodes, the superintendent, and you are being blackmailed by elements of organized crime, and have been for some time.'

'What? That's a joke.' Silence would've been smarter.

'Apparently a federal grand jury subpoenaed your personnel records and the superintendent's. The U.S. Attorney believes he has proof.'

'She.' I shake my head. 'They say anything else?'

He shakes his too, no more leery of me than before. I keep squeezing Chief Jesse's hand like it will help. No one's blackmailing me, so the G's lost on that rabbit trail. But they *will* stumble into my truth sooner or later, or at least close enough. And although they can't pin Chief Jesse with Calumet City, they can use me to ruin him.

I glance at the doctor. But if I kill Roland – *bullshit* – when I kill Roland and he dies big, maybe Roland and I and his horror show becomes the focus and they leave the superintendent alone.

The relief lasts a full second because that's not how it works. Everyone connected to me will burn unless I can turn this into *Taxi Driver*, where the psycho becomes the mistaken hero – But it could happen, couldn't it? Politicians spin absolute fantasy into fifty-year careers. Religions spin it into holy robes and gilded rule books.

The doctor interrupts with his eyes; they skip over my shoulder into the hall and land on the nurse who stopped me. She's talking to a man in a blue suit, Special Agent Stone. Agent Stone smiles at me. I have no idea how many doors there are in and out of ICU, but there's only one door – Chief Jesse's – between Agent Stone and me.

'Any other ways out of here?' I ask the doctor.

'Several, if you can get past him.' He glances left and smiles with his eyes. 'Back in the far corner. Door'll be open.'

I pat Chief Jesse's hand, want to kiss him on the cheek, but don't with the FBI watching. 'Take care of him, okay? He was your driver that day, you and Elfego Baca.'

The doc is genuinely surprised and breaks into a little black kid's grin. 'Karma.'

In the hall, Special Agent Stone stands between me and my

escape route, either because he knows where it is or because he intends to arrest me. We stare. He says, 'You'll be indicted on Monday.'

Le Bassinet opens on Monday. I don't answer or try to pass. He seems surprised.

'Obstruction, evidence tampering; we'll add more before the weekend's over.'

He's right but doesn't know why and hasn't mentioned Evanston yet. Not that my little scene was federal, but he'd mention it if he knew. 'You got a whole day, Special Agent Tough Guy. Give it hell.'

'Get an attorney . . . Or we can go over to Dearborn and try to work something out.' He glances past me into Chief Jesse's room.

My face reddens, my neck too. I can feel it in my legs, the muscles bunching. 'You are a serious bunch of motherfuckers, you know? You want me to front him, my friend, while he's dying. What kinda fuckin' world you live in?'

He waits to see if I want to be stupid and hit him. I don't and he says, 'The real one.'

We stare from twelve inches. He has no backup and no cuffs out, so I bluff back at him, 'You done? I got places to go.'

'Today I can help you. Monday – by noon, say – nobody can.'

A loud buzz lifts three nurses out of their chairs. I wheel to Chief Jesse's window. Two nurses loop us, the last one says, '*Out. Now,*' and grabs us both. Special Agent Stone has his phone out and follows, not realizing I haven't moved. The black doctor is met at another patient's door by more nurses and they're all sucked in like a fast drain. I bolt around the nurses' station for the left corner, find the door, kick the stopper out so it'll close behind me, and run the stairs. Two flights down my thigh muscle cramps or it's my phone vibrating. Door. Street level.

Outside, the parking lot's dark wherever the overhead lights don't flood the pavement. I run to my Celica, trying to be less obvious than I'm being. With luck Agent Stone will figure me for the bathroom or Chief Jesse's room and by then I'll be on the highway. Ignition. Gears. Gun it. But to where? Evanston? Are we doing a B&E after all, one we don't know how to do? My thigh vibrates again. I answer my cell and run the light, turning south onto Michigan.

It's Tracy-the-nervous, but right on schedule. 'Meet me at Midway.'

The ambulance charging at me changes lanes. 'What? At the airport?'

'General Aviation Terminal. Now.'

'Why?'

'Big news on the PI. If we're fast and lucky, your son may be alive tomorrow.'

Chapter 18

SATURDAY, DAY 6: 11:30 P.M.

Demons and ranches and death by fire and I'm jolted awake. Plane. *Small* plane; hands white on the armrests; cheek cold near the window; blink; glance – the earth below is held together by giant screws? The screw is missing and the hole's on fire. Fast cabin glance – Tracy in her seat, eyes out her window. Calm the fuck down.

Calm down. Desperation and half a sleeping pill got me on this plane and now we're landing, not crashing, in the Sonoran Desert, over the missing screw. I crane at my window; the round hole has to be fifty or sixty square blocks, the size of the Chicago Loop. Ridges descend inside the hole where the monster screw was removed; what's left glows purple-gold in the moonlight. We're making a midnight approach directly over it – right, right, I remember the plan – into Ajo, middle-of- nowhere, Arizona.

Ajo's airport lights rush at us. I hear Tracy say that the airport is a combination rifle range, country club, roping arena, and runway. The landing gear hums and the plane jolts sideways. The wing dips on my side. Less than a mile away, and way too close to the missing screw, a stunted mountain range is burning without flames. The entire formation is purple–gold like the screw hole, but with a white phosphorescent vein as tall and long as Navy Pier.

I confirm that I'm sober, ungrip my hands, wipe nightmare–drug sleep from my eyes, and fast glance Tracy again. Miss All-Everything still looks edgy, no better than when we boarded, and knowing what's supposed to be out there, maybe she should be. I asked for better detail; what little she explained en route didn't add up to baby shit, not the right response considering the stakes and effort. 'Stakes' whitens my knuckles. She had a magic word that got me on the plane.

Six hours ago Miss All-Everything scammed this eight-seat King Air from the *Herald* for an overnight trip to Why, Arizona. Why is a fifty-six-person suburb of Ajo, which according to Tracy, was a mining town until twenty years ago. I'm light-headed from the cabin pressure and sleeping pill and about to add Ajo's missing screw and burning mountains to my list of unanswered questions, but we slam into the runway. My eyes and mouth jam shut. We don't die – by impact, fire, or collision – and hurtle down a dark runway until we slow, then turn and taxi toward the silhouette of a metal building with two head-lights. A gentleman I've heard two sentences about named 'Bob' is waiting on the fender of a 1979 Cadillac Seville that was ugly when it was new.

Tracy and I deplane into crisp night air and a chance to stand up straight. I bury the nightmares. 'Bob' grins when Tracy makes our introduction. I don't grin, nor am I getting in 'Bob's' car until he explains who he is.

Bob says he's a reporter for the *Phoenix Sun* and that he's known Tracy 'since that thing we did in Costa Rica.' I'm guessing Bob is mid-fifties, and I'm guessing Tracy has promised him something beyond the Wild Turkey in his hand or he wouldn't be out here at near midnight. That, or he got a good look at her in the Miss Costa Rica Pageant.

I ask why the mountains are Technicolor and why the big screw's missing. Bob points to the mountains that from the ground now look more like the battlements of a fortress and says, 'New Cornelia mine. Copper.'

'That's a mine?'

Bob nods. 'Tailings slag. Seven billion cubic feet of poison. World's largest manmade dam. Made the *Guinness Book of Records.*'

We don't get a lot of 'tailings' in Chicago, but I can taste the metal on the sides of my tongue. 'What about the hole?'

Bob takes a sip of Wild Turkey and slips into hillbilly: 'That'd be your mine, Missy. Thousand feet deep, mile wide. Mondo bizarro, huh? *Burrrrrp.* Looks like we threw a screw, those roads cut into the side of it?'

Tracy winces at 'Missy,' then stretches for her and Bob's benefit and eases into the Seville's passenger seat. I take a good look at Bob's eyes. I've seen worse and get in the back seat. The back seat will have a seatbelt and two ways out if we crash. Bob fires the Seville, then bumps us past the gateless airport fence and onto the two-lane – maybe lane-and-a-half – Ajo Highway. His headlights illuminate mile after mile of nothing, not even fences, before they light up Ajo Town. At sixty miles an hour in the dark Ajo Town appears to be constructed of gravel, scrap wood, and trailers. We follow railroad tracks for a mile that he says belong to the mine and we don't stop at the American Citizen Social Club even though Bob says it can be fun. Town lasts another ten or twenty seconds before we're surrounded by blazing rock massed on both sides of Highway 85, rock that's somehow on fire without flames.

This goes beyond Rod Serling and reruns of *The Twilight Zone* – it's Jules Verne, *Journey to the Center of the Earth*. Bob rambles while he steers ten miles south to Why, mostly about the history of the area, the Indians, outlaws, and cactus. As the flameless glow of the tailings mountains and slag heaps disappears behind us, the Sonoran Desert goes dark. Bob stops the car in the middle of the road on a low ridge, quits talking, and the desert goes to dead quiet. Spend your life in a city and real 'dead quiet' will knock you off balance worse than Chinatown.

Shiver. Don't think about Chinatown. Not where we're going.

My eyes adjust and the land sort of *silvers* in places, like the ground's on a low dimmer. Very strange, and it's also full of twenty-five-foot prickly-green cactus. Those I've seen in the early Clint Eastwood movies. Tracy calls them *saguaro* and rolls the 'r' like she's still in Costa Rica modeling bathing suits from her back.

Tracy still hasn't looked at me since we got off the plane.

Bob veers off the pavement and onto a hard dirt road. His Seville's bright lights don't define desert from hardpan. Tracy suggests Bob tell me the 'story.'

Bob tells me his surname instead. It's Cullet, French, he says, by way of Gibraltar and his mother's marriage of convenience to a Phoenix car salesman. Bob Cullet is also drunk. How drunk is one issue, the other is whether or not the Sonoran Desert has cliffs. From the backseat there isn't shit I can do about any of it, other than bounce and listen. And try to prepare for another trip to the basement with Roland Ganz.

I have been blocking that thought till now, waiting for Bob

Cullet to explain what Tracy couldn't or wouldn't. She'd determined that this outpost was Roland's and likely his hideout since he put Annabelle in the wall. This was the reason I got on the plane.

Bob drives another minute in silence, then says, 'The Pentecostal Ranch is now called His Pentecostal City.' He burps again and adds, 'Eerie,' as if answering a question, then takes a slow drink. 'Smelled like sulfur, and crazy, every last one of 'em—' pause '—all of 'em livin' out here ten miles deeper into the Sonoran and Indian nowhere. A square mile of paradise, six hundred sixty acres of mostly unfenced desert ranch, built by Reverend A. A. Allen, *Triple A*, like the antiaircraft guns.'

Bob bounces over something that throws Tracy bracing into the dash. This would not be a good place to break down. He two-hands the wheel and continues.

'Triple A was a tent-show evangelist back in the late '50s, a God-fearing lunatic from North Carolina who had trouble accepting denominational structure; had trouble with his reproductive organs too. Rumors of progeny.'

My teeth grind. Gee, there's a new story.

'But Triple A could find water without arsenic and fluorine in it – that's a big damn deal on the res or off – and in ninety-some years no one else had. He found it, he said, with "God's divine ordainment."' Bob uses his chin to point beyond his side window. 'Compared to his square mile of sand and scrub, Triple A's "divine" well was worth double or triple.'

I ask, 'What's a res?'

'Reservation. Injuns.'

Outside Bob's window, low mountains rise and blacken the sky. They seem to be rising on all sides now but appear and disappear as we bump through washboard scrub and moonlight. I shiver once and for the first time, realize it's cold – assuming that I'm not dreaming. Dull–silver light brightens only odd patches. The stars are just a couple of miles away and closing. I try to imagine water with arsenic in it that you'd drink anyway. Not to mention what tailings mountains might do to your daily intake of minerals. Bob is oblivious, either warming to his story-teller role or the Wild Turkey.

'Reverend Triple A held desert baptisms. The profits from his well's "106-degree Holy Water" built the ranch's three frame buildings – slant-roof *cobertizos* like you see out there on the res, bunkhouses God needed to house the pilgrims who didn't succumb on the trip.' Bob stops explaining and bends closer to the steering wheel, then cranes over his pudgy hands to see something. '. . . lost souls who stayed, who couldn't catch on with permanent work elsewhere. Not that there's permanent work out here. Ain't nothing in this part of Sonoran Arizona but rock and poison.'

That's not hard to believe, and neither Tracy or I argue.

'For his *main* customers, the baptisms were a shorter–term pilgrimage—' Bob glances at Tracy '—not unlike the Yankees up on Route 66, stopping to see our three-headed snakes and UFO evidence, thank y'all very much.'

I can't decide if Bob is a real southern boy or just hillbilly drunk, so I ask. 'How long we been drinking today, Bob?'

He checks a watch he can't see. 'Far as I know, Missy, today just started.'

It's unlikely that Bob's had a woman put a pistol in his ear this week. That will change if he stays with 'Missy' or his driving worsens. We veer away from the moon and Bob goes silent again, this time for two miles and ten minutes of endless starry dark. Then out of the vast desert and Wild Turkey nowhere (Bob's term) he starts talking again.

'The '70s and '80s were less godly, likely due to cocaine Triple A said, and the Reverend had to supplement his ranch's income by touring. His circuit was the Colorado River mining towns – Nevada, Old California, and Utah – preachin' about apparitions in the desert, promisin' salvation to those who undertook the trip.

'Triple A regained momentum in the early '90s after hiring him a Utah preacher who'd gone pissy with the Mormons. This fellow brought a daughter, too, and Triple A put 'em both to work, sowing the Word. Got popular, the daughter did – that's what the townies said – but was damn near a prisoner. Triple A promoted her like had been done with that child evangelist Marjoe Gortner. A damn shame, frightened child circus–talking for God. Horseshit, if you pardon my French.'

Preacher with a daughter. I flash on the cleaning woman at the Lazarus Temple describing little Gwen, '. . . pretending she was a preachin'. Child was a ray a light.'

'Earning better now, Triple A brought out contractors from Yuma after Highway 8 was finished. They built him a house with indoor plumbing. How about that? Contractors stayed a year, doubled the generator's capacity, and installed window A/C in two of the *cobertizos*.'

Bob pauses, thinking, trying for a thought he can't quite find. 'Then it began to get weird.'

Tracy turns to Bob and looks down her nose. He's squinting out past his side window like something out there in the dark is pacing us.

'The folks from Why began to talk – they will talk in the

desert, God bless 'em. At first no one listened – these were complaints from citizens who *chose* to live in a furnace, so far from civilization that the U.S. government had trouble giving it to the Indians.'

Bob turns back to Tracy and jolts when he sees her frowning at his progress.

'But the good residents of Why were persistent. They told anyone who'd listen: "People went out there to that damn ranch and just never came back. *And* they weren't out there hidin' neither, ask the sheriff. And they married each other, brother and sister, father and daughter. And the preacher's son – hell, he was proof, wasn't he? Him full grown and too slow–minded to find his way home from an Idaho revival for two damn years."'

I'm listening to Bob's second impersonation in a half mile, feeling Roland coming to life in the words, seeing his face out there in the dark, hearing his breath on my shoulder. The more I hear, the more this bizarre place becomes his home.

Bob continues: 'Triple A wasn't stupid. He bought goods and paid on time and that gave him allies in Why and Ajo, albeit quiet ones. But not a Baptist widow who'd survived skin cancer and "those godless doctor charlatans." She had a cousin who'd been a one-term state representative from Fort Thomas and she pressed her cousin until he got the state involved.

'The Staties went to the ranch – this was in 1994 – found nothing stranger than what one would expect in such a place, but pressed Triple A anyway, and for more information than Triple A cared to provide. His response was to incorporate the ranch/church into a city and hire a private investigator to investigate his detractors. The PI was an Indian from the Tohono O'odham nation named Delmont Chukut.'

Tracy looks over the seat at me for the first time and says to Bob, 'The one you said the state police stopped on this highway with a minor named Gwyneth?'

'The same. She's the little girl preacher I mentioned. Almost lost his license over it.' Bob pauses for a sip that lofts his voice. 'Then, miracle of miracles, the state investigation stopped.' Bob pats the dash the way an old prospector might slap his thigh, 'Two years pass. Triple A stays busy: God tells him broadcast TV is the answer. Direct from the ranch. Triple A contracts with a company in Tucson for a small satellite-station setup – a metal tower and satellite dish with its own generator. Then suddenly he sells out, does not offer a word of good-bye, and he's gone. His boy stays – the one who'd been up in Idaho. The tower and dish were never completed.'

Tracy glances over her shoulder again, then screws up her nose into a polite show of suspicion. Something akin to hearing a husband's alibi when his wife goes missing.

'With the preacher gone, His Pentecostal City and Why elect to get along. Hearts and flowers lasts six years. "Incidents – this time with children," according to the Baptist widow, are happening again and she files another complaint with the state police.

'Delmont Chukut returns to poke into the widow's business, as well as that of her friends and family. Nothing comes of her complaint and she files it again in April of this year. And this time the state is interested, as is the media. Me in particular. So, my own self and a coworker buy a baptism for each other – a warm one, I might add, and done by a young woman in white who'd either been voodoo–tranced or she'd spoken to God one too many times. My coworker and I return to the *Phoenix Sun* and write a story that a rival at the *Tucson Star* said sounded "strikingly similar to Waco and Ruby Ridge with cactus."'

Bob laughs. I notice his cadence has lost the drunk singsong and hillbilly component.

'A number of state agencies get involved, each trying to avoid involvement while pretending to do their job. That's how it's done here. The Tucson TV tabloid shows jump in and that forces two of the agencies to get serious.' Bob hesitates, looking over both shoulders for effect. 'And then ten days ago the entire place emptied. Poof, like they were never there.'

On the plane Tracy repeated that last line almost verbatim, said we could only get the rest of the details when we landed, then tucked a small pillow against the oval window and either went to sleep or pretended to. I thought about an exodus only ten days old and visualized rats scattering from a crewless sailing ship when it drifted into harbor. Exhaustion and the sleeping pill finally closed my eyes but didn't block the nightmares of Roland's vampire castle in the desert. Right now I don't see, hear, or smell anything resembling a castle and realize I can't smell Bob's Wild Turkey either.

Bob Cullet slows to drop down into a steep turn that crosses a wide ditch they call a wash instead of what it is, a dry river. He looks both ways like he's expecting something, and tells his windshield, 'So, last week they found a cemetery here, the Pima County M.E. did; he guessed forty years old from the body they exhumed, but not much else. Had four investigators sifting through the papers in the main house while we all had cameras clicking from the fence line. But the sifting and the digging quit when the media did. If there's a "smoking gun," no one found it, much to my everlasting chagrin.'

Bob has a drink on that.

'But, shit, we got more mobile homes than books in Arizona. No telling what a smart man would find.'

I tap Bob on the shoulder. 'Pass me some of that Wild Turkey.'

Bob balks at the request. Tracy whiplashes the seat with red hair. I grab the pint before she can, spilling bourbon on her hand and a camera she was adjusting. Definitely bourbon; I can smell it now and hand it back. Bob is confused and looks at Tracy drying her camera and then over his shoulder at me. 'Or a smart woman, of course . . . Crazy son of a bitches, though. That's for damn sure, the reverend *and* the flock. Dead or alive.'

Clouds cover the moon and the Caddy goes dark other than the dashboard. We climb higher, skirting a deep rupture in the desert – the cliff I've been worried about for an hour. Bob slams the brakes and jolts me two-handed into his seat back. Dust trail envelops the car and blows into our headlights. Blocking the road is a black metal arch, padlocked and threatening in the scrub. Ribbons of Sheriff's Department tape flutter from the frame. The breeze is cold. 'HIS Pentecostal City' is arched across the iron gate. I shiver, inhale deep, and touch my Smith. Tracy leans over the seat and says something.

She says it again, 'Can you pick a lock?'

'No.'

Bob Cullet throws his column shifter into Park. This feels wrong; I draw the Smith – Bob steps out and walks uneven into the headlights. At the gate he looks up and down the ravine, then does magic I can't see, and the heavy chain rattles to the ground.

I tighten on the Smith; Bob does not look to be the 'magic' type.

Back in the car, he drops the shifter into Drive and doesn't explain as we pass through the gate. The desert rises slightly, obstructing our near-vision. Nobody talks and we bounce to the top of the rise and over – three buildings silhouette against the lowest stars. To the structures' right is the unfinished broadcast tower, rusting and out of place. I shiver again and press back into a colder spot on the seat. The few horror movies I've seen play across our car's windows. I reach for the door handle, the confinement is—

QUIT IT. If he's here, or has people here, don't give them fear to beat you. You're the new girl not the old one. He can't do shit this time but kill you. I squeeze the Smith. The car bumps forward and up, blocking our vision again. I hear a rush past my open window that's too fast and shadowy to see. Bob's head jerks to the sound, dislodging his hat.

Tracy points at the windshield, 'Something's moving, right there.'

Bob slows and cranes over the wheel. 'Where?'

'*Right there, damn it.*' Tracy jabs with her camera, then fires the flash. I lurch back, night blind. The car bounces left, veers higher, and stops broadside twenty feet from the nearest structure. Tracy flashes again. I bolt out blind into the scrub. We're in a night gunfight without the noise. Car doors pop. My vision recovers to half. Tracy faces the building and machine-guns her flash. Bob winces sideways. I aim left at headlight shadows; then right at another building fifty feet away; then behind me at the desert running downhill into black.

Tracy says, 'What was it?'

I pivot to her voice, the Smith braced. '*You saw it.*' The ground's dry and squishy at the same time.

'I did?' Tracy clears her throat. 'Yeah, I did.'

'*And?*' The wood siding on the nearest building might be red.

Wind adds a faint whistle and smells like a dried-out cedar chest.

'I don't know.' Tracy's still trying to see something she can't. '*Something* ran past.'

'Mountain lion.'

We both turn to Cowboy Bob Cullet, standing unsteady. '*What?*'

'Cub probably, or a javelina rootin' garbage these folks didn't burn.'

I don't know shit from mountain lions or 'javelinas.' As far as I know javelinas are lizards. Lizards that'd have to be the size of dragons if Tracy could see them run in the dark. Tracy and I shy in different directions. She asks Bob Cullet how big javelina get in the Sonora.

'Sixty, eighty pounds.'

Both of us quick-check near our feet. I wanna ask what else is guarding Roland's castle. Bob explains that javelinas are wild pigs. With tusks that will hurt you if you make 'em. I step back and miss a furry cactus by inches. Bob says I want to avoid that too.

'Jumping cactus, cholla, very nasty.' He nods at my pistol. 'Nobody's here. At least no one we care about.'

'And you know that how?'

Bob frowns and pats for his pint. 'Border's hot down at Sonoita. Imm'grants that make it through stay on 85 till they hit Phoenix. Folks from Ajo and Why don't come out here at night, at least they didn't when we were all here before.'

I don't lower my pistol. 'And why is that?'

'Shit, Missy, we're two six–packs from God *or* his adversary.'

Tracy notices her proximity to the nearest building and retreats toward Bob, 'Hand me your flashlight.'

Bob has a large one in his non-whiskey hand. He declines Tracy's request and says, 'We'll look up at the house first' but doesn't move.

Nor do I. Roland has been in there. I do not want to smell Roland again. My stomach agrees and I force it down. Or touch things he touched. Or be where he's been. The desert breeze chills my neck again and I fast-glance behind me. Bob and Tracy stare uphill at what has to be the house. Deep shadows cover a discernible porch with a low roof.

Bob points left and says, 'Cemetery.'

My eyes stay on the porch, but I move toward the cemetery and its shadows. Like in Chicago, dark cemeteries don't scare me; their ghosts are my homeys. Bob follows me to the cemetery instead of approaching the house. Tracy notices she's alone and hurries to catch up. I can't tell how rattled she is, just that she's battling between panic and the insatiable reporter mode. It's how addicts feel – we can't get enough of the shit that will kill us. Until it does.

The cemetery has a knee-high fence of scrap metal painted white. Sharp-edged, purple rocks are piled along the base where a landscaper would plant flowers. The rest of the plot is sand. Eleven crosses stand cockeyed and in no particular order. Beyond them, facing us, a parched acacia tree rustles. Under its branches is a six-foot crucifix rising out of pocked concrete. Christ's feet are missing; the ankles are faded red.

Two of the graves have been opened. I remember being told only one, not two, and notice tracks, wide channels in the soil.

Bob says, 'Backhoe,' swallows Wild Turkey, then points beyond the two open graves toward a group of three crosses. 'Those over there were the oldest, their worldly remains buried without boxes. After the first body came up in pieces, the M.E.

had 'em dig the other'n by hand. Mexicans. The good people of Why weren't up to it.'

I long-glance Roland's house to our right, then point Bob and his flashlight past a fresh pile of earth to the first hole. It's four feet deep and the edges have caved in. 'Who were these two?'

Bob says, 'Who knows?' and shines the crosses instead of the hole. 'Folks, all adults, though, according to the inscriptions. We ran state birth records but got nothing. Sheriffs in Ajo ran missing persons and got a match.' Bob shifts his light to the farthest of the two holes. 'Joseph V. Smith. But how many of Joe Smiths are there worldwide?'

'From?'

'The Mr. Smith in *this hole* – who knows? The J. V. Smith that matched was from Blythe out by California, a Marine Corps deserter in the '70s.'

The wind whistles shrill; Tracy and I snap to face Roland's house. Bob doesn't notice because he's already pointing his light at the house. Instead of splashing it back and forth, he keeps it on the door, too long to be anything but expectation.

The wind quits with a low moan, and it gets colder. Tracy's voice fakes confidence. 'We're playing BASH in twelve hours, let's finish with this,' and she heads uphill for the house. Bob follows her. My feet don't move. The cemetery wants to keep me. People came out of these holes in pieces . . .

Tracy and Bob and his light are gone. Something's moving low in the dark, changing the shadows just beyond the fence. I squint as my heart ramps, can't see, and run uphill. Roland's house stops me. It will have a special room. Roland isn't on his porch kneading his cotton briefs; the door's open; hungry. The room will have special tools, special toys.

My foot won't step up onto the porch; I force it, then the other. The wood planks creak, announcing I'm here. The open door sucks me across the threshold. Inside, it's, it's . . . I can't feel him. Or smell him. *Oh, man, that's good.* So good I'm dizzy. But it's wrong; he should be all over me, making me puke. And he isn't. Tracy and Bob are at a stack of boxes. I stay statue–still, wearing the room, waiting for it to smother me.

C'mon, motherfucker. Come and get me . . . If you can . . . I sound fourteen in my head, not armed and dangerous.

I look left, then right and fight the memories I invited. This place isn't a black castle, it's just walls. Windows. Furniture. Be a cop. *Kill the motherfucker.*

Roland didn't live here. *What?* If he did, where is he? I don't feel it, him, at all—

'Look at this.'

I snap sideways but don't shoot Tracy. She's looking at Bob and doesn't see me do it. Bob is in front of an open file cabinet. His flashlight's shining on a page he holds above a box of dumped papers.

Tracy says, 'Patti, c'mere' without looking behind her.

I force my feet to move. From behind her shoulder I peek. Bob's whiskey hand is wobbling the beam. The page is typewritten. Below it on the floor is another page, handwriting, a child's or a lunatic's:

> *The Cradle Will Fall.*
> *The Cradle Will Fall.*
> *The Cradle Will Fall.*

'Oh my god,' my knees buckle and I grab for the page. 'A bassinet is a cradle.'

Tracy sees the page and grabs for my arm. 'Easy, Patti.'

I speed-add dates, times . . .

'If Roland knew, he would've gone there right after they ran out of here.'

Bob says, 'Knew what? Who?' He shines his light on the handwriting. 'What?'

Tracy holds my arm tight and smiles into a lie. 'Bob, honey, we're partners, right?' She touches his upper arm – one hand now on each of us. 'The Chicago job's yours after we put this story together, done deal, but we have to do it my way.'

Bob doesn't look trusting or horny. He checks me, but I'm mostly shadows. I start to relax; Tracy's right, if this meant what I thought it did – that Roland knew about Le Bassinet ten days ago – John would already be dead. But how do you *know* John isn't dead? You haven't seen him. That stumbles me back into a chair, screeching the legs on the plank floor. All three of us jerk at the noise and Bob splashes me with light.

I straighten. 'Sorry. Must be the . . . hell, I don't know what it is. I'm fine.'

Bob looks at me, then begins a house–layout explanation speaking slower than necessary. He has new respect for my lack of self-control. Bob highlights with his light beam, pointing around the room, down a short hall, and out a window. 'Bedroom's back there; two of 'em. Sheriff found papers on the original owner's son, Triple A's son, the one who wandered from the flock and was lost up in Idaho.'

'Meaning what?'

'Dope. While on the revival road, the reverend's son fell victim to illicit narcotics and the company of women, women of

271

low virtue. His return was heralded as biblical – the black sheep returning.'

'What kind of dope?'

Bob says, '$C^{10}H^{15}N$,' like I would my star number.

I stare. Bob takes way too long to realize I'm waiting for the English version.

'Methamphetamine hydrochloride. Arizona's cash crop. One of our sheriffs said there was a period, not too long ago, where they thought His Pentecostal Ranch might be brewing crystal meth. For sale. Big with the Indians and PI Delmont Chukut.' Bob raises his chin toward the reservation. 'Not so much now.'

Well, there it is – Gypsy Vikings, Pancake the meth chemist, and an *Arizona-Idaho whiteboy buying torches* at the Cassarane Bar. I already know the answer but ask anyway. 'What's his name, the son?'

'Balanter Joseph Allen, son of the right Reverend A. A. Allen.'

Idaho Joe. A fifth grader would've had that the first time Bob mentioned Idaho. So Idaho Joe blew out of here with Roland . . . one big happy fucking horror family.

Tracy asks, 'What about his father, Triple A?'

Bob says, 'Not a word in years. No IRS filings; no Medicare claims; no credit cards; no telephone. Not-a-peep.'

'He's dead,' I say.

'For sure.' Bob says, and nods down the hall toward the endless desert beyond the bedroom window. 'For sure.'

'Who'd the reverend sell this . . . establishment to?' I ask.

Bob and Tracy make eyes at each other. Tracy tells him, 'I didn't get that far on the plane. Fell asleep.'

Bob shifts to me, stares, but doesn't answer.

The guy who steps out of the shadows says: 'He sold it to you.'

SUNDAY

Chapter 19

SUNDAY, DAY 7: EARLY A.M.

'DO NOT FUCKING MOVE.'

The apparition doesn't. 'Hands on your head. Slow.' He does. 'Turn around. Face the wall.' He does. I hard-glance Tracy and Bob, then back to the apparition's shoulderblades. 'Who the fuck are you?'

He takes a breath, making me wait. 'Colleague of Bob's, at the *Sun*.'

I keep the Smith aimed at his back and glance down the hall at rooms I can't see. 'That so, *Bob*?'

Bob doesn't answer, but I can feel him nodding. My voice grinds down to ugly, matching my heart rate and the rooms I can't see. 'Anybody else here, Bob? You and them gonna die if there are.'

Tracy says, 'Easy, Patti. Easy.'

'How 'bout it, Bob? Anybody else?'

'N . . . no.'

I have six bullets, multiple threat locations, and no options. 'Bob, if this asshole you hid in the shadows has a gun and a badge, I'm gonna be awful unhappy.'

Tracy tries to purr. 'E . . . easy, Patti. Easy.'

'Okay, colleague-of-Bob's, I'm gonna step in behind you and cuff your—' He spins. I fire twice. The room lights up. Wood and plaster splinter. Bob's partner hits the floor. I stomp him flatter on his stomach and hear his air go, knee his back hard, and aim the Smith at Bob's face. Bob's frozen; I fan at the rooms I can't see – nothing comes – then jam the barrel into the guy's neck. 'It's cocked, asshole. You decide.'

He slow-moves his right hand toward his back pockets. I use my cuffs, ram his arm under my knee, grab the other hand and cuff it too, then stand to wheel on Bob, the dark, and my good friend Tracy Moens, intending to shoot them all one at a time.

Tracy guesses. 'C'mon, Patti. Don't. You're scaring me.'

I jump sideways to keep the hallway in front of me, '*Scaring you?*' then glare Bob into the wall, then back to Tracy. '*You fucking bitch*. What is this?'

'I had no idea. Honest.' She grimaces at Bob's partner rolling over on the floor, 'About him . . . being here. I thought he'd be at the airport. I was about to tell you—'

'Tell me what?'

'Bob's nervous about . . . you. Since you're the real owner of this . . . place.'

Bob is suddenly as far away from me as the wall will allow. I aim the Smith at him and frisk his partner with one hand – a pistol . . . cuffs, and a star. Phoenix PD. My teeth clamp. 'Well, *Bob*, guess you'd better explain your colleague.'

Bob is sucking short breaths. I step up off his partner and closer. Bob decides to answer. 'I was . . . ah, worried . . . You being the owner who bought out—'

'*I don't own shit*. And I didn't buy out anyone. And I don't want to hear that outta your fucking mouth again.' Gun–barrel glare. 'Who's your friend?'

'A policeman, that's all. Please, take it easy. Just here to make sure . . . you don't hurt me, us.'

I look at the man on the floor. Either a rookie, a drunk like Bob, or he lifted the badge from a real cop's dresser. I'm going with drunk. Tracy interrupts my assessment.

'Patti, the papers we found say you own it. That's why we're here. One of the reasons.'

'*I don't own shit*. How many Patti Blacks do you think live in America?'

Tracy tries hard to look understanding in the flashlight shadows. Bob tries for invisible. I eye the dark hall and rooms beyond, then kneel and strip his partner's cell phone and wallet. I tell Bob and him to sit facing a post column like it's a campfire. They do. At my direction Tracy cuffs Bob and his partner to each other using both sets of handcuffs, their arms ringing the pole. A cell phone falls out of Bob's pocket. Tracy tosses it toward the table where I put his partner's phone. Both fly off and the cop's phone shatters. I almost shoot it.

Deep breath. 'Here's the deal, Bob. If there's anyone else hiding down the hall or in the other buildings, this is your last chance to tell me. I find 'em and live through it, you don't.'

'N-n-nobody else.'

'If there's anything else I need to know, tell me now.' I glance at Tracy. '*My friend* and I will steal your Caddy, drive to the airport, and fly home. Six hours from now we'll call and have you rescued.' I small smile at the cop. '*By the locals* so you aren't embarrassed shitless for losing your weapon. It'll be on the table. If you don't tell, I won't.'

Neither man answers. Tracy tries to intervene as their agent. I'd love to shoot her and bury her here. She sees that in my face and stops mid–breath. I look back at the men.

'Talk to me, *Bob*. Any more surprises?' I look down the hall while he shakes his head. 'Okay, then, what else are we supposed to see?'

Bob glances at the door and semi–whimpers, 'There's a bottle of Turkey in the trunk. Think I could have that?'

I know the blackout comfort a bottle can bring. 'Could happen. If I'm happy after we finish the inspection.' *Bottle* and *blackout* hang in my head longer than usual . . . like a set of crime-scene murder shots in Calumet City—

Oh my God, *have* I been here . . . too? I stumble into the wall. No way; no way—

Bob starts talking, telling us where to go and what to look for. But I hear *blackout* and *been here before*. I bite my lip until I taste the blood. No way – I haven't been here. No way—

'Patti?'

I spin with the Smith. Tracy flinches. I fake stable and point at the hallway. Never been here before. Never. Not one fucking time. Tracy's still staring. I need to get out of this room and point us to the hallway again.

Tracy leads with Bob's flashlight. Every step is Halloween. There's two bedrooms, a bathroom, and no basement.

How would I know that? I've never been here.

My hand brushes the cop's pistol in the waistband of my Levi's, Tracy's Levi's actually. She bumps a chair; I taste the dust drifting through her flashlight beam.

All new. Never been here.

Each bedroom yields nothing but high pulse rate and the

feeling that this house belonged to someone other than Roland Ganz. The bathroom is the last room; it's stale and dirty. Two mice are dead in the corner. This building's clear; I take a long, deep breath and relax my shoulders but not the Smith. 'There's another house somewhere.'

Tracy stops her retreat back into first bedroom mid–step. 'Another house?'

'Roland isn't here.'

She shines the light near my face but not in it. 'Right. We know he isn't here. He's in Chicago.'

I shake my head, feel my jaw muscles bunch. 'This place doesn't . . . vibe; it isn't his.'

'How do you know?'

'*How do I know*. I'm a fucking girl. *I know*.'

Tracy moves away in the general direction of a bedroom porch door. 'You're right, that's fine. Fine. Let's look at the other buildings then.'

A thought stops me. I realize I just said I was a girl; in a house they say Roland Ganz owned. Me, a girl. I almost smile and that bumps Tracy into the rear door. She fumbles with the knob behind her and backs outside. And keeps backing until she's traveled as far into the night as she's willing to travel without protection.

I step through the dark bedroom and out into moonlight. Tracy has a tough choice – search these buildings alone or with a madwoman who has an ugly history of blackouts. Tracy stays in front with the flashlight; we don't talk because I'm focused on shooting the next surprise before it surprises me. We find nothing but more dust and decomposed mice – like Bob said we would – and stop under the incomplete broadcast tower, both of

279

us doing slow 360s at the ground and the air immediately above it.

Tracy scans where we've just been and semi–whispers, 'There's a boatload of strange here, for sure.' She pats the metal, 'But this the cops probably missed.'

I finish my 360 and don't feel any safer, hadn't thought about the tower either, and ask how anyone *could* miss it. Her eyes follow the metal to the sky. 'Not physically, they missed it financially. Right here's where the money is. All of it.' She pats again, as if the iron grounds her in more comfortable wave-lengths she can understand. 'If you intend to run a salvation enterprise – baptism and pilgrimage – it requires distribution. TV. This tower would've been like owning a bank.'

As she finishes the sentence I hear *PTL Club* on Roland's Magnavox. It's twenty-three years ago and Tammy Faye is pleading for money. Roland is . . . *I have not been here*.

'No way this makes sense.' Tracy's staring at the cables dead on the squishy ground. 'This preacher Triple A had the goods and didn't use it.' She's deep into reporter thoughts and no longer afraid of me or what's out here in the dark with us, human or otherwise.

'Had this tower but quit before Roland got here, right?'

She nods at my statement, looking around.

'Or maybe . . . *when* he got here,' I add, thinking cop thoughts. Tracy cuts back to me, staring hard, and we both figure it. TV might be money, but it's also notoriety. And some folks can't afford notoriety.

She says, 'You and Bob are right; the preacher's dead. Had to be Roland who the preacher brought back from Utah, Roland and little Gwen helped him boost his business, and when the preacher wanted to go satellite, Roland murdered him.'

Little Gwen again, trapped out here in ... this ... vampire fucking castle. It makes me want to puke, but it fits. I add, 'Then Roland stayed on ... all those years, till now. When the last round of state investigators started poking ten days ago, he hit the road. But why go back to Chicago? And why's he after me again, and John ... at all?'

Tracy bites at her lip. 'You really didn't know you owned this ... right?'

I look away and hear my teeth grind. *You have not been here, ever. Period.* While I'm not looking at her, shadows move. I jump back to fire ... it's clouds covering the moon; light that in a city wouldn't register, but out here scares the shit out of me until I figure it. I follow one shadow running away and up a distinct path. The shadow runs around a low hill and into the dark. The tops of larger hills are silhouetted higher behind the path and hill. I look back at Tracy watching the same thing.

She tiptoes. 'Wonder what's back there?'

I'm thinking *bitch* and say, 'You've got the flashlight.'

'I'm sorry, okay? I was just trying to help us, you. There's nothing we can do till Monday morning anyway.' Tracy sprinkles what little fairy dust she has. 'The FBI's not here; that counts for something.'

Miss All-Everything wants a gunfighter on that path with her. We'll go, but I'll let her lead and hope for a hungry mountain lion. I wave her forward without adding my sentiments and she inches toward the path. Surely the state police covered this ground in the daylight and found zip. We walk higher, lower, darker, lighter, and the path ends abruptly on a plateau. We're a foot from the edge. Way, way in the distance low lights twinkle in the black. It could be ten miles or fifty, Mexico or the Indian reservation or whatever's on fire festering in the bottom of that screw hole.

Tracy sees the lights too and says, 'The superintendent's an Indian, isn't he? What kind?'

I answer, 'Hohokam,' but only because I'm concentrating on moonlit, unending western landscape seen for the first time, landscape that's sort of like a blood pressure pill . . . and maybe why people live here.

Tracy draws back from the plateau's rim, glances at me, then down the nearest edge. 'If you wanted to hide something on this ranch, where would it be?'

According to Bob this place is a square mile. Eight city blocks in every direction. Searching it all will be impossible and I say so.

Tracy nods. 'What's the most valuable thing out here?'

I'm a street cop, not a detective, but this is one I can figure. 'Water. The baptism well. You don't die of thirst and it cashes your checks.'

Tracy says, 'Let's go.'

'Like the Staties didn't think of that?'

She stops, stumbles for balance, and falls down the plateau. The flashlight goes with her doing cartwheels that I hope are a match for hers. I hear her land but can't see. When she doesn't call out, I peek, not wanting to join her more than wanting to save her. My shoe tumbles rocks down the face and I jump back. They hit bottom in a muffled flurry.

'Quit it, for chrissake.' Miss All-Everything-but-Mountain-Climber has survived.

'You okay?' I'm actually smiling, which feels like the

landscape looks, and think I remember that Clint shot any wounded who couldn't finish the trail ride.

'Give me a hand.'

'How? I can't see anything.' I hear rocks moving and Tracy bitching. After two minutes of scrabble noise, the top of a red-head materializes. I step farther back and reach to help. She gets closer and I step back again, arm extended. When she gets an elbow on the level ground I step forward, grab her collar, and drag her bitching to 'safety.'

The flashlight is still lit at the bottom but I ask if she has it. She's sitting, rubbing her knee, and spitting desert and doesn't answer.

'You were saying something about the well when you fell.'

She thanks me for my help. I ask if she can walk. She stands with difficulty and brushes her designer jeans, torn at both knees.

'There's something down there.'

'Yeah, our flashlight.'

'Fuck you, Patti. You know? Just fuck you.'

The first rise I have ever gotten out of Ms. Moens.

'There *is* something down there.'

'I read *Tom Sawyer* for the first time last year, bought it instead of your book. You want the flashlight, be my guest.'

Tracy turns away from the edge, then retreats down the path toward the first hill and civilization beyond, but stops short. I don't bump into her because I haven't moved. I know this act, have seen it on the field and on the sidelines. She turns fast and says, 'I'm going back down.'

If I were a guy, this would be my cue to assist her by jumping into the lion's mouth. I stay put when she passes me. Nor do I speak when she crawls down over the plateau lip and disappears into the shadows. I hear the rocks moving and imagine her fingers bloody to match her knees. This is a good moment in a shit week.

The flashlight's beam moves and she yells from under the plateau, 'Take a look at this.'

Out of nowhere 'this' lands at my feet and I jump sideways. I avoid falling over the rim by going to a knee and slamming the plateau with my gun hand. No one but me sees this and I bite my teeth to keep from yelling.

'This' is near my shoe. It's a tin can that up close reads ... I can't read it. Another can lands behind me, then another. I'm wondering why they were worth Miss All–Everything clawing her way back down the cliff, or ravine, or whatever it is.

She answers my unasked question in a muffled, roundabout manner, talking to herself. 'The state police or the sheriffs didn't search this. Why would they? No one had proof anything happened here, other than the ranch's people are gone. So they'd look around, go through the papers – some of them, and write it off as a media weekend. When the authorities go home, so do the cameras.'

Although I'm not party to the conversation, I agree that it makes sense. Not enough to crawl down there, but it makes sense and she continues from the dark below.

'They dig up the one grave, make a show, but don't need to spend more county money on a crime that hasn't happened.' She pauses, then states with conviction: 'They didn't look in the well. Probably drove a few acres of the six hundred sixty and never left their cars.'

I've seen a number of detectives 'windshield' a crime

scene and write a report; some from five miles away with a bourbon-and-water in hand. The 'one grave' comment kind of hangs there and I wonder if I'm the only person who can count to two. I answer loud, down what sounds like a two-story basement. 'So? The Staties are lazy and you found the trash dump.'

'I found a safe.' The word *safe* echoes. 'Under all this crap, just where a Waco or Ruby Ridger would put it.'

I ease closer to the rim and peer past the overhang, considering how a city cop might descend. Cans and debris clank in the dark. Her voice echoes again.

'And it's open.'

My descent is not athletic either. I arrive scuffed and sandy in a trash ravine that doesn't feel like a basement. Tracy's safe is big, old, and buried in a concrete vault like the bodies in the cemetery should've been. She's scraped back the layers of burnt trash and desert to expose the safe's metal door. The door is scorched gray – black, ajar six inches, and blocked open from the inside. Whoever opened it didn't bother to close or hide it after. What little hiding the safe got when they were done was likely from Bob's javelina rooting through the trash until Tracy slid in and rearranged the pile.

She tightens her light beam to just the door handle and what trash-pit lighting we had, quits. Now we're knee deep in a dark trash pit with whatever desert creatures eat and sleep here. That thought motivates me to throw open the door and I use both hands when one isn't enough.

The safe's interior has an odd odor, letter-size metal boxes, and loose papers. Both of us politely wait for the other to reach. When that doesn't happen I look for a stick, find none, take a deep breath, and reach.

Nothing bites me at first so I grab a box, then the flashlight from Tracy before she can react. This leaves her hands free and I shine my flashlight back inside. She hesitates like she can't decide which cherry to pick, and grabs. Her hand returns with a box that matches mine and a six-inch centipede. The latter makes her toss the box and me flinch. Before I take my turn – we seem to be taking turns now – I use the light to check as much of the dark metal hole as possible.

We take our turns reaching until we have four metal boxes, a sheaf of loose papers, and one last look to be sure the safe is empty. Whatever's in the pit with us, hidden under the trash surrounding our feet, must be asleep at 2:00 a.m. Only Tracy is happier about this than me. We and our boxes scramble back to the top of the plateau, then alternate with the flashlight, checking our legs and contraband for creatures.

We sit Indian style with the boxes between us. Tracy grabs the flashlight and shines it on the box farthest from her. It's not lost on me how strange this is. I'm one of two city girls sitting on a low plateau in the Sonoran Desert, washed in dull–silver light a Chicagoan only sees at outdoor concerts. This is stranger than the two of us walking *ghetto ho* yesterday after the rain.

Jesus, that was *yesterday*?

Tracy is not as taken with our surroundings and says, 'Open it.'

I do; it's a box full of . . .

Watches. Maybe fifty. Old ones. I immediately think dead people. A serial killer's souvenirs. The preacher Triple A did this? But where are the fifty bodies? Only eleven marked graves up front and they were showy – probably part of the new pilgrim tour. I glance at the desert beyond our flashlight that goes on forever — a cemetery no psycho could fill in one career.

That answers the *where*, but why kill your pilgrims?

Tracy fishes through the watches, inspecting two, then a third. None bite her.

I answer my own question. 'Maybe he didn't kill them. Maybe it's give up your watch, join the ranch, screw the grid. A symbol, you know? These bullshit artists love that shit.'

Tracy's reading an inscription and says, 'Huh?' I repeat both thoughts — serial-killer dead people or just off the grid.

'He . . . they killed all these people?' She hesitates with that thought while trying to 360 her shoulders. When she comes back she says it again but with less reporter glee.

'Could've.'

'That would be . . . messy.'

We try to read the inscriptions. Only two have any, and neither of them are names. I toss the last Timex back in, an old one with a fake alligator band. Tracy reaches for the next box. It's sturdier than the others and empty, other than two crumpled pages and a rock. No, not a rock, a nugget of massed cubes. We both hit Lost Dutchman Gold Mine in the same instant — flashing on the calendar that was pinned above Roland's file cabinet. I'm dumb enough to say it out loud.

She sneers and says, 'Long way from here, east of Phoenix,' but continues to examine the nugget. It shimmers against the light and she says, 'Could be something,' then hands it to me to assay in the dark. I try while she reads one of the pages with all the flashlight.

'It's an assayer's report: "Pyrite". Fool's gold.' She looks up and frowns at my attempt to polish "pyrite" into gold ore. 'Probably why the "divine" water made 'em all smell like sulfur.'

Uh-huh. I'm thinking I might need to peruse that page myself. She reads my mind because the bitch seems to be able to do that and hands me both pages, then the flashlight. Page one says what she said it did and I hand it back, but keep the rock . . . nugget. She notices; I smile her pageant smile.

Page two is more interesting. It says the first assayer's report may be wrong. Unfortunately, the stationery heading is gone, as is the bottom half of the page, so it's tough to know what the paragraph means out of context. I put the rock and the page back in the box and stack it on top of the watches box.

Metal box three is cinched with leather clasps. Tracy fights it open as the breeze picks up to wind again, and colder still. I don't like the timing and check a phosphorescent desert on low-dimmer that runs as far as Mexico and maybe outer space.

Voodoo.

That's my first thought when I turn back – after I peer into box three, after seeing Tracy's face go blank. *Voodoo kit.* Inside box three are bleached bones that might be four–toed feet, incisor teeth – one of length and sharp – two talons with reddish tips, a nine-inch curved backbone, and another nugget. Behind the nugget is a compass and under it a red cloth that shines like velvet does when it's wet. Tracy pulls and half the cloth falls away in red flakes. The cloth must be hot because she drops it, recovers, then shrugs. 'Beats the hell out of me . . .'

I frown at memories that aren't good anywhere, even here. 'Relics.' My chest tightens and I'm hot and cold at the same time. 'Circus bullshit if you're selling religion. Make your "holy artifacts" from weird animal parts.'

Tracy mimics me and asks the box, 'We found His Pentecostal City's Shroud of Turin?'

I didn't need to hear that; I absolutely hate organized religion's false hope. Hate it to the point I can be violent. I *want* the shroud to be true, to believe that God is out there and She gives a shit. And in a place like this it's easier – somehow the weirdness of it all, the brilliant . . . emptiness suggests She's possible. But all the bullshit relics in the world don't change one day with Roland, not a fucking minute of his hands and—

'Patti? *Patti*.'

I snap back to Tracy shining the light in my eyes. I block and twist sideways. She lowers the light but keeps in on me.

'We okay?'

'Keep the damn light out of my eyes.'

She does but continues staring at me and my tone. These little side trips I keep taking must be painted across my face. If that's true, and I know it is, one has to give Miss All–Everything credit for staying with me.

I ease up on the tone. 'I'm fine.'

She shines the light back on the box but her eyes linger on mine, then finally follow the light. She rummages, shrugs again, and hands the voodoo box to me. I stack it for later, or never, and wait for box four. It's definitely getting colder, not just my imagination. The wind has a new scent too, blooms of some type. Sweet but sharp, like spices burned in a pan. I smile. Julie had a sous chef from Charlie Trotter's do a 'spices' charity demonstration once at the L7. She paid more attention to Julie than the spices heating in the pan, took a face full, and gassed herself.

The L7 and Julie. My old life. Maybe when I save John, I could hide out here after . . . in this nothing. My back flexes so hard it hurts. I realize I'm considering a future. One I don't have.

This isn't real – not for me – I'm going to murder Roland Ganz and if I win, go to Joliet forever.

Tracy says, 'Well, that's . . . ah, *different*?'

I blink from my latest side trip and see her looking inside box four from as far away as her back and neck will stretch. I lean toward her; she and the box lean away.

'What?' I notice the box is different from the others, newer. 'What?'

Tracy blows air through her lips. 'Take it easy, all right?'

I stare.

She's still hoarding the box. 'All right?'

I nod, not sure.

She eases the box across our nonexistent campfire, then follows it with the light. Inside are two hands connected to forearms. Small hands with manacles.

'Ohhhhh, *shit*.' I drop it and twist away, '*The fucking monster*.' Then jump to standing. '*Motherfucking monster*.' My right hand has a pistol in it. Tracy backs up like I'm burning. And I am, *God damn him*, I am.

I'll B&E Le Bassinet even if it takes dynamite. *He will not get John*. I pivot and sprint. The path leads toward a car that leads to a plane that leads to saving my son from the fate I know will be his if I don't. I flash on the hands and realize they could belong to Gwen's son—

'Wait. Patti, wait.'

After two stumbles and one fall I'm semi-panting and passing the house. From inside Bob Cullet yells for Tracy. I get to the car and – no keys. Bob has the keys. I have his partner's weapon. I need Tracy in order to find our pilot. I need a lot of shit and better calm down until I have it. Deep breath. Another. Desert air, try more, I do and lean against Bob's four-door. I can't remember what Gwen said—

Tracy struggles up with the boxes and sets them on the hood. Bob yells again. She produces the keys and pops the trunk. From inside she retrieves the bottle of Wild Turkey I promised Bob, then wipes at her face and sneaks a look at me. She decides I'm not too dangerous to address and does.

'Those . . . hands and manacles make this a murder scene, at least it could be, based on what we know about Annabelle's body and . . .' she takes a second to think about it, 'and you. Do we call the local cops or not?'

That's a question for a real cop. I'm not a real cop anymore. 'Put all that in the trunk. We'll read the papers flying home. Gimme the bottle.'

Inside, Bob is not happy to see me. This is a telling moment for his future if I'm actually part of the ranch. I notice the raw grooves on the pole and both men's bloody wrists. Bob can't do anything but wait and see if I intend to execute them. The cop starts to speak and I wave him off with Bob's bottle. The cop is happy to see his weapon laid on the table instead of pointed at his head. I drop the bottle between them so Bob, with the cop's help, can get at it.

'We found stuff Tracy will explain tomorrow. She wants you to look for the preacher's body, Triple A, the original owner. I'm taking the papers that say a Patricia Black owns a ghost town so I can prove I don't. We'll be in touch. Say six hours or so. You two take a good look through the rest of this shit while you wait.'

Bob is max-happy and focused on the bottle.

I walk to the papers that have my name on them, hoping there aren't any others, and move all the other boxes to within Bob's reach. A broke-open first aid kit falls out of the last one, spilling syringes and gauze rolls. I leave those within Bob's reach too. The boxes suddenly have energy. Now this house feels more like Roland's and I want to leave. But I can't, yet.

'Delmont Chukut. Tell me what you didn't in the car.'

Bob checks his Phoenix PD partner, stutters from adrenaline and heart rate, licks his lips, and says, 'Ah . . . priors for crystal meth, like I said, and smuggling – marijuana and illegal aliens, but no convictions.' Two deep breaths help his cadence. 'Did a stint with the Army Rangers, then Tucson PD after being booted from the res.' Bob checks to make sure I'm happy. 'More than one rumor of murder, the most recent a bail jumper he chased into Mexico. He's Hohokam – "the nomad vanished ones" – so the desert is —'

'What did you say?'

Tracy fills the doorway and Cowboy Bob flinches at my tone. He checks her, then me again but lots slower, then repeats what he said. I turn my back to Bob and face her. She uses the doorway for support and says it quietly, and with great care, but repeats what I already told her.

'Superintendent Jesse Smith's a Hohokam.'

Chapter 20

SUNDAY, DAY 7: 10:00 A.M.

Turbulence. The King Air ducks. My eyes pop open as we veer lower around a cloud mountain. I rub my eyes awake and check my wrist. Manacle scars, no watch. Wrong hand. My left wrist reads 10:00 a.m. Sunday. Twenty-three hours till I can brace Le Bassinet.

The clouds break and Midway Airport's crisscross of concrete is visible. We've been in the air six hours, the last two bouncing toward a series of 'nasty weather conditions' that back in Arizona Pilot Tim warned would put Chicago into storm shelters. I boarded anyway, too scared for John not to; Tracy boarded because I did. In the air, I made two calls to Delmont Chukut that he didn't answer, then hid my face in a pillow and passed out, surprised that I could.

I rub my eyes again; if this is how awake feels, then sleeping didn't help. Tracy is facing me from across a drop-down table. She and I have not discussed 'Hohokam' or its gut-wrenching implications, denial being my favorite food. Nor have we discussed the *real* reason she took me on this trip. She's cornered and so am I; now's a good time.

'Why the trip? The real reason. And don't bullshit me.'

The plane bucks and Tracy grabs an armrest. 'You needed perspective, still do, and it kept you from doing anything stupid here – which you were about to, don't tell me you weren't. Two, I figured that seeing the ranch might shock you into facing the truth. Maybe telling it.' She leans away as she finishes.

I don't lean away. 'Yeah? What truth is that?'

Her eyes are a mixture of apprehension and proximity. 'You own Roland's Pentecostal City, Patti. And have since 1996. I checked your vacation records. You were off the same week the papers were signed. We haven't validated the deed signatures yet, but if they come back as yours—'

I reach before I know I'm doing it and the plane hits the tarmac, jolting my hand away from her neck. She gets both hers up and now it'll be a fair fight.

'*How'd you get my records?* Who . . . fronted me? Sonny? Kit Carson, that—'

The plane shimmies as it becomes a too–fast land vehicle.

'Doesn't matter; I have 'em and you were off duty. And if I have this stuff, so will the FBI as soon as they put you in Roland's foster home.'

'You *honestly* think I was on that ranch before? That I'm *part* of this?'

Tracy's not flushed, but she's as far away as she can get. 'You are. Think about it. Try to remember. Try—'

'I don't need to remember!' The plane brakes hard and plasters me into my safety belt. '*I live with that motherfucker every day.*'

'Did you sign something in '96, anything like a deed?'

'I've never been in *fucking* Arizona. Never.'

The plane stabilizes and the engine noise drops. 'You're sure?'

It's like she won't stop slapping me. *I have not been there.*

'Answer me, Patti. Are you sure?'

'We get outta this plane I'm kicking your ass—'

'Maybe. But you'll still have to answer the question . . . to somebody. Why not me? I'm helping, aren't I? Risking my career; hell, my life.'

The pilot says something to the back of Tracy's head while he social–worker smiles beyond her to me. He can't hear us, but he can see my expression and posture. Tracy's eyes stay with mine until I answer the 'sign something' question without thinking.

'I bought my half of the duplex from Stella.'

'When?'

'Nineteen-ninety . . . two.'

'How about Arizona?'

I lean at her again, but slowly this time. 'I told you. I've-never-been-to-Arizona. Or Utah. Or Idaho.'

Tracy blinks once, drops her hands an inch, then cuts her eyes while she thinks reporter thoughts. When her eyes return they're still that witch-hazel green Julie can't shut up about. 'All right, I believe you.'

'Hooray.'

'You've been sober every day since we've known each other – and that predates the sale. If it wasn't a blackout trip, the big question is, why?' She smiles, surprised, and drops her hands to the table. 'Why, just outside of Why?'

Hardly funny, but at that moment between us, it's Comedy Central and we both laugh. There won't be punches between us in the near term. Tracy produces a Mont Blanc pen and scribbles a name and a number.

'Cindy Olson Bourland. A lawyer, the one who beat the State's Attorney in the *Killing Condition* case. She's paid five thousand in advance for ten hours. Talk to her about the FBI and IAD.'

Girls like me don't get many $5,000 presents so it pays to ask, whether you intend to keep them or not. 'She my lawyer or yours?'

'Yours. A union lawyer will get you a prison term.' Tracy takes a long calculated pause. 'And if your friend the super-intendent's in this, a union lawyer may get you the death penalty.'

'Illinois doesn't currently have a death penalty.'

'Yeah. *Illinois* doesn't.'

I block the implication because . . . because I don't know how to deal with a betrayal like that. A death threat so crushing, so beyond my ability that I can't, won't accept that Chief Jesse is a bomb in my pocket. But Tracy and I both know he is. We can hear it ticking.

Bullshit. Chief Jesse is not part of Roland Ganz and Delmont Chukut, not part of . . . I flash on my superintendent meeting out-side the Berghoff – the perfume in the car, not five hundred feet from the U.S. Attorney's office, a woman's office. Then my showy breakfast in Canaryville and the photographer. My trip to Chief Jesse's office at headquarters, the two phone transfers in two days . . . No one sees the superintendent that often other than his secretary and his wife. And he doesn't have a wife.

Tick. Tick. Tick. But the mayor does.

Tracy's staring at me. The plane parks and she punch-dials her cell phone. In an hour Cowboy Bob Cullet and his backup will be free. The pilot walks past us in the narrow aisle and pops the cabin door. He smiles and waits for us to deplane. Tracy smiles back, waves him out, and turns to me.

'I read the rest of the papers from the safe while you slept.' She hands me two pages. 'These mention a will, Roland Ganz's will, but there's no copy. They also mention LaSalle Bank. The bank administers the trust that owns Gilbert Court, remember?'

I remember.

'Try this. You own the ranch, but if he faked your signature to buy it, then he fakes a sale deed too, also with your *matching* faked signature. He can't own the ranch in his name, so he uses yours; your name's just a convenient blind, same as the LaSalle trust is for his ownership of Gilbert Court, just much, much sicker.' Tracy pauses, trying to talk herself out of it, but doesn't. 'Ten to one, he filed your sale deed for the ranch inside the trust with instructions to record it on his death. Tax dodges and cheats do it all the time.'

I nod, happy for any port in a storm. She continues.

'So, when he leaves Arizona headed here because he's spooked by the state investigators coming, he only grabs the papers that he knows he needs and—'

'No.' *Grab* doesn't fit. I glance at the boxes strapped into the seat across from me. 'If he'd had the time Bob Cullet said Roland did – not just minutes or seconds – Roland's safe would've been empty. There wouldn't be trace one of Roland Ganz on the ranch for anyone to follow. He's an accountant, Tracy, an anal retentive, piece-of-shit monster who's covered his tracks and God knows how many bodies for at least thirty years.'

Tracy glances out the window. 'Then someone's chasing him, too – we thought that was a possibility. He's not cleaning up his past to reemerge, he's removing evidence. It's . . . it's—'

'The blackmail angle.' I nod harder, remembering the side of the bus with Denzel behind the title, the recent notes in the margin of the Cal City PD file. 'Gotta be blackmail. Somehow, Roland's shooter *and* target.'

Tracy leans away into her seat, shaking her head. 'If it is, it's not the two lightweights in Calumet City freelancing Delmont Chukut for more money, or Chukut blackmailing Roland Ganz. Think Hohokam, Patti. Think Superintendent Jesse Smith.'

'No fucking way.'

'Awful big coincidence then. About the size of Rhode Island.'

I want to hit her again. 'Reporters always have to have a bigger story, don't they? I got one for you, one you've been walking by blind for three days: Forget about who *lived* in Gilbert Court for ten seconds. Who *owned* it first? Who must've sold it to Roland Ganz? And why?'

Tracy's face blanks. She's been to this spot before. Now she's trying to see what I see, what seems so obvious to me, the billboard everybody's missed. She scrunches her eyes to search mine. The search becomes a stare, then her mouth drops as she puts it together.

'Holy shit. The three shots weren't at Mayor McQuinn. They were at his wife.'

Tracy's still staring. There isn't a reporter prep school for those moments. On the Northside they call them *epiphanies*, the kind of sudden clarity that sets you back on your heels. Epiphanies often explain the previously unexplainable but add new confusion to ruin the moment. And that's what we have – a whole new set of possibilities. But they don't feel possible; they feel probable. They have weight. Confusing, but in this muck, and for the first time, I know the mayor's wife is part of this. A big part. *I know it.*

Chief Jesse is another story. The FBI says he's part of 'blackmail, murder, and continuing police corruption dating back to Calumet City.' I just can't go there. And if that kills me today, then it does. Tracy will see it different; the same killer instinct that will blitzkrieg the mayor's wife will also bullet–train Tracy to ICU. That I can't stop. What I can do is get Sonny out of bed on his day off and hear what he's found on Delmont Chukut and Idaho Joe in Chicago. Then I too will go to work on the lovely and talented Mary Kate O'Banion McQuinn.

Tracy shakes her head, tapping fingernails on the plane's table. 'Mary Kate, Mary Kate . . . what are you into, girl?' Tracy's smiling again, then checks her watch and surprises me sideways. 'Are you playing?'

'Huh?'

'BASH. At noon. Are you playing?'

Like Julie, Tracy's devotion to rugby outpaces reason. The same has been said of me, but that was the old me. 'Ah . . . on the off chance your side of the cabin wasn't pressurized, no, I'm kinda involved in this.'

'Here's my key. Take the boxes to my place. I'll see you right after.'

'You're kidding, right?' This has to be a move of some kind.

'Tim the pilot will get you a Town Car.' Pageant winner smile. 'I'll think about Mary Kate.' Tracy pats my hand as she passes in the aisle. 'And don't go to Evanston; it won't work. We'll find Delmont Chukut first – he's our key – pump him this afternoon or tonight, then talk our way into Le Bassinet first thing Monday when they open.'

I stare and she stops when I don't answer.

'Promise, Patti.'

Like that would mean shit.

'Promise, Patti.' Her hopeful tone ceases. 'Or this is going to cave in and kill us both.'

She's probably right and I lie to make her feel better. 'Promise.'

SUNDAY, DAY 7: 11:00 A.M.

The Town Car's leather is clean and cold. Sonny's on my cell phone and not happy. He starts the conversation I just initiated, saying, 'The Ayatollah's poking, asking why you stopped Wardell Scurr in the first place.'

I do not need Alderman Gibbons and his pickets in my face today and Sonny agrees, saying he doesn't either. Next, Sonny bitches about the 'PI/Pentecostal City' voice mail assignment I left him yesterday. Then he jumps back to Wardell Scurr. 'When we booked him, Wardell had a piece of napkin in his sock, had '10026' scribbled on it in blue ink.'

The five numbers on my license plate are 10026. I flash on the GD at Leon's RideBrite, his cell phone tight to his mouth even with my pistol pointed at him.

Sonny pauses to let '10026' soak in as if I need the punctuation, then ghetto–speaks: '*About yor man, Delmont mulfuckin' Chew-cut.*'

Roland's boxes bounce next to me in the backseat – the little hands wrapped in manacles. I push them toward the door and check the back of my driver's head.

Sonny says he's only semi–happy to make the following report, provided I forget where I heard it. I agree.

'*Delmont Chew-cut*. Upstanding citizen. The Indians threw him off the reservation on a rape complaint that he beat. Was a copper for awhile, till Tucson PD tired of defending him on aggravated battery. Did get an honorable from the Army Rangers, though. He's been implicated in two murders, has two pages of assaults related to bail enforcement, and if he isn't in the dope and smuggling business, he should be, given all the time the G has invested.'

The highway bumps the phone off my face and I notice the driver's eyes on me in the mirror.

'So tell me again, P, why are you and Mr. Chew—toy sharing air.'

'Can't talk right now, I'm in a hired car.'

'Convenient.'

'Wanna talk to the driver?' I push the phone up by the driver's cheek and ask him to say hello to Sonny. He does and I pull it back.

'Satisfied, asshole?'

'*I'm* an asshole? The guy who's got his neck on the block and the G up his ass? No, I'm a fucking idiot, Patti. There's a difference.'

Sonny's got a point. 'Sorry. Anything on Idaho Joe and the bar?'

Silence, then, 'Stop and call me . . . the number at Eighty-seventh and Hamilton. Five minutes.'

It's a landline pay phone we use when cell phones don't cut it. I say, '10-4,' and tell the driver pull off the Stevenson. We're in Cicero and I ask him to stay in the car with the engine running. The Exxon station isn't busy but the pay phone outside has a half —cover that blocks too much of my vision. I drop two quarters, eye the street – even Cicero is full of SUVs – and punch the number at Eighty-seventh.

On the seventh ring Sonny answers.

'We were talking about the bar and Idaho Joe.'

'Could be something. Me and Cisco – he's out of the hospital and too stupid to stay out of this – me and him braced the bar owner and his license. He's got a silent partner he shouldn't have, a dude sergeant over in 7. We explained that the price for continued silence was his license and the sergeant's star. They both pissed on our shoes like they had steam, then folded and braced their bartender. Bingo, a description.'

' "Idaho Joe" was Mr. Chukut?'

'Nope. Mr. *Chew-cut* is in the six-four range, pushing two-fifty, if he's still eating right.' Sonny goes ghetto for the bartender's quote, ' "Idaho Joe" he a whiteboy, you know? Arizona-white, maybe twenty-five . . . and rangy, you know, twitch-eyed like them bikers get.' Sonny laughs at his impersonation. 'Fuckin' bartender's as white as you and me and sounds like Ice-T.'

'I just came from there.'

'Where?'

'Arizona. They've got a missing, probably murdered, preacher out there who Delmont Chukut PI'd for. The preacher has a son named Joe who fits your description. Balanter Joseph, last name Allen, A-l-l-e-n. Can you run him?'

Pause. 'You know all this 'run him' shit is gonna come back to us, me. I better have a real good explanation.'

Ten feet away the Town Car's engine stalls. I notice the driver looking at me instead of the scenery. Sonny's right, this isn't fair. 'Forget it, okay? If I'm still in Intelligence, I can run him. If not, I'll find another way.'

'You're not.'

'Not what?'

'On the job. They suspended you this morning.'

My shoulders slump and I lean into the phone cover. This isn't a surprise, more like the steak dinner arriving on death row, final reinforcement that your fears are real. You'll be dead shortly. Just like the person or persons you killed to reach this moment.

'They say why?'

'Not to TAC. But then the first deputy don't care for us much anyway. Our team has another round with IAD on Monday, then me and Cisco sit with the G again.'

'Shit, Sonny, I'm so sorry—'

'Trust me, you ain't the only one.'

There's nothing I can say, nothing that helps him or Cisco or Chief Jesse. 'How's the superintendent?'

I hear Sonny breathing and a truck passing him. 'You don't know?'

I brace for it, but can't make myself answer.

'The G says they got him cold. Dropped it in the *Herald* from "highly placed sources inside the U.S. Attorney's office."'

'But he's alive?'

'Huh? Oh, yeah, shit, I thought you knew. Yeah, better too. Not good, but he came outta the coma twelve hours ago and the G tried to serve him. Motherfuckers. Two HBT guys, Tommy Moore and Babe Catenzo, were there in the waiting room – you remember Catenzo, big, giant dago, he was uniform in 6 way back. He and Tommy Moore damn near killed the Gs, wrinkled 'em up good, then threw their asses in the elevator.' This time Sonny's laugh sounds so good it's food. 'Gonna be some shit over

303

that. But they're both legends now. They'll get cush city jobs somewhere when they get out.'

'The G's not bluffing, are they?'

Sonny's tone loses its street–cop triumph. 'They're gonna pop you tomorrow a.m. That ain't bullshit, honey. If you liked Arizona, I'd go back.'

At this moment, and God knows I don't know why, I want to tell Sonny the whole story. So at least someone I care about knows. Not just Tracy and the parts she has, but the whole thing and how I feel about it, what I hope to do. A confession, I guess, before I step off the cliff. I suppose I want to be the old me one last time. The good guy.

'Sonny, I—'

But I stop because I'm not *her* or the good guy anymore. I will save my son, and Gwen, and her son if they're still alive. I will murder Roland Ganz because no one else will or has.

'Patti? You there?'

'Yeah. Thanks. Listen, uh . . . like I said before, if you can get away from me, do. It won't hurt me and I'll understand even if nobody else does. Tell Cisco and Eric too. I'm gonna go all the way on the guy who's after my son. No matter how he and I meet, he's over.'

'Shit, Patti.'

'And about Chief Jesse, listen to me, okay? I don't want him to be dirty. I don't want anything ever to be bad for him. Ever. He's my dad, the closest thing I ever had to one.' The air in my lungs is real thin. 'But—'

It goes silent on Sonny's end too. Not even trucks and horns. Nothing. I shouldn't say what I'm about to.

'The PI, Delmont Chukut, and Chief Jesse are the same brand

of Indian. A tribe I've heard of only twice in my life. The Hohokam. They're from the Sonoran Desert in Arizona and northern Mexico, the quote 'vanishing people,' and they need to be 'cause there ain't shit out there but sky and cactus. Chief Jesse lived in the building at Gilbert Court. We found my foster mother's body in the basement. Twelve years after she goes in the wall, her husband is hiding out in Hohokam country.'

There's just no way to say how much I hate saying what I'm saying. Just-fucking-hate-it and my hand pounds twice on the phone cover. But I keep going, pouring gasoline on my mentor's future.

'Chief Jesse sends me, a TAC cop, to Joliet and then Calumet City, and then two phone transfers and a meeting in his office and another one in Canaryville with a photographer there. And somehow there's another photographer waiting for me when I show up at Ruth Ann's porch. Chief Jesse loves me, but it ain't right, Sonny. As much as I hate saying it, it ain't right.'

'You told anyone else?'

'C'mon.'

'That reporter?'

'Why the hell would I do that?'

'I don't know. Why the hell would you bring her to 6?'

The hair stiffens on my neck and I feel the prickles on my forearm. Somehow Tracy got my vacation records from personnel. I spin, losing the phone, and draw the Smith. Nothing but air, not even a stray or a leaf or a . . .

The dangling phone is a disembodied Sonny saying my name.

'Sorry.' I start to say something spooked me but don't. 'Dropped the phone.'

'What're you gonna do?'

305

'Do? Shit, I'm gonna kill Roland Ganz. Nothing else I *can* do.'
Saying that out loud, on the phone, is as big a shock to me as it is
to Sonny.

'I didn't hear that. Must be a bad connection. How 'bout we
meet and talk this out in person. Possibly you need advice you
don't seem to be gettin'.'

Meeting him was my plan but now it isn't. 'Stay away from
me, okay? Nothing good's gonna happen in my neighborhood.
And the Chief Jesse stuff . . . I said it 'cause I want you safe.
Please don't hurt him with it if you're . . .'

Sonny's voice drops two octaves. 'If I'm what?'

The hair is still tight on my neck. This man has saved my life
and sided me in life-and-death encounters for seventeen years. I
have never, ever known him to screw over anyone in uniform,
ever. Beat the shit out of few, yes; criticize and insult them when
he shouldn't, yes; but never burn them, ever. And now that's
what my instincts are telling me. No explanations, just instincts.
I want to tell him those same instincts *know* the mayor's wife is
part of this too. But I don't.

'Gotta go. Love you, bye.'

I'm walking to the car when I realize I just said, 'Love you,
bye.' I have lost my mind. No question about it. And where I'm
going that can't be anything but good.

Chapter 21

SUNDAY, DAY 7: 1:16 P.M.

At 1:16 p.m. Central Time, the Chicago Cubs began playing their last game of the season, a game that could clinch them a playoff berth as the NL wild card. North of the river, not far from Tracy's town house and the L7 Bar, the city was already balls-of-their-feet drunk.

At 11:16 a.m. Arizona time, ace reporter Cowboy Bob Cullet and a crew of off–duty Arizona civil servants dug up the first of five bodies buried together in His Pentecostal City. The grave was unmarked, other than the small rupture caused by a magnitude 2.6 earthquake not uncommon in the area. One body had suffered two bullet wounds to the temple and one to the sternum. The first two bullets removed half the skull and all the upper teeth. All three rounds came from a revolver found in the grave.

Prior to his phone being confiscated, Bob Cullet made two calls to Tracy Moens. Tracy's cell phone was on, but it was packed in her kit bag, safely in the trunk of Julie McCoy's car while they warmed up for BASH. An unfortunate set of circumstances for everyone involved.

I'm pacing in front of Tracy's plasma TV. The Cubs are on but I keep glancing at Roland's boxes. They aren't just boxes; I know better. They're little metal demons. The Cubs go down in order. Tracy's phone rings in the kitchen. I pace her living room instead of answering, then walk around the boxes to the bathroom and avoid the mirror. The bathroom smells like an expensive department store and feels like a cell. I step out and stop.

Avoiding the mirror? Why? You're a ghost, remember? The girl who never was; mirrors don't matter. I check my hands, not sure why. *What am I thinking about?*

The mayor's wife.

Why her?

Voodoo. She's gangster legend Dean O'Banion's granddaughter.

Roland's boxes. Animal parts, watches, nuggets ... don't think about the manacled hands; don't look at your wrists.

So what if she's Dean O'Banion's granddaughter?

Watches, rocks, and bones. And manacles. I open the watches box.

Those three gunshots were at her, Mary Kate, the mayor's wife. Chief Jesse lived in Mary Kate's building at Gilbert Court. The mayor, her husband, appointed Chief Jesse – a street cop – to superintendent. The watches box looks different here than it did in the desert. I fingertip each watch and stare, still wondering if it's a dead person, still expecting one to talk, to tell me how to find the monster hunting my son.

Thirty–one watches, not fifty, and none talk. None are running either.

Mary Kate O'Banion McQuinn.

Casino license.

Gangster's granddaughter.

So what?

I check the clock. The G and the U.S. Attorney will have their warrant in twenty hours; Le Bassinet opens in nineteen. That will be a gunpoint showdown with Le Bassinet's two codirectors. Scaring the shit out them will be simple; getting out before a secretary calls the Evanston police won't be. I'll have to 'calm' my way inside, then get in to see—

Shit, that'll never work. The first secretary who sees me will 911 with both hands. Parking lot. I'll grab Codirector Marjorie Elliot when she exits her car. Except I don't know what she looks like. And what about Pinkerton? Didn't Ms. Meery say they open the lock with her, or do they just have an emergency override?

I try to remember and can't.

The mayor's wife is from where? The Northside, like her gangster grandfather Dean?

Okay. Plan B. I'll grab the other director, Mrs. Trousdale, hop in her car when she pulls into the parking lot. Stay there with her until Marjorie Elliot and/or Pinkerton opens the vault. When they leave, Mrs. Trousdale and I will walk in, smile for the cameras and secretaries, and hit the vault. Ten years in Stateville, minimum.

Yeah, but if I can get out of Evanston, it'll work long enough to warn John—

A reality moment jumps in. But if EPD can stop me or come close, John won't be warned . . . I don't want to think about outright failure or a police confrontation where I have to choose between an officer and my son. My plan just has to work.

I glance at the TV. The Cubs are down one run in the third. The mayor and his wife gotta be at Wrigley.

What the hell is it about her?

My phone vibrates. I recognize the number but can't place it until my thumb slides off the screen's corner: 602. Delmont Chukut.

'Patti Black.'

'It's my pleasure, Ms. Black. Delmont Chukut. I'd like to talk to you.'

Relief. It's not Roland's voice. 'About what?'

'There's a matter of an inheritance. Money owed you if I can confirm you are the correct Patricia A. Black.' He doesn't sound like an Indian, although I have no idea what Indians sound like.

'Gee. That's great.' I don't bother asking who died, since the story's bullshit and we both know it. 'Where are you? I'll be right over.'

Delmont laughs too smooth, like the street pimps do, like his boy Harold J. J. Tyree did. 'It's customary that I come to you, verify your address, your phone, electric bills, bank statements – all the elements that make up an identity in the modern age. A birth certificate, your Social Security card, voter ID, that type of thing.'

'I'm not at home. Maybe I could pick up that stuff – it's all in my locker at the station; we could meet there.'

'No. I don't think that will work. I need to see your home, verify the meter numbers match the bills with the name, things like that. Why not pick up the papers and bring them home. I'll meet you in . . . an hour?'

I take the deepest breath I can, trying to drive the anger toward my feet and away from my mouth. It doesn't work.

'Here's the deal, Delmont. In three minutes I can have every cop in this city looking for you. I'll recap this conversation as part of a long list of violent felonies we're currently investigating. When I'm done my fellow officers will believe that you intend to kill me. This will dramatically reduce your chances of surviving the arrest.'

I give Delmont a chance to respond that he doesn't choose.

'Then I'll call the U.S. Attorney at home – she and I are chums – that's one-stop-shopping for the FBI, DEA, ATF, and INS. Should you escape our city, Phoenix and points south won't be where you're going.'

He clears his throat. 'All that because I want to help you collect your inheritance?'

'We both know what you want. We're gonna trade, you and I, in person and right now. Like I said, when I hang up it better be because I'm headed your way.'

The silence lasts thirty, forty seconds, a long time when you're bluffing.

Delmont says, 'Do you know the Lamplighter Inn on Lincoln?'

'Sure.' I don't.

'Room 121, on the far end. Wait out front in your Celica. I'll be by.'

I'm squared up on Tracy's TV like it's an oblong Delmont. 'You're kidding, right? In sixty seconds you're gonna be a citywide.'

'You tell me, then.'

I look out the window at Lincoln Park, which you'd think was on Lincoln Avenue but isn't. 'Try a coffee shop full of people.'

Delmont takes a moment, then, 'Should I have a problem, or be arrested, or assaulted at this meeting, *none* of your inheritance will find its way to you. *None*, if you get my meaning.'

I assume 'my inheritance' means John and want to strangle Mr. Chukut instead of the phone.

He says, 'A houseboat, docked in slip E26, Diversey Harbor. The Yacht Club there's full of people. The *Schofield's Too*. Come alone, no follow cars, no radios. We'll talk, see if there's a way to work this out for everyone.'

I'm almost positive he was playing toward this from the beginning. And if he's running a game on his employer, Delmont will have someone else there who'll either explain where I fit in the scam or tell me where Delmont really is, so Delmont can explain. That or they've wired the boat, prepping for this: I step aboard and BOOM.

'When?'

'Four o'clock. No negotiation. Alone.' Pause. 'Could be I have someone for you to meet.'

Click.

Click? I'm still bracing the TV. *Someone for you to meet*, my ass. Wait till four o'clock? Guys don't hang up on you when you have the upper hand. I notice the Cubs score, we're tied, Soriano's up. Four o'clock. Maybe I don't have the upper hand.

Instead of watching Alfonso's at-bat, I google 'Diversey Harbor.' In three clicks I produce a map. Diversey Harbor is at the other end of Lincoln Park, twelve blocks from where I'm standing – close. God loves me today.

Tomorrow will be different.

Before I go to hell, I need a plan, a way to survive this meeting in order to reach the one that matters. That will require some

312

sort of Lincoln Park yuppie disguise. I mount Tracy's stairs two at a time and hope I don't get lost in her closet.

Rummaging through what would be a decade of cop salary on hangers, I hear a *creak*, then the *whoosh* weather stripping makes on an expensive door when it's opened quietly. Too quietly to be an owner. I visualize Delmont Chukut and Idaho Joe, rubber restraints, their employer grinning – my Smith's in my hand. I spin 360 for an exit: bathroom window – too small, big window in the bedroom. And twenty–five feet to the street. Trapped – only one stairway to this floor. If whoever's downstairs has a machine gun or shotguns, I'm already dead. The door downstairs closes and something hits the floor. Nobody yells; it's too soon for the BASH game to be over. I hold my breath and listen to movement. It stops, or hesitates. A stair creaks. *Here they come.* My best chance is to shoot through the wall—

'Patti?' Tracy's voice wavers, like it might sound if she had a knife at her throat.

I soft-step to the doorway but don't peek. 'Up here.'

My gun hand trembles. The stairs creak, fast like two at a time, not how you'd feel after you've played against BASH, win or lose. I duck out the doorway into the hallway's blind corner, brace fast into the stance, ready to shoot whoever has her. The fast footfalls keep coming; Tracy's face speeds around the corner like she's been pushed, sees nothing but gun barrel, and yells, *'Jesus!'* She ducks and slides sideways past me into a small table. I step past her to the corner, aiming chest – high at whoever pushed her.

'I'm alone. *I'm alone.*'

The stairway's empty.

I lower the Smith, exhale, lean my shoulders into wallpaper, and glance at her piled in the hallway and wide-eyed. She's still in shorts and jersey and asks, 'What . . . happened?'

'Talked to Delmont.' My tone's dry, not I-almost-shot-you. 'Shouldn't you be playing?'

She jumps to standing. 'Julie kept calling your cell and you didn't answer.'

'*You* left the match because I didn't answer my phone? This story *must* be a Pulitzer.'

'The FBI was at the pitch. An ASA, too. *And* a rep from the mayor's office. Couldn't focus, kept thinking about Mary Kate—'

'*You* couldn't focus on BASH? Mary Kate beat you in a pageant or something?'

Tracy uses both hands to artfully restrain red hair. 'The only way it could be better than Mayor McQuinn's wife is if it's Hillary Clinton.'

I can't help a small laugh that feels better than it sounds. 'Julie'll make you suffer if we lose.'

Tracy smiles and now I'm sure she and the mayor's wife have pageant history. She says, 'I told Julie I couldn't let you face this alone.'

Right; Meryl Streep couldn't make that line believable in Tracy's mouth. Tracy rights the table she knocked over.

'Ever consider we might be friends? Like you and Julie; like me and Julie?'

I stare, pistol still in hand. 'Uh . . . no?'

She frowns. 'Well, you might,' and walks into her bedroom. Her walk is nonchalant but her voice isn't. 'So, what did Delmont say?'

I follow and stop at her doorway. She strips en route to her

314

bathroom. I hear the shower and she yells over it. 'Delmont say anything about Mary Kate?'

Her closet's in the bathroom, forcing me to walk past the steaming glass to resume sliding hangers for my disguise. 'He's meeting me at Diversey Harbor.'

'Five minutes. I'm going with.'

Sure thing. Five minutes will be forty–five. And safe in the shower 'she's going.' Once we take a brief reality walk, she'll be doing something else of equal import that doesn't require murder or suicide.

The shower quits and the door pops behind me. I hear, 'What're you looking for?'

Miss Centerfold is wrapping a white towel. A small Pink Panther logo finishes perfectly above her left breast. If I were a guy, she would own me at this instant. I can't tell if this is a move, an invitation, or an accident.

I turn back to the hangers and my search for a disguise; she keeps standing there, toweled up in white like Sharon Stone. 'You're going through my closet?'

'Yeah. Sorry. Need a coat and hat, something that looks yuppie.'

Tracy frowns. I explain:

'If I make it past the harbor meeting, I'll do Le Bassinet next; need to look like I belong here instead of Seventy-ninth Street.'

'Where in Diversey Harbor? The sky over the lake looked pretty ugly. Another storm's coming.'

'A houseboat.'

She steps in front of me, grabs pants first, then a blouse, and on her way out a sweater. Over her shoulder she says, 'All the coats and hats are downstairs, the closet off the kitchen. What slip number?'

I say, 'E26' and turn for the door, toward the stairs, the stairs that were life-and-death minutes ago. Funny how things change.

'Great.' She drops the clothes on her bed and reaches for a hairbrush. 'A gentleman friend has a cruiser in F21. We can get in and on the dock using—'

'I'm a cop; we get in and out without a "gentleman friend"' My tone sounds like a third grader and Tracy makes that matching face as I pass.

Bitch, now I want her to come. I'm halfway down the stairs and hear: 'It's more than one gentleman, actually. It's five.'

Two third graders at the water fountain. I say 'Fuck you' only loud enough for me and focus on searching the kitchen closet. Inside, it has two leather jackets – one is dead-on if I were an Outfit guy wearing a black shirt and neck chains. There's a serape or wool cape, four long coats for winter, a letterman's jacket from Northwestern she probably won on her knees. *Jesus*, she has clothes. More jackets and ten pairs of boots underneath. I want the Outfit jacket – natch – but go for the serape since I'd never wear that. Need a hat. Above the coats is a hat rack the length of the closet, triple pegged, and stunning in its selection. How much freakin' money can you spend on this stuff?

'That's a surprise.' Tracy is bug–eyeing the serape. 'Looks . . . nice, though. Try the leopard print,' and points at a something she calls a 'Russian round hat.'

Tracy's playing dress–up, I'm sure with the intention of making me look as stupid as possible. I grab the hat anyway; she grabs boots with heels and holds them out, nodding a silent leer and floating her eyebrows.

'I'm not gonna fuck the guy, I'm gonna kill him.'

Miss All-Everything personal shopper stalls. I said it honest, matter of fact, not a hint of bravado. It's so obviously true that she steps back.

'Delmont Chukut? Not Roland?'

'Delmont Chukut if he's stupid, and that's eighty-twenty. Roland Ganz for sure, and anyone else who makes me.'

The boots drop but she doesn't move. 'For real?'

'Murder One, honey. At least once.'

'I'd be an accessory, like you said.'

I smile. The Pink Panther finally gets it.

'You can't do that and save your son.'

'It's the only way I *can* save him.'

My new serape brushes her as I pass. She's behind me but silent. I find my gym shoes in the living room. They're dry, a bonus I didn't expect.

'Patti, look, you can't just . . . you can't . . . 'cause you can't.'

Tracy's Northside fairy-tale life hasn't prepared her for pre-meditated murder. Mine has. Seventeen years of ghetto will do that to most people. But I'm not even most people. I turn to Tracy's mirror and stare right at it. Daring it. Instead of the ghost reflection that never quite forms, there's . . . less. The new me.

I check my two speed-loaders, then face her. 'Do I look like I can't?'

Tracy doesn't answer, but her face votes. She backs to the front door, puts her butt on it and says, 'Just think . . . a minute. Maybe there's another way.'

I wait for the minute. Out of courtesy for the expensive clothes I'm going to ruin and the explaining she'll have to do when this is over. But by then she'll have the story and when it gets messy in the morning, she'll be the only one with all the answers.

She exhales through lips shaped to kiss or whistle, but does

317

neither. 'War correspondent. Not an accessory. Piece of cake; I'm in.'

I hear a silent drummer rim-shot the punch line.

Being a dumbshit, I'd just decided that her 'you just can't' was honest concern for me. 'War correspondent' is much better. The Pink Panther's in this on her own, hence her life is only half my responsibility. Now I can focus on Delmont Chukut, Army Ranger, bail enforcement officer, drug smuggler, kidnapper, and probably killer.

SUNDAY, DAY 7: 3:00 P.M.

The air's electric. Lake Michigan is churned up in whitecaps and splashing over the buttresses of Lake Shore Drive. I'm worried and so is Tracy as we approach Diversey Harbor from its western edge. The harbor is inland three hundred feet from the lake and shaped like a pork chop. To the north, south, and west is leafy Lincoln Park, beyond that it's all high-rise city.

From the passenger seat of Tracy's Jaguar I count fifteen long piers bobbing with chop and hundreds of boats. Tracy says there's a yacht club too. She points north toward the parking lot she says we'll use just as the lot materializes downhill at the fat end of the pork chop. The lot faces a low, bridged channel that tunnels under Lake Shore Drive to the lake. The channel has rough water and no boats in it.

I glance at the sky out over the lake. Tracy wasn't lying about the storm coming. She adds that these yacht clubbers are her people, hers and Mary Kate's, although I don't recall seeing pictures of them above Tracy's refrigerator. She also says that the houseboat is unusual; one of only two in a harbor of five hundred-plus boats. And although she knows everyone and everything, she doesn't know who owns either one.

We pass by on the north end of the harbor, climb higher out of the park onto the southbound ramp of Lake Shore Drive and make a cop-pass from the slow lane. Tracy points down at the general area of slip E26 and what might be a restored mahogany houseboat midway out on a long pier surrounded by bigger and smaller boats tied down tight in the chop. Tracy says that if a storm weren't threatening and it weren't twenty degrees colder than normal, all the piers would be empty. She adds that our approach would've been obvious from the deck of any boat still docked at the north end.

Really? Wonder if Delmont missed that or just doesn't know shit about yachting. One would guess a desert Indian nomad might not; so why pick a one-way-in/out marina if you've never seen a boat before? To face a Chicago cop?

We exit Lake Shore Drive at Fullerton, make a U-turn in dense traffic, take the Drive north back to Belmont, then southbound again, rolling slow in Lake Shore Drive's close lane. Our two passes take twenty minutes. One hour left. No people are moving on the houseboat's deck, if it's the right boat. Delmont said he might have someone he wanted me to meet — someone who's got to be part of his scam angle, if that's what this is. And I still haven't figured who.

Since we have no other way to do this, we pull off the Drive, make two right turns and a veer into the park that buffers the harbor on three sides. Instantly we're out of city and driving through an oil painting.

Leaves gust across the windshield, bits of green mixed with fallen red and brown. Tracy slows and drops her window. The

Jaguar fills with air unpickled by fried animal fat, exhaust, and four-inch speakers cranked past their limits. A damn shame people in the ghetto don't get to see and smell this. We've got parks, some on the lake, but you need an army to walk through them.

I know John has seen this park, or one like it. He and his mom have strolled through the leaves and fed the birds, and now he does the same with his girlfriend, pointing at things his mom showed him and laughing at the memories. I know this in my bones and lean back. The butt of my Smith catches a rib and I adjust it the way a civilian would their pager. John's mom wouldn't have a pistol; she'd have a paintbrush or a harmonica. And she'd be nice all the time. And never murder anyone.

Tracy pulls off the boulevard and into the farthest corner of the harbor's parking lot. The oil painting quits; my heart adds rate. She points and says her friend's cruiser is over there in F21, buttoned up one pier south of Delmont Chukut's houseboat. From here, I can't see either one in the bobbing congestion; just boat tops and gulls and dark water pushing in from the lake. Tracy looks at me, takes a deep breath that flexes her neck, then exits the driver's side. Have to wonder about her; she's taking risks for her story that I wouldn't.

I climb over the console into the driver's seat. Our plan is risky but simple: Delmont doesn't know her, so she'll recon his houseboat by walking down his pier to a yacht just past him, a yacht that she'll pretend is hers. She'll do a bit of fiddling – securing it for the storm – then return to tell me what I'm going to face when I approach Delmont directly and alone. While she's doing the recon, I'll sneak to the next pier and her friend's boat, close enough to watch and maybe act as backup if Delmont Chukut gets ugly.

It's not a good plan and we both know it, but if Tracy's careful and lucky we might make it work. If she isn't, Tracy's a strong swimmer and that's Plan B; cold, congested water will be her escape route should Delmont somehow decide she's part of this and not a civilian boat owner.

Through the Jag's windshield I watch her walk the almost-empty lot downhill to the water and the security gate fronting Delmont's pier. At the gate Tracy punches the keypad using a master code given her by the commodore so long ago she can't remember why. I glance ahead of her out on the pier. Delmont's 'someone you should meet' echoes in my head.

What if it's not a scam partner?

The breath catches in my throat. Jesus Christ—

What if it's Roland Ganz? All his divine insanity on that house-boat? I lever the door to yell but Tracy's already past the gate and walking the pier. My heart starts to ramp; how the fuck did I miss the obvious? A gust stumbles her off balance. She'll never see that psychopath coming. Tracy grabs her cap and steadies with a piling. The wind quits and she balance-walks to the end of the pier, hesitates with her back to the houseboat, then boards a cruiser bobbing bow–first opposite the *Schofield's Too*.

Shit, she's trapped. And it's too late to abort.

Go with the plan; make it work. I drive the lot to the pier with her friend's cruiser, park between two SUVs – neither one dented or the right color – and run to my gate. *Please, no Roland near Tracy. Please.* The wind's directly in my face and the concrete's littered with wrinkled, slippery-green Tootsie Rolls. Beyond them are fifty geese honking in the water. The pier's security gate won't unlock – I'm in the open, obvious as hell to any Delmont accomplice, and I've forgotten the code. The lock's too good to jimmy. The geese keep honking, telling each other and anyone else that I'm here. My backup for Tracy is toast. Even in a yuppie disguise I can't loiter ... I pat my pockets, showy, then pat them again. I make fists, pump them in more frustration, then turn to run back to the car and locate a lost code I'm too stupid to remember. A man yells from the piers. I twist back to draw, but miss the Smith's grip covered by a serape I don't ever wear. He's waving from the water side of the now-open gate. I run back, say, 'Thanks so much' without stopping, and run the lurching pier toward the cruiser. The pier bucks, my feet tangle, but I don't fall. The gate man has to be staring but I don't look back and hope I pick the right boat. And hope it's empty. And hope to God that Roland Ganz doesn't already have Tracy.

Slip F21 is full of tall, bobbing white-on-white fiberglass, maybe thirty feet long, open deck with a cabin in the center. I jump on, don't fall, and the cabin door's locked. I duck, hoping I look like I went inside. Quick breath, then peek around the cabin's edge into a mishmash of wind and bobbing ships. I can't see Tracy. She's wearing red; she should be easy to see if she's okay – *BOOM*. Lightning drills into the lake. *BOOM*. The second thunderclap almost puts me in the water. I check for Tracy, don't see her, then the sky again. A twenty–mile line of lightning crosshatches the sky. Tracy said this was the second storm Tim the pilot was sweating; one wide enough to blanket the whole city.

A siren wails. Still no Tracy in a boat or on her pier. Not a cop siren, the old Civil Defense warning. In Chicago, that almost always means *test*, not tornadoes, but no one would be testing on Sunday afternoon in this neighborhood. I 360 for a funnel cloud and don't see any. Could be it's for the front coming in, telling idiot boaters to make for the harbor, or people in the park to seek shelter before it's too late. A flash of red between the boats on Tracy's pier. Then more red and moving fast. It's Tracy running full out, way too fast for the footing.

Roland Ganz.

I fan to fire behind her. Fifty boats bob and block any shot. I jump to the pier but slip, aim and – *Shit*, lost her. *Wait*: Boat . . . space . . . boat . . . space . . . red. *Red*, there she is, running again. Boat . . . space . . . boat . . . *Red*— She flattens at the gate. Fighting it. I aim two–handed and know it's Roland Ganz. *Die, you motherfucker*. Tracy fights the gate open and bolts through. Roland doesn't claw behind her. I sprint my pier, trying to watch her and not be bucked into the water. Tracy's into the parking lot and still running. I can fire six fast and scare— She and I reach both sides of my gate at the same moment. Her eyes match my heart rate. I get through, push her behind the Jag's fender, and twist to kill Roland Ganz and Delmont Chukut—

From behind me she yells, '*Maniacs*—' the rest is buried in thunder.

I aim at her gate and all things in between. My heart's in my throat. *C'mon, motherfucker*—

Tracy's voice goes shallow, 'Cut to pieces,' then she vomits. The wind stiffens and rushes past me. The siren wails again. Tracy pants and stammers, 'God almighty.'

C'mon, Roland, right now—

'On . . . on the deck. Blood – God, everywhere.'

Nobody charges. Heart rate. Heart rate. Nobody charges. '*Who*, Tracy? What blood?'

She doesn't answer.

'Who, Tracy! Who's chasing you?'

'Was a body. Just a body. Blood. Pieces.' Her voice steadies. 'Freaked out . . . I guess.'

'You're alone? You sure?'

'No. Yes, no one's chasing me.'

Her gate's still shut. I glance at the lake. *A funnel*, south and sucking water into the sky. Swelling like a serpent. We're too low to tell how far south or which way it's going. I wide-eye Tracy. 'Anyone else on the boat?'

She shakes her head, starts to steady, and sees the funnel. *'Oh my God.'*

'Gimme the gate code.' She doesn't; I grab at her but miss. 'The code, give it to me.'

She's focused on the funnel draining Lake Michigan into the sky. I slap at her hands and step between her and everything else. *'Give-me-the-code.'*

'Right, right,' and she mumbles it.

The siren, wind, and the funnel are emptying what few people were on their boats. I don't hide my pistol and run to Delmont's gate. Lightning cracks again; thunder pounds right behind it. Lincoln Park and Diversey Harbor are about to get their asses kicked. I make the gate, fight it open, and sprint the pier trying to avoid power cords and water hoses.

Tracy could be wrong. Roland may be waiting on that boat.

That slows me a step. And what if the dead man's not Delmont Chukut? He could be waiting too.

Thunder hammers and car alarms go off. I land on a knee, scramble to aim . . . and there's the restored houseboat sucked down in its moorings. I step closer. The deck of the *Schofield's Too* is splattered red-brown like Tracy said.

All over. And body parts. Ragged wounds – a leg torn off

above the knee, a foot, a half-shirted torso with a headless neck severed at an angle. A hand still duct-taped to a severed chair arm, another hand with only two fingers. Richey's body had severed fingers. Butcher-shop surreal.

The cabin door bangs open.

I duck and fire. The *Schofield's Too* bobs up on a gust. I aim, already squeezing another round at . . . The cabin's empty? The door swings shut then open, vanishes down, then up again. *Squeeze* – the cabin has a light on – small cabin, too small to hide a shooter. My feet jump onto the deck. I slide in the blood, trip on a booted foot, and smash shoulder-first into the outside of the cabin. The door jerks open next to me and I try to shoot it.

My finger jams on the trigger guard. A strip of red flashes on my left; Tracy's five boats down and crouching on the pier. I kick a deck chair past the door and draw no fire, suck big air, and rush in low: Big shadow on the left; I twist at it, stumble, and gun-barrel the corners. My knee buckles and I fan again. No shooters. I rush past and slam my back into the wall facing the door I just entered.

It's a slaughterhouse inside too. He . . . they . . . it . . . did the torture in here, the pieces tossed out onto the deck as they went about it. Reveled in it. The blood splashes are still screaming. I can smell the lust, taste the copper. This isn't human, it's . . .

Thunder pounds the boat and water. Roland the devil. The son of a bitch is always ahead of me. Always—

Part of the lower torso is still tied to the remainder of the chair, a syringe buried to the hilt above the hip. A cleaver lies upright in the corner, pliers and a hacksaw beside it. My stomach cramps; I fight the vomit down. There's the head. Rolling in a corner.

Delmont wanted me to meet someone.

The head's gagged. The eyes are gone. *Jesus Christ*, this is awful.

Deep breath. Mistake. Steady, Patti, steady. Judging by the amount of body, all this . . . flesh likely belongs to Delmont Chukut. Sonny said he was 250+. But massacred, Delmont seems twice that size. This is bad beyond what I've seen before. Wind roars over the boat. The CD siren wails and I remember the tornado. Bad too; I crane my neck, semi-frozen but can't see the funnel. I can see what's tied to the chair. The chunk resembles a pair of Bermuda shorts, only full. I know what I have to do, look away, and reach through the gore, hoping to try all four pockets if I can force myself.

Pockets one and two have car keys and a thin wallet. I toss both at the door. Pockets three and four are empty save for a pen that sticks me. My head's starting to fog and I gasp from holding no breath. The siren won't quit. Hard to think. The wind pitches the boat and stumbles me into the wall. I get the whole scene again, framed from the opposite corner. Lightning streaks just beyond the windows. My hand and fingernails are covered in Delmont Chukut.

I part bolt, part stumble out of the cabin into the discarded body parts. The wind knocks me to a knee and I slide in the blood. A quarter of the Southside's sky is now funnel. The thing's huge but no closer. Thunder hammers again. I land on my ass – *Jesus Christ* – both hands braced on the deck.

Tracy yells, but I can't make the words. I can make the bloody wallet and keys, grab both, fight to my feet, and jump onto the pier. My handprints and shoe prints are everywhere in the blood. Tracy and I sprint for the gate. She jumps an overturned dock box and a gust sails her sideways. She falls and I can't avoid her without swimming, and go down too. The wallet and keys hit the water. I get both hands in. The keys are gone; the wallet sinks slower. I get it, lose it, and get it again. Bigmouthed fish come up and gulp at my hands.

I beat them to the wallet. My arms return harbor-water clean to the elbows. Lightning rips through the sky. Tracy tugs me up, yelling. All I hear are sirens and wind. We run for the gate, then to her Jag. She jerks her door open and dives behind the wheel. I round the hood and scramble in. Rain lands in a wave. We both wince *'Jesus'* in unison.

But we don't move.

'Need to get away from here, Trace.' Lightning explodes into the park. The air is water. We're swimming or will be if the funnel catches us here.

'Can't see—'

I push Tracy up into her seat; she's blinking. *'Hell with seeing.* Crank your window.' Her side's on the back side of the rain. She could see inland if we don't have to turn. The Jag inches backward. I slam her knee and we catapult backward into the lot. 'Go!'

She hits the brakes. I bounce into the dash.

'For chrissake, go! Roland cut that guy to pieces. He could be on your bumper!'

She hits the gas blind and accelerates me into the seat. Her head's out the window with one hand blocking the rain, the other steering serpentine through the lot. She brakes and turns left toward the park, away from the lake and jolts to a stop.

She cranks her door open. *'Can't see.* Have to run,' and stumbles out. I round the hood semi–floating and catch her sleeve before she's sucked away in the wind. We pack back into the car, me behind the wheel, and I hit the gas. An invisible low curb bounces us left, downwind of the rain. I miss an elm tree by accident, swerve, miss a bench, and land us on a six-foot-wide walkway. A row of trees blocks rain; the windshield's suddenly functional. I gun it, hoping no escaping jogger gets in our way.

Four hundred feet – then another hundred – then the path veers into the storm. I lock both arms and bounce us blind off another curb, jump it, and land in the middle of the oil-painting boulevard we drove before the sky fell. The wind pushes us sideways, then catches us like a sail and we're semi-flying past a monument's corner. The corner blocks our tailwind; we decelerate, the tires grab. I steer left again and land behind the monument. Instantly the wind quits. The rain slows by half. I'm death-gripped on the wheel and can't feel my hands. I can see them, though, blood clots and gore under my nails. I'm gasping from holding my breath.

Tracy says, 'Headlights. Behind us. Back by the parking lot.'

I see a glow diffused in the rain and stomp the gas. We chew grass uphill, then down and through willow trees whipping themselves into green shreds, skirt the edge of a huge pond with whitecaps, and skid into a street littered with branches and a foot of water.

The Jag stalls.

Oh, shit, baby, c'mon.

It starts.

Tracy jabs at the windshield, 'Diversey's up there.'

We make Diversey and the park becomes city. A snarl of people are fighting into a hospital building tall enough to be in trouble if the funnel picks this path. I veer left, away from the lake. Both of Diversey's two lanes are empty. We hit sixty semi-blind and Tracy yells to slow down. I do, with both feet, miss an ambulance parked without its lights on, slide twenty feet broadside down the center stripe, kill nobody, and the Jag stops.

My heart's pounding. The rain's pounding. A man's pounding too, on my hood, drenched, deranged, bearded, and beating it with both fists. I hit the horn and he jumps sideways to Tracy's door. She lurches into me and I hit the gas. We pass the guy still screaming and confront knotted headlights facing us from three directions. I veer into ... an alley, gun it again, miss all the dumpsters for Duffy's Tavern but one, bounce off its overflow, find another street, turn us left and back west away from the water. Away from the devil.

But not far enough away. The ground's shaking. I can't hear the engine. Suddenly the roar outside is so loud I can't hear anything.

Chapter 22

SUNDAY, DAY 7: 5:00 P.M.

I heard a guy once say God owned parking garages.

We're in one on Clark Street, an old three-decker that could stop artillery rounds. It's raining in three directions. Tracy's out of the car and hugging herself warm, protected by the garage's outer wall on the downwind side. She's looking out at what wanted to kill her and me two hours ago. The Jag's radio works. WLS says it was a water spout – a tornado on the water, nine hundred feet high like they get in Miami. It came within a quarter mile of Thirty-first Beach before the storm's own squall line swallowed it.

The DJ promises that the worst is over, then jokes that all the fish in Chicago's end of Lake Michigan are dead – drop down to any beach and pick up dinner. He has a laugh track to go with the patter.

Past Tracy, the rain has slowed and the last of the afternoon starts to look less like soup. The Cubs game was rain-delayed and finally postponed when it became clear that everyone in Wrigley would die if they stayed there, and they would – Cub fans have a stranglehold on stupid. The DJ says the Sox lost

330

yesterday, so they're toast for another year. Win or lose, at least we outlasted them.

I wipe residual water from my eyes and notice my fingernails; they'll be sore but clean as soon as I can find a knife or paper clip. My jeans and Tracy's serape are blotched with Delmont Chukut's blood – I think it was Delmont.

And I remember the wallet. But it's not in my lap or pockets, or in the seat, or in the console. It was a tough trip from there to here, but I know I fished it out of the harbor just before the fish and sky attacked us. Tracy's walking back, her arms still hugging her chest. At the passenger door she leans in and looks a little better, not good by any measure, but better.

'That was . . . harrowing.'

Harrowing makes me smile. On the Northside, near–death by weather requires three syllables. Miss All-Everything has had a tough two days as my sidekick.

'Who did that . . . to him?'

I wipe at my nose and eyes again. 'Gotta be Roland.'

'But why . . . like that?' She pales out again and turns away.

That's not a tough one either. 'Roland's a monster. A long-term hunter-killer. The fucking devil.' I feel him in the words, shiver, and reach for the high-heat buttons.

Tracy leans on the Jag with her hip to me and squeezes wet red hair into a ponytail. When she finishes, she turns, only her chest in the window. Her voice's half reporter, half assault victim. 'No. They slow down when they get older. Everything I've read says so. Less testosterone, less murder.' She shivers and shakes water off her hands. 'And that boat was a lot . . . of murder.'

Since I don't work serial killers, I don't know. I do know

Roland Ganz, though, the earlier version. But Tracy has a point – why like that? That was madness and rage. A bunch more than paying back a dishonest employee. The storm hadn't hit yet and Roland's tossing body parts out in plain sight? Any boat owner on the far end of that pier could've seen them. And if it was torture – *and it had to be, at least at first*. Roland wanted answers to something at the beginning, after Delmont was subdued with the syringe, answers that Delmont was withholding. If it was Delmont.

Where's the damn wallet?

This is the blackmail scheme or schemes unraveling, the employer declining to be blackmailed or pay more for information he already bought.

Where's the damn wallet?

I reach around under my seat and find only a pen, then reach under the passenger seat and find the wallet. The leather's wet, but thankfully with harbor water. I open it in the passenger seat anyway, not my lap. Credit cards are layered on the left, a wad of business cards on the right. *Confidential Investigations* in bold type, his name underneath with the Arizona phone number. All the credit cards have his name. Two driver's licenses – one Arizona, the other California. Different picture, but the same guy, big blockish head and shoulders.

I flash on the gagged and severed head rolling in the cabin – there's no obvious resemblance, but there wouldn't be. It's the same guy, gotta be, given that I fished this wallet out of the chunk of him still tied to the chair. It wasn't Roland; I know that in my bones. And that's too bad. The wallet has nineteen one-hundred-dollar bills and an oddly familiar folded paper wrapped in plastic.

Tracy says something I don't quite hear, then, 'Patti?' that I do.

'Huh?' I look up, trying to place the feeling rushing at me. 'What?'

'We've got company.'

It's an SUV, the right color, and the driver's side headlight is smashed like it should be if it hit a TAC car in 18 four days ago. I eject and draw before the SUV finishes the turn into our aisle. Tracy jumps fast and lands alive behind our rear bumper. I level at the SUV's windshield using our fender as semi–cover. A .38 will kill the driver but not four tons of metal.

The SUV rolls at us, then jolts to a stop that sprays water off the hood.

Three . . . two . . . one . . .

Its back tires smoke and squeal in reverse. Thirty feet back it slams two parked Hondas shattering their windshields, wheels left, and fishtails down the ramp it just climbed. I hear the engine gun; there's no way to tell if it was a civilian scared shitless by me and the pistol or the grab team that took Richard Rhodes to Roland.

'Get in. We're outta here.'

Tracy requires no convincing. She hip-checks me and takes the driver's seat. I loop the front, grab the wallet off the passenger seat, and make it in just as she floors it. We take the ramp fast and don't stop for the gate arm. It smashes across the top of her windshield and makes us both duck.

No SUV there to T-bone us. She slides left at the intersection, hits no one, and speeds north. I flash on the folded paper inside the wallet I'm holding. See it plain as day inside a yellowed envelope taped to the back of my mirror at home.

My adoption agreement with Le Bassinet.

The burglars left my envelope in place but took the agreement; I just touched the envelope to be sure it was there – I rip at the wallet, tear open the plastic. 'Le Bassinet' is the fourth word I see. 'John Cougar Black' are the first three. *Harold Tyree knew*. Delmont knew. Now *the devil knows*. 'Oh my God.'

'What? Patti, what?'

The phone fumbles out of my hands to the floor. Our car veers to the curb and throws me into the dash when it stops. I shoulder the door. Tracy grabs my arm. I find the phone, bang the door open, and stagger into the rain. Night's coming and Roland knows where John is.

Tracy grabs both my shoulders, her face inches from mine. 'Patti!'

It's like I'm . . . lost. 'Roland knows. About the adoption agency.'

She grabs the paper in my hand, covers it from the rain, and reads it. She says: 'When?'

'Huh?'

She shakes me. '*When*, Patti? How long have they had this paper?'

'The B&E . . . last Monday.' My fingertip tries to punch-dial Le Bassinet but misses. 'Harold Tyree. Gave it to Chukut.'

'They don't have John.'

'Yes they do. Yes . . .' The phone won't work.

'That's six days ago. You've been there since.' She's shaking me again. 'Roland doesn't have him.'

'What?'

She slaps me. 'THEY-DON'T-HAVE-JOHN. Think about it. Think.'

I blink at the slap, then think long enough to see. She's right. *They don't have him*. I was at Le Bassinet Friday. Delmont Chukut never told Roland; Delmont had gone into business for himself. Blackmail or ransom. Just like I thought.

John's reprieve is a river and gushes over and through me and suddenly I'm sitting on the wet concrete, empty and full at the same time. My watch is fogged but it looks like 5:15; Le Bassinet opens in sixteen hours . . .

Tracy tugs at me. 'C'mon, get out of the rain.'

I stand but don't move. Tracy pulls me to a print shop doorway, checks the street, then checks me again.

'Are you all right?'

I nod and shake off the water, take three level breaths through my hands, and scan the street. My watch lights the scars on my wrist. I can't wait sixteen hours; there's no way I can wait sixteen hours—

Tracy notices. 'Talk to me, we'll chase this from the mayor's wife. Her, I know we can find.' Tracy starts matching up Mary Kate and Roland Ganz history like she tried yesterday at her town house. 'Mary Kate sold him Gilbert Court in '76. What else happened in 1976 that we care about?'

I lean against the storefront, processing John's reprieve, catching breath, and scanning for the parking garage SUV. The SUV had to be a facsimile or we'd be wearing it. I need to call in the houseboat homicide – *shit*, can't do that, my prints are all over . . . they're only all over the houseboat *if* it's still afloat. Plus there's the rain coming down just beyond my face – there'll be no evidence an ASA could use anyway. At least on the deck.

Tracy's voice: 'Patti. What about '76? Or '83 when Roland put the building into the LaSalle trust?'

She's keeping me busy, keeping me from *doing*. I answer without thinking and mumble, 'John,' making sure the engine noise I think I hear isn't the SUV returning.

'What about him?'

The engine noise belongs to a Datsun sloshing low in the street water. 'John was born in '83. I told you.'

'Born . . .' Tracy steps back, then cocks her neck like dogs did at the kennel when they were working it out. 'What about '76? Who was born in '76, the year Roland gets the building?'

I shrug and feel the rain. A train that has nothing to do with 1976 hits me in the heart. I go bolt–straight and flash on Delmont. *He talked.* Oh my God, he talked. Even if he kept the adoption agreement, he talked. You know he did – the missing fingers, then the hand. Then he talked. Then Roland lost it and slaughtered Delmont into cat food.

Roland is at Le Bassinet.

Tracy's eyes go half fear and half surprise. 'Patti?'

'Gimme the keys!'

She doesn't. I draw the Smith to hit her in the face. 'Gimme the fucking keys!' I grab; she slips it, runs to the street and puts the driver's fender between us.

'*Delmont talked.* The missing fingers. He talked. Me and your car are going to Evanston. I'll call you an ambulance,' and aim at her ankle.

'I'm with you; you need me.'

'Gimme the fucking keys.'

I intend to shoot her, not argue. She jumps in the driver's seat and fires the engine. Then I'm in and we're northbound on Clark. My hands are shaking.

Call Evanston Police. Call Evanston Police . . . No . . . even if they get involved at Le Bassinet's Ridge address, there's no guarantee that anyone will warn John. EPD will arrest me, I'm the psycho biological mother. John'll have no warning.

'Easy, Patti. We'll get there.'

My left hand balls. The right has the Smith. Both have been pounding my thighs. The pain is substantial, now that I notice. My mouth asks me, *What am I gonna do?*

'Roland can't get in that vault, Patti. He's an accountant, not a bank robber.'

I stop mid-breath and turn to stare at Tracy. In her fantasy world, accountants do tax returns. My lips slide back over open teeth I can't feel; I see her but don't. My eyes narrow and tighten down to their corners as the words form. I feel the words before I speak; they've been forming for twenty-three years.

'He's the guy who raped us while he prayed, and when his dick didn't work, he used candlesticks, handfuls of candlesticks.'

Tracy shies toward her door.

'He's the guy who put his wife in the wall alive, who beat Richard Rhodes to death, and tore the legs off Delmont Chukut, a two-hundred-fifty-pound Army Ranger.'

Tracy runs a light and gets horns from both sides. 'Sorry, I didn't—'

'He's the guy who wants my son. *MY SON.*'

Tracy shies again, but there's nowhere to go. 'I know, Patti, I know. We'll get there. We will.'

All I can do is rock in the seat, a mental–patient felon jacketed up tight, counting minutes in a horror movie that won't end.

Chapter 23

SUNDAY, DAY 7: 6:00 P.M.

Too much time.

Evanston can't be this far from Diversey Harbor, can't be. Tracy swerves past two weather-related accidents. It's six o'clock and looks like midnight. The rain quits at Howard Street, but the Evanston side's a mess of downed trees and power lines and pitch black the farther north we try to drive. No streetlights, no window lights. Cops and fire trucks block each of the four streets we try.

Neither Tracy or I know any back way to Le Bassinet. We're wasting time. It could've been five hours since Roland was at that boat.

Tracy says, 'Easy, Patti, he can't get in until they open.'

I try to believe that. But he'll find a way.

How? How would he do it?

He'd find the women, the codirectors with the keys.

You couldn't.

A PI could. Delmont Chukut.

Oh my God. 'He's got the keys.'

Tracy turns onto another side street littered with branches but no power lines or squad cars. 'No he doesn't.'

'He's already got the keys!'

Tracy guns it instead of arguing. Tree limbs and street debris are everywhere. She serpentines a course at speeds that make me pay attention and stiff-arm the dash. *Roland has the keys.* SQUAD CAR. We miss T-boning it by inches. His siren slaps at us after we're already past. Tracy hooks a left. We race away from him for three blocks. She cuts back north on a commercial boulevard. Three cars are backed up at a light. I check for the squad. She guns it across the intersection but skid-stops at the southbound driver's window.

'Where's Ridge Avenue?'

The guy answers instead of speeding away. Tracy floors it north, takes a right that avoids an abandoned van, then a left into water cascading as high as our axles. We slosh sideways until she mounts the crown of the street. Ridge Avenue. I remember the corner – Le Bassinet is a mile farther. A squad flashing its lights loops us before we see or hear it coming. The light in front of him and us is yellow. He brakes hard and fishtails toward the lake. The light goes red and Tracy runs it. She believes me. She knows Roland Ganz has the keys.

Two EPD squad cars are parked outside Le Bassinet. Two is a big response to any call right now, given that a storm just tried to kill half their citizens and left the rest without power. Tracy grabs a small flashlight from the glove box and says, 'Let me talk. We'll both be reporters.'

Seventeen years on the street says I'm looking at a crime scene. A homicide. Either Mrs. Trousdale or Mrs. Elliot. Getting to the vault will be close to impossible without— An EPD uniform stumbles out the front door into his headlights and pukes in the bushes. He goes to a knee with his pistol drawn and heaves again. It's dark everywhere his headlights aren't. Tracy and I use a high hedge for cover and run to the building's far corner. The side door's propped open. A second cop's voice tells the sick one, 'Jesus, Tommy, call it in. We need the dicks out here.'

Tracy and I slip through the side door and into a lightless hall. I whisper to give me the light and let me lead. She does. The door being propped open isn't right, no way the cops did it. I draw. This crime scene could be seconds old – I'm bumped from behind and lurch sideways. Tracy gasps. Either I slowed or she's scared shitless of being swallowed by the dark after watching cops puke. Sick or not, this is a fresh crime scene to the cops – they'll shoot us if we startle them.

Ahead of us forty feet a down-only stairway is bathed red by the EXIT sign above. Between us and the stairway are three doors, all closed, all with very bad possibilities. I shine Tracy's tiny flashlight on each door, then the carpet leading to the next one. My heart's ramping. The devil is here, behind those doors or down those stairs. Those dark stairs. There's no choice. No time.

Fuck it. Just run past the doors, down the stairs, and hope.

That's what we do. And if Roland's trapped, he'll see us coming, see the light beam, wait till we're close and – At the bottom of the stairs the light catches an open door, a vault-type door. I hear a muffled voice and spin to it. Tracy takes my shoulder on her chin and grabs my shirt before she falls. She doesn't yell. The voice is above us, up the stairs, maybe down the hall. Could be a cop, could be Roland. I cut the light and it's instantly black; all fears become real. Tracy keeps her handful of my shirt; we're both frozen. The voice fades; I button the light, duck, then rotate the beam from above our heads. Inside the vault the beam shines across file cabinets built into three walls, floor to ceiling. One cabinet's open and speckled with dark stains. I edge closer. The drawer tag reads '1980–1984.' My knees weaken; the air's thicker than it was. Tracy bumps me again and reaches past my hesitation. Her hand enters the light, fingering folders in '1983.'

The year is smeared. Tracy fumbles to the 'B' tab, then a green suspension folder behind it. The folder's empty. She whispers, 'Shit,' and grabs the next one. It has a heavy binder labeled 'Duplicate-2' with a log-out sheet stapled to its face. No entries, no smears. She opens it to an empty divider, then mimeographed reports, then the front page of one I recognize. My name. And John's. And his parents – M/M T. L. Bergslund. His address is 2507½ Ridgeway, Evanston, Ill.

I shove Tracy out of the way and rip through the files, looking for the original. She steps back and stutters, 'It's g . . . gone, c'mon.'

I keep searching. The dark smears flake onto the top of my hand. Flakes . . . ? My breath catches short. Tracy tugs at my arm, but she no longer needs to, I'm with her now. I understand. Roland isn't here anymore; he's at 2507½ Ridgeway. The flakes and smears are blood. Dry. He's been there for hours.

Tracy's doing sixty down a main east–west artery marked Central Street.

It's blackout dark and has to be like driving blindfolded. We're missing most of the tree branches and trunks and other vehicles doing the same. Most of my heart's in my throat – 411 matched the address to a current phone for 'T. L. Bergslund.' John and/or his parents *still* live there. No one at their number answers my call. Tracy's flashlight juggles in my hand. I try to read the file while we charge through glare, horns, and debris.

Tracy's voice: 'What's the file say?'

'Can't read it.'

'What's it say?'

'*I said I can't read it.*'

'What's it say?'

I jerk to slap her. She's vise-gripped on the wheel, neck jutted over her hands, face contorted into *shock mouth*. She's probably looked this way since we left Le Bassinet, since we stumbled past the body parts. In a bucket, propping open the side door we'd entered. A gray head with a bullet hole and eyes staring up at us from the bottom, a severed hand with two fingers missing twined into the hair. Whatever the cops saw upstairs was the main massacre.

An EPD squad car flashes red-and-blue into our face. The lights snap Tracy's shoulders into her seat. He barrels past sans siren. Her Jag slows. I flat-palm her chest. 'Tracy.' Her heart's thudding under my hand. 'Tracy!'

'Yeah . . .' She swallows and leans toward me like she's on a couch. 'What?'

'*You're driving.*' I shove her upright and she brakes hard. We skid to a stop mid–street. Horns blow behind us. I jerk the wheel toward the curb. 'Park. Outta the road.'

She eases off the brake. We limp to the curb. She's so white in the blackout dark she glows. I slap her. Twice, then a third time until she jolts away into her window, both hands up between us.

'Wha—'

'Lemme drive.' I snatch the keys, pop my door, and arrive at hers before she moves. She handles her seat belt with three tries then shuffles through our headlights to the passenger side. Definitely in shock. Another EPD squad approaches, lights flashing and heading east. He brakes hard to eye us. I wave him off – a woman not in distress. He hits the gas and the siren.

The siren jolts Tracy. She mumbles, 'Where're we going?'

A woman in serious distress says, 'The house. Ridgeway. John's parents.'

Ridgeway's streetlights are on when I turn, but dim, the old-style ones with the thin panes and liberty crowns. The clouds break and moonlight shadows big trees with broken branches. Small neat houses are set back from the curb. I cut our headlights and park, wishing for a shotgun. Wishing for courage too. Most of all I wish for John and his family. They would've never seen this nightmare bearing down on them, never imagined they could be connected to something like Roland Ganz.

Tracy follows me out of the car. Ridgeway's as quiet as it is dark and Tracy doesn't slam her door. I check her eyes; she's better and paying attention. Only five cars are parked on the street; must be an alley; 2507½ will be on the east side. Roland would have come at them from behind. He came at everyone from behind.

I stumble over a rupture in the sidewalk and into a wide tree. The bark smells smoky bitter – 2507½ is three houses down, a two-story brick with a high roof and a tree in the yard's front corner. Where is everybody? Tracy bumps my shoulder. I realize I've stopped, that I don't want to know what's inside John's house. I'm too late; Roland's had too much time.

'Is that it, the house?' Tracy points at the white clapboard next door.

Deep breath. *Face it, Patti. Face it.* 'C'mon, we're going to the alley.' I pull her left through a long yard, past a house with vines and a detached garage. The alley's narrow, lined tight with garages and strung with telephone poles. We step slow with the flashlight off, crunching branches with leaves, and try to stay in the alley's center. If Roland's hiding here, our reaction time will be zero.

A light flickers on, upstairs on our left. Tracy and I flinch into each other. A candle? Then another in the same house. Watching us? Where is everybody?

We count three buildings and stop at a dark garage with a low gate to its right. The gate is chain–link and blocks a narrow concrete walk to the north side of John's childhood home. I ease the gate open and it doesn't squeak. The walk is an inch deep in water and roofed low by the neighbor's trees. No candles burn in the windows of 2507½. No lights in the yard. Thirty feet ahead of us on the walk the house's side door is propped open.

The quiet's so loud, it's deafening. Be a cop. The door's propped open. I pop the empty brass from my revolver and reload. Be a cop. Be a cop. Wind gusts through the treetops. Tracy startles; I sprint up the walk. The door's propped with a broom, not a bucket. I listen plastered to the bricks, hear nothing, peek, and jump back. No shots or stabs. I peek again: short, wide entry hall – right leads down a dark set of basement stairs; I go low and left and into a small kitchen, fanning my Smith and the flashlight.

Moonlit windows on two sides, a porcelain sink facing the backyard we just crossed. No blood. And no sound. Nothing but the wind. Perfume. Tracy's perfume, she's behind me. The room bristles, hair tightens on my arms. I point the flashlight at another doorway, beyond it a dining room table, beyond the table a double window draped heavy and dark.

Go. I step in fast, duck, and fan right: open stairway, white metal railing; next to the first tread an archway. My beam dies before it reaches through. Sweat beads on my neck. Everything's pitch-black where my light isn't. Move. I bump a table's corner. Me and the flashlight jerk left. I don't shoot an arched-wood front door, duck, and twist back to the stairway opposite.

No one.

Tracy's breathing at my right shoulder. I'm blocked; can't shoot toward the dining room or kitchen. I ease into her, pushing her back behind me and both of us into the arched-wood front door. She shuffles until we reach the door. I cut the light. She gasps and we both duck.

This is a 'no choice' tactic. Whoever's in this house – in the dark, behind the furniture, in the closets – now can't see any better than we can. My eyes adjust while my pulse worsens. Windows form beyond the archway to our left, dark gray rectangles backlit by the streetlights outside. The trees shimmy. Light squirrels across the panes. Furniture shadows.

Sweat. No sound of struggle. My rugby knee aches into my hip. Dim shadows flicker on our right five feet from the kitchen doorway we just walked through. *Shit*, the dining room opens even farther right and into another room. I missed it completely. The walls I can see are mostly glass . . . an enclosed porch maybe. I lack choices and decide to fear it the least.

Stairs.

Save John.

Wind and shadows flutter on the windows. Don't shoot the wrong person. Be a cop, save John's family. Be a cop.

Stairs.

The stairs are five feet wide and carpeted. Up eight treads is a landing dim lit from behind by a window where the treads change direction and climb through the ceiling. From the second floor the window would backlight anyone climbing the stairs. Any gauge shotgun would work.

John and his room are up there.

And so is the devil.

I swallow part of a shallow breath. 'Stay put till I'm at the landing.'

Tracy doesn't answer but doesn't move when I do. I lie on my back and use my heels to slither up the treads head first, arms and pistol extended at whatever weapon will be aiming back. My head won't be visible until my pistol is, and none of me will be silhouetted by the window.

Roland Ganz will be firing from twenty feet. If he has the shotgun, I'm dead; if not, we're 50–50.

The carpet smells deodorized-florid, probably a dog or cat. At tread four the bottoms of second-floor balusters materialize. Be a cop; eyes wide, Smith tight, hammer back. Tread five rubs my neck. The balusters top out at the railing. No shotgun aims; no hulking shadows jerking into . . . *There*. Fire. *No. Don't kill John.* Don't. The Smith's stiff-armed at level railing – fast breath – and more rooms. Tops of doorways, four total – two left, one right, one facing the stairs and me. All open. Four more doors to go through. Not counting all the places I didn't look on the first floor.

I want to use the flashlight but don't. At the landing I flip to my stomach, wait a two–count, then rise to a crouch against the wall. No shotgun. I slide up the last five treads to door one at my

left shoulder. Deep breath, stand, suck in one more and . . . lights
pop on. I duck a shotgun blast that doesn't happen, and charge
the room: four walls, aim, two windows, pivot, furniture, door.
Closed. Spin back to the entry door. Empty, lights on
everywhere.

'Patti?'

No blood. I level on the closet door and flatten on the wall. The
closet stays shut. The room shrinks. Tracy appears at my shoulder.
I silently point at the closet doorknob. She hesitates, then steps to
the knob from the far side and jerks the closet door open. The door
covers her; I spin low and . . . just clothes. Girl's clothes.

Three more rooms.

Everybody can see everybody coming. We do the same in
room two – don't die, then a bathroom, then another bedroom,
closets in each. We finish max–jangled. But alone on the second
floor. And no blood.

I think we're alone. Tracy starts to speak and I wave her silent,
listening to the first floor. Two minutes of no creaks or bumps
and I return us to room two.

John's room, heaven and hell in a package. Trophies, movie
posters, a 2004 University of Chicago calendar, rock posters –
Cowboy Mouth and Farm Aid, book stacks and a desk with a
little metal Corvette under the lamp, a single bed with a Cubs
poster above and signed by the '95 team, a dresser with a framed
8 x 10. The photo's John – has to be – dark-haired and
handsome, and his mother with an aging German shepherd.

John's boyish and . . . and . . . and, oh God there's no trace of
Roland Ganz in his features. John's arm is comfortable around
his mother, his hand messing her hair. She's smiling, comfortable
with John's hand, and— And . . . this room is too neat.

John doesn't live here anymore.

I check fast . . . and sigh to my shoe tops. Tracy steps in from the doorway and grabs at my waist. 'Patti, c'mon.'

John isn't dead here. Just his past kept pretty by a mom. I sit on the bed. *John's not dead here.* His picture blurs through tears I can't stop. So do his posters . . . my heart and lungs actually ache. I want to curl up with his pillow. Tell him . . . It's like having him again. It's like—

Whisper, 'Patti, c'mon. Patti—'

Hand on my shoulder. My name. John's room. I wipe at the tears and stand off balance. A softball trophy by his picture. It's inscribed 'Special Olympics: J. C. Bergslund, 2004 Sports Person of the Year.' I lurch back and into Tracy. She fumbles not to fall, then looks at the trophy too. The inscription doesn't change. I scan the room again, this time looking for . . . Is John, did I . . . ? *Oh no, God*, did I cripple him? Is he a . . .

Tracy's eyeing the door to downstairs, but has the same 'special' thoughts on her face. I search for crutches and make too much noise, then pull out his books, try to open his drawers, try to . . . *How the fuck can I ruin so many lives? I'm* the devil, not Roland Ganz. Red burns my face; my stomach's expanding. No. *We* are the devil, Roland *and* I. Father and mother. Me.

The vomit stops me from screaming. I do it on my knees in the bathroom, head in the toilet, pistol in hand. Tracy has her back to me, eyes on the stairs. She's whispering, but the words don't matter. I'm the devil, the fucking devil. My pocket vibrates. I wipe at my mouth instead, not sure I can stand. Tracy eases back from the stair railing. 'There's something down . . .'

I snap fear-rigid and jump up – Roland's on the stairs. My feet charge past Tracy at— The stairs are clear; landing's clear. *The son of a bitch is here.* I leap to the first floor and aim at everything, don't shoot a lamp now lit in the living room or a plant in its shadows. I fan toward the outside door where we entered. A light's on in the kitchen. Wall phone, next to it a note, big – a full sheet of notebook paper. The handwriting's childish. 'YOUR FRIEND GWEN CALLED.'

Tracy rushes up behind me. 'Smell that?'

I'm locked on the note, but look at Tracy when she says it again. I smell her perfume and look back to the note. *Gwen called?* Tracy bumps into me with her back, shying again from something I haven't seen. I look back at the note – pinned to it is a business card with John's name and an address on South Michigan.

Tracy says, 'The smell's in the basement.'

She tugs me toward the basement and won't let go. I knock her hand away, but balance makes me stumble and follow. Just beyond her shoulder the basement stairs are lit dim. She points to the bottom. Now that the lights are on I can see the blood.

Chapter 24

SUNDAY, DAY 7: 7:00 P.M.

The basement's cold; four walls of concrete. The floor's painted, as are the walls. An orderly room, utilitarian – a washer and dryer in the corner, shelves. Cast iron pipes run through the rafters; a metal pole supports a painted beam. Boxes. A thick throw rug. Animal toys. A food and water dish. And an old German shepherd ripped to pieces.

I jump away from the stairs and aim up at the top. Nothing. Tracy staggers to the pole and uses it to remain standing. The air is light copper and intestines. The shepherd's blankets are soaked. His gray muzzle is beaten flat, the eyes frozen in his last minutes.

No creaks on the floor above us. No one on the stairs. Tracy is sheet white, but standing. She mutters, 'Roland . . . these aren't people.'

'Now you get it.' I remember the card upstairs by the note, say, 'C'mon,' and grab her off the pole. She doesn't let go and I don't blame her. 'Tracy, I'm going upstairs; you need to come with me.'

She's staring at the shepherd.

'C'mon.' I jerk her hands free. We mount the stairs into the kitchen. I read the phone number on John's card and use the wall phone to call. His voice answers for the first time since he cried on my stomach. He sounds like music, young and smooth, but mature. His message log beeps out and disconnects. I forgot to speak, just held the phone to my face. I dial again, hear him again. It's like . . . like he's talking to me. Me and him.

Tracy coughs. The message log beeps out again. I dial again; this time I say, 'Run. Now. Do not—' and the message log beeps out again. The son of a bitch is broken or full or— My cell vibrates my pocket again. I don't answer this time either and use the wall phone to redial John's number. My cell vibrates again and continues until I fumble it out.

'*He's got us alllllllll.*'

I jerk the scream away from my ear. 'What?' My cell doesn't answer, it's dead. Gwen? John's recorded voice is telling my other ear to leave a message. I yell, '*Gwen!*' at my cell.

Tracy goes wide-eyed, looking in every direction at once. I slam the wall phone and punch Talk on my cell. It rings back at Gwen's number while I try to follow Tracy's eyes.

No answer.

Tracy's eyes land on everything. Still no answer. Still no answer. I punch Redial. *He's got us all*. Back trace the number. The operator says it's in Chicago, and gives me an address on South Michigan – 2301.

My eyes are two feet from John's card; 2301 S. Michigan. It's a different phone number but at the same address. Oh my God. Roland Ganz has John. Her. Them.

Call in HBT or a TAC crew. Now. I thumb at the 9 of 911, miss, and the cell vibrates my hand. It's Gwen, crying, hysterical: '*Help us, Patti, help us. He's right here*; he'll trade – you for John and us.

351

He'll do it. Just you. He wants you. Please. No police. *Please, Patti. Help us.*'

The phone quits again. I hit Redial. No answer. I grab the red marker by the wall phone, tear off the 'Gwen called' note, and scrawl: 'RUN. CALL THE POLICE.' Then sprint out the door with a terrified Tracy on my heels.

I'm driving way too fast for conditions when the remainder of Evanston's houses all light up at once. Debris shadows go three-dimensional – trash cans, downed trees, people silhouettes who weren't even ghosts a second ago. High–beam headlights glare out of nowhere; Tracy flashes rigid in the passenger seat.

Trade me for John? Roland and me – That cannot *happen.* Ever. *Give up your son? Again?*

I scream, 'He can't keep John!' at the windshield and Tracy flinches away.

How do I out fight the devil?

GOD DAMN IT, HOW?

Call Sonny – leave your phone on with his, connected like with the Gypsy Vikings; he calls in a TAC crew the second I see that I can't trick Roland out on my own. My cell vibrates. I can't get to it and steer too. It vibrates again and I fumble it out. Nobody there. I speed dial Sonny. His voice mail answers.

'Sonny, it's me. I gotta have help. Sorry. Sorry. But I gotta. He's got John. At 2301 South Michigan; you know what I'm gonna do. Roland wants to trade. Any cops and he kills John. I'll be there in fifteen minutes; call me. Come over; stay outside like with the Vikings, unless . . . Unless it goes bad.' I stutter; realizing this cell-phone tether won't work if Sonny doesn't call before I go in. 'If we don't talk before I go in, if it goes

352

bad and I don't kill this motherfucker, you can call in a 10-1.'

I punch off without saying thanks and concentrate on not wrecking the car. I feel Tracy's eyes on me and flash her a glance. She looks just as scared of me as she does of the road. 'W-what's a 10-1?'

'Officer down, needs assistance.'

Her eyes are wide and white.

'Yeah. I'm gonna kill him. Already told you that. Murder One; dead forever. He isn't coming back again.'

Tracy leans forward against the seat belt, blinks in my face, and passes out.

South Michigan Avenue is deserted, as is the neighborhood. The west side of the street is an empty half block fenced tall and topped with razor wire; 2301 is opposite and on the corner, a five-story warehouse painted white twenty years ago. It's an old car dealership from when they still had indoor showrooms in the South Loop. A construction sign attached to the building reads: 'Lofts. February.' Hard to believe this neighborhood will be livable by then. John's name and number is under the Contractor/Broker heading with six others. Under the numbers the sign reads 'Office on site – 2nd Floor' and lists the hours.

'2nd Floor' hits me – *John's not crippled, retarded* – the message at his house, the childish handwriting, the Special Olympics trophy 'Sports Person of the Year,' the girl's clothes and crutches in the other closet – *John's a coach; his sister wrote the message.*

Tears well behind my eyes. *John's okay . . .*

Was okay. Deep, sickening breath. Be a cop. The building's beat to shit, same for the neighborhood, John's probably in with a group of young guys pooling their money; they probably live in the building to cut costs. I hope to God they don't, but they probably do.

I make two fast trips around the building's block and see no lights on any floor, no movement, and . . . an SUV parked just off the street. The driver's side headlight is mashed. Jolt. Roland's here. He's watching me. Waiting. It's true; he wants to trade.

I hit a curb and park out of sight on Twenty-third Street, marshal the flashlight, and touch Tracy's arm. She jerks upright. '*What! What?*'

'Easy. Take a breath. We're downtown. South Loop. Take a breath.'

She does and stays pressed into the door. Her eyes flash the neighborhood, then me, then the car. 'What're we doing . . . here?'

Her tone knows. I feel the adrenaline coming, swallow it down, and eye the building while she remembers

'You're . . . going in there? To kill him . . .'

'Listen. I called Sonny, my sergeant you met in 6. He's coming. If this goes bad, he'll call a 10-1. You stay out of it; go down the block by that Exxon station. But stay out of sight.'

Tracy shakes her head.

'*What?*'

'Not out here . . . alone. And I'm not leaving. My story—'

I refocus on the building and hear her being stupid to the back of my head. 'Get outta here. Now. I gotta go in alone.'

'No.'

I turn to her staring at me. 'Now, Tracy. This ain't a game.'

'No.' Tracy screws up in her seat. 'No.'

John's life has no time for this shit. 'Fine, then. C'mon. You know what's in there.'

She hesitates.

I draw and take three fast steps out of the car instead of hitting her. She follows, skirting the car like she does tacklers on the field. She's not reporter-crazy after all, or rugby-crazy; she's just plain insane and I never realized it until now. The building stops us at the sidewalk. Finding a way inside that isn't a door Roland left open will be difficult. My hands are slippery. This is not . . . good . . . at all. Fifty feet down the long north side there's a door. It's locked. Another door, fifty feet farther east through the puddles. Up close the door's rusted metal and locked. Further east I can't see anything but bricks and boarded glass.

We retrace our steps two hundred feet back to the front. Next to an empty bottle and a urine stain a dirty face protrudes from dirtier blankets. I aim and splash with the flashlight. The man doesn't respond. Ten feet south two more shapes are completely cocooned in their blankets. No bottles. No urine stains. A shopping cart separates them, empty, not full. I shove Tracy back, aim, and kick the first foot.

'Smana nanan bamma.'

I kick the feet again and step aside, ready to put two in Roland's head. A dog's muzzle and another filthy face I don't recognize uncovers and blinks at the rainy dark, then covers again and quits mumbling. I do it again with the second shape. It's a she, and legit homeless too. The door past them to the south is locked, as is the next one. At the corner, the narrow bulldozed lot next door is being used as a wide alley. Its front is blocked by a twenty-foot trash container under a chute connected to the second floor. Tracy and I hug the container, sneak around, and see Roland's invitation one hundred feet down the wall – a new, steel-door construction entrance that's wedged open. I glance above the entrance at painted windows that run half the block to the east. Roland Ganz is watching us. Tracy senses him too and splashes back to hide tight to the building.

I flatten next to her, eyes on the construction door. 'Get out of here. Dead's forever.'

She grits her teeth and shakes her head. Tracy is scared shitless and doing this anyway. I'd slap her if I didn't have both hands on the Smith.

'Stay back, out of my way. I'll be shooting . . .'

No response. Just the 200-mph face.

Deep breath, light the flashlight, duck, aim, and— Do the door— Everything's fast – column, wall, floor, debris, *stumble*, *spin*, *twist*, column, dark, light, shadows – *there, there – shoot! Shoot him!*

I squeeze but don't kill him. He doesn't move. Or speak. I jump left, aim at . . . nothing and pivot back. Still hasn't moved. Or spoken. I duck, spin to the right, aim at columns that don't shoot back, spin back to him, and . . . not a twitch.

He's right there where I can't miss him, in a chair. Head down. Could be John. Could be Roland. It's a trap. For sure. A trap. My heart's at max. Don't shoot him. Look at his face. Don't shoot him. Don't . . .

Right behind me. I spin and FIRE. Tracy silhouettes in the flash and roar. The huge space swallows the explosion and the light. Night blind. I duck behind a column, spin back, and can see zero. Hard to hear, impossible to see. *Threat. Threat. Threat.* Who's there? The room shadows. He's still in the chair.

Is Tracy dead?

No. Yes. She's crouched, not dead. I yell, 'Stay down,' no idea whether she's hit or not. My vision improves to half. From the column I scan as much cavern as possible. Other than spaced columns, there's nowhere to hide – the entire floor is wide open and abandoned. Other than the man in the chair we're alone. What kind of trap is this?

I wait. So does Tracy. So does the man in the chair. My eyes blink out the last of the flash. I notice the man has a purse spilled at his feet. Both feet are manacled to the chair, as are his hands. Under his chin, a long screwdriver has been driven through his chest.

The purse has a gold buckle that matches his right shoe, a three-inch pump.

Maybe it's not a man.

Tracy whispers, '*Schofield's Too.*'

She's okay enough to talk. I don't get the connection to the 1920s houseboat where Delmont's body parts are. But I now know whose face is hidden by the medium blond hair. Those are trademark shoes. Their owner isn't John and it's not Roland.

Tracy says, 'I get it now, the flower shop. Schofield's on State Street . . . famous.'

Schofield's is a Chicago crime landmark. Now I get it, too – this murder victim is who Delmont 'thought I should meet.' The houseboat was hers. Her grandfather, gangster Dean O'Banion, owned Schofield's Flower Shop until he was murdered there in 1924. He also built the building at Gilbert Court in 1922, and he owned the houseboat from the same decade, his last.

I take a final, careful scan of the empty expanse and approach the chair.

It's a long walk for fifteen feet. I lift the woman's head by her matted hair. The face shocks me sideways. The makeup, not the face. The makeup's the same as the photographs from the Calumet City crime scene – the murder of Burton Ottson – it's Tammy Faye's makeup.

I'm trembling, staring at the makeup, not the gray features of the once-radiant Mary Kate O'Banion, wife of Chicago's mayor.

Why's the makeup *here*? If I did it in Calumet City blackout drunk . . . I *know* I didn't murder Mary Kate.

Mary Kate's mouth has yawed open. A number of her teeth are broken and her tongue is missing. I hear Tracy say, '*Oh fuck*,' then feel her step forward. Mary Kate's coat looks misbuttoned. And her shoes are on the wrong feet. There will be serious trauma under the clothes. Mary Kate was killed elsewhere, then repackaged here.

And since I didn't kill her I couldn't have done this makeup. It's the sudden implications that has my attention, not the murder. Not Mary Kate's murder, anyway. *And maybe not Burton Ottson's makeup and murder nineteen years ago in Calumet City?* I release the hair and Mary Kate's head drops slowly on a stiffening neck. It's surreal, me still staring at a corpse reacting as if it has life. I hear Tracy stumble. I fan to shoot Roland Ganz swinging an axe.

Tracy is five feet from dying at my gun barrel, unhurt, and all alone.

She's frozen. And in that instant I realize she knows about me and Calumet City or guessed – the part I didn't tell, the part about Patti Black being a murderer. She's known all along and now sees the Calumet City crime scene again with me and Tammy Faye's makeup at its center. And sees my pistol in her face, one squeeze from ending her ability to testify.

'I didn't do it.' My words are whispers, a half-question, half-statement. Gradually, I lower the Smith.

Tracy doesn't move.

I start to smile. There's a dead woman with a screwdriver through her chest next to me and she's not who I'm thinking about. '*I didn't do it.*' Calumet City wasn't me. This time it's a statement of fact and bathes me like a baptism. I nod with mounting enthusiasm. '*I didn't fucking do it.*'

The Pink Panther can't love her geography – we're in the middle of a trap and have just taken the bait. But she can't help herself and ekes out, 'Ah . . . then who did?'

Noise. I duck, twisting to fire. A rat runs between two columns. Columns that hold up a high ceiling. I never looked up until now. Tracy does and begins to scream.

Chapter 25

SUNDAY, DAY 7: 9:00 P.M.

Two fifty-five-gallon drums crash to the floor. Gasoline drenches us and everything in our vicinity. Tracy sprints for the door. I spit gas and suck fumes. A metal cube twinkles, falling in slow motion. Zippo lighter.

It lands open, then clinks on the wet concrete unlit and bounces. *Oh, shit—*

No spark. No fire.

I sprint half the building to an open elevator encased in concrete. The buttons are the only light; my finger jams at the 2. All I smell is gas. *Run. He'll just toss in a book of matches.* I spin out of the elevator and cop-brace the adjacent fire stairs. The stairs leading up from me are crammed with lumber and Sheetrock. The down stairs aren't. Dim light spills from below. On the first landing there's a long bag, a stained painter's tarpaulin tied with rope. It squirms. The bag is the size of a human.

It's John.

Too small.

Gumdrops.

Gumdrops. A trail. More bait, only now you're a human

candle, easy to control, easy to trap, *easy to have*. I jerk back from the stairwell, fanning pistol and flashlight at the open space behind me. No killers there, no Tracy, just Mary Kate in her chair.

A smaller rat scurries along the far wall. I hear a groan and look back. The bag squirms again. I inch down the stairs, my back to the wall, expecting an attack from below, or from above once I'm trapped on the landing. I have no knife; it will take both hands to untie the knot. Roland can toss his matches into the enclosed space. I stop inching. He'll threaten that – tell me the bag is John, make me give up the gun . . .

Don't do it – listen and ease down three steps. The light's dim but brighter, like it's coming from the stairwell's door into the basement. The bag hears me coming and squirms harder. It's blotched with paint. Or blood? I jump the last three treads, land crouched, and swing my gun at the lower doorway, then back up the stairs. The bag rustles into my ankle. I one-hand at a knot, eyes on both doors. The bag stops. Two very bad thoughts bubble: What if the bag holds a bad guy with a gun? Worse, if I fire mine, will the back-blast ignite me?

I jump away from the bag and up the stairs two at a time, fan the entire floor again, then quick-strip to my bra. From the waist up I'm dry other than my face, hair, and hands. If I fire stiff-armed away from myself I might not torch. Back to the bag. I re-fan the stairwell, push the bag toward the lower stair, and rip at the knot until it comes loose. No motion. I prod with my foot and whisper, 'Kick your way out,' then climb the stairs to bolt or fire around the wall if the captive is a bad guy.

The bag does nothing at first, then begins to fight. The wrestling takes more than a minute. It's a woman, younger than me, blond, on her stomach, hands tied, face painted, mouth gagged, and so scared I can see her eyes from here. I wave at her to stop moving. She does, but stays glued on me like her neck is going to break. I pat the air, trying to relax her but it doesn't, then ease down two treads. I point at her feet and motion 'Get up.'

She tries and can't. She tries again and reaches her knees. Total deer in the headlights. This must be Gwen. I keep waving her up toward me. 'C'mon, you can do it. I'm a cop.'

She notices my star hanging over my bra and tries harder. The wall helps her up. She's taller than she looked in the bag, the blond hair matted like Mary Kate's. The face paint is Tammy Faye Bakker at Halloween.

'C'mon, baby. Up here. You can do it.' Her legs aren't working well. 'It's me, Patti Black. C'mon, Gwen, seven steps and you're safe.'

We both hear a noise below her. She sprints up the stairs past me and hits a column that knocks her down and the gag partway out of her mouth. I aim, waiting for the downstairs noise to become an attacker. It doesn't. I look over my shoulder. The girl is a pile. I ease back to her, eyeing the stair, and untie her hands.

She flinches into a ball, shivering like it's ten degrees and mumbles, 'My son. Has my son.'

'I know, baby; I know.' I have one hand undoing the gag and the Smith on the stair doorway. 'We'll save him.'

She wide-eyes me and I remember the look; Gwen was a child then, but it's the same look, just with way too many years of Roland's torture built into it. Every inch of her is quaking.

'Get up, honey. You gotta get out of here. There's a girl outside who can help you.'

'My son. No. My son.'

'I'll find him. Run. Now,' and I grab her belt to lift. She shies so hard it wrenches my elbow, then crouches to all fours to defend herself. She's terrified, a mother fighting for her child but lost in Roland's madness.

'I'll find him, Gwen.'

'But, but . . . I know where they are. I know where they are.' She says it so fast her tongue can't keep up. 'Has your boy too. HE'S GOT US ALL.'

Gwen is as scared as I have ever seen anyone. And screams; terror bounces off the walls. I spin, aiming at everything. Then turn back to her. 'Where? Tell me where.'

From her knees she points downstairs. The basement. Roland always loved basements. 'Where in the basement?'

Gwen cringes. 'Go with you. Show you.' I can't tell if she's shaking her head or shivering.

'No, honey, you can't. Just tell me. I'm a cop. I can save them.'

'Won't work. Won't work. Won't work.' Gwen's stretched tight under the face paint.

'Calm down, baby. Calm down.' I make the best lie-face I can and pat the air. 'We'll do it together.'

'The basement. He's . . . they're . . . it's sooooo bad.'

I stumble a step. *God, please don't let this happen*. Please. I'll do anything. Anything. Please. Gwen wobbles to standing. Her hands stay cupped at her chest like they're still tied. She stares right at me as if she knows what we'll find but can't say it.

'I'm going now. You just go as far as you want, okay?'

Gwen doesn't move an inch until I do, then shuffles chain-gang steps. If John wasn't down there, I would still face Roland Ganz and kill him for Gwen. Kill this fucking monster. Face him. Kill him. Over and over. Kill Roland Ganz, Patti. It's worth life in prison.

Gwen and I hesitate at the door. She's at my shoulder, a trembling mixture of sweat, cigarettes, and cheap perfume. Roland loved cigarettes and cheap perfume. I feel him in her, on her, on me. Again. 'I'm going down first; you stay back till I call, okay?'

Gwen nods, cow-eyed.

I do the basement stairs down to the landing, hesitate, then do the rest and flatten inside the stairwell against the doorway wall at the bottom. My heart counts it out. Going through the door is my only option. Not good, but if Roland wanted to trap me right here, he would've used the stairwell. But he hasn't. I want to ask why but bolt through the doorway while I still have the nerve.

Low ceiling. Columns. Pipes in both directions. Dim. Mildew. A boiler clanks; I spin, duck and . . . don't fire, jerk left, right, left – right. Empty? Columns – short, fat ones. Rows and rows of columns in every direction. Dim light. Straight ahead, to the short side of the basement. The light is coming from a doorway fifty feet away. I creep out into the open, loop left then angle toward the doorway. The basement's a rectangle, maybe three or four times as long as wide. Far to the east of the elevator and fire stairs, there's a maze of vertical pipes and metal boilers. I smell oil and grease as strong as the gasoline soaking my jeans and then perfume crawling up my neck.

I duck backwards and into Gwen. She pancakes hard onto the concrete. I snap back to the column forest. Nothing moves. I aim at the silent maze of pipes and boilers; the noise we heard on the stairs didn't come from these boilers and isn't audible now. Gwen's panting half–breaths from her back. I use one hand and wave her to standing; I use the other hand to aim at everything else.

Her perfume reaches me before she says to my shoulder, 'Through there.' Her head nudges mine back east one hundred fifty feet toward the pipe maze and a wall now visible just beyond. 'My son is in there.'

'Where's John?'

'In there.' Gwen sounds like she's twelve.

'Where's Roland?' I'm focused on the nearest columns and the low ceiling getting lower even though it's not. 'Where's Roland? How many are with him?'

I have to strain to hear: 'Joe. A boy. Man, from the ranch.'

'One or two, Gwen? A boy *and* a man?'

'Joe ... from the ranch. The preacher's boy. Joe is evil too.'

'Where's Roland?' I don't have to ask where Joe is. It had to be him dumping the gasoline through the hole in the second floor. 'Where's Roland, honey?'

She mouths something I can't hear. I ask again and the elevator rumbles. We both jump and run one hundred fifty feet to the pipe maze, bounce off a boiler, slide between two others, then crouch into a dark corner. The elevator motor stops. We can't see the elevator when it opens. Door noise. Light spills forward into basement. The doors rumble closed and the light quits. We listen; all I hear is Gwen breathing and water dripping. Or gasoline?

Gwen whispers, 'Next door,' into my ear.

'What?' I'm concentrating on shooting the elevator's passenger before he can toss a Zippo at us.

'Roland. Through there.' She trembles a finger through the

maze at an unseen, double-wide passageway/tunnel framed in dirty white tile. 'Next door.'

A number of Chicago's older buildings are connected below street level; why these two are I don't know. Now, even if Sonny gets my message and decides to help, he and HBT will go to the wrong building.

'He . . . made me . . . at the ranch. I didn't want to. He made me.'

I fast-glance Gwen – she's in another time zone – then whisper 'Easy, honey,' still expecting the elevator passenger to charge. 'I'll stop it all, okay?' I lift my chin at the tunnel, knowing we have to go no matter what she says. 'Is he in there?'

'We're . . . married. I had his baby.'

'We gotta go.' I grab her hand, we slip through the pipes and sprint into the tunnel. Three strides and it's pitch-black. We run ten more before I trip and we both tumble to wet concrete. She wails and I grab her to me, covering her mouth with my gun hand. The tunnel mouth is silhouetted behind us; when the elevator man chases in after us we'll see him. If I wasn't flammable I could shoot him. And I may have to anyway if he has a flashlight and a weapon.

Flashlight! I pat at my pockets.

Must've dropped it. My empty hand flattens in cold liquid, probably water. I cup, smell stale grime and no gas and splash it in my face. *Focus, now.* I holster the Smith, wash my hands and wrists, then my face again. The water tastes like shit but now I have a 50–50 chance of not igniting if I have to fire.

The far end of our tunnel where we're headed is impenetrable dark. 'Where's Roland, honey? Down there?'

I feel her nod.

'Is this tunnel clear? Can we walk down the wall?'

She doesn't answer or move.

'Gwen, baby. C'mon. Is it clear? Can we walk down the wall?'

She hugs against me. 'Maybe.'

We push up till we're standing. She's shaking so hard it trembles my leg. No, it's my phone, but I can't get my hand through to it. 'Let go, honey. I gotta get my phone.' The phone stops; Gwen doesn't. I wriggle and she holds tighter. Both my arms are pinned. The phone vibrates again. I try, but she's terrified-strong and I don't get to it this time either. 'Baby, you gotta let go.'

She doesn't and the phone vibrates again. I jerk hard out of her hug and hear her stumble. 'It's okay, Gwen. It's okay.' I pat air until I find her, grabbing at limbs from behind until I reach her shoulders and whisper, 'We're okay, baby. I got you. I'm not leaving; I promise.'

'Please.' She's whimpering. '*He's got my son.*'

I slide my hand down to her wrist, grab tight, and step out from behind her to flatten on the wall. 'Follow me, stay on the wall.'

Behind us the mouth of the passage is still clear. Maybe the elevator was a ruse, part of the trap to drive us in . . . here. Gwen and I take baby steps, then bigger. We stumble over conduit that rattles, but neither of us falls. The air gets staler and the light behind us at the tunnel's mouth fades out. Gwen's crushing my hand. Our backs are sliding on the dirty tile.

Noise. Behind us.

Dead stop. Squint hard. Listen, listen, listen . . . Someone or thing *is* there, already in and past the lights, and closing. And Roland's up ahead, waiting. We're trapped, bookended, squeezed ... Gwen whispers words I can't hear. Forward or back, but don't stay here. I lurch us forward and Gwen follows, taking half steps.

She whispers again and I stop to hear, 'He's ... going to burn us. Purify us.'

I whisper, my lips touching her ear, 'Is he close? In here?'

Gwen stutters, then says, 'No. There's ... a ... trap. First.'

Every bit of me freezes. I think trip wire. 'Where?'

'At the end ... at the doors.'

But there aren't any doors. I can't see a thing. No doors, no 'end,' just dark.

'D ... don't go through the door. The ... the door with the l ... light behind.'

'You sure?'

'Uh-huh.'

'You'll have to show me.'

We inch down the wall, thirty more feet of black-dark, and bump into a closed door. The collision doesn't kill us. I recover, put Gwen's hand on the frame, and ask if this door's okay – a good door. She says yes. I feel for a trip wire to be sure, then grope higher, find a knob and a latch, throw the latch – *too loud* – turn the knob, and creak the door open an inch. Rusted hinges add echoes and corrosion to stale air. I fast–glance the dark and whatever's moving behind us, then shoulder the door hard. It opens with a loud *screeeech* and I stumble into an odd space like a large kitchen but ending in a curving concave wall. I gunpoint in a stumbling 360, get balance, and 360 again.

Empty. No Roland Ganz. My heart's in my throat. A string of naked construction bulbs illuminates three doorways set into the concave wall at four-foot intervals, each with puddles in front

368

and scaffolding support instead of doors. All three are hallways that end in dark. I could be staring at a shotgun right now and never see it.

The hallway on the far right has the only light. Has to be the 'trap' if Gwen's right about the light. Thirty feet down the hall a doorframe's edges are backlit in the wall, beyond that the hallway's black. I push Gwen back into our tunnel, listen for whatever's behind us, hear nothing, and whisper, 'Roland? Which way?'

She shies and points to the hallway with the door's dim silhouette, then squeezes her chest to my back. I wait and listen; her breath is what I hear and my heart racing again. I smell the rank water and corrosion air, and the gasoline that still soaks my jeans and shoes. Time to go . . . no choice . . . have to jump out, sprint down the hall to the silhouetted door that has Roland Ganz waiting. I could get lucky; he could jerk it open, thinking I passed, then it's whoever's better with their weapon. I pat for my speed loaders and bump my cell, then remember it vibrating – the call could've been Sonny. *Shit*. I flip it open, hiding the light, peek at Roland's hallway, and hope I still have a signal. Four messages, all from Tracy. Gwen presses tighter to my back. Tracy's first two messages are panic gibberish. The third is a series of gulped breaths and clearer words:

'Roland Ganz is dead. He's *dead*, Patti. Bob Cullet found him. Ganz and four other bodies. All dead a week or more. Murdered, *before* all this started in Chicago. There's a will. Bob found Roland's will in a—' The message cuts off.

Roland Ganz is dead? Then who's ripping people to pieces? Arson, SUVs . . . I stare at the phone's tiny screen like it will answer. Bob Cullet's wrong. Roland Ganz isn't dead; he's right here, down that hall, behind that door with . . .

I turn to look at Gwen and a shape charges out of the black. I duck, twist and a man smashes Gwen into the wall. A thick tug wrenches my arm and the man's all over me, hands and feet and – I duck again and two-hand the Smith. My left arm doesn't work and I fire one-handed. Three feet away he silhouettes in the muzzle flash and dirty white tile. I don't ignite, he spins into the wall, and I stumble down the other. My left forearm screams at me. So does Gwen. The man lunges and I fire again. He pretzels back into his wall. Pain rips up my arm; blood pumps in my mouth. The man falls and curls into a ball. I wheel to grab Gwen and all that's left are her screams trailing back into the dark. My arm's gushing from a ten-inch slice and I squeeze it against my stomach. The man groans; I jump over him and out of the tunnel, aiming at the three hallways until nobody comes at me, then step back to the tunnel's mouth and kick him in the face. Gwen's screams die. The man at my feet mumbles again. He has an earring and a biker bandanna covering stringy blond hair. I aim at Roland's hallway until the silhouetted door doesn't open, then belt the Smith and rip off the man's bandanna. This has to be Idaho Joe, the preacher's son; he groans something to my shoes. I spin to put four into Roland's door.

But Roland's dead.

No fucking way. No way. I pat for the phone I no longer have. *Roland's been dead.* That's why you didn't feel him in Arizona. *Bullshit; he's behind that door.* I hear scraping ahead in the hall-ways and bolt back deeper into the tunnel until I fall. My arm's throbbing; I squeeze it hard against my stomach, flatten the rest of me against the cold tile, draw and aim shaky at the tunnel's mouth.

My phone's in the water, lit where I dropped it. My arm

bubbles blood. I belt the Smith and cinch-wrap the gash with the bandanna, then stuff my hand into my belt and don't scream. I didn't frisk the guy I shot. If Roland's dead, who's got John? This is a trick, part of the trap – Tracy's taking the word of Bob Cullet. Bob Cullet's a drunken idiot working with Roland Ganz and Roland's alive in the next room and ripping people to pieces. Gwen's been Roland's captive.

I armpit the Smith and grab my cell. It smells like gasoline and won't work no matter how hard I punch it. Choose door number one; use the .38; it'll work. That's the only answer. Kill Roland Ganz hiding behind door number one. I pocket the cell, draw the Smith, and ease back up the tunnel toward the mouth. Idaho Joe is prone at my feet. His hands are empty; I peek past him to door number one.

It's no longer shut. I jerk back. Was it ever shut? It's open now, but no brighter.

Run.

I can't. Have to find John. Find John; don't die first.

I do the corner low and sprint into the confined hallway toward Roland's door. Thirty feet down I've hit no trip wire, stop, wheel, and kick Roland's door the rest of the way open. It bangs into the wall. The room's empty. I lurch back out into hallway – left is lights and the prone Idaho Joe; right is shadows.

No, IT'S ROLAND.

No, it's nothing. Silence and me panting. I run right, slam into a T dead end, bounce left and run lighter shadows to another T junction I see before hitting it, turn right for no reason and skid to a stop twelve inches before falling into the lowest level of a double–basement boiler room. Two bulbs light the deepest part of the pit and shadow where I'm standing. I jump left along the edge and slip into the spaghetti of pipes and furnaces above the pit. I'm panting and can't stop. *Call for help; building's too big; won't find John.*

I aim at the room until I can safely belt the Smith and try my cell again – still won't dial out, but Tracy's fourth message blinks at me. It starts with: 'The will, Patti. John gets it all; if he's dead, then as his mother you're next in line; if you're both dead, Gwen inherits it all. It's *her*, Patti! She's a nutcase, was a psycho even before—'

My piece-of-shit phone goes dark. Wait! *What?* I fumble at it again. The screen lights, then quits. I hear scraping and duck. *It's Gwen* – who the fuck are you kidding? *Gwen's killing all these people, ripping them to pieces?* My left arm jerks out of my belt to help and the pain buckles my knees. The hand makes a reaction fist. I press the phone into it. Gwen, Roland, Idaho Joe – too much. Gotta find John. My heart keeps pace with: Gotta. Gotta. Gotta.

I hear Tracy talking to my jeans. The phone's lit again. She's in broken reporter mode saying, '. . . she's Mary Kate's daughter. Illegitimate. Born in '76, the same year Roland bought Gilbert Court. Diagnosed as brain damaged. Never adopted. Institutionalized in '82 for fires and juvenile assaults. It's her; I just talked to my crew. The records were sealed, but my crew got 'em. Roland worked at that hospital; he'd been blackmailing Mary K—'

A *whoosh* sucks the oxygen out of the room.

Fire! I scramble into the open and an airborne Gwen screams into me. I land on the concrete with her nails clawing for my eyes and teeth at my throat. I swing with the Smith and lose it. Her weight's on my stomach, both hands pounding. I swing into the screams and saliva and Tammy Faye makeup. Both her hands are beating the shit out of me. Her left misses and she slides off. I land a right on her temple, roll with it, and she falls to her back.

The Smith is next to her hand.

In one perfect fluid motion she grabs it.

Chapter 26

SUNDAY, DAY 7: 10:00 P.M.

Gwen fumbles and fires. I duck, leap into pipes. Doorway. Locked.

The pipes are a maze. I spaghetti through and pop out in a hall. No idea where I am. Run.

Another door. Locked too. An animal is roaring behind me; a madwoman with my gun. Metal doorway. Open and wide. I leap through it, stumble, and pancake on the wall. Wrong side! My useless left arm is nearest the opening. My good hand grabs the metal door and slams it. The door wedges into the jamb, stuck midway. I stumble back, stop, and throw 130 pounds at it. The door screeches into the frame and I crank down a twelve-inch lever-latch.

No windows, no other doors. I'm safe – if the fire in the subbasement can't reach here. She's only got three bullets or maybe it's four . . . if she doesn't have another gun. But she probably does. There's no way out of here. I'm trapped. In shadowy dark. John's going to die and so am I.

Gwen screams outside my door. I flinch, stumble on debris, and see the light source. Above me, a ragged hole in the ceiling is filled with a four-foot-wide corrugated tube, a chute like the one outside. The tube's bent at the end, making a lazy *L*. Inside, it has block and tackle. And light. And whatever the tube's purpose, it has to go somewhere. But the chute's too high to ever reach. Gwen hammers the door. 'The trust fund's mine! The ranch is mine. *He's* mine. Not Annabelle's. Not yours. MINE!'

The room is four concrete walls and construction trash. And no way to reach the tube—

Gwen stops yelling; her voice goes stern-placid. 'Want your little bastard boy back? I'm almost done with him.'

I stop scanning the room and stare at the door. Words form, but my mouth won't let them out. I have to keep her here . . . away from John.

'Gwen, I'm sorry. I'll come out, we'll talk, okay?'

'Talk? About *my* husband and your Tammy-sex with him? The sloppy little-girl Tammy sucking and fucking you gave him?'

The picture stumbles me backwards.

'On your hands and knees? I watched you, WHORE. I—'

Gwen falters, fights through a series of coughs to a controlled silence, then continues. 'You were so special, all made up. The big girl. The *special* one. You ran, and I stayed. You ran away, I stayed, and you got everything.' Her voice ramps loud and wilder, 'And I got nothing! You fucked him, cried for him, those *so sad*, itty-bitty Tammy tears.'

The picture's too vivid and I clamp my good hand to one ear. *It's not true*. Not true. I survived – nothing more. I was fifteen years old.

'You'll burn, Patti Black. You and your fucking spawn. You and Annabelle. She's in hell waiting.'

'Gwen, he hurt us . . . all of us.' I try to say it loud, but can't.

'It wasn't your fault. Or mine. It was Roland and Annabelle.'

I smell smoke and get no answer.

Gwen whispers, 'He thought Annabelle ran away, like you. But she was mine. I went down to the basement every day and watched her mess herself. I made her cry.'

God, Roland. What did you do to this child?

'You and Annabelle, the two unholy cunts. *I* preached His word, did you know that, Babylon Whore? *I* brought glory to Him and resurrected His ranch. Resurrected it! *My* hard work. *My* charisma.'

I'm on my knees, looking for anything I can use. Gwen's voice changes to singsong: 'The ranch in Arizona had lots of little boys and girls for Roland.' Now she snarls, 'He had them. He had me. Oh, but he missed you.' Fists pound the door. 'Now there's NOTHING for me. I kept pieces of the others for you, their watches and ribbons and bows. And their pretty hands. It was fine. Because he was mine. It was *all* mine, all of it.'

Fingernails scrape down the door. 'And then it wasn't fine.'

Roland's dead; Gwen killed him. I'm dizzy, dealing with that and 'the others.' Oh, God, don't say 'others.' I cover my ear again and chant, rocking until the visions stop. Slowly I uncup my ear. It's quiet, soundless. I stare at the door – either she's baiting me or – or . . . *she's gone to get John.*

'Gwen?' I stagger up and to the door. 'Gwen?' She doesn't answer and I run at the chute, jump, and miss by a foot and jump again. 'Gwen? Please. Say something.' Gotta climb up the chute. I smell smoke – the fire in the subbasement – and look at the floor. Debris under my feet, not a lot, maybe stack all of it, pile it, ramp it. 'Gwen, are you there?' I make my left arm help pile debris. The arm hurts so much it's almost useless. 'Gwen? Talk to me.'

I hear rustling outside; could be her or rats running from the fire, or Idaho Joe wounded and crawling down the hallway.

Keep piling debris, make a ramp.

'Gwen?' My pile rises twelve inches higher than I thought I could make it. Stretching one–handed I can almost touch the chute. More rustling outside the door, but heavier, then a low moan and the odor of gasoline. Liquid dribbles under the door. *Oh shit, no.* I stuff rags from my debris ramp under the door. The gasoline stops. The rustling and moans don't.

Please, please, don't let it be John. Please.

'Gwen, I'm coming out.' The gas soaks through the rags and begins to puddle. I stuff more debris but it only slows the gas.

Gwen's voice becomes a preacher's, but soft, like her lips are on the door: 'Fear not the flames. There is salvation in the fire.' She shifts back into singsong, now like a little girl: 'Play with the boys; play with boys. Show them your pants.' She pauses and defaults into what must be her 'normal' Gwen voice: 'I have John here, *Patricia*. Time to play.'

'Don't hurt him, Gwen. Don't. He's . . . John's not part of this. He's—'

'Oh, yes he is. Roland made him part. You got my ranch; he gets the building insurance. My trust fund at the bank. Everyone gets what's mine.'

'You can have it all, Gwen. I promise. I just want John. If you killed Roland, I'm happy. I don't want any of his stuff. You can have it all.'

'Does not work that way. There's a will. You made a bastard. To steal from me.' Gwen pounds on the door and shrieks something about being 'the wife.'

I lurch back, trip, and land butt-first in the gas puddle. The fuel wets my hands and soaks my pants to the belt. I jump up and spin for a fantasy way out.

'I'M THE MOTHER, I'M THE WIFE.'

'Gwen, please—'

'Want your boy? I'll skin the rest of him now, peel his face for you—'

'Don't, Gwen. *Please*. I'll do whatever you want. Anything.' I jerk the latch up hard and yank. The door won't open. I jerk again, and again. My left hand tries to help but just spins on the knob. 'Don't hurt him!'

'The whore wants her pretty boy?'

Another shriek. Not Gwen's. I rip at the door. The scream becomes agony and feet kicking the metal, and finally a gurgle. I pound on the door, kick it, and fight the knob. It's wedged too tight for me to one-arm it open or it's now locked from the outside. The gas flow builds at my feet and rivers away one of the rags. The color's changing, red streaks ribbon through the pale pink gas. A thin length of steel rebar pokes under the door, pushing away the bulk of my blockade. The rebar withdraws and in its place a bloody mass washes under the door. Thin and fleshy, a mask, except this one's slaughterhouse real.

Gwen's little-girl voice says, '*Ick*, boys are so messy.'

The face has half its hairline and an ear.

'But, Mommy, Johnny's teeth are still pretty. We'll need them for i-den-ti-fi-ca-tion.'

Oh, God . . . no.

An earring glints. The hair is bleached blond.

Idaho Joe. He had an earring and stringy blond hair. Gwen just skinned her partner, boyfriend, acolyte. Gwen becomes the preacher again, stern and angry. 'The price of the Pentecost is devotion. Purity from lust. Search out the fornicators making bastards who steal. Burn them as they—'

Burn. My dead left hand brushes my belt; pain buckles my knee. *Belt*. I look at my belt then my shoes, pink and red in the bloody gas, then the door I can't budge. Then at the chute. *Use the belt, Patti. Pull it down*. I strip my belt, and suddenly see Gwen's plan in the gasoline and psycho sermonizing: Gwen *doesn't* have John; she's waiting here for him too. She doesn't have him *yet*. JOHN IS NOT HERE. The thought's like amphetamines. I jump the buckle bend of my belt at a bolt protruding from the chute. It misses.

'Gwen, sometimes you are the dumbest bitch, you know?'

No answer.

'Roland wanted Tammy Faye, not me.' I jump again and miss.

Gwen's grown-up voice says, 'Tammy Faye is not in the will; she's not stealing from the family. Tammy Faye did not make a bastard child. Tammy Faye did not sleep with my husband. Tammy Faye did not sleep with my father. Tammy Faye did not—'

'Hell she didn't.' I try again and my buckle clangs off the metal. 'John's not my son, he's Tammy Faye's.'

'Liar!'

'Ask him.' The impossible is happening; I'm saying this shit out loud and she's listening. 'Ask John.'

'He's your son, and you can't do a thing to save him.'

'I never had a son, you stupid bitch. Fucking your husband, or father, or whatever, was fun though.' The words bile my throat, but the buckle hooks the bolt. I jerk as hard as I can. 'We used to laugh about you, what an idiot, retarded shit you were. No wonder Mary Kate gave you up at the hospital.'

She sings, 'I know where Johnny is.'

The block and tackle rattles, but the chute doesn't budge. 'She leave you in a trash can or the maternity ward?'

Gwen coughs again. Her voice levels to fake sanity. 'You pretend we're different, don't you? That you're not me, that you're "better" now.'

I jerk on the belt but the chute holds, rattling dirt in my face.

'Do you still hurt yourself? Whose razor do you use?'

The belt slips out of my hand; I grab and try not to hear that.

'Bedtime with your clothes on, still? Even in August, hoping not to fall asleep. Annabelle wanted to play at night. It's so very dark at night, isn't it?'

Shut the fuck up, Gwen.

'And when you get mad, do you get *really, really* mad? How many men have you had – lots? None? You *can't* have them, can you?'

I grab for the belt.

'And the hate. Oh, the hate, hot and sticky wet. It throbs between your legs doesn't it? Where little bastard Johnny lived. He's like his daddy, you know.'

I scream at the door: '*No he's not.*'

Gwen singsongs: 'I know where Johnny is. I know where Johnny is.'

I want to rip through the wall and kill her. 'Sure you do, bitch. You're fucking crazy. Shit, you just murdered your mother and your only assistant. How fucking stupid are you?'

Gwen goes stern, 'I'm the mother. You're the birth-whore.'

'Upstairs you stuck a screwdriver in your meal ticket, Mommy.'

'J . . . Johnny's on his way. He'll watch you burn. Then I'll eat him . . . but not his teeth. We need his teeth . . . for the i-den-ti —'

The gas at the door ignites. The flash knocks the belt out of my hand but it stays hooked to the chute. I hear 'Do the police bring fire hoses too?' and my shoes catch fire. I land on my pockets and beat my shoes to just smoke, smoke that's filling the room. Smoke and fire adds painkillers to my left arm. I add my 130 pounds to the belt and the chute buckles, bending down. The tackle inside is a handhold; I grab, leap in, and try to claw up the thirty-degree angle. Flames and smoke chase me. Hand over hand, push with both feet. The tube's hot, hotter, hard to breathe. Ten feet to the ceiling; crawl, fight, claw. My hands are scalding.

And I'm out. On the first floor. And then the tube is a chimney pouring smoke. I crawl to a wall and pant until I can stand. I'm soot-black everywhere, camouflaged so . . . but Gwen would've heard no screaming as I burned alive. She'll know I'm out. She'll be running up here anyway; she started both fires. She'll—

A twenty-foot metal wall section screeches open on rollers at the far end of the building, the end that connects John's lofts to this building. Smoke pours out of that opening too and from John's side. A man sprints through it. On my side of the door smoke erupts through huge holes drilled into the floor. Flames crackle up under the smoke, spitting sparks into the ceiling. The ceiling ignites and flames race across the rafters in a rolling carpet.

The man running at me is fast and young. He's yelling but I can't hear. Gwen bursts out of the stairway aiming my pistol. I lunge. My forehead hits the pistol, then her chest. She staggers.

I head butt her and swing both fists. She falls and I go with her. My left hand rips useless into hair; I pound with my right. Someone knocks me sideways into the door of the stairwell. My left arm jolts pain to my shoulder. I gasp. The boy's helping Gwen. I gasp for air, yell at him not to help, to get away, to— Gwen helps him, kicking away from me with her heels. She pushes to her feet and into his arms. '*John, it's me, Gwen*. I called to warn you. That naked crazy woman, she's trying to kill all of us, she's—'

My son struggles Gwen farther away. I point but can't get a word out. John 360s for a way through the flames. Sirens scream outside. Gwen wobbles, holding on to John. I see the pistol that he can't. John points her toward a plywood-boarded window. I reach my feet. Gwen turns; the smile is soft, angelic, and she points my Smith at the back of John's head.

A huge flame snaps and he flinches. Gwen fires. I charge an instant too late, but the bullet passes his ear and chips plaster. She pivots, fires at me, and my shoulder drives us into a flaming hole billowing smoke.

Tongue.

Licking my face. I cough, roll, '*Owww*,' and spaz with my hands. The left hand hurts so much I grab it. The tongue licks my face again. I swat but it keeps licking. My eyes crunch open and I bat again. Smoke and fire and sirens and lights and, 'Quit licking me!'

It's a Labrador and she doesn't quit. I see my stomach and hands – still black – and the Lab starts licking them too. A ragman pulls her back and to his chest. I think he's one of the homeless guys I saw on the way in. He looks sooty too.

He says, 'You were on fire. I put you out.'

From the weeds surrounding us he shows me an empty water jug and his scorched sleeping bag. His Lab tries to lick me again. I push her away and look at the inferno two buildings north. A five-story building is pouring flames and smoke at the base, but not the upper floors. Fire trucks and hoses are everywhere.

'Your pants was burning. Woulda burnt you up.'

John's building. *John*. 'Anyone. Get. Out?' I cough and grab at my savior. 'Did they?'

The Lab growls; her human swats at my hands. 'Leggo.'

I do and scan for John. Smoke rolls out of the boarded window. The one he pointed out for Gwen. I get up to run but my rugby knee buckles. The Lab licks me again; her human points to Michigan Avenue. TV lights, squad lights – lots of heavily armed cops who aren't fighting the fire. I look east. Same thing at the other end, but no TV. My homeless savior says, 'I saved you.'

I nod and keep coughing. 'Did a boy run out? *Anyone?*'

Gwen went into the fire with me; no way she got to John. He could be out – he's gotta be out. I cough and it rolls me to my knees. I spit into the weeds and hear the Lab barking at men with pistols; they're at two hundred yards and coming our way from the east side. The men are staccato lit in the squad car's flashing lights and intent on the building. A 10-1. Sonny or Tracy called the cavalry. I look back at John's window, then Michigan Avenue. A reporter is doing a stand–up bathed in brilliant TV lights. To the reporter's right and not coming our way two men are talking at the edge of the TV lights. One big, one slender. Sonny Barrett's the big guy. I choke and smoke tears stream out of my eyes.

My son John is the other one. The Lab steps between me and the prettiest picture I have ever seen. We're both on all fours and she's licking the tears off my face and I don't care.

Sonny pushes John's shoulder and John squares up. *What? Why do that?* They stay face-to-face until John steps back. I try to stand again and fall. The Lab barks. Sonny looks our way and John turns to leave. Sonny says something. John shoots him the bird and keeps walking until a woman with a camera crew stops him.

'See that guy.' I point my homeless savior at Sonny. 'Bring him here, okay?'

'I saved you.'

'I know. Thanks. Go get him.'

'I saved you.' His canvas-gloved hand is out.

'Right.' I give him all the money in my pocket. 'Go get him. Hurry, okay?'

I have never seen Sonny Barrett on his knees. I've never seen him close to crying either. He's got both hands on my face after pushing my hair aside and he doesn't know what to do or say. So he's just frozen there, a great big bear with wet eyes staring at me while I bawl like a little girl. When he touches my left arm I almost faint.

He looks it over without removing the bandanna. 'We need to get that looked at.'

'We need to,' I sniffle, 'get outta here.'

'I called it in when I got your message. They already know it's you.'

That feels like a knife. 'What . . . do they know?'

Sonny lets go of my face. 'They know it's about something. Somebody trying to kill your kid.'

384

'You told 'em?'

He shrugs. 'What am I gonna do? Half the district don't rally without a story. There's twenty guys out here looking for a cop in trouble.' Sonny pulls a radio from his coat pocket and buttons it. 'Paulie.'

'Yo.'

'I saw her. Patti's out.'

'*No shit. You got her?*'

'No. *I had* her. She ran to a 1994 Bonneville.'

'How bad?'

'Didn't look good, but a least she could run.'

'10-4. She give a location on the shooters?'

Sonny looks at me for an answer. I shake my head, make 'two' with my fingers, and point down at the east end. He buttons the radio. 'Two of 'em. Firewood. In the basement on your end.'

'10-4. Paulie out.'

Sonny stares at me, then says, 'You got five, maybe ten minutes to make serious decisions. Let's get your arm looked at and decide before they dope you up.' He helps me up using my waist, the second time he's touched me there. I dry at my eyes, feeling his hands. He scoots an arm around my waist and limps me south into the shadows toward Mercy Hospital.

'I'm not going to Mercy.'

Sonny tightens his arm. 'Yeah you are. We're done hiding all this bullshit.'

I jerk semi-free. 'We? When did you become me?'

Sonny does his Irish face. 'Listen to me for once in your fucking life. Your ass is in trouble. You cannot run from it anymore. Period. And neither can your friends.' He reaches for my arm and I wobble back. He glares, takes a deep breath, and says, 'At least get the arm treated, then do whatever the fuck you want.'

'Not at Mercy.'

'Fine. We'll go to the Mickey.'

I stagger, trying to add space. 'Promise not to front me?'

Sonny holds up both hands. 'We're going to the Mickey. You can ghost it from there if being an idiot makes you happy.'

The Mickey is Michael Reese Hospital. I went in alone, half naked, and that's the last thing I remember.

Now I'm in an apartment, a man's apartment. Actually, I sorta remember the emergency room; I was too weak and dizzy to run or I would have. This apartment's warm and dry and has decent music . . . Stephen Stills and someone much less talented singing:

'When you see the Southern Cross for the first time . . .'

I blink but don't move. The lights are restaurant dim and almost rosy. I smell corned beef and cabbage, not gasoline. I'm covered in . . . stadium blankets? The coffee table by my face has seen better days as have the books stacked on it. My hand's by my face; I sniff . . . clean? And don't remember how it happened.

Under the blankets I seem to be dressed in a man's robe and lying on his sofa, no idea how that happened either, but I know I'm on it. A huge fireplace stares at me – strike that, it's a soundless TV pretending to be a fireplace.

From a La-Z-Boy Sonny Barrett in a sweater and snap-brim cap notices I'm awake. He flusters, re–tough–guys, and says, 'Doc said you lost a pint of blood, tore up the tendons. He filed a report but left me out of it.'

Sonny Barrett in a sweater? I look at the bandages on my left arm and rub my face. 'What time is it?'

'You mean what day is it?'

Did he say *day*?

Sonny angles his head at a window. It's dark and I get the feeling I missed something. No telling how much dope they gave me at the hospital. *Jesus*, or what I said. I check Sonny again.

'We, ah, have coffee?'

'Yeah, sure.' He dismounts the La-Z-Boy. His pants are pressed; the sales tag's still on them. Lumbering toward his kitchen he points back to the coffee table and a folded stack of clean clothes topped by a new Cubs hat. 'Your pal the Pink Panther was here. Said she isn't filing till you call, as long as it's by tonight.'

I glance at the clothes, blink twice to make sure I'm taking all this in, that it's real, then ask, 'And today is . . . ?'

From the kitchen I hear, 'Monday night. Miami game's on in a minute.' Sonny swears at something in his kitchen, grumbles, and adds, 'You slept all day; no-showed IAD. And, man, they is pissed.'

The last twenty–four hours are starting to come together, as is the pain in my arm. I'm afraid to ask, but do. 'My son. Is he . . .'

Sonny returns with a blue coffee cup that reads: 'CPD Homicide: Our day begins when yours ends.' He sets it on the table in front of the still–prone me and says, 'The G has a warrant out, too, just like they said—'

'Is John . . . Is he . . .'

Sonny buttons the TV from 'fireplace' to WGN and sits back in his chair. 'Cops and media know they got three charred bodies, but that's all they know.' Sonny raises a can of Old Style from the floor to above his cardigan shoulder. 'You said it was two. Moens told me one of 'em's definitely the mayor's wife. That's somethin', ain't it?'

I see the screwdriver, the face paint, the fire . . . and start to shrink under the blankets.

'So far, you two ladies are the only ones who know Mary Kate sleeps with the fishes.' Sonny grins, then frowns at his joke. 'Strange Mary Kate ain't been reported missing yet.'

'W . . . what about,' my eyes shut tight and I shrink a little more, 'John?'

'Fine; shit, they run his interview every ten seconds.'

'*He's okay?*' I grin to my limits, sit up so fast I'm dizzy, then I flash on John talking to Sonny by the TV lights, the two of them shoving. He *is* okay.

'Here it is. See? Every ten seconds.' Sonny buttons the sound and my son has the fire for a backdrop. He's smoothing hair out his face and talking to a reporter I know.

'. . . she was going to shoot me, can you believe that? And the other one grabbed her, then dove 'em both into the demo hole.' John rubs a soot streak that smears his face. He's handsome anyway and I feel my skin blush. 'The one with the gun had makeup. Mardi Gras weird, man, very weird.' John wipes his hands on his jeans and shrugs. 'Two crazy ladies. Maybe they just hate loft redevelopers. Who knows?'

The reporter tilts the mike to her face. 'Did you recognize them, either one?'

John grimaces. 'Ma'am, I don't know that type of woman and don't want to.'

Sonny looks at me and the happy tears filling my eyes. John's alive, unhurt, and what he said rings so true – he doesn't ever need to know women like me.

'Gwen, is she . . . ?'

'DOA at County, gun grips burnt into her hand.' Sonny nods at John on the TV. 'They found his sister's dog dead since this was taped yesterday. Moens said they'll be tying the dog to that

388

adoption agency you told me about.' Sonny pauses and I feel his eyes. 'Some *Richard Speck shit* over there.'

The tape cuts to a studio anchor. 'John Bergslund and his partners are being questioned in the three deaths at 2301 South Michigan.' The tape cuts to daylight; reporters and cameras are following John and three other young men into an office building. The anchor speaks over the video, 'Without presales in a strong market, arson is suspected—' and Sonny speaks over him.

'Moens's people at the *Herald* put it together late, pretty damn good. She said the Gwen girl was in the foster home with you; crazy even then, was like six or seven when she torched her own orphanage in '83, that's how Moens clocked her. Moens said Gwen found Ganz's will, got pissed, and murdered . . .'

I try to listen to the TV and don't answer.

'She was Mary Kate's kid, you believe that? This guy Ganz who . . . ah . . . messed with you was a coat-and-tie accountant at the hospital where Gwen was born. Looks like he used his admin connections to get Gwen into his foster home; been black-mailing Mary Kate for thirty years.'

'Yeah.' I shrink back into the sofa. 'Tracy told me.'

The TV video cuts back to the anchor with a PIP of last night's fire inset over his left shoulder, then a smaller picture of me when I was Policeman of the Year. 'Sources inside the Chicago Police Department say details of Officer Patricia Black's involvement in the suspected arson are unknown. But they do confirm that Officer Black was working directly for Superintendent Jesse Smith at the time of the blaze. Superintendent Smith remains in critical condition at Mercy Hospital. CPD News Affairs spokesmen deny—'

Sonny harrumphs. 'Assholes. Cut you loose the minute you're heavy.'

None of that is unexpected, nor is the anchor's next line: 'The U.S. Attorney's office *has* issued a warrant for Officer Black's arrest in connection with the death of Assistant State's Attorney Richard Rhodes. Attorneys representing Officer Black say she is innocent and will turn herself in tomorrow morning at the Dirksen Federal Building.' The anchor turns to change cameras. 'In Evanston, the brutal murders of—'

I lean into the TV, losing the blanket. 'My attorneys, huh?'

'Your pal Moens had a chic lawyer answer for you; Cindy Somebody, supposed to be a player – dressed like it at least, her number's on the table.' Sonny nods at the note by the folded clothes.

I feel threatened instead of protected, but finally have to admit that Miss All-Everything must be my friend after all. And that's almost as strange as me naked in Sonny Barrett's robe. But it's true and the Tracy thought adds a hint of a smile.

'What else did Tracy say?'

Sonny slips into street sergeant. 'Thought maybe somebody oughta slap the shit out of you. Wake you up some.' He shrugs and sips the Old Style. 'Me, I know you don't listen no matter how hard you get hit.'

The tone's got a funny edge, like there's hurt in it. I glance at him, big and better-dressed than I've ever seen him, and realize that the tone's been there all week, ever since this started. I scoop up the clothes right-handed and stare at a guy who never looks away, but he does.

'What'd my son say to you? At the fire.'

Sonny Barrett dressed as Phil Donahue doesn't answer.

'What'd he say?'

'Kid was confused; he didn't know shit about what he was saying.'

I lean at him like he needs to answer me. 'What'd he say, Sonny?'

Sonny's eyes narrow as he returns to my face, all the Phil Donahue gone. 'You gonna brace me, Patti? For saving your ass. Again?'

I grab his arm, digging in with my nails and he doesn't move. I lean into his face and watch it harden. 'What-did-he-say?'

Sonny cocks his head, fights with his temper, and loses. 'He said ... he hoped those two psychos hadn't made any kids; the world didn't need any more mental patients.'

At first I laugh, 'cause it's what I'd say. Then I see WGN running John's tape again and realize he's about to find out who his parents are, that they did make a kid.

Sonny removes my nails from his arm. 'You gotta tell the story. The whole thing. Tell your kid before the TV does. Then tell me and your lawyer. Make some kinda show before the G loads up the whole city against you.'

I blink at the tone and the words. 'Why would they do that?'

'What are you, a fucking child? *Somebody's* gotta pay for the mayor's wife and it ain't gonna be the mayor. Chief Jesse ain't gonna help you, he's in too—'

Sonny stops so fast his beer bobbles. I look at the TV like it has answers to the old questions forming on my lips, but the TV's now full of bikinis, frat boys, and beer.

'Chief Jesse is "in too what?"'

Sonny's nostrils flare and his neck bulges, but he doesn't answer.

'What! Damn it.'

'They say they got him cold, Patti, on the casino license. That bitch lawyer from the old First Ward – you know her, she works for Toddy Pete; she rolled on him and Chief Jesse.'

I remember the perfume in Chief Jesse's car. Shit, she was in my hospital room too, after the SUV almost killed Toddy Pete's kid. She patted my hand—

'The G says they flipped her, had her wearing a wire. If Jesse Smith survives the hospital, they say he's toast. And so are most of our bosses.'

'Tell me you're lying, Sonny.'

'Ain't no way Chief Jesse's guilty. But the G thinks so and they think you know all about it. That you, him, and all this bullshit from Calumet City was being used on the mayor, making Mayor McQuinn agree to casino shit he otherwise wouldn't.'

'That's a lie.'

'Is it?' Sonny's rubbing his arm.

'You don't believe me? You think I'm into that?'

'Hell, you don't ever answer; don't explain.' Sonny doesn't sound right; he's not mad, he's . . . 'What're we supposed to think?'

'*We?* Who's "we"?' The answer hits me. 'Are you wearing a wire on me, Sonny? That why you're dressed for a costume party?'

Sonny flashes teeth and stands. ' "We" is your fucking crew, asshole. Your friends.'

The whole week of revelations freight-trains in my face – John, the career, prison, lawyers, microphones. The cameras. Patti Black victim, Patti Black liar. I killed two people today, yesterday. Roland Ganz is dead. All of Roland and Gwen's victims have my fingerprints around them. My entire Calumet City past, everybody but me and Danny del Pasco doing life in Joliet, is dead.

'I didn't kill the guy in Calumet City. Back in '87. Gwen did.'

Sonny crushes his beer, says, 'Whatever you say,' and walks toward the kitchen. He palms the snap-brim cap off his head and tosses it in a trash can as he passes.

I watch, start to yell something shitty, and stomp to the bathroom with my new clothes instead. Inside, I put on Tracy's hand —delivered jeans and the sweatshirt with my back to the mirror, then the Cubs hat. A credit card receipt falls out. It has Sonny's name, not Tracy's.

Five twenties are in the jeans, so is a key to Tracy's town house, and a note that reads: 'My deadline is midnight, Monday. Call or come over by 8:00. Remember, we have a deal.'

We have a deal. I lace up my tennis shoes. This must be what it feels like to be important – everybody waiting for your next step, except my fans and paparazzi will be armed with leering tabloid questions, then pistols and handcuffs. I spin on the mirror, glare right at it, dare the son of a bitch to look back.

The shock is total, the face much older than thirty-eight, someone whose lack of courage has killed innocent people, buried them tiny and young, and shallow in the Sonoran Desert. I . . . I . . . I'm not butch enough to face this. My eyes blur and my gun hand starts to shake. I steal something from Sonny. And I do what I've been doing since I was fifteen.

I run.

CHINATOWN

And keep running. Toward a last dark cocktail with the ghosts of Wentworth Avenue. Seventeen years of Friday nights.

In real time the journey's an hour race from Sonny's apartment, but almost two and half decades if you count back from my parents dying in that car wreck. My final confrontation with Wentworth Avenue won't settle my whole life, just the nightmare half, the half with no reflection and all the hate.

Roland Ganz has to be dead for the nightmare to end. Chinatown will be my proof. I have to know it here, feel it on my skin just once before my life runs out of gas and time.

Winded, I skirt Ricobene's parking lot and the worst of its shadows, then slow to a walk at the south end of Wentworth. Chinatown's pavement looks almost clean stripped of its litter by the heavy rains. The storefront neons glare a smeary '40s feel, hazy like me and all four blocks are smoking opium. The sidewalks bustle, busy for a Monday night.

As I pass through the narrow–eyed hawkers fronting the bars and restaurants, they tell my shoulder why I need what they have. I hear sailors, girls . . . promises. Noncombatants crowd the sidewalks and don't notice me.

But I notice them. I'm looking for Roland Ganz in their faces, in their hands. In the cheap perfume and cigarette smoke. A man bumps me; we share an angry stare and he moves on, figuring me for the transient hustler he is.

Roland took me here twice. Chinatown suited him, he said. They understood things in Chinatown. My first time here was so he could explain the blood in my underwear, that I was a woman now with a woman's responsibilities. We had noodle soup and fish balls and he fucked me in the car.

Roland and I will be news very soon – he with Mary Kate and Gwen. Me with John and the will. The G and the media will put me in Roland's Calumet City foster home; they may guess the devil was John's father. But they won't *know*. Not if that secret dies tonight.

Tracy will have plenty else to write about – and none of it Patti Black, hero cop. Now it's Patti Black coward. Patti Black victim, Patti Black dirty cop and owner of His Pentecostal City. That's where Chinatown ends you if you lack the guts to end it else-where – a prison 6 × 9 that never sees sunlight. Me and Danny D and the nightmares. Forever.

At Twenty-third Street I step into the restaurant. It's dim and empty and when she sees me, the old woman inches back in her chair. She knows something isn't right. I sit facing the window. The same boy who works Friday nights brings my tea. I surprise him and the old woman by ordering wrong and too loud, 'Noodle soup and fish balls.'

I know I'm not going to prison – I've known it since I left Sonny's; I'm not going to trial either, not making transcripts to sell leery scandal sheets in the supermarket. And I'm not running. I'm keeping the faith tonight, the old promise that's kept me pieced together since I made it out of Calumet City: no capture – no more attics, no more basements. Ever.

For seventeen years I've come here every Friday and re-affirmed that promise, making it true, making it strong enough to sustain the unsustainable.

The food comes, steaming the stale air between me and the window. Roland and I sat at this table the second time we came to Chinatown, me in this chair, and I looked out that window in a daze. I was fifteen then, and already showing; Roland was buying me a present for our baby, telling me I was his special little girl, telling me he was my father and my husband, and that I would understand when I was older.

I'm older, but I still don't understand.

I don't understand Chief Jesse taking money either, being mixed up with the old First Ward crew and the casino license. And I don't believe it. His accidental brush with my past could bury him and his career – every decent thing he worked for – even though he and my past have nothing to do with each other.

I don't understand why John will have to suffer for all of it.

I don't understand. But I know what to do.

The restaurant's door bangs open. I don't look; I'm frowning at the window, at my reflection that won't ever be there, won't ever be completed.

'No more bullshit.' Sonny's voice is hard and angry. 'Time to talk.'

I force my eyes not to cut. How Sonny found me is a mystery; no one knows I come here. I feel his size looming at my shoulder and look up. He's in gunfighter-don't-fuck-with-me mode. In the Outfit, it's your best friend who pulls the trigger. That would be easier. I just wish it wasn't him.

'Talk about what?' The steam from my soup smells old.

Sonny has his new cap on and angles it at the kitchen. 'Cisco's out back. You got a piece?'

He knows I only carry one gun and it's lost in the fire. If Cisco really is blocking the back exit, then Sonny has shrunk the restaurant to the length of his arms. He also knows I have a terror thing with confinement and doesn't step any closer.

I pull the .38 Airweight I stole from his apartment and rest it and my hand on the table. 'Badass Sonny Barrett afraid of me?'

Sonny takes a breath that he exhales slowly. 'I'm gonna tell you somethin'.'

I wait, but he doesn't speak. I feel strangely lighter looking at him, less afraid of where all this has to go. He shifts his 250 pounds, takes another breath, and still doesn't say anything.

I check the window, then the kitchen, then back to him. 'What?'

'I know about this place.'

'Yeah, I can see.'

'You gotta tell the story, Patti.'

We both know that isn't gonna happen. He can tell by looking at me and I can tell by looking at the window. Sonny and I are saying good-bye. He knows it; I know it.

Sonny seems smaller, almost manageable. Boyish. His eyes read funny too, like he's a photograph from the early days when we were in our twenties. I'd forgotten how he looked at me then, protected me. I'd forgotten. He asked me twice to go for 'coffee or somethin'' back then, and the weight of those requests hadn't registered until just now. At the end of everything and there it is.

'How'd you know? About here?'

Sonny swallows small. 'After that shit by St. Rita's. Thought you might start drinking again. Followed you here.'

I squeeze the .38 and sit back to see all of him. 'That was a long time ago, Sonny. I come here every week.'

He nods, embarrassed, like he knows. Street criminals nod like that, copping to the cheapest of the felonies they face. For some reason I remove the Cubs hat and show it to him. 'You buy me this?'

He nods again, another felony in Sonny Barrett Tough–guy Land.

I smile, surprised that I can, and the smile chokes at my air. '*You?* Badass Sonny Barrett has *a thing for me?*'

Sonny harrumphs and cuts his eyes. It's knee-jerk and he stops halfway, hesitates, and tells the floor, 'Maybe. If I didn't know better.'

'*Me?*' I'm still choking. 'Damn, Sonny, I figured you for smarter.'

He shrugs the big shoulders. For sure boyish now, stripped of the armor – then flexes his neck to recover the macho he just tossed in the river. I stare because I don't know what else to do. Three quarters of me knows she has to go, to face the Airweight finish; one quarter wants to stay, see what the boyfriend I never had feels like. Sonny Barrett, my boyfriend – no possible way I could've seen that.

Except every way . . . if I'd been a girl before just now. I tighten on the pistol before I lose my nerve. I owe my son a clean slate. 'Gotta go, Sonny.'

His face flushes and real hurt fills his eyes; he shakes his big head.

'I gotta. And you have to let me.'

'Am I so bad . . . that I ain't even worth trying? That ain't fucking right, Patti. I could be better. As good as the other guys.'

'That's not it, Sonny. Not you; it's me. It's this . . .' The .38 waves itself at the room.

Sonny snarls, 'Fuck this place and whatever it means,' then nods at the window. 'Them too.'

Outside, two sets of flashing lights are double parking. *Shit*. I jump up to run. Sonny shoves me back into the chair. I try again and he puts his weight into it this time, splattering me to the floor. *Big panic*, then anger, then more panic.

'*I gotta get, Sonny*.'

'What you gotta do is face this thing. Dying's chickenshit.'

Then I see it, the betrayal, the . . . 'You fed me to the G? *You mother—*'

I scramble to stand. Sonny puts a size-13 boot on my chest. I shove him off balance and use the wall to stand. Everything's a blur, not the moment of clarity the shrinks say will be there when you finally decide. Cisco charges from the kitchen, yelling, 'Don't!' Sonny pancakes me into the wall. His hand covers the Airweight but doesn't rip it out. We're face to chest; I can hear his heart. He whispers, 'I'm going with you in the car. Everybody from the crew will be at the station. You ain't doing this alone.'

My hand tightens on the gun. His hand tightens on mine.

'Don't say shit outside; don't answer shit. Far as they know you were giving yourself up, just having dinner first.'

'I . . . I can't.'

'Got to. Lotta people you care about go down if you don't.'

'I can't.'

'Gimme the gun; we walk out proud. Together.'

Every pore is burning. I can't surrender; now, here, later. I just can't— The ghost at my ear says yes you can. I hear Cisco move; this place will be flooded with cops any second. God says trust me in Sonny's voice.

He has to say it twice. And louder.

I let the Airweight slide into Sonny's palm. Sonny steps back and without showing it to the window, pockets the pistol. 'Kit Carson's out there, he and his ASA buddy wanna make the big play for the cameras. We walk out, me in front, if Kit says shit, he goes to the dentist.'

I look at Sonny, then Cisco, then the flashing lights. I'm about to be blinded in the cameras. Then locked in state or federal handcuffs – the beginning of living Calumet City all over again. All of it. Surrender. Confinement. Saliva.

'What about my son?'

'You saved his ass, what else you need to do?'

'I need to . . . know, to . . .'

'Patti, the kid's a fucking adult. He can take it. Once you lawyer–up, you tell the story, loud. Kit and the G and these other assholes will run for the fucking exits. You do that, you walk.'

'No.' I shove at him.

Sonny drives me back and flat, and tells my ear: 'Moens says she can front-page their asses. Splatter 'em all, including the Ayatollah.'

'Not John. I won't tell it.'

'Yeah you will, 'cause I'll tell the little Northside fuck what happened if you don't. Ask your boy if he wants the woman who saved his ass to die in prison.'

'No!' I lurch at Sonny's chest, slug at his kidneys—

Sonny smothers my hand. 'If he's worth a shit, what do you think he'll say? *Let her die? I don't care?*' Sonny pins my head with his chin. 'I ain't lettin' it happen, Patti. If that means you and me got no shot, then that's what it means.'

'I trusted you, goddamnit. Don't.'

'Too late, your kid's out there in a squad, gonna ID you for the fire. For the stiffs.'

'John's out there?' I try to look out the window but can't move. 'Does he know? *Does* he?'

'You gonna do right or do I knock your ass out?'

'Does he know!'

Sonny's chest expands into mine and the longest silence I can remember. 'No. Not yet.'

I slip and squirm and stomp at Sonny's shoe. 'Don't you tell him. Don't.'

Pots and pans clang in the kitchen. Cisco shouts, 'Let her alone.' This has to be the G coming for their prize. Tracy's voice adds to the commotion, out of place and getting louder. Then she's at my inside shoulder, away from the window.

'Hey, fly half.'

I can't move to look at her but can smell the perfume.

'You Southside girls can throw a party; this guy bothering you?'

Sonny's chest hiccups, maybe a choke or a laugh without sound.

'Do *not* tell them, Tracy. Not about John.'

'Honey, we have a deal.'

'Bullshit. Don't tell. I ain't kidding. I'm warning you—'

'You're warning me?' Tracy's tone leaps to anger. 'Pinned against a wall by a gorilla and you're warning me? I saved you every way a woman could. I gave you my friendship; you used it for firewood. I risked my career, hell, *my life – way* past what we agreed – and you *still* haven't said thanks.'

'Don't tell. Not now, not ever, not—'

'If I'm not printing this story – *like we agreed* – why'd I do all that?'

I fight against Sonny's bulk.

'Why, Patti?'

'I don't know why, but you aren't writing it.'

'In some other universe I'm not. Tell me where that universe is and maybe we make a new deal.'

Sonny's too strong to move; my knee lands on his thigh instead of his balls and I get slammed hard into the wall. I can hear, but it's hard to breathe. Tracy says,

'For God's sake, Patti, wake up. This is real here, we can beat 'em; I know how.'

'Not . . . with . . . John.' I twist my head from under Sonny's chin and catch Tracy's eyes. She jolts, either at my dark circles and tears or the panting breath I can't catch. Patti Black, victim.

Tracy cuts to the window, scanning lights and people I can't see. The perfect lips purse, then peel back, and she blinks twice. She nods to an unspoken decision and leans closer to my face. 'You don't look good. No way I'd go on camera if I were you.'

From deep in his throat Sonny Barrett, gunfighter, says: 'Fuck 'em. She's going out the front door, with me. Fuck the cameras . . . and anybody else.'

And anybody else means Sonny has reached his line in the sand. Not only are his career and pension over, he's gonna go to prison for me, a terrified little girl in a sundress. Because of me. Because I won't—

'All right,' Tracy tells Sonny and my cheek, 'I'll do it – no John, not a word. But I write whatever your lawyer and I decide has to be written for you to beat this. And before you bitch, you need to know that if you back out – *again* – I'll tell the whole thing. All of it.'

I hear her but there's too much adrenaline and not enough air. This is it if I agree; I'll be naked out in the lights. Everybody will know.

'Yes or no, Patti? Now.'

I stare at her eyes and don't see the lie, don't see the career–at –all–costs town house owner. 'What about your—?'

'I'll win the Pulitzer later.'

'You'd do that?'

'If you never, *ever* mention it, especially to me.'

Sonny's heart is ramping with mine. He really does mean to save me, regardless of what Tracy says. This is that moment at the school dance that I never had, the boy I wanted asking me in spite of how I look. This boy – this big, huge Irish man – wants Patricia Black, even though he knows I'm crippled, even though he knows my history will cripple him too. His heart beating honest against my cheek decides for me.

'Okay.'

Sonny leans back, gripping my shoulders. He stares but doesn't speak, making sure I'm in for real, not prepping to go stupid. Surprise softens his face. Caused by the tiny smile in mine, the hint of girlish in the tears and eyelash flutter. Tracy interrupts our first date.

'The quicker we go, the fewer feds.'

Cisco agrees from behind her; Sonny says, 'Cisco. Hop out front. Tell 'em we're going to the alley. They bring the kid around back, he does the ID, then *you and me* are taking her uptown.'

'Th, the G . . . G won't like that.'

'Fuck 'em. Tell 'em I said Ruby Ridge.'

'Da – damn, Sonny—'

'Tell 'em.'

I can feel the power in Sonny's body, the mass of it readying for battle. It's another first–time 'girl' moment that feels . . . good, instead of clammy and threatening. It's humid in here; I'm sorta dizzy . . . and, man, my arms hurt.

'. . . all right?'

'Huh?' Sonny has me by the upper arms, nose to nose.

'Are you all right?'

'Yeah.' I blink and swallow and glance. 'I think.'

Cisco comes back in and whispers to Sonny. He listens, look-ing at the window, then turns to me.

'Get ready. Cisco says they're doing the ID in here – it'll be CPD pimping you for the condo fire. You be cool, let me and Cisco play it.'

I don't answer; don't have an answer for facing my son this way. Any way.

'Say yes, Patti.'

'O . . . kay.'

Sonny straightens me up, steps behind my shoulder, and grabs a handful of belt. The front door adds commotion and John walks through, shouldered by two uniforms, followed by the Watch Commander from 21. The four of them stop at fifteen feet. My son looks into my eyes for the first time since he was a day old. John doesn't grin, frown, or blink. Only the splattered chairs separate us. Sonny's holding me up. I don't have enough air.

'She in here?' The Watch Commander takes charge.

John scans the room and its wreckage, then fakes a smile in my direction. 'Uh, hi.'

Ghetto instincts tell me to duck; my son just said 'hi' to me with my eyes open. I need to run. The window's full of lights and there's nowhere left to run. I avoid John's eyes, then can't help but look. He's . . . grown–up. And so close. *So right there*. I wish . . . I wish for a way—

'So that's her, the one?' The Watch Commander hard-eyes me.

'Could be, I think.' John checks me out the way a guy would a girl. 'But, you know, the woman last night was covered in soot, had on a bra, flames all over, the other one shooting—'

'Take your time, kid.' The Watch Commander was once Sonny's partner. He and I know each other fifteen years and he hasn't smiled an inch. He's a boss now.

John shrugs. 'Could be her.'

Cisco hides a smile and it hits me. This ID is a trap. I glance at the window. The ASA's apeshit and being restrained by uniforms. I check the Watch Commander, still dead serious. My son doesn't get it, but I do. His ID, even if it had been solid, is useless. No lineup. The Watch Commander just gave me my birthday present.

John shifts his weight. He doesn't know he's standing by his father's old chair, IDing his mother. He has no idea that a monster was his father, that the tabloids will swallow him whole if I tell. More lights flash outside, blue and red and white, but John's eyes don't leave me. I want to touch . . . but I'm paralyzed. Another squad arrives, then another. I hear Eric Jackson yell, then see him lean in at Kit Carson now backed by two uniforms.

My crew is buying me and Sonny time even though they know IAD will crucify them.

My son glances at the window. He's not sharing my tidal wave of emotion. His eyes are calm, deep black, and forever; and don't say what's inside. I search for Roland Ganz seething under the beautiful face. *Please don't let Roland be there. Please.*

John's surrounded by cops and confusion, but his hands are quiet. Not a speck of Roland Ganz in the hands. He reexamines the wreck of me. No expression; we're strangers, two passersby in Chinatown. Tears stream down my cheeks. He doesn't understand where this leads. I check a last time for any trace of Roland Ganz . . . John stays; Roland isn't here.

Tracy whispers, 'C'mon, fly half, you can do this.'

But, but . . .

But in her voice and John's eyes I see that it's possible . . . for him. He doesn't have to know. I never named Roland as the father, not in the maternity ward, not at the adoption agency. No one but me and Roland knows that for sure. *That could be the bargain, couldn't it?* My one, sanity-sparing gift to a kid who someday will be sideswiped by his parentage, a side trip he didn't know was realer than horror movies.

In that bargain I catch a whiff of hope – it's not Thursday night at the animal shelter in South Holland, all the abandoned animals don't have to die tomorrow when the killers come. I remember hope. It's the feeling I had when I'd set the animals free.

The Watch Commander taps John's shoulder and points him at the door. John looks relieved and should, then says to me, 'If it was you last night, I'd like to do more than just say thanks. If not,' he nods at my tears and circumstances, 'good luck with this. Maybe get some professional help.'

Sonny flexes all over; Tracy hugs me hard at his shoulder.

I say the only words I've spoken to my son since his birth, 'I'll do that.'

And he turns to leave. Gone forever is best, but I want him to stay, to love me, to understand. To turn right now, grin big, and say: *'Bye, Mom, be back for dinner.'* But he doesn't; he just leaves, silhouetted in a blast of flashes out front.

The sunbrites splash the window and its paper lanterns. Sonny steps him and me a pace closer to the door, eyes still hard from where his head and guts have been, then softens a bit when he looks at my eyes.

'Proud, now, Patti. Magnificent Seven. You one of us.'

I wipe at the tears, see Tracy quit her cell phone and prep to own the stage, then Cisco jumping ahead to run interference. Tracy follows Cisco and tells Sonny:

'Give me three minutes to do my stand-up – I'll bury the alderman's case first, then the U.S. Attorney's. Bait 'em both for tomorrow's front page.'

Sonny nods, teeth bared.

'Don't let Patti say a word. My article's the only person telling the story. Cindy Bourland, that's Patti's lawyer, she's on her way. Here's her mobile; as soon as you know where Patti's going, call. Cindy'll be there when you get there. She's a bunch tougher than she looks, Sonny. Let her handle the legal stuff.'

I'm listening like we're talking about someone else.

Tracy retreats to me and kisses my cheek, hard like she's mad and happy, like we won a match we shouldn't have. 'You owe me forever.'

The Pink Panther walks out and Chinatown ignites. I can see Sonny's reflection at the edge of the window. My reflection's next to him, shoulder-to-shoulder. My reflection's turning, like the pretty girls do when they want a boy's attention. I have a face . . .

And I have a man with his arm around my waist. 'We going on a date, you and me?'

Sonny Barrett, gunfighter, actually blushes. 'Maybe after we get out of prison, if the GDs don't kill you first.'

I smile back; first at him, then at Tracy owning the cameras, then at the window: me, Patti Black, with a boyfriend and a pretty girl's reflection. No way you could figure that.

THE END

ACKNOWLEDGMENTS

Writers
Don McQuinn, Denny Banahan, and Easy Ed Stackler. Without these three fellows and five years of their mentoring, *Calumet City* wouldn't have happened. And after every agent in two countries said no, Simon Lipskar said yes.

Cops
Patti Black, Denny Banahan, and Matty Rzepecki. Matty Rzepecki is the most fearsome man I've ever met; he taught me how to behave in the street. Denny Banahan introduced me to Patti Black and taught me everything I know about cops in Chicago. Patti Black walked me through hell and showed me you can survive it.

Friends
Brian Rodgers, Sharon and Doug Bennett, Beth Steffen, Billy Thompson, Jim Barlow, Holly Kennedy, James 'Sears Tower' Levy, and Bill Owens. They read and reread every manuscript, and critiqued and stayed with me when I told them they were full of shit.

AUTHOR'S NOTE

Patti Black is a ghetto cop in Chicago and has been for almost twenty years. This is a work of fiction. The true story of her life is both worse and better, and someday she'll tell it.

DEDICATION

In 1959 there was a hurricane in the Libyan desert. They don't get many of those there. *Calumet City*, like the others that preceded it, is probably for her.

Shutter Island

Dennis Lehane

Summer, 1954. US Marshal Teddy Daniels has come to Shutter Island, home of Ashecliffe Hospital for the Criminally Insane. Along with his partner, Chuck Aule, he sets out to find an escaped murderess named Rachel Solando, as a hurricane bears down upon them.

But nothing at Ashecliffe Hospital is what it seems. And neither is Teddy Daniels. Is he there to find a missing patient? Or has he been sent to look into rumours of Ashecliffe's radical approach to psychiatry? As the investigation deepens, the questions mount. How has a barefoot woman escaped an island from a locked room? Who is leaving them clues in the form of cryptic codes? And what really goes on in Ward C?

The closer Teddy and Chuck get to the truth, the more elusive it becomes, and the more they begin to believe that they may never leave Shutter Island. Because someone is trying to drive them insane . . .

'Chilling, thrilling and so clever you'll be chewing it over
long after the final page'
MIRROR

9780553818277

Nothing to Lose

Lee Child

Two small towns in Colorado: Hope and Despair. Between them, nothing but twelve miles of empty road. Jack Reacher can't find a ride, so he walks. All he wants is a cup of coffee. What he gets are four redneck deputies, a vagrancy charge and a trip back to the line.

Mistake.

They're picking on the wrong guy. Reacher is a big man, and he's in shape. No job, no address, no baggage. Nothing, except bloody-minded curiosity. What are the secrets the locals seem so determined to hide?

A hard man is good to find. Lee Child's ex-military cop Jack Reacher is today's most addictive hero. Now he pulls on a tiny loose thread, to unravel interlinked conspiracies that expose the shocking truths behind America's greatest scandals.

Because, after all, Jack Reacher has **nothing to lose**.

'A **high-testosterone** adventure with a thoughtful nod to what is going on in Iraq . . . a **page turner**. **Thrilling**'
OBSERVER

'**Classic** Child . . . **brilliantly** paced . . . his **tough-but-fair** creation, Jack Reacher, both a **man's man** and a **ladies' man**, proves once again that he's also **his own man**. And no one is going to get in his way'
MIRROR

9780553818116

Written in Bone

Simon Beckett

I took the skull from its evidence bag and gently set it on the stainless steel table. 'Tell me who you are . . .'

On the remote Hebridean island of Runa, a grisly discovery awaits the arrival of forensic anthropologist Dr David Hunter.

A body – almost totally incinerated but for the feet and a single hand – has been found. The local police are quick to record an accidental death but Hunter's instincts say otherwise: he's convinced it's murder. Indeed it appears Runa might not be such a peaceful community after all – and a burned corpse but one of its dark secrets.

Then an Atlantic storm descends, severing all power and contact with the mainland. And as the storm rages, the killing begins in earnest . . .

Powerful, unpredictable and shocking, *Written in Bone* is a nerve-shredding crime thriller from a brilliant British storyteller.

'Beckett cranks up the suspense . . . unexpected twists and
a gory climax'
Daily Telegraph

9780553817508

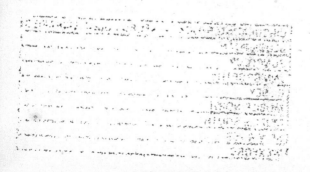